Barring Some
Unforeseen Accident

Barring Some Unforeseen Accident

by

Jackson (Tippett) McCrae

ISBN: 978-09715536-5-1

LCCN: 2007939107

Printed in the United States of America on acid-free paper

First Edition

Published by
Leo Press
P.O. Box 2008
Norwalk, CT 06852

Book cover and design by Leo Press

For Laura

Acknowledgments

I would like to thank the following people and institutions for their support, either with this book and my other writing endeavors, or by way of their friendship and loyalty:

The Bluestocking Society of Georgia for their generous support, Bread Loaf Writers' Conference, Middlebury College, Northwestern University, The University of Philadelphia, the Missouri book clubs, the book clubs in Canada, the Arizona and California book clubs, the New Zealand book club, the book clubs in Florida, Pennsylvania, and New York, Concordia University, UCLA, the Georgia school system, The New Canaan Dog Park People (and Kit), Leah Beckman for her excellent comments and attention to detail, The Stamford Yacht Club, The Rye Yacht Club, Laura Edwards, Earlean C., Mary S., Laura Inman, Joyce Dixon of Southern Scribe, Rita Potochick, James Waller, Jeff Cabral, Pam, Amy McMurray, Holly, Vegas, Missy, Bessie & Piggy, Louise Weiss, Donald Harter, Peter M., and my cousins Lynn, Sandy, and Trish.

. . . til sock be snug

Part I

I am a part of all that I have met …

—Lord Alfred Tennyson, from his
poem *Ulysses*

Note to my editor: By the time you receive this manuscript, I will have committed suicide.

Demise by my own hand was never something I foresaw, but the trials of this book have been too much to bear. I sit here now, in an enormous antebellum mansion in the Deep South, writing this to you with the hope that what follows will explain my present state of mind and the decision to end my life. It was either this funereal route via my present writing and delving into places better left untouched, or prison, for when the story comes to light I will undoubtedly be hunted down like some rabid raccoon by yokels looking for sport and lurid gossip which, if not found, will be manufactured.

Persons of authority in Chalybeate Springs have no problem with what I've done—how could they as they are all dead?—but I'm sure that officials at the state and federal levels will intervene and make my life a living hell (more so than it has been for the last month). I'm not even sure what day it is at present. All I know is that it is sometime after this year's Fourth of July.

We agreed that I would get you a book within the last thirty days. I am, however, delivering this manuscript slightly late. What you do with it is up to you. Not that I will know, having gone to a better, or at least less stressful place (this based on my meager Sunday school teachings and my lack of belief in the evils of self-annihilation.)

As far as worrying about lawsuits—don't. Everyone of any consequence in the book (and a few others that no one would care about), are quite dead.

A note about the house I am in at present: I leave it to you, as it was indirectly left to me—the thing seems to get passed around more than a Hollywood starlet with no future. It is in need of some work (the house, not the starlet), but I'm sure that you will find it comfortable and a good retreat from the noise and confusion of New York.

My trip back to the South was, for the most part, an enlightening one, and the month or so that it took to glean this tale from the good (and not-so-good) people of Chalybeate Springs was an experience I shall never forget, short time that I have to remember it.

Exactly how I will end my own life is not yet known to me. My revisitation (I think that's a word I made up—my homage to Faulkner and his penchant for invention and warpedness—another one) of the South has given me more book material than I ever thought possible, a lot of which was, and is, disturbing to me; so much so that I cannot live with what I know.

Perhaps my death route will include pills, perhaps a gun. I tend to think pills would be less untidy for whoever finds me, but a gun seems so final—I suppose that *is* the point—and here in the South, a tad more masculine, don't you think? I do fear for the antiques in the house should I miss while using an artillery device—really nice stuff (the antiques, not the guns) which, if not to your liking, can be auctioned off at one of New York's major houses—lots of John Henry Belter and Duncan-Phyfe: top drawer, all of it—the real thing too.

Hanging is another possibility (for me, not the furniture). I've checked out the rafters in the attic of this old mansion as I've been spending as lot of time there—solid, sturdy cedar things that are a good foot square thick, and quite capable of handling my weight. But I've had a bit of a time managing the noose. I stole a car the other day and drove to a nearby town, questioning the locals on how exactly one accomplishes such a complex knot, but the inquiry elicited more than a few raised and disapproving eyebrows from some, and overzealous reactions from others. Human beings are an uneven lot.

As you may have guessed (or will from reading the manuscript), people—for lack of a better term here in Chalybeate Springs—*had* taken quite a shine to me, while others would have been more than willing to help with my demise—nay, some actually attempted it for me once or twice. But I'm not one to give those who might hate me the satisfaction of aiding my trip to the great beyond, choosing instead to personally take charge of my last moments here on earth. It's one of the few things I will actually have control over in these last days and I'm looking forward to the experience.

I do dislike the thought of leaving this house though. It's what I've always wanted, and perhaps that's fitting—getting what you really want in the end. But then, where do you go from there, when you finally attain your goal? My objective *initially* was to live in New York and become a famous writer, garnering enough money to allow me to move back to the South and live in seclusion like some hermit with only pen and paper and a lifetime supply of Scotch.

Then my fantasy progressed to a farm in Connecticut. Years ago, when I pictured myself as a writer, I imagined my broad-shouldered torso, expertly fitted in a custom-made tweed sports jacket, sitting before an open window, puffing my pipe while ideas flowed—waterfall and torrent-like—to such an extent that I was forced to find less lofty distractions.

"Be sure to shear those sheep early this year, Bill," I might throw out at some farm worker of mine, between the incessant clacking of typewriter keys (I was imagining this long ago) and sips of imported tea.

But, for the most part I found myself traveling across the country from sea to not-so-shining sea, staying in seedy hotels, eating questionable fare, getting no sleep, listening to chatty housewives go on about the characters in my books, and as of late, trying to make sense of one town's flagrant and blossoming idiosyncrasies that led it down a most unwanted path. It wasn't what I would have imagined for myself, but then, what is?

So here I sit, writing this in the one place I've always wanted to be—a twenty-room house built before the Civil War. It has remained untouched by the hands of time: no indoor plumbing or electricity, but the fifteen-foot ceilings and original furnishing more than make up for the lack of modern amenities. I've often walked about the place at night after I've put some finishing touches on the manuscript you're about to read. My work is all done by the light of hurricane lamps, fueled by kerosene—very old-fashioned. And I've been scanning the collection of books that are in the house's library—first editions of Dickens (my, he did like a comma, didn't he?), and even Poe and Proust. Who would have thought that anyone in this area cared for Proust?

Lately, the vicinity that the house sits in has been having those tremendous thunderstorms which seem so very Southern and add to the general gloom and doom of not only my life, but the story I'm sending you as well. You couldn't order this stuff up from Hollywood if you tried. And the thunderstorms gave me an excellent idea: I've thought of flying a kite, à la Benjamin Franklin, seeing if I could be electrocuted. But it's been done before and I'm a real stickler for originality in matters where death is concerned.

While pondering the many ways I could do myself in, drowning came to mind. But that would entail a long walk as the nearest pond is a mile away and only accessible on foot. (I am, if nothing else, a lazy person, and the well on the property—while deep—is not filled with enough water.)

It was then that I considered drowning myself in my own urine but realized that I would have to fill a bathtub (remember, the house has no plumbing), and even if I could find a receptacle large enough, the process would take weeks before I would be able to stock it with the necessary amount of my own juices. Peeing on an electric fence was out as I *have* no fence (or electricity for that matter), though the urination theme seemed to be ever-present that particular day.

Next stop was death by hari-kari. Unfortunately, for all the house's Southern ambience, the "help" I've recently had here absconded with the solitary knife that had taken up residence, so disemboweling myself was out. Plus, there's that clean-up factor again. On the same note, I nixed the idea of a wood chipper since, a) it is noisy, and, b) the nearest one is in Bugger Hollar (yes, there is such a place), which is a good forty miles away. True, some have put it to good use here, but I'm looking for a solution that requires less energy and no gasoline. Besides, who would turn it off once I'm done? Again, the lazy factor raises its unsightly head.

Slitting my wrists seemed like a bad cliché, and strapping explosives to my body would damage the structure of the house and that lovely furniture I've told you about—I do have some semblance of respect for the past.

I thought of giving analingus to an AIDS-ridden hooker, but Chalybeate Springs doesn't have prostitutes (any longer) or AIDS (just about everything else though), and I don't particularly want the general reading public to know the last place my mouth has been. In addition, the dying process might take months, even years. And what self-respecting (oxymoron alert) prostitute is going to actually tell you she or he (I'm not picky at this point) has AIDS?

I hope you won't find it too morbid; me giving this house to you after I've done away with myself *inside* the thing. It's nothing personal—I just want to finish what I've started in a comfortable, albeit drafty locale, where I feel I really belong.

As for the citizens in the surrounding towns, you'll have no problem. I'll leave them a note explaining who you are and how this whole endeavor came about. Trust me, they'll understand. In the meantime, I'll keep trying to come up with a creative way to shuffle off my mortal coil. The latest method I have dreamed up is to read a book by Hemingway and be simply bored to death (the man was a complete idiot and pulling the shotgun with his big toe was the most creative thing he ever did).

In closing, I hope this last epistle of mine finds you in good health, and, when you come down to Chalybeate Springs to claim the house, take my advice—bring a gun.

Parenthetically yours,

Jackson (Tippett) McCrae

P.S. Please do not

Eatables Psych-Ring

Here I sit, at the Chalybeate Springs Inn, starting my latest literary effort. The room is comfortable enough, and for the time being I expect few disturbances. We shall see what happens, but first, let me start from the beginning or at least somewhere nearer the point in my life where the idea for this book came about so as to better explain how I got where I am.

When my editor called me in New York and asked what I was working on, I searched my desk at home, looking for some subject that I could incorporate into a lie. "I'm working on a story about Eskimos who were transferred to South America now that global warming has reversed the climates," I said, seeing a carved Walrus tooth as it rose, Pike's-Peak-like, from a pile of bills and first drafts. (It was imitation— the tooth, not the bills or drafts.) But the idea seemed forced. He wasn't interested anyway.

"How about a novel on the history of the enema?" I mused into the receiver. He waited, not even bothering to answer that one. I tried to coerce the wheels to turn, thinking of the friends I have and their occupations. I always try to keep people around me who are not a part of the book world, finding that it gives me a great deal of fresh ideas. And it's healthier. My closest friend works in a lab, performing chemical tests, soil and air analysis, and experiments on various products, looking for lead toxicity or other elements in common everyday items. It sounds boring, I know, but it might come in handy some day. Another is a computer programmer—a bit dull but convenient when you have problems as I so often do with my laptop. And finally I have one who is a furniture designer.

"How about a book on the history of the Eames chair?" I ventured, but Mr. Editor would have none of it. Then my sight fell to the right of my desk; to a pile of mail I had just received that included a letter (I get so many) from a woman, requesting that I come to her town and help put together a cookbook. Before I could fathom the lack of interest this sort of thing would generate sales-wise, I blurted it out.

"Sounds like hell," was the response, "but you might as well go down there and see if you can make something out of it—you know, find out who these people really are and write about them. Just make sure *they* don't find out what you're doing," he said.

"Well," I responded, "barring some unforeseen accident, I should have the manuscript to you in about a month."

I gazed at the letter from the Southern housewife, now open and in my hand, and gave it a once over.

The correspondence from Chalybeate Springs—from a Miss Henrid—was straightforward enough. About the only thing that struck me as odd was the handwriting—not very feminine and with a touch of, well … something I couldn't quite put my finger on. Nevertheless it was an invitation, and having just been harangued about my next book—of which there was none at present—I accepted the summons, even though it was to a town of only three hundred people and in the middle of the Deep South. I thought that surely something would come from the experience. As I had pulled the letter from the envelope, something had fallen out that I had previously missed. And as I hadn't bothered to read her note all the way through days before, I had overlooked a valuable money reference.

Here is what the note said:

Dear Mr. McCrae,

I am quite a fan of your work and would like to present you with a proposition: Would it be possible for you to visit our fair town for a few weeks and help the Junior League put together a cookbook of their favorite recipes? My way of thinking is that you could add in some historical facts and maybe even an essay or two for good measure. I must be up front and tell you that I, personally, am not in the Junior League—just yet. This town *did* have *another* Junior League over a hundred years ago, but it has long been disbanded. If you could do this favor for the town, perhaps they would look upon certain persons (myself comes to mind), more favorably. I won't try to hide the fact that I have an ulterior motive in making this request, but my way of thinking is that you might also find some new material for a book—in addition to the cookbook. I hope you will consider this request—it would be such an honor to have a great author such as yourself in our midst. I am enclosing a check for $25,000 in the hope of seducing you to come to Chalybeate Springs.

Very truly yours,

Miss Tuck Henrid

Seduction indeed: of the most glorious kind. And there *was* a check accompanying the note, just as promised. I wanted to kick myself for missing it previously and actually tried to perform the act. It's very difficult and I don't recommend it. The outside of the envelope, as well as the letterhead inside, bore the name Chalybeate Springs. The invitation was two-sided in my mind (not literally as that would have been bad form for any Southern woman, but figuratively.) First of all, the chance to get out of Manhattan for a while was inviting. But I was an unsure traveler. Would this be a *Southern Homes and Gardens* visit (shameless promotion), or would it be *Deliverance?* While visions of well-appointed chintz-stuffed antebellum bedrooms, and breakfast in bed served by a pretty woman who called me "Sugar" and "Honey-lamb" danced in my head, I was also aware of the possibility of no air-conditioning, snakes, and people lacking front teeth who asked not-so-innocuous questions such as "You funny, boy?" while fingering a twelve-gauge shotgun and looking for a place to aim their latest gathering of tobacco spit. And they weren't inquiring about my sense of humor either. Besides, I had absolutely no idea where Chalybeate Springs was.

So I looked on the map for the town.

Nada.

Still, I needed material for the next writing assignment and my editor had been calling each and every day. "Why don't you just pay me an enormous advance?" I had asked him. "That's sure to get the creative juices flowing." But it didn't happen. And Miss Henrid was offering dollar signs—nothing to sneeze at. I wrote her back—after cashing the check and waiting for it to clear—letting her know that I'd be there in a few days, and set about packing toothpaste, hairbrush, contact lenses, and laptop computer. Surely they had electricity.

I stopped.

What was I thinking? I had grown up in the South. I knew that everyone was acquainted with each other, that you could find culture and civilization right next to towns that barely had phones, and that the gamut of intelligence and manners ran from Antique to Zealous. In short, I knew what the general atmosphere was like. But years of never venturing outside Manhattan's safe confines had taken their toll and I found myself being overly critical of any place that didn't offer a sushi bar or massage parlor where the staff spoke twelve languages—or both. I was used to New York now: its manic bustle and throw-around style; its way of talking (a simple jerk of the head upward was all that was needed to say "Hello" where anywhere else it would have been a five minute conversation); its foods, theaters, and united or not-so-united nations of peoples. It's been said that over one hundred and seventy different languages are spoken in New York. That was the nice thing—that you could remain anonymous and alone, even in a city of eight million proper, choosing to communicate with no one if the mood hit. Yes, it was now home. A trip out of it would clear the head and make New York look new again. Especially a trip to some remote town like Chalybeate Springs.

I tied up what loose ends I could in the city and prepared for my trip. I cleaned out the mailbox in my apartment building's lobby and alerted the doorman that he would need to collect my letters for a while, telling him that I'd be out of town. He seemed his usual overjoyed self at being asked to perform one more task for no extra money, and grunted. On my way back up to my apartment—to get my bags—I glanced at the incoming correspondence. Nothing too spectacular. But then an unusual envelope postmarked "Chalybeate Springs" grabbed my attention. Was this the illustrious Miss Henrid taking back her invitation? I hoped not. The idea of writing the history of the enema was not an appealing one. But wait, the letter was from someone I'd never heard of—a Mrs. Helen Weems. Here is what it said:

> Dear Mr. McCrae,
>
> It was so good of you to offer your services in the planning and editing of our Junior League's cookbook. I cannot tell you how happy I am that you are coming to our town, and I would like to extend an invitation for you to stay at my lovely home. My husband is the mayor and we have more than enough room. And what a thrill it will be to have a real-live author in our presence!
>
> My best wishes, and may God speed.
>
> Mrs. Helen Weems

"What the ...?" I thought. How did she know I was coming? And it sounded as if she thought *I'd* written *her*. It was strange, but I had to be on my way to the airport and figured that I would address the issue when I got to the town. And stay in her home? I'd never met the woman! How did she know I didn't walk in my sleep or that I didn't have thirty body piercings and green hair? For that matter, how did I know she didn't? Perhaps she was just being kind, displaying Southern hospitality. Or perhaps her invitation was a hollow one; not really meant to be acted upon. I would figure it out when I arrived in Chalybeate Springs, so I made my way out of Manhattan and began the journey.

By the grace of God, nothing remarkable happened between the time I made my plane reservations and the wheels of the 747 touched down at Atlanta's airport. A labyrinth of such enormous proportions so as to confuse even the most learned student of geometry or professional surveyor, Atlanta's hub of air transportation activity is not for the faint-hearted. I somehow found my way to one of the airport's areas where smaller planes took off—for smaller places. This was nothing new to me. I'd been home to visit relatives several times, but at least *those* towns had more than a couple hundred people.

I unzipped my laptop case to take out my cell phone—to let my editor know that I was on my way and to check and see how the sales were on my latest book.

It wasn't there (the cell phone, not the book).

I looked again, panic-stricken. I had forgotten my phone. "Stay calm," I said, as they called my fight to board. "You can always get in touch by regular phone or use e-mail," and I took a deep breath and boarded the plane.

When the twin engine propeller aircraft finally bumped to a stop in some place called Swillville (swear to God—I could see the sign from the plane), I disembarked. The plane's exiting gear wasn't exactly what I was used to as it was one of those fold-down step things. You know, made for presidential photo ops or old film reels of Marilyn Monroe gently making her way earthward while her knees rub together and Jo DiMaggio scowls in the background.

Just as I reached the tarmac, a rather burly law enforcement person of considerable size and attitude did a toe-to-toe dance with me. I backed up. He came forward. I noticed his badge. It said simply, "Sheriff." Very Western.

"You that McCrae fella?" he asked, removing the salami-sized cigar from his lips for a moment, then replacing it. It bobbed no more than a quarter of an inch from my face. I felt, nay, heard three eyelashes singe and curl up. I tried to ease back.

"That would be me. Anything wrong?" I asked, holding on tightly to the one bag and computer case I had.

"Naw." He waited, eyeing me up and down. "Ain't nothin' wrong." He waited again. It was all coming back to me now—the pregnant pauses in the South, either designed for maximum discomfort of the other fellow, or simply because the person one was having repartee with needed time to think. I wasn't sure what the reason was at that moment, but didn't care; I just wanted to get to my hotel and rest. Sheriff Big-Smoke Cliché continued after taking the cigar out of his mouth once again and flicking two inches worth of ash onto the asphalt. "Sent here to collect you up," he said, turning his head to the side and squinting. He removed his hat and scratched his balding head, all the while surveying a line of trees to his left, on the side of the small airstrip.

My nerves were getting the better of me. I wasn't sure why someone had been sent to "collect" me, and the guy didn't look like he was going to ask me to join his poker game (I don't play), so I moved from foot to foot, squinting at the harsh sun.

"Wouldn't have thought a town of this size would have an airstrip," I said, attempting nonchalance. Unfortunately, my voice broke on the word "size" and I sounded all of thirteen. The sheriff squinted. I went on. "I mean, I couldn't find this place on the map and ..."

"Ain't no *real* airstrip," the man said, readjusting the hat atop his head and rolling his cigar between two sausage-like fingers. "Pig field. Belongs to Old Man Reynolds. (Double puff, deep inhale, thirty-second wait, exhale.) "Just leveled it off last year," he finally managed.

"Must have been expecting me," I tried to joke. He eyed me again as his tongue lapped around the end of the Havana smoker. There was a pregnant pause again, only this time he was evidently expecting twins.

"Musta been," he said, never taking his eyes from me. "And this here's Swillville. You's goin' to Chalybeate."

After a set of triplets and two miscarriages, he gestured toward a police car. "Better get goin' if you're to get rested up afore you get started."

"Guess there's no rental car in this place," I said sheepishly, trying to add a smile to my face.

"Nope. I'm it."

At that moment, a nice-looking man sauntered over toward where the sheriff and I were standing.

"Well, speak of the devil," the sheriff said, and grasped the man's hand, pumping it up and down. "I's just tellin' this here Mr. McCrae that this used to be your pig farm." Then My Collector turned to me: "Mr. McCrae, this here is Mr. Reynolds." Then to Reynolds: "This here is Mr. McCrae."

"I'm pleased to meet you," the new man said, extending a firm handshake and a smile in my direction.

Mr. Law Enforcement broke in: "Reynolds here might have had to move his farm, but he sure does have some fine sows. Ooooooooo-weeeeeee! And got a damn fine slaughter and smoke house too."

"Then why ain't you bought any pork from me for the last five years?" Mr. Reynolds asked the large cigar that was attaching itself to the sheriff.

"Now, you know I come over from time to time to *That's All Folks* and pick me up some good chops and ribs."

Reynolds looked at the sheriff. "Not near enough. And I don't know who you've been buyin' your contest pork from ..." and he turned to me, "but the sheriff here makes the best chili in seven counties. Wins the cook-off every year." Then he put his hand to the side of his face, pretending to shield his comments from the officer. "Personally, I think he's been using beef, but I can't prove it."

The sheriff piped in, toward me: "No, ain't used no beef, and he's got some good pigs," he said, indicating Reynolds, "but man, he's high on the price."

I couldn't hold back. "Your pig farm and slaughter house are called *That's All Folks?*" Both men ignored me.

"Tell you what," Mr. Reynolds said to the officer, "you come on over this year and I'll match any price you get, *anywhere*. I guarantee I'll give you a lower price than anyone else—that is, if you promise to buy from me."

"You know what?" the big armed-with-gun man said, "Let's shake on that. It's a done deal. You give me the best price and I guarantee I'll use them fat pink snortin' things this year in my chili recipe."

"Deal," Reynolds said, and both men shook. Then Taxi & Co. turned to me, putting his hand on my shoulder. "Got to be gettin' Mr. McCrae here on his way."

"Any hotels in the town?" I asked.

The sheriff looked at me sideways. Then Mr. Reynolds spoke: "You ain't got no place to stay, with folks, I mean?"

"Well, I did get a sort of invitation, but I'm not sure if it was serious or not. I thought if there was a motel or something that ..." I started to say to Reynolds, but my personal chauffeur held up his hand and shot me a look.

12

"I know where I'm a-takin' you." (Twins again.) He looked around at the leveled pig farm. "You just put yourself in my hands and everthin'll be okay. I'll take care of you. Got it? Know just the place where you can stay."

I heard myself say the words and they shocked me as I'm not one to offer them up easily, but out they came nevertheless. "Yes, Sir," I said, and followed his pair of overly beefy buttocks to the patrol car as Mr. Reynolds waved good-bye.

3

Banal Creepy Sights

"**E**ver been in a po-leese car 'afore, son?" the sheriff asked to the rearview mirror. It was all very *In the Heat of the Night*. At least he wasn't chewing gum.

"No, Sir," I said leaning toward the Plexiglas and wire mesh partition, trying to squeak my voice through.

"Huh?"

"No, Sir," I repeated more loudly.

"You got to speak up 'cause I'm deaf in one ear—the left one. Gun went off right next to my noggin and can't hear a damn thing outa that side." He turned his head to the right, closer to the partition, while still looking in the mirror, then continued. "That's good—that you ain't never been in one of these 'afore. We don't want no trouble down here. Not a good thing if you's too familiar with the inside of one of these here cars."

"You do have a point."

"Huh?"

"YOU DO HAVE A POINT," I said a little louder, leaning forward.

Realizing that conversation was not going to be the better part of the trip, I preoccupied myself with what scenery lay about. Miles of cotton fields stretched until their verdant rows seem to bend with the horizon, and the clearest blue-June-sky effortlessly wrapped itself about the whole area—a comforting shroud of peace and warmth. Perhaps it wasn't going to be such a bad experience after all.

Along the sides of the highway, watermelon peddlers sold wares resembling miniature Hindenburgs, and faded and tired women clad in sackcloth dresses offered up the ripest tomatoes and largest cucumbers known to mankind. The people and their oversized vegetables whizzed by us—or us by them: a sped-up movie reel with no rewind button. At one point, a flock of fifty or sixty crows shot upwards simultaneously from one of the fields, and careened, all in the same direction, over two-hundred-year-old oak trees lining a nearby farm. In the distance I thought I saw a plantation house. The occasional worker in the field looked up and waved, and the sheriff waved back.

"Everybody must know everybody else here, I guess," I said.

"Purt much."

Attempting camaraderie, I finally asked, "Uhhh ... *you* know who *I* am, but I didn't get *your* name." My driver had not introduced himself—a major *faux pas* in the Southern book of etiquette. Then again, he was in law enforcement. I knew from having relatives in that line of work that explanations were seldom offered—they didn't need to be as the employee almost always had a gun, and that pretty much said it all. This time the sheriff was in labor for a good thirty minutes. Finally the baby came.

"Salinger," he said, not bothering to look in the mirror or take the cigar from his mouth.

"Oh, like the author?" I said, after translating what had come out of his mouth, taking into consideration the cigar's impeding properties. The result was something like "Allengur," but I regressed back to my youth, remembered how people in this area spoke, and made the translation.

"What author?" he asked, glancing out the window at a mule cart that ambled alongside the highway. A washed-out woman slumped in the driver's seat, casually cracking a whip half-heartedly at a pokey mule. We left her and moved on. She receded into the background, blending in with the soil, the farm plants, the trees, the highway.

Cigar out of mouth for a moment, and seeing another of the area's townsfolk, Salinger let me in on some local lore: "That there's Smoot Hawkins. Lived here all his life. Knowd him since he was knee-high to a grasshopper." Then he shook his head. I watched the ash build at the end of the cigar—it was the size of a grown man's thumb. He hung the lighted instrument over the car seat. The interior of the automobile smelled faintly of burning rubber and I did the proper calculations: the man was none too careful with where he let his cigar droppings land.

"Salinger. The author. You have the same name. You know, the guy who wrote *The Catcher in the Rye*?" I said, returning to my initial literary comment.

"Ain't never read no *Catcher in the Rye*. Some farming book or somethin'?"

"Uh, no. It's ... never mind."

"He a friend of yours, this ... Salinger author person?"

"I wish."

We were coming near the town now. Three-story rows of century-old brick structures stood side-by-side with the occasional 1950s dime store thrown in to break up the monotony, its slick flesh-colored tile façade a marked contrast to the older concrete-festooned buildings that sported embedded stone names such as "McIntosh Pharmacy" and "Myert's Dress Shoppe"—mortar signs set in brick, a hundred years old themselves and still quite visible even though the actual stores now sold hardware or housed a beauty parlor and a small café. An occasional cement planter, thrown in for good measure, dotted the warped sidewalk, accommodating wilting petunias and sweet potato vines that attempted to escape their hot, dry jail. A lone stoplight swung at the main intersection and scampering newspapers and other litter outnumbered what townspeople were visible, the paper news items seeming to posses more life than the actual inhabitants of Chalybeate Springs.

Sheriff Salinger, sensing my dismay (or actually seeing it in his rearview mirror) commented: "Everybody's inside. Too hot."

I nodded and continued to gaze out the window. The entire downtown area was a whopping one block in length. As we came to the end of it, my chauffeur turned off onto a side street.

"Hotel's down here a-ways" he said, then added, "but first just want to make a stop if you don't mind."

Who was I to argue? Besides, he had a gun and knew where we were going.

After two right turns and one left (passing the very place where I was to stay), Sheriff Salinger motored up next to a small quiet cemetery. He maneuvered the patrol car easily along the curb and came to a stop at the bottom of a hill. Looking into the cemetery I could see enormous cedars as they swayed in the wind. I listened: They gave off an odd other-worldly music. Other than that, the place was eerily quiet. Tombstones of every slant and century jockeyed for position, some crowding, some standing apart; a now departed ghostly peanut-munching crowd of mutes awaiting any and everyone. I watched from the car as the sheriff made his way a good sixty feet up the hill and stopped at a pinkish granite number (small urn on top, slight carving around the edges). With hat in hand he bowed his head and his lips seemed to move.

While he paid his respects, I looked around the inside of the car. Not really that much to see; nothing that unusual except a police radio, the partition, and the smell of coffee from the sheriff's large plastic cup. Then I looked at the seat I was sitting on. It was new and the fabric didn't match that of the front seat. Strange. There must have been some accident or maybe one of Chalybeate Springs's criminals had gotten out of hand with a knife, or worse, thrown up. Or perhaps Salinger had set it on fire accidentally and it had been replaced.

Finally the sheriff donned his headgear and bounced toward the car, regaining his police-like attitude.

"Sorry about that," he said to the sun visor as he readjusted himself in the front seat. "Little ritual of mine. Hope you don't mind."

"No, no problem for me."

"We small town folks like to stay connected with everything and everyone, even if they *is* gone."

I wanted to ask who the dear departed was but thought better of it. (I also wanted to correct his grammar.) But I figured that if he wanted to tell me, he would. And he wasn't offering up any further explanations so I let it go.

"Passed your hotel on the way," he went on. "Now listen, if you need anything, or anyone bothers you while you're here, you just let me know. I'll take care of you."

I had to wonder at his kindness—what was in it for him. I knew people from small towns (I had grown up in one) and I knew people in places like New York. They weren't that different deep down—the same fears, the same hopes, the same kindness, and the same covered-up meanness. The accents were the only real difference.

The car finally stopped. As the only luggage I had was a small bag and my computer that I had carried on the plane, I pulled them and myself from the back seat and onto the sidewalk, and waved good-bye to the sheriff.

"CHALYBEATE SPRINGS INN," the white sign with black lettering read. Rows of neatly trimmed boxwoods—a good century old—surrounded the white clapboard structure. It could have been in any-town anywhere with the exception of the burning sun and the accents of the natives.

Making my way through the door (proverbial overhead jingling bell meant to announce newcomers), I rolled up to the front desk.

"I have a reservation for …"

"McCrae, Jackson," the man answered without looking up. He was dressed in a white shirt with garters on the sleeves and a green visor cap. A regular Mr. Druker from *Green Acres*, this one, even though the nameplate on the counter read "Percy Abel Hastings." I secretly hoped for his sake he didn't nave a brother named "Cain."

"But, how did you …"

"Only person to stay here in five years," he responded, still not looking up. Then added, "That we admit to. Read about you coming in the paper."

I waited. "Then how do you stay in business?"

It was his turn. He waited. He did what I had by now termed the "Chalybeate Springs baby shuffle." This time, however, he was quicker. The baby, it appeared, was premature by Chalybeate standards. "We manage," he snapped, and smacked the bell that sat on the counter. The ping brought out a large African-American man, no less than seven feet tall and a good three hundred pounds.

"This here's Jecko," the front desk man said, gesturing to a substantial specimen who had arrived and taken possession of my carry-on bag. I held onto the laptop as an elderly lady would hold onto her purse on the D train in New York at three in the morning. "He's the cook too, so don't make him mad," Mr. Hastings added.

Jecko grunted—an indication that I was to follow. I did.

Up one flight of stairs and past two doorways I was ushered into a modest and comfortable room. The decoration was straight out of a 1930s movie—the only things missing were Joan Crawford, a seedy plot, and an oversized cigarette lighter. I had the immediate inclination to turn to Jecko and say, in an overly dramatic voice, one hand resting behind me, leaning back slightly, "I know where you were last night. Why do you insist on embarrassing me with this horrible charade?" I could have added the high arched eyebrows and sultry Crawford look too, but thought the moment would be lost on him. He hadn't said one word and so far there was no sign of a sense of humor. I settled on tipping him five dollars and thanked him for his troubles. He bowed slightly and exited the room.

I looked around and was just about to set my laptop down on one of the room's tables, next to a potted African violet, when I saw a small hand-torn piece of paper. I picked it up and read what was on it: "Eatables Psych-Ring." Ordinarily I wouldn't have thought much of it, but looking over at the bureau, I noticed another. "Banal Creepy Things." Same scrawl, same paper. After pondering what they could possibly mean, I shrugged and stuck them into the side pocket of my computer case. And with that, I found myself in the land of Chalybeate Springs—an adventure that would prove most interesting.

4

Single's Cab Therapy

It was the next day and I was still there—no, it wasn't a dream. I entered the small dining room at the Inn and sat down. The room might have held ten people but no more. No one else was in sight, and within minutes Jecko arrived with a plate of scrambled eggs and bacon—extra crisp. And coffee. I was about to ask to see a menu, thank him, or, well, say anything when he abruptly walked off. Not wanting to make waves, and actually thinking that I would have ordered scrambled eggs and bacon anyway, I ate what was given to me and then made my way to the front desk.

"I need to get out to ... (I consulted a piece of paper I had dug from my pocket) see a ..."

"Miss Tuck Henrid," the front desk man answered. He had yet to look at me.

I leaned forward on the counter, my arms crossed. "Let me ask you something." I waited, practicing my Chalybeate incubation period. I wasn't that good at it yet—the rabbit was only slightly sick; nowhere near dead. I continued: "Does everyone know everything about everybody in this town?"

Twins on Mr. Hastings's part. "Pretty much," he said, stapling a group of papers together. It occurred to me how odd this was, what with the Inn having no business. What was there to staple?

"You'll find the sheriff just outside, waiting to tote you around."

I looked confused. He saw this. "Like I said," he started, but I held up my hand.

"I get it," I answered, and began to walk toward the door. "Everybody knows everybody else," I muttered under my breath.

But I hesitated before I left the Inn, turning back to the man at the desk doing his Mr. Druker imitation. "Say, not to be nosey or anything, but what's up with Jecko?"

"Big nigger?"

"Well, yes, if you insist on using that word. I mean, it's the twenty-first century, don't you think something a little more politically correct would be ..."

"Nigger's a deaf-mute," the man answered. "Always was, always will be." He paused, then for the first time he looked up. "And we calls 'em they way we sees 'em down here. He can read lips if you look right at him. Can't read regular-like or write."

"How very Carson McCullers," I said.

"Who?"

"All-righty then," I responded, and stepped lightly out of the Inn to my waiting equipage.

"Serves as the town's cab service too," Salinger offered up as I swung open the door of the police car. He had his cigar in his mouth. It, fortunately, hadn't been lit. "Yes sir indeedie, I'm the po-leese, livery service, and even the fire department. Though the last fire was when Old Lady Childers left the grease on the stove, heating it up to fix that drunkard husband of hers some collards—so she said. I'll tell you, she's a loon. Only damn woman in the county who fries collards instead of cookin' 'em."

I got in. Then I noticed another piece of paper—just like the ones in my room; cryptic message included, though this one made a bit more sense: "Single's Cab Therapy." I relegated it to my pocket and said nothing of the find.

"I'm guessing I don't need to tell you ..." I started to say, not getting a chance to finish.

"Nope. Miss Henrid. Got it all down. Just thought I'd show you about the town first, if you're interested," he said, and shut my door. Then he mashed himself into the front seat.

"But my appointment is for ..."

"Son, I don't want to pull rank on you or nuthin', but I'm the sheriff in these here parts and, just trust me on this one. Miss Hereid will do *what* I tell her and *when*. I done told you, I got it all down. Now, do you want to see where everythin' is or not? Seems to me if you gonna be writin' that cookbook and make us all famous, you gonna have to know who's who and what's where."

"How did you know about the cookbook?" Before the words were out of my mouth, I knew the answer.

"I thought y'all Yankees was supposed to be quick," Salinger said, eyeing me in the mirror now that we were on our way.

"Right. Everybody knows everybody," I said, and settled back.

"Well, you got it *part* right. Everybody knows everybody ... but *you*. Now that makes for a right interesting equation, if you ask me."

"Right interesting," I said to myself and stared out the window.

After a moment or two (short by Chalybeate standards), Salinger spoke. "How was the bacon and eggs this mornin'?"

"Man, you guys keep up with everything," I said, shaking my head.

Salinger waited, laughing to himself. "Not all that much," he said.

"What do you mean?"

"Scrambled eggs, bacon, and coffee is the only thing they serve at the Inn. Way I look at it, you didn't have much choice."

"Amazing," I said, and let out a sigh.

The car turned the next corner and we found ourselves in a rather nice section of town. Enormous oaks and tulip trees towered over two-hundred-year-old homes, and azalea bushes the size of Kansas vied for attention with sprawling boxwoods and rhododendrons that could easily have filled an airplane hanger. Smatterings of maple, sycamore, and willow accented the properties— the effect being that of a garden district rather than a small town. Scarsdale, Greenwich, and Oyster Bay had nothing on these few blocks.

"First house up here on the left ... that would be the Weemses'. Weemses is the big people in town, you might say. The husband is mayor of the town. Big ole fat guy with the gout. Got it all sewed up as far as bein' on top."

I thought maybe I had heard wrong. "Gout, or gut?" I asked.

Salinger paused, then looked in the mirror. "Yes," he said. "Weems is my boss, so I can't say too much about him, but that durn wife of his is another kettle of fish altogether."

"How do you mean?"

"Well," he said, reaching over with his right hand to scratch his left arm that was steering the car. "First off, she weighs about four hundred pounds."

"You're exaggerating, of course."

"No, I ain't. Four hundred if she's an ounce. And got this big ole beehive hairdo. Thing's at least three feet high. But boy does she think she's some kinda snooty-patooty. Let me tell *you*. Nose so far up in the air I'm surprised one of them big ole planes hasn't flown up it. They travels a lot too, the Weemses. All over." He swung the car onto a side street beside the great house and put it in park. The lawn sloped down to the sidewalk and the view was a picture postcard. Great white columns stretched from the ground floor to the second-story, and an enormous side porch (obviously added on sometime later) nestled to one side. The landscaping was beautiful and offset the house perfectly.

"Yes sir," Salinger went on, "they're the big money in the town. Got to say one thing though."

"What's that?"

"He didn't get rich paying his employees well."

"You're talking about what he pays you, I'm guessing. I mean, since you work for him, at least indirectly."

"You got that right," Salinger continued. "Oh, you know, there's the odd jobs—security detail for their parties, that sort of thing—but nothing to speak of. And, hell, there's not a lot going on in this town anyways." He put the car in drive once again and we moved on.

"Next house I'll show you belongs to the Brandyworths. Not as big, but still a nice place. Sort of what you'd call a Colonial type. Not my taste, but wouldn't say no if you gave it to me. It's just about a block away," Salinger said, as he dug a meaty paw into the back of his pants and adjusted some unseen article of clothing.

I couldn't help but ask: "I really appreciate you showing me around and all, but why the tour? I mean, I'm here to help some ladies with their cookbook."

"Son, you just don't get it. I'm showing you the places where these ladies live for a reason. That last one—the Weemses' house—that lady's President of the Junior League. You'll have to do some major ass-kissing on that one, and let me tell you, it's one *very* big ass, so you better get them lips stretched out."

"I'm not really sure about this whole thing ..." I started to say, but stopped. I remembered the note from Mrs. Weems—the one I had received just before leaving. Now it was all falling into place—this tour of the neighborhood.

"Aint' nothing to be sure or unsure about. You's here. It's a done deal. This next house—we're coming up on it now, that Colonial—belongs to the Brandyworths. Man, let me tell you, the wife is really the 'C' word."

"Cunt?" I asked.

Salinger's forehead furrowed, then he spoke. "Naw, Christian." He waited, still looking confused. "Come to think of it, your definition might just fit a tad better. Anyways, her old man is Reverend Brandyworth."

"A preacher."

"Only got one. Brandyworth Church of Christ. Hell, they won't let no other churches *in* the town. Now, you'd think we'd at least have a Baptist church; but no, Old Man Brandyworth and his wife won't hear of it." Salinger brought the car to a stop across the street. In the front yard, monkey grass and camellias dotted the lawn. Salinger went on: "The wife drinks. And boy-howdy, do I mean *drinks*. I've had to pick her up more times than I can count, but hell, can't do a damn thing about it."

"How come?"

"Hell, she's best friends with that Weems woman—mayor's wife." Salinger turned halfway around in the seat to better look in my direction. "See all them trees we passed back on Lee Road? Them big ole oaks and such? Every single one of 'em got a chunk about so big," he said, making his hands form a space big enough to encompass a basketball, "taken right out of 'em. That'd be Mrs. Otis Brandyworth. Drunk as a skunk all the time and can't do a thing about it. And get this: Seventeen kids."

"Excuse me?"

"Yeah. Seventeen kids."

"Well, we know that they've been doing."

Salinger turned back around and addressed me via the rearview mirror. "Don't kid yourself, boy. There ain't been no sinkin' the sub in that house for quite a while. Adopted—all of them, they did."

I thought for a moment as I gazed out at the two-story Colonial. It could have sat in Connecticut and not been out of place. "Well, I suppose that's something to be said for them, taking in all those orphans."

Salinger reached over and scratched his left arm again. Then he shook his head.

"What?" I said, seeing his reaction.

"Somethin's up if you ask me. Who the hell wants seventeen kids? And them taking trips all the time down to Orlando and places like Fort Walton Beach. Now, don't get me wrong—these Brandyworths got money. Hell, they ought to, the way they pass that collection plate around at church, but something just seems wrong."

"You're the sheriff, why don't you ask?"

"Like I told you, when Mrs. Brandyworth ain't hooked up to a vodka I.V. she's busy being best friends with Old Lady Weems. My hands is tied."

"See your point. So she would be another of the lovely ladies on the Junior League?"

"Now you're catching on, my friend," Salinger said, and turned the car in another direction.

5

Cigar Bashes Plenty

The drive to the next area of town (the whole place was only thirty or forty square blocks) was short but not quite so sweet.

"Well, this is certainly different from the last neighborhood," I said as Salinger maneuvered the car around streets that bordered well-manicured but not overly posh lawns. Smaller but still tasteful houses sat side-by-side—a little closer than in the previous wealthier neighborhood.

"Observant for a Yankee," Salinger said, not even bothering to shoot the comment in the direction of the mirror. "This here," he went on, as the car turned slowly onto a shady lane, "is the home of Mrs. Shelby."

"That's her last name?"

"Not exactly," he said, pulling the car over about two houses away. "It's her first name. I don't want to stop too close. Had my eye on her for years and don't want to arouse any suspicion."

"What's she done?" I asked.

"What's she *not* done, is a better question," Salinger said. Then he lit his cigar for the first time that day. I had noticed that he had been chewing on it since the beginning of our trip, but not bothering to actually smoke it. "Well, let's see where to begin with this one," he continued. "First, Shelby was married to a Mr. Dipsey, or as he was loving known around these parts, 'Dipshit.' Sorry for my language."

"I'm from New York, remember?"

"Well now, you're originally a good ole Southern boy, am I right?"

"Yeah, but you keep calling me a Yankee."

"So, just because you lived up there all them years ain't no reason to give up on your manners. 'Sides, why else you think you's asked to do this here assignment?"

"How do you know who asked me?" I said, my curiosity piqued.

"Let's just say that I have my ways." He paused. The usual childbirth period followed. The day was beginning to get sultry and Salinger offered to start up the air-conditioning.

"Please," I said, fanning under my arms.

"Gonna get a lot hotter than this after you been here a few days," he went on, exhaling a long column of cigar smoke. The air-conditioning caught the haze and shot it toward the partition. The section of the separation that was heavy wire mesh allowed the smoke to filter back.

"Hope the smoke don't bother you," he said.

I choked back a cough and tried to reply, though nothing came out.

"As I was sayin', Mrs. Shelby is what we *call* her. Lives in that smallish stucco number with the high pitched roof. Kinda cute but outa place in Chalybeate if you ask me. Originally built by some doctor. Shelby is the head ly-*berr-ian* at the Shelby D.E.A.T Memorial Ly-berry. She thought the name 'Ly-berry' was too ordinary, so she renamed the place. Now Shelby's first husband was a Dipsey. Oh, yeah, already gone over that. Darnell Dipsey. Went to school with him. On the town council and had a bit of money but lost most of it on some invention designed to take your temperature."

"A thermometer?"

"Not exactly. Well, kinda. It was this here contraception what you inserted into your ... what's the word I'm a lookin' for here ... anus, I guess, for lack of a better adjective, noun, whatever. Anyway, it ran some line up to your watch and you could check the time and your temperature all at once."

"Sounds charming."

"Fortunately, for Shelby, and the rest of us, he died." Salinger exhaled another column of smoke and gazed at the house. He pointed the cigar and one meaty finger in the direction of the white stucco building. "Yes sir, that lady's a piece of work. Never could determine exactly what old Dipsey died of. He'd been hit over the head with a blunt object but no murder weapon could ever be found. Gave up on that. It's been a sore point ever since in the town. Next husband she had was Frank M. Ewell, of the Tennessee Ewells."

"Never heard of them," I said.

"And why would you? They's good for nuthin' if you ask me. Ewell was nothing special—into feed and grain. Trouble was, we's a cotton and bean place, 'cept for them pigs, so his business petered out."

"So Shelby's still married to him?"

"Not so, my friend. Dead. Two in a row. Poisoning, that one."

I waited, wondering why he was telling me this. "So she's on the Junior League also?"

"Right-O. But that's not the least of it. Husband number three ..."

"Wait a minute," I said. "Husband number two ..."

"Ewell."

"Ewell, was poisoned, and nobody asked questions?"

Outside, two kids on bicycles, squealing to one another, whizzed past the police car. Salinger watched them. "Damn little rug rats," he spat out. He flicked the end of his cigar toward the ashtray, completely missing. "Guess I shouldn't complain. Other than the Brandyworths' kids, that's about all we got in this town. Guess you could say we's short on the young ones."

"Any reason?" I asked. Salinger looked out the window and had a miscarriage.

"None I can think of," he said.

"You were saying about Shelby and husband number two, Ewell—the one who was poisoned."

"Couldn't do nuthin'. Again, Shelby is on that Junior League and tight with Weems and Brandyworth. What Mayor Weems didn't sweep under the rug, Reverand Brandyworth put away with a sermon on the evils of feed and grain distribution."

"You've got to be kidding me."

"I'm funnin' you about as much as a one-legged man trying to kick down a screen door in a submarine," Salinger responded.

"I'll hold that image for a moment, if you don't mind."

The sheriff continued: "Tried everything, but couldn't get a confession out of Shelby. Was up at the library ever day while she was stamping them books and re-shelving them things. Still couldn't get no info outa her. Then the trouble really began. Sent my best deputy over to try and *woo* it out of her. Um-boy-howdy, let me tell you. He was successful, but not in getting a confession. He got sometin' else outa her, if you catch my drift. Next thing I know, they's married."

"He didn't suspect anything?" I asked

"Oh, he suspected plenty, but you know that saying, 'When the pecker stands up, the brain turns to poop.' "

I squirmed in my seat. The sheriff caught my reaction.

"Oh, sorry. Sometimes I forget my manners. But the truth was, he was just plain seduced. Pure and simple. And Shelby's a looker, that's for sure."

"So, two husbands are dead and she's still walking around?" I asked, eyeing the small house now with more than a modicum of interest.

"Just wait. It gets better. My deputy—Charles G. Adams, best damn deputy I've had in years—well, he liked to drink, if you know what I mean. While he and Shelby may have had a pretty good roll in the hay from time to time, she didn't take kindly to his carryin' on with Jim Beam."

"He was gay?"

Salinger turned slightly to look at me. "Boy, Jim Beam's a drink."

"Oh, right," I said, embarrassed.

He went on: "Adams come home one evening and they got in a spat about somethin', and old Charles, well he pops her one. Nice shiner, too."

"No stereotyping there," I said.

"Now, don't go there. We's all human. Hell, the woman had two husbands die on her, and you can bet they wasn't natural deaths, so she had something a comin' to her."

"I'm just saying …"

"Now, don't get your panties in a wad. Let me finish it. I'm tryin' to fill you in on this here Junior League bunch so's you can help them out with that there cookbook."

"Yeah, here's the thing I want to know. What's in it for you? I mean, you're driving me around this town, filling me in on all the dirt. What do you get out of it?"

"Son, you ask too many questions. Don't you know we Southerners love to talk, but we don't give a rat's ass about listenin'?"

I sat back in the seat. While Salinger had said that the police car doubled as the town's taxi, it wasn't completely lost on me that the determined areas of seating were cleverly disguised as a power play. He was, after all, sitting in the front, driving—a real sheriff—and I was, for all practical purposes, in the back, a prisoner. He had a captive audience. I decided to play along. Besides, money was at stake, and personally, I'd have listened to Satan's ramblings to get some of it at this point in my career.

"You were saying," I started up again, feigning attention.

"Cigar's gone out," he said, looking at the ashen end. He shook it off and relit. "Where was I? Oh, yeah." A rhythm had been set up with Sheriff Salinger. He waited—a good Ceasearean in length. "Husband number three was my deputy. At that point, I started gettin' mad (puff, puff, glowing end of cigar). Hell, who wouldn't? So, right after the black-eye incident, Charles comes up dead, again with poisoning. I'd just about had enough, so I said to hell with Weems and

27

that gang and did my own investigation. I interrogated and cajoled—is that the right word?—and whatnot, but nothing. Finally, in desperation, I called over to the courthouse and got the county coroner to come out—explained the whole thing to him. Everything was fine for about three weeks. He's out there doin' his job and such and before you know it, that damn woman strikes again. Now, how in the hell she done it, I'll never know."

"Let me guess …"

"You got it. The *Chalybeate Springs Times* read 'Siegfried Tellerman marries Shelby Dipsey-Ewell-Adams. Lord God, baby Jesus, and the plastic sheep on the courthouse lawn at Christmastime. You coulda knocked me over with a feather."

"Please tell me that Mr. Tellerman is alive and well," I said, my head in my hands. I shuddered to think that this woman, along with the mayor's wife and the Reverand Brandyworth's, were all in the same Junior League. I was starting to see a pattern emerge and it wasn't pretty.

Salinger cracked his window to let some of the smoke out. "Look a-yonder," he said, sinking down in the seat, "there she comes," and with that I glanced up to see a very pretty woman of about thirty-five dressed in a tailored yellow suit with matching bag and shoes. Salinger waited until the woman had gotten in her car and driven away. "She's a looker, I'll say that much for her," he said. "And to answer your question, No, Tellerman is dead now too."

"Should I even ask how he died?" I ventured.

"Well sir, when the coroner from the *next* county come over—seein' how we done lost our own—I insisted they do an autopsy. Shelby raised Cain over it, but I said 'No way, I'm gettin' to the bottom of this.' Well, she squirmed and squawked, and had Mayor Weems and the Reverend Brandyworth on my tail, but I's like a pit-bull on the nose of a steer. No sir, one of my best deputy's gone and now the coroner. I had them take that man Tellerman apart until they could find out what killed him."

"I'm guessing you didn't find anything," I said, "hence her walking about."

"Oh, they found something all right, but it twernt nothin' we could put her in jail for. He died from some God-awful concoction of food she'd prepared, but Lord Sweet Jesus, none of it was illegal. There was Lime Jello, beef fat, old noodles, pudding, beer, breast milk …"

"Breast milk!"

"Breast milk, an entire loaf of bread, cream of asparagus soup, cream of broccoli soup, cream of bean soup, cream of celery soup, cream of mushroom soup, and get this ... even some old suppositories. It was the coroner's opinion that no *single* ingredient killed the poor bastard, but somehow, the combination did him in."

"Suppositories?" I asked.

"Hey, don't shoot the messenger."

I looked around at the leafy green suburb—placid and serene. One would never guess that such goings-on were, well, going on. "So she's single now," I said, seeing another of the neighbors amble out of his front door to retrieve the paper.

"You'd think so, now wouldn't you?" Salinger remarked, looking at me via his mirror.

"Oh, Jesus."

"You got it. This one's named Hatton. Josh Hatton."

"Any pray tell, what does he do?"

Salinger chuckled to himself. "Man, you wouldn't believe it. But I suppose that after you've gone through half the town, who's left to marry?"

I waited. Salinger read my eyebrows going up.

"Used-car salesman," he finally said. We sat in silence for a few moments as I tried to put it all together.

I mulled over the list, thinking there must be some connection. Finally, it hit me. "Dipsey, right?"

"Check," he answered.

"Then Ewell, then Adams."

"So far so good," he said.

"Finally, Tellerman, and now Hatton."

"I'm waiting, son," he said, drawing a particularly long piece of smoke from his stogie.

"D.E.A.T.H.," I finally said. "The list of her husband's initials spells *Death*."

Salinger smiled, neither to the mirror nor to anyone in particular. "See now, you may have been up North for quite a while, but you still a Southern boy at heart. I knew you'd come around soon enough," and with that he started the car and pulled away from the curb.

6

Reb City's Phalanges

Sheriff Salinger parked in front of a nice but smallish house on the other side of Main Street—the street separating the Weems and Brandyworth houses from the less affluent neighborhoods.

"Ain't terribly big, but it works," he said, leaning his head down to look at the front of the small abode. A white picket fence graced the property and one enormous oak tree—no less than four feet thick—stood in the front yard. A halcyon charm seemed to inhabit the place.

Salinger sat in the car while I got out. "Stayin' put, if you don't mind—want to finish my *see-gaar*," he said.

Just as I was wending my way up the front path (snapdragons and sweet peas on each side), a rather pretty woman opened a squeaky screen door and came to meet me. She extended her hand and smiled.

"I'm Tuck Henrid," she said and shook my hand. "You must be Mr. McCrae."

"Yes, ma'am," I said. "Quite a grip you got there," I added. Then I took a step back. The resemblance was uncanny. If the woman had spent hours in makeup, she couldn't have achieved the Joan Crawford look more accurately. I immediately thought back to my room at the Inn and how I had been tempted to offer up some Crawfordish repartee to Jecko. And there was something else; something about her mannerisms and the way she carried herself—as if I'd met her before. Perhaps I was just remembering all the old Crawford movies I'd seen.

"Well, so many of us Southern women have that mealy-mouthed-Melanie attitude that I like to counter it with whatever I can," she responded to my comment about her handshake. "You come on inside now, Sugar, and I've got some iced tea waiting. You like it sweet or unsweetened?" she asked as she reentered the house. I followed her as if she were a draft from the pull of an eighteen-wheeler, and found myself in a tastefully decorated and air-conditioned home.

"Now, don't let my cold air out," she said, motioning for me to shut the door.

"Sweet tea," I said, answering her question, shutting the door and looking around. A soft green carpet covered the living and dining rooms and practical Duncan-Phyfe reproduction furniture filled what I could see of the house. One large green velvet armchair sat next to a table sporting an original Tiffany lamp (I know about these things), and a fireplace grounded the space, obviously not enjoying its vocation. Fake logs—the kind with a hidden light bulb and colored paper in the openings, attempting to reproduce artificial warmth—sat stoically, awaiting winter or at least the next whim for ambiance.

"Got your letter ... obviously," I said in the direction of the dining room. Miss Henrid was just beyond, now in the small kitchen. I could hear her cajoling ice cubes from their plastic trays. They popped into the glasses unceremoniously and proceeded to emit cracking noises as the tea was poured over them.

"Glad you wanted it sweetened," she said, entering the room with a serving tray and the promised beverage. "I had my fingers crossed since I'd sweetened the whole thing." She sat down and shrugged. "Have a seat. You probably think I'm awful for the deception."

"Not really. I've seen worse," I said, and sat.

"I just wanted to meet you face to face and explain a few things since you were so nice to come all the way down here." She adjusted herself on an Empire-style sofa and settled her head back a few inches. It gave me a chance to take her in fully. While her hair was perfectly coiffed, set off nicely by two solid but slightly large clip-on earrings, and her overly-frilly day dress was a bit gauche, she was more put together than anyone else I'd seen so far in the area. Bright-red finger nail polish drew more than the needed attention to her hands. I noticed that, for all her feminine charms she had sturdiness about her—something gawky, as if she'd been the perpetual wall-flower at the prom dance of life and had worked day and night to fight the image.

Either the good people of Chalybeate Springs were exceptional at reading other's expressions, or they could simply read minds. She caught me glancing down at her feet (encased in 1930s pumps even though this was the first decade of the twenty-first century) and commented on the tea being served: a foil designed to bring my stare up and away from her lower extremities. The transition was smooth enough.

"I brought some fresh lemon out with the tea," she said, changing my thoughts back to the land of beverages. "Some people like it, but some don't. Personally, I can't stand that fake stuff that you can get—you know, in that little plastic lemon? I grew up on a farm and everything was fresh, fresh, fresh," she said as she handed me a glass (amber-colored and overly-textured with squares—a rather garish seam completing the design).

"I had to work all my life—picking cotton, milking the cows; the usual farm chores. I have to say it built character, but it sure does a number on your hands," she said, holding them up and then curling her fingers in toward her, giving them a look that reflected a sadness at how they must have been before the cotton and the egg-picking took over and aged them prematurely. " 'Fraid I was a bit of a tomboy, too. Daddy loved that … at first. But then later, when I was courting age, he tried and tried to get me into one of those frilly dresses, but just couldn't do it." She smiled demurely—pure Southern charm—and added, "Now you can't get me out of them." Each hand went symmetrically to a shoulder and she adjusted the ruffles even though they didn't need it.

"You grew up around here?" I asked, taking a sip of tea. While I liked mine sweetened, this particular beverage was going to require an insulin injection if I finished the thing. I squeezed one of the aforementioned lemons into the glass, careful to hold my hand over it so as not to spray Miss Henrid or her faux Duncan-Phyfe side tables.

"Heavens no," she said, rolling her eyes. "Grew up way down in the southern part of the state. Lived all over. Birmingham, Atlanta, Memphis. Guess you could say I'm a real international traveler of sorts. Not like some of these uppity socialites around here. Well, with the exception of Mrs. Weems. She's been all over and makes sure *everyone* knows all about it."

"You like to travel?"

"That was ages ago, and I don't want to even discuss it now. No, I grew up in the southern part of the state and worked on a farm. Oh, we had money; that much I found out *after* my daddy died. But while he was alive he made me work as if I was one of the hired help."

I said nothing. She read this as boredom even though I was simply taking it all in.

"You need more tea?" she asked.

"No, fine. Thank you."

"As I was saying, I've lived here and there. Moved to Chalybeate just about a year ago and it has been *absolute hell.*"

"How do you mean?"

She leaned forward, setting her iced tea down on the tray, confident in the fact that she had my attention. "Well, where do I start? I don't have to tell you that Chalybeate Springs is not a big place, and everybody …"

"Knows everybody," I said, finishing her sentence.

She looked shocked for a moment and I thought I had offended her Southern sensibility by cutting in, but it was something else entirely. "How did you know?" she asked. She was completely innocent in her questioning.

"Word gets around," I said.

"Well, anyway, as I was saying, they all know each other: the Weemses know the Brandyworths ..."

"Mayor's wife and the wife of the Reverend."

"Yes. And then there's that Shelby woman. We would call her by her last name but life is short—especially for her husbands, I might add—and we just don't have the time. We just call her Shelby."

"Yes, Sheriff Salinger was nice enough to show me around earlier and give me a little background information on the three ladies."

"Well, there's more than three." She paused, deep in thought. "Now, mind, not a lot more." She paused again. "Actually, there's only two more."

"Oh?"

"A Mary-Ellen Killchrist (she pronounced it 'Kill-Christ'), lovingly known as the village idiot."

"Salinger didn't mention her."

"Honey," she said, reaching over and touching my knee, "the day is not *that* long."

"You said 'Kill-*Christ?*' How do you spell that—Mary-Ellen's name?" Miss Henrid spelled it for me. "Are you sure it's not pronounced "Kill-*crest?*""

I got a blank look. "Guess not," I said.

Then Henrid made a face. "I'll fill you in, but first you wait just a minute and let me get some more sugar from the kitchen. This tea is a little bitter for me. How's yours?"

"Fine, mine is fine," I said, thinking that she must have stock in a sugarcane plantation in Costa Rica. No wonder she was practically bouncing off the walls with energy.

While she got up to procure more white granules, I turned and looked around the room. My gaze went to a window that was behind the green velvet chair and Tiffany lamp. Leaning over, I was able to see Sheriff Salinger reclining against the side of his patrol car, smoking his cigar. I wasn't sure if he was keeping an eye on me, or just being polite and waiting until I was finished.

33

"Sure you don't want some more?" Miss Henrid offered, as she swung into the room with a sugar bowl the size of cantaloupe.

"I'm fine, really," I said, and felt the buzz from the caffeine taking hold.

7

Teachably Pressing

"W here was I?" It was Miss Henrid, attempting to pick up where she had left off with her history of the Junior League.

"You were telling me about the other two members—Mary-Ellen and ..."

"Oh, yes." She smoothed the front of her dress and squeezed her knees together. Then she folded her hands in her lap and looked up at the ceiling as if trying to recall some difficult chemistry formula from high school.

"Now. Mary-Ellen is the town whore. She's never been married and has not a brain in her pretty little head. She was Homecoming Queen ..." but she stopped as soon as she said it. Some trigger had been pulled and her expression changed. "Let's not talk about that." She began fumbling with the iced tea tray, arranging glasses, the pitcher, and the lemons even though they didn't need it. Again her tone changed somewhat—it mellowed. "Mary-Ellen used to be a nice person, many years ago," she went on.

"This is what people have told you," I said, taking a sip. Miss Henrid looked confused.

"Why would you say that?" she asked.

"Well, you said you grew up in the southern part of the state so I'm guessing you didn't know her in high school."

"Oh. Yes. Yes, that's right." She fanned herself with her right hand. "How silly of me. Yes, you know, in a small town, people so like to talk. And everyone says she *was* nice. I wouldn't know personally, but that's what I'm told."

"So what happened?"

"Evidently being head cheerleader and Homecoming Queen went to her ... head—what there was of it—and she got a wee bit above her station, as they say."

"In what way?"

"Well, once you sleep with everyone in town, you tend to get *on* a bit in life. She now coaches the cheerleading squad at the Chalybeate Springs Killchrist High School ..."

"This town has a high school?"

"Hmmm," she said, tea glass to her lips. Then she swallowed. "Forty students total."

"That big?"

"And, she teaches home economics. I don't have to tell you, in a town this size, that qualifies her as a celebrity. She got them to re-name the school for her. Conceited little bitch," she finished, muttering it into her iced tea.

"Shock," I said.

"Exactly."

I pondered the situation concerning Mary-Ellen for a moment. Good-looking woman, cooking skills, probably perky. It didn't add up. Finally I asked. "If she's so hot-to-trot, can cook, and keep house (I'm guessing here), and is so popular, why isn't she married?"

Miss. Henrid looked from side-to-side but said nothing for a moment. "Let's just say that she's ... different."

"Different how?"

"She had a bad experience with a, uh, man once. Long time ago. I don't know all the details," she went on, one hand touching the back of her hair, adjusting the style even though no modification was needed.

"You mean she's a ..."

"I'm not saying anything bad, mind you." She looked down at her hands, now folded in her lap.

"But you said she was the town whore," I reminded her. Henrid waited, rather uncomfortably.

"I really shouldn't say that. I'm just jealous, I suppose. After all, she is a member of the Junior League and, well," she looked up and faced me directly, "I'm *not*."

"Which would be the reason for my visit here."

She nodded but said nothing, giving a long, slow blink. Then she continued. "There are those who make up stories about other people in an effort to throw them off the trail, so to speak. Do you know what I'm talking about?"

"Maybe. But—and I'm not changing the subject here—you said there was a fifth woman in the group. There's Weems, Brandyworth, Mary-Ellen, that Shelby with a list of dead husbands. Who's the fifth one?"

Miss. Henrid got up and uneasily walked over to the fireplace mantel. Her overly-full skirt swirled about her legs. As it did so, I noticed her calves and ankles. She was a very pretty woman and obviously kept herself in excellent condition. I noticed how comical her

1930s pumps looked on her feet—oversized almost, giving her the appearance of Minnie Mouse. She absent-mindedly fingered a reproduction Staffordshire figurine on the mantel for a moment, then looked out the window at Salinger, who was still leaning against his car, arms crossed.

"Mrs. Childers. She's the final one. She's the maid for the other four women in the club," she said, addressing the figurine, "and *pure-dee* white trash."

"I don't understand." She turned toward me.

"Now do you see why it galls me that I'm not allowed into the League?" She was becoming angry, her face turning red.

"But how did a woman who is a maid get into the Junior League when all the others are ..."

"Society women?"

"Well, if you want to call them that," I said.

"And whores?"

"I guess ..." I added.

She was fuming now, her emotions spilling out as they can from a woman who has been socially rejected.

"I'll do anything it takes to get into that Junior League, Mr. McCrae. You can't be anyone in this town or do anything without acceptance here and I'll do whatever it takes."

I looked down at the carpet, not wanting to bring up the money she'd sent, but it seemed like as good a time as any. "Let me guess: that's why the monetary inducement."

"I wasn't sure you'd have come otherwise." She toyed with the figurine once more—her back to me.

"Look, I don't want to seem greedy, but my publisher hasn't offered me an advance and ..." I was going to say, "And I was thrilled to get the $25,000 from you," but she didn't let me finish.

She turned to me, full face again, straightforward. "Mr. McCrae." Her tone was firm, almost hostile. "I've read your books. I know what you're all about. I know how you write. I know what you're capable of."

Evidently she thought I wanted additional compensation. I made a face and looked around. She was making me uncomfortable. "I'm not sure whether to be insulted or take that as a compliment."

"You'll get more money if you can come through with what I propose," she said, turning back to the mantel and re-adjusting the figurine. "You see, many years ago ..." but she stopped.

"I'm listening."

She hesitated, then sat down and tried to collect herself. She took a deep breath and let it out.

"Many years ago, my family was wronged. Land, money, oh, it doesn't matter how, but they were done . . . *I* was done a great injustice."

"But you …" I started to say. Her upheld hand cut me off. The ultimate Southern belle, she could go from perky innocence to Scarlet O'Hara in one-point-five seconds. And right on cue too.

"As God is my witness," she said (I tried not to laugh—the only thing missing was the turnip, the silhouetted tree with fake orange sunset, and skirt swinging in the breeze), "my family was wronged. Many, many, many, many …"

"I get it," I said.

" … years ago. It was *long* ago and most people have forgotten about it. But the family that ruined my relations lived in this area," she finished.

"Which ones? Who?"

"Oh, it's not important who—it could have been anyone. It doesn't matter so much now. And there was more than one family." She took a deep breath. "Dipsey, Ewell, Reynolds …it was a long time ago."

I sat and thought. So much had happened since I had arrived, my head was swimming. "Dipsey," I said out loud. "Wait a minute."

"Shelby," Miss Henrid offered up. "But I'm not saying it was her family in particular."

"Oh, that *death* person, I think Salinger said?"

"That would be the one. I see you know your Chalybeate history. As I was saying …"

"But wait a minute. Her first husband was named Dipsey."

Henrid paused for dramatic effect. It was long but not *that* long—an ultrasound in the scheme of Chalybeate time. "Mr. McCrae," she said, leaning on the arm of the sofa with the panache of a movie star, "if you want to focus on Shelby, fine, she married her brother, Darnell Dipsey."

I knew this sort of thing happened sometimes, in some places, but the actual fact took me by surprise. I simply couldn't believe it. I looked up at Miss Henrid's smirking face, her svelte frame draped over one cushion, her hip stuck out for the added seduction factor.

"People actually name their kids 'Darnell?' " I managed after a few moments.

She paused. Then delivered the rest: "And his middle name was Udder."

"Like the cow part?"

She said nothing but waited. I waited. We both waited.

"Oh, my God. The poor bastard," I said. "His initials were D.U.D."

8

Change Prissy Table

Ms. Henrid was back in the kitchen. I had gotten her off track with regards to who had wronged whom. She had been baking when I arrived, and as that task needed attending, she forgot her past family problems for the moment. She was calm now—less dramatic.

"You want some of this fresh gingerbread I just baked, Hon?" she cooed from the safe confines of the small culinary area.

"No, I'm fine, Miss Henrid," I said.

"Call me Tuck, if you don't mind. I just know we're going to be good friends," she went on. I could hear the sounds of pans being shuffled. "Burned a couple, but the rest are still good. Sure you don't want any? Put these in before you came."

"Maybe one … Tuck," I said, trying her first name on for size. "Tuck Henrid," I thought, "Now there's a name you don't hear every day in the South."

She returned with more iced tea and the warm cookies. I picked up one of the sugary pastries and turned it over, looking at the shape. Either something had gone horribly amiss with the cookie cutter, or Tuck was playing games. I had to wonder if the shape was intentional. Some people say Southerners are slow, but Tuck was pretty quick to pick up on my angst.

"Made the outline myself," she offered, snipping off an end with her perfect white teeth. She chewed with relish, closing her eyes and even adding the necessary "Ummmmm-mmmmm!"—a pointed exclamation point on the end. It was all very June Cleaver.

I turned the small cookie over in my hand. Tuck noticed.

"Colt .45. Salinger's gun of choice. Standard issue for police officers is usually a .357 Magnum or a .38 special."

"Amazing," I said. "And very Southern."

"I spent two whole days getting one of those Santa Claus cookie cutters pulled out of shape and then molded into this one. Do you have any idea the trouble I had getting the gun barrel just *so*?"

"I can imagine."

"Only problem is, I have to use a screwdriver to get the hole where the trigger goes, just so it looks real."

"How do you get the texture on the handle?" I asked, seeing a crosshatching that decorated the lower end of the gun.

"Old piece of screen wire. Works wonders."

"Well, I certainly can see why you're interested in the Junior League ... and that cookbook," I said, gently setting the cookie down. Then I nudged it slightly so that the barrel was pointed toward a Boston fern that cowered in the corner.

"Oh, there's plenty more, so don't be shy about taking all you want," Tuck offered, shoving the handle of the sugary morsel into her mouth. She swallowed hard and then washed the cookie down with a large helping of iced tea.

"Now," she said, dusting the crumbs from her dress, "I want to talk to you about this cookbook."

"I'm all ears."

"My idea is this: You can put together this book of recipes for the "ladies" (she made rabbit ears with her fingers at this point), and if things go as planned, you, simply by way of being who you are and what you do, will give them enough rope to hang themselves. Oh, not literally, but just to take them down a peg or two. You see, Mr. McCrae, I'm new in town and they have completely ostracized me. I had thought at one time that I might bring something, some culture to this place, but every idea that I've come up with has been thwarted. I tried organizing a bake sale at the Brandyworth Church of Christ, but since they don't allow me actually *inside* the place, that brainchild was nixed. My next plan was to have a movie night—you know, show old movies at the Town Hall? We don't have a movie theater in town in case you haven't noticed. Nearest one's over in Bugger Hollar and that one's closed. Well, the first movie I picked was *Mildred Pierce* and ..."

"I love that movie," I said, jumping in.

"Oh, me too. It's my favorite!"

I tried a quote from the film: "I'm sorry I did that ... I'd rather have cut off my hand."

"Weren't the pies bad enough?" Tuck chimed in. We both laughed and then she continued. "As I was saying ... nixed. All of it. My last try at acceptance was decorating one of the rooms at the Chalybeate Springs Inn. I did it in this really nice 1930s pale blue and light beige ..."

" ...wallpaper with Hepplewhite furniture?"

"You've seen it?"

"I'm *in* it. I was wondering who did that. I just assumed it had been that way for decades," I said.

41

"Heavens no, that was my doing. That nice man at the front desk let me decorate it. Bless his heart, he's not really on anyone's side about this social thing in Chalybeate, so he really didn't care. But as I was saying, even *that* didn't impress them."

"So, you think that by organizing this cookbook indirectly and having me as the overseer of it, you'll garner points with these women and be allowed into to The League after they've torn each other to bits?"

"Nail on the head."

I looked about the room and rolled the plan around between my ears. It was starting to make sense. Tuck would, if successful, get into the Junior League—a goal that she, for a reason I could not fathom—wanted more than anything, and I would be getting a nice piece of pocket change. Not a bad proposition.

"I'm on board so far," I said, but there was an uncertainty in my voice.

Tuck smirked and folded her arms. "You want more money."

"Well, I ... already cashed the check."

"But you want more," she said.

I actually didn't, but she read my pause and discomfort in the situation as greed and jumped in. Who was I to correct her? Her first check hadn't bounced so there was little fear that the second one would. But where was she getting this kind of money from?

"How does another $25,000 sound?"

It sounded too easy and I almost choked. There had to be some other angle but I couldn't figure out what it might be. I asked if we could go over exactly how and what she had in mind, and how she proposed to get me in to see each of these women. After all, if they were the pieces of work she and Salinger said they were, it wasn't going to be a walk in the park. Then again, maybe that was why she was offering so much money.

"What exactly do you have in mind," I asked, "with regard to how I go about this?"

"Not to worry," she said, picking up another gun pastry and running her finger around the barrel. "They're all expecting you."

"Wait a minute, you told them about this?"

She hesitated. "Not exactly," she said, setting the cookie back down. "They each got a letter from you, offering your services to do this, well, cookbook—to oversee it and put your stamp of approval on it."

"But I didn't ... send any ... letters."

"I know that. And you know that. But they don't know that."

This was not good news. "You're telling me that you sent letters to these women, from me, *signing* my name?" Then I remembered the note from Weems, just as I had recalled it when Salinger was showing me about the town—the note I'd received before leaving New York. Now it all made sense.

"Indeed," she said.

Any elation that I felt at the thought of receiving $25,000 up front with another $25,000 to follow, faded. It was a helium balloon that had suddenly slipped from my hand. I watched it sail upwards, getting smaller and smaller.

"That's forgery, Miss Henrid," I said, my voice becoming tense.

"Tuck."

"I don't care what your name is. You had no right to do this." I was standing now, pacing about the room. "You've got some nerve, bringing me here under false pretenses, using my name without my permission, offering me more money that probably doesn't even exist." I couldn't imagine she could come up with an additional $25,000.

She was oblivious. "And you know, I can just see it now. Me, as President of the Junior League and ..."

"I don't give a damn ... Tuck ... Henrid, whatever ... I'm not going to stay here and listen to any more of this. This town is one step away from a mental hospital. And I resent being used as a pawn just to further your attempts to get into some two-bit Junior League, for whatever God-knows-why reason I can't imagine."

"If you'd just calm ..."

"I don't *have* to be calm. I'm leaving. I can't tell you how insulted I am over this."

"Mr. McCrae?"

"What?" I said angrily. I was standing in the middle of the room, fuming at the latest revelations. Sure, I wanted the money, but at this point I wasn't sure there *was* more of it. This woman had lied and used my name without my permission. I had turned my back to her, facing the front door, and was thinking of making an exit.

"Would this help?" I heard the words behind me and spun around to see Miss Henrid's hand holding a large envelope.

"What's this? Another trick?"

"Take it," she said, and I walked over to where she was sitting. The envelope was unsealed and fat. Lifting the flap told me that at least some part of her story was true. There, inside the white paper fitting

43

was a series of hundred dollar bills. A *lot* of a series. While I didn't stand there and count them, it was obvious that the amount was probably somewhere in the $25,000 range. (I counted it later—it was.)

"You weren't kidding," I said, my voice half filled with shock, half filled with embarrassment.

"No," she said coolly. "And besides ..."—she picked up a cookie and nibbled at one end—"how do you think you would get out of town anyway if you didn't accept my offer?"

Once again my momentary elation at gaining a large sum of money faded. This rollercoaster of emotions was getting exhausting. I wished she'd either come clean or shut up. As it happened, she did neither.

"I'm sure Sheriff Salinger would be more than happy to take me back to the airstrip," I said, then added with extra venom, "And he'd be glad to know of your little scheme and how you committed fraud and bribery."

She got up and once again dusted off the few crumbs that were clinging to her dress. "Oh, Mr. McCrae. Poor Mr. McCrae. I wouldn't worry too much about that." She was now tending to the Boston fern in the corner—the very one I had pointed the cookie toward. "You see, Sheriff Salinger is a dear friend of mine. In fact, you might say we're quite close." She fluffed several fronds in an attempt to liven the thing's appearance. "Needs water," she said to herself.

"Oh really? Just how close?"

She turned from the fern and faced me. Then she let me have it with a power equal to that of one of her doughy confections, only this time, the ammunition wasn't sugar-coated. "Mr. Salinger is my fiancé," she said, and as I turned and looked out the window at the burly sheriff leaning against his car, he too looked up and, quite friendly and with a large smile, saluted me with his large cigar.

Part II

Tell me what you eat, and I will tell you what you are.

—Anthelme Brillat-Savarin

9

Lisp Betrays Change

My note to Mrs. Weems—on Chalybeate Inn stationery, if you can believe there actually *was* such a thing—seemed appropriate since I had (at least in her eyes) written to her. Fortunately, Miss Henrid had seen fit to provide me with copies of my, uh, *her* correspondence to the ladies of the Junior League and I was prepared (as well as one can be in these circumstances) for what was to follow.

I wrote this:

Dear Mrs. Weems,

As I said in my earlier correspondence from New York, I would welcome the possibility of coming to your fair town to interview you and help put together a cookbook that would include the culinary delights that Chalybeate Springs has to offer. It is my understanding, from a source who shall remain nameless, that you and your highly cultured group of ladies would like to share with the world the many great Southern recipes that have graced the tables of your lovely homes for years. It is with great trepidation that I ask for an invitation to your beautiful home in Chalybeate for the purpose of getting better acquainted with you and The League. I don't want to impose upon your precious time, and therefore am declining your gracious invitation to stay with you and Mayor Weems; this, only out of respect for your privacy. Please let me know if this meets with your approval—the request for an invitation—as I am most anxious to get started on the cookbook.

Your faithful servant,

Mr. McCrae

I tried not to choke on my own vomit as I sealed the letter and sent it, via Jecko (he looked as though he could use the outing), to the house that so superbly imitated Tara. Evidently Mrs. Weems had poor Jecko wait, for her response came back at once (well, seven to ten minutes later) on very expensive and personalized stationery.

Dear Mr. McCrae,

    It is with great pleasure that I am able to invite you for tea today at four o'clock. As this is our first meeting, I hope you won't mind that the other ladies will not be present. I do so want to share some of my ideas about this cookbook with you before the others have a chance to steal you away. Please know that we are *thrilled* to have a great author such as you grace our town. And remember, four o'clock sharp!

Best,

Mrs. Helen Weems

    The handwriting was most opulent and florid, resembling an overfed and out-of-control Kudzu vine that had been exposed to radiation. The capital letters were especially large and her signature alone took up most of the page. A handwriting expert's head would have exploded on the spot, so rife was the scribbling with psychological problems and repressions, narcissism and emotional bloat. And I love it when people sign things, "Best." What the hell does that mean? Best what? In short, I could not wait to meet Mrs. Weems.

    But something else was odd. When Jecko returned with the note, a slip of paper was stuck to the back. It said, "Lisp Betrays Change." I asked Jecko if Mrs. Weems had given it to him and he shook his head "No." Strange, this one—this note. Plus, the others I had been collecting—"Try Passable Change," "Cigar Bashes Plenty," and "Reb City's Phalanges," had all found me—either left in my room, in Salinger's car, or stuck to some *other* note. I'd kept each and every one, and had started typing them in the computer file I was keeping on the town. What they meant, I wasn't sure, but some message was definitely being sent my way.

    At exactly four o'clock I rang the bell to the Weemses' house. An assortment of chimes to rival Big Ben clanged for such a length of time that, even after the manservant had answered, ushered me into the drawing room, and begged me to have a seat, they were still going. The last note hung in the air as Mrs. Weems swept into the room, resplendent in evening gown (it was more like a sequined kaftan) even though it was still afternoon. Earrings the size of small chandeliers hung from each lobe and a diamond necklace, which wrapped itself around her neck, could have easily been auctioned off to feed the entire country of India. On one of her fingers was a diamond the size of Rhode Island.

"I'm ooh vewy peesed to meep you," she said, offering me only her fingertips. I took no offense, assuming that it would have been impossible to wrap my hand around hers while it sported such a large stone. I was standing, as is customary for persons playing the part of the Southern gentlemen to do, and even managed to bow slightly, adjusting my navy double-breasted blazer in the process. I had left off the tie, thinking that I might have been overdressed. I wouldn't have been.

"Pees have a teat," she said, indicating the least comfortable chair in the room. "I'll justh wing for tea," and with that she pressed a buzzer at the side of an enormous marble fireplace. I guessed she must have just recently had some type of oral surgery or accident as her speech was odd, completely without several members of the alphabet in sight ... or sound. Letters seemed to get dropped from time to time. There appeared to be no consistency in her pattern as "Ls" would emerge, then disappear like a Macbethian ghost, and "Ts" and "Ss" came and went with a whimsy not heard since Marie Antoinette's flippant remark regarding cake and who should eat it. There was also something definitely odd about her appearance though I couldn't quite figure it out.

"You have a lovely home," I managed, trying to keep the conversation going. Why, I now have *no* idea.

She tilted her head and paused. "Why, tank you." She seated herself on a Chippendale sofa (I'm assuming it was the real thing) and attempted polite pre-tea conversation.

"Ear is ut I'm hinking," she began, gesturing dramatically, chin up, speaking more to the vast room than directly to me, and leaving off a very important "T." It was all very Gloria Swanson after too many face lifts. "De book shou be fe-ud with ony the most de-ectable Soudhern dishes."

"The book should be filled with only the most delectable Southern dishes?" I said, just to make sure I was getting what she was trying to say—*trying* being the optimal word here. I scrutinized her face, intent on seeing what made her speech so odd. She caught my look and I glanced away at a four-hundred-year-old Chinese vase.

"You know, sadd-ah of amb?"

"Lamb? Saddle of lamb?"

"Ha-iday fare—hings at everyone wan ooh read abou. And I've poken ith a ew of the other adies—noh all of em, mind—and they all (there, she managed that) seem to agwee tat you oud offer tome ort of in-toh-duction for each reci-ee."

"That's fine with me," I said, having no idea what she had just said and thinking of the additional $25,000 dollars that had come from Henrid. Otherwise I might have bolted from the room. Pride was one thing. Making money was something else entirely. Plus, no one was ever going to read the pile of junk I was going to prepare, so I was willing to go along with Mrs. Weems on just about every point.

"Hen, I'm hinking, hat after duh reci-eee, we would each ave a itt-uh urb abou ow we came to ave it—the reci-ee. You know, a itt-uh istory."

"How it was passed down from generation to generation or how you all had refined it—that sort of thing?" I said, hoping to finish her painful sentences and save myself the need for translation. "I like that idea," I went on, having no intention of doing any of it.

Just then, the butler appeared with tea and an assortment of *petit fours* and finger sandwiches. I scanned the tray: no gun-shaped cookies and the crusts were trimmed from the sandwiches. Mrs. Weems's stock was going up.

"Do ooh take meok or emon?" she asked, having poised the silver teapot over my cup. "A gift rom de de-hendents of Heneral Obert E. Eee's re-uatives," she said, smiling at the silver object in her hand.

"Meok. Pease," I said, indicating what I wanted in my tea, not meaning to, but unconsciously imitating her.

"Oust of our siu-ver is pee-war. Eee do ike to keep ah Toutdern ta-dituns a-wive." ("Most of our silver is pre-war. We do like to keep our Southern traditions alive.") … You're welcome.

"Indeed," I said.

She went on, unfortunately. Her speech sounded more Chinese than Southern. I managed a stare or two at her face, trying to figure out just what the matter was.

I couldn't.

"It muh be fat-in-ating, being a rihu-uh. You know, I ave tome ideas, if ooh ev-uh un out."

"If I ever run out? Oh, boy," I thought, "Here it comes." Every time someone finds out you're a writer or that you have a friend of a friend of a friend who works in publishing, they try and get you to read their awful manuscript.

49

"That so?" I said, taking one of the finger sandwiches: egg salad. "Tay-teee," I offered, my mouth half full. "So you've read my books," I said, after I swallowed. Then I stuffed the remainder of the sandwich in my mouth.

She hesitated. "Well, no, nah exacte-ee. We're toh busy, you know, with trav-uh and mee-ings and tuch."

This was getting out of hand. At least if she'd dropped all her "Ls" or all her "Hs" I might have been able to come up with my own quick dictionary as to what she was saying, but her inconsistency in the way of (excuse the term) talking was like trying to put together an ever-changing Rubic's cube.

"Oh, what kind of meetings do you have?" I regretted the question as soon as I'd asked it. Listening to her was about as much fun as being poked in the eye with a stick.

"Eell, uh, we aven't rea-ey had more tan one mee-ing toh far."

"You mean your Junior League has only met once?" I was getting a little worried. I imagined five women who did small town charity events, but one meeting was scary. And knowing Chalybeate's penchant for pregnant time lapses and the like, I was worried that this infant hadn't even been a gleam in someone's eye, much less incubated. Then there was the intimidating idea that Mrs. Weems was President of The League. I imagined her presiding over each session, taking a full three months to say something where only an hour had been needed. In the end, her decision to raise money for charity might be misconstrued as drug-running for communist lesbian dwarfs with Down Syndrome.

"So, what has your league been doing?" I asked. I needed to know, but regretted the decision to ask as soon as it exited my mouth.

Mrs. Weems looked more than slightly uncomfortable (she couldn't have been more so than myself). She got up (quite gracefully for her elephantine weight, I might add) and waddled to the mantel. It seems that walking to mantels in order to think was the thing to do in Chalybeate and I couldn't help but feel it had some preoccupation with fire, but I put it out of my mind as coincidence. Perhaps it was a hearkening back to caveman days when that utilitarian and yet destructive substance had been discovered and the knowledge of what it could achieve had been made known. The residents were, after all, rather primitive in ways. Besides, the Weemses had real logs on the grate, not those faux ones with colored paper and light bulbs like Miss Henrid.

While she stood in thought, I once again tried to make sense of her way of talking. Not wanting to come right out and ask—my Southern manners showing—I had a moment or two to try and analyze her odd way of speaking. There was zero consistency in her discourse. Every now and then an unharmed word would escape, and when it did I felt like once again believing in organized religion. At other times the words were so hacked to pieces that it would have taken Rosetta Stone-like antics to make sense of them.

"Tat's haat I anted to tak to you ah-out," she said. ("That's what I wanted to talk—[loose term]—to you about.") As there were no figurines on the mantel, Mrs. Weems was unable to do her complete Henrid impersonation.

I was grateful.

She continued: "Eee have five members [Oh, my God, three words in a row that made sense!] in da cub, most of oom are a-teck-table."

"Acceptable," I translated.

"Wite." She went on. "Oost ec-tept un." She turned, sat back down, and concentrated on the teapot again. By this time my money was on the fact that she'd had a stroke. Mrs. Weems was no spring chicken and it occurred to me that I shouldn't be poking fun (in my mind) at her afflictions.

"Except one," I said, translating again. I felt the need, in order to make sure we were on the same ... tongue. This entire meeting was like a bad high school production of *Children of a Lesser God*.

"You want to ask me to include the recipes for only four of you, and to leave one person *out?*" I ventured, hoping to save her the trouble of talking.

A nod confirmed this.

"And which one might this be?" I said, reaching for a sugar cookie whose shape was, thankfully, simply round.

"Isses Chiu-ders." The reply came quickly and was almost curt, though no less hard to understand.

"Mrs. Childers? Does she know about this?"

"No, and I ould ery much ike it if you di-nut teh her."

"You'd very much like if I didn't tell her. May I ask why?" Again, I thought before I spoke. Major Discomfort was heading his troops in our direction. Ah, the pleasures of asking questions to those who so don't want to answer them. Unfortunately, Mrs. Weems was one of the more talkative in the town—a pity.

"I'd ra-duh noh say."

"You'd rather not say." I pondered another finger sandwich for a moment. "If you don't want her to be a part of the book, then why is she in your Junior League?"

"Duh tooth is, we ahh fee-uh so-eey foh her. You tee, she attu-ee orks for me, ah my maid. Tee ah-so orks for Me-es Bandyuth, Miss Killchrist (a full name!), and Mrs. Iipsey-Eweuh …"

"Adams-Tellerman-Hatton, E-I-E-I-Oey. Yes I know the story," I said, finishing the woman's many-hyphened name.

Mrs. Weems looked aghast. She drew back and put her hand to her breast—a dramatic movie-move if ever there was one. I thought I had offended her by jumping in. At the same time, I once again noticed the enormous ring on one of her fingers. It had to be eighty carets at least and the light reflected off of it to such an extent that I narrowed my eyes.

"What? What's the matter?" I asked, seeing her response.

"Ooo-wah not Eewish, I ope," she said, her head a good three inches back beyond its normal position.

"I'm not Jewish, you hope? No, why?"

"Eell … ou-ted 'Oey.' (Mrs. Weems was nothing if not well traveled and this one Jewish word was right up her alley, narrow though it may be—the alley, not the word.)

"I live in New York," I said. "Things rub off. You were saying?" (Damnit, I did it again.) But I jumped right back in, hoping to save her the trouble. "Mrs. Childers—you all feel 'sorry' for her and made her a member, of course thinking that she would never dream of attending meetings or …" But I waited, realizing something she had previously (no other word for it) said. "You just mentioned that you had only had *one* meeting."

"Eell, that's ust de point."

"Huh?"

"Tee came. De woman came to de mee-ing, so ee've only ad un. Tee actually ants to be a pah of the Junior Eeague!"

"She actually wants to be a part of the Junior League? Is that right? And let me guess, you can't have a black maid being part of your club?"

Mrs. Weems looked confused (on top of everything else.) "Ahat are you tah-king about? Mrs. Chu-ders isn't back; tee's why."

"She's white?" I asked, hoping the conversion from "why" to "white" had been correct.

Mrs. Weems nodded. I thanked God and sat still, taking in the opulence of the room, the steaming teapot, Mrs. Weems herself. Then I remembered Miss Henrid's words: "*Pure-dee* white trash." They had zoomed right by me. So Childers was white. "I honestly don't know what I was thinking, Mrs. Weems. I do hope you will forgive me for assuming."

"Eell, you're kite forgiwen. Oow, if you woud, ooh mut tie un of hese petit oours—hey're simpy ex-skis-it and so, eellll … petit!"

"Anything else I should know—before I start helping to compile these recipes?" I asked. I kicked myself for once again for attempting to continue the witty badinage we were having. For the remainder of the (conversation is the only word that fits, but you get the idea …) Mrs. Weems told me (you can pay me later for translating) that Mrs. Brandyworth was the Reverend's wife and that she was, how should I put it, a little more down-to-earth than one would like. And she also liked to drink. Then there was Shelby and her husbands. Mrs. Weems couldn't say she approved, but Shelby was pretty much all the Junior League could find when trying to scrape up someone decent. And she *was* the town librarian. Last and *certainly* least was that Killchrist woman. Never been married. Mrs. Weems apologized for the lack of cultured people in the town. (I'm making a stab here. She could have actually said that she was Hitler's offspring and that she and Vincent Price played Parcheesi with kitchen spatulas for all I know.) She also insisted that, while the order of recipes in the book was important, she didn't want to be first.

"How magnanimous," I replied. At that point she had felt about her bosom, obviously thinking that the term had something to do with flattening one's breasts between two large plates for the purpose of finding lumps—who was I to correct her?

"I'm guessing you don't want to seem too self-serving," I said, as she poured herself another cup of tea, forgetting to re-fill mine, completely missing the irony. (Think about it.)

"Ee-tatl-y, I tan tee tat eee under-tand each oter perf-etee Mitah Muh-Tahy."

"My God," I thought, "she was sounding just like Buckwheat. The only thing missing was the dog with the black patch on his eye and Spanky and his beanie."

"You can see that we understand each other perfectly?" I asked, just to make sure. The Muh-Tahy part I could figure out on my own.

"Yes." (Manna from heaven—a complete and understandable word!)

"Well, I'll certainly do what I can," I said. The wheels were already turning.

While the woman was a nightmare to converse with, she could obviously handle a pen (think, previous note to the Inn), and that was all that I really needed. I would avoid her in person now at all costs, or at least hope for situations where so much food was involved that conversation could be kept to a minimum.

10

Gin Betrays Chapels

Returning to the Inn on foot—the same way I had gotten to Mrs. Weems's house—gave me a chance to catch my breath and clear my lungs of the amount of wealth (and ignorance) that had accumulated in them. Besides, the town was so small you could walk to almost any spot in a matter of minutes. One had to wonder just how much taxi business Salinger's police car actually performed. As it was getting late, I inquired about food and was told the dining room was expecting me. This would be my chance to sample some of Jecko's cooking, other than his bacon and eggs. But before I could, Hastings called to me and then handed over a piece of folded paper. "Gin Betrays Chapels," it read. Okay, that was it—I'd had enough.

"Do you know who's been putting these notes around where I can find them?" I asked him.

"No idea," he quipped, totally uninterested, and I sulked over to the dining room in the hope of enjoying some decent food.

I had just sat down when a plate was put before me. Roast beef—well-done—mashed potatoes, and string beans. None of it was anything to write home about, but it was edible and I was so exhausted that I didn't question the selection or lack of a menu.

After dinner I made my way to my room, thinking of Miss Henrid and her deco decoration, and fell fast asleep. I dreamed that Joan Crawford was my mother, always talking backwards and baking pies shaped like AK 47s, while a large black man slowly turned into a hydrangea bush and drove me around an imaginary town—hey, this is dreamland; it's not supposed to make sense.

Morning came in the version of a car horn being loudly sounded just below my window. I rolled out of bed and over to the small dormer window, parting the Cape Cod curtains. Below was Sheriff Salinger, looking as though he'd been up for hours. I raised the sash and stuck my head out.

"Better get ready, boy. You got work to do!" he shouted up toward me. I glanced back at the alarm clock: Eight-thirty. Before I could turn back around I heard his voice again. "And don't worry about Jecko's breakfast this mornin'. We's goin' to Mrs. Brandyworth's for somethin' to eat—least-wise, you is."

"Great," I said to myself as I fumbled for my clothes and slouched, cow-heavy and baby-blue with white-piping-covered pajamas, into the bathroom. I shaved, showered, dressed in record time, and barely had placed myself in the back of the police car when Salinger took off.

"Couldn't we just as well have walked?" I asked. "The town is only a few square blocks anyway."

"Got to go in style," he said. " 'Sides, Tuck wants me to take real good care of you."

"You mean she wants to make sure I do what I'm here to do."

"That too," he said, turning the car's siren and lights on.

"What gives!" I shouted over the din.

"Jus' wakin' up the town," he said, and smiled into the mirror as we pulled to a stop in front of the Colonial he had shown me earlier. Then he turned around and spoke through the mesh. "How was the roast beef?"

"Huh?"

"Last night, for dinner—the roast beef. How was it?"

"Jesus Christ! Isn't anything safe around here?"

"Son, you're getting yourself all upset for nothing," he laughed.

"Then how did you know what I had for dinner?"

He sighed heavily and looked out the window, squinting toward the house I was about to enter. "Roast beef's the only thing they serve for dinner at the Inn."

"I thought Jecko was supposed to be a master cook," I said.

"Is. But only for special occasions." He scratched himself. "You might want to get along now so as not to keep the Reverend's wife waitin'."

I paused, my hand on the door handle. "Question," I said. Salinger looked at me in his rearview mirror. I continued: "Hastings— the guy at the front desk?"

"Percy? At the Inn?"

"Yeah. What's his story? He's a bit of a grouch."

Salinger looked out the window, then straight ahead. "Cancer. He's had it for four months now. Nobody knows how long he's got. Took it real hard. We're all tryin' to pretend like it's nothing. Least wise that's the way he wants it."

"Oh. Sorry. I didn't mean to pry, it's just that . . ." but I didn't finish my sentence, choosing instead to exit the car; feeling embarrassed that I'd stepped into some territory that I'd no right to. Salinger held up his hand as if to say, "No problem," and I walked up to the house we were parked in front of.

This time no butler greeted me as had been the case at the Weems house. I was instead shown in by a rather dour and jowly man of about sixty. He neither spoke nor offered to shake my hand, and it was only after Mrs. Brandyworth came into the entrance hall to escort me onto the back patio that I discovered it was the Reverend who had answered the door.

"You'll have to excuse Mr. Brandyworth," the matron said. "He's working on a new sermon and his mind is somewhere else."

"Yeah, okay," I said, still groggy.

"Let me get you some coffee," she offered, and instead of performing the deed herself, yelled rather loudly, in the direction of the kitchen.

"Delilah, get some coffee—for me and Mr. McCrae." While the Brandyworths didn't have a butler, they did have a cook. When Delilah appeared, I took her in with my eyes, trying not to be too obvious. She was the very definition of sturdy. A large woman with size-thirteen feet, she wore a uniform and a scowl, completing her outfit with the largest pair of sneakers I had ever seen and sporting bright yellow rubber gloves on her hands. The coffee was served, and after taking a sip I almost choked to death.

"Oh, dear," Mrs. B apologized, "Delilah must have mixed ours up. I'm so sorry about that. I always have her put my medicine in first thing."

"Medicine?" I thought to myself. "The thing was ninety-percent Dewars with one or two Columbian beans thrown in for color." I looked at Delilah, who was standing, waiting. Her head made a "Z" one way, then the other. The movement pretty much said everything. Then she left.

Mrs. Brandyworth: "I did so want to meet with you—to get to know you before we started this project. And I must say it was so nice of you to write each of us personally, offering your expertise in this area. I have so many recipes that I'm sure you'll love."

About this time, Delilah appeared again and set our plates out before us. No one had asked what I wanted and the meal consisted of grits, eggs (sunny-side up), and sausage. I was in the process of picking up my fork, ready to compliment Mrs. B on the lovely breakfast when she stood abruptly and threw her head back.

"Stand up, Mr. McCrae!" she commanded. Her personality had so suddenly changed that I thought for a moment that I had committed some horrible *faux pas* . . or worse. "Stand up and let us *thank* the Lord God FOR ALL HIS BOUNTY! Delilah, you too!" she shouted, eyes closed, head still back. Delilah obeyed, gloved hands at her side.

Then Mrs. B let loose: "Lord, sweet *Jeeee-sus!* Praise *God!*" she said, shaking her fist skyward, "WE THANK THEE for this *blessed* food and for the fact that you sent your SON TO DIE for us, praise his HOLY NAME! Lord, we ask that you bless these grits and the corn they were made from, and Lord, *forgive* us for our treatment of our Indian brothers who *showed* the first settler how to plant this vegetable! And Lord, we THANK THEE for these blessed eggs! PRAISE GOD, praise his holy *name* and we ask that he take care of the *bless-ed* chickens and the *bounty* that they have provided! And Lord, we KNOW that the Bible says thou *shalt* not eat the animals with a cloven hoof, but Lord we ask that you FORGIVE us these sausages, as they forgive us, and grant Mr. McCrae strength to help us with your work, and spreading the word of GOD through this most bountiful cookbook that he is going to edit. In your name, dear sweet Lord God, we pray, AMEN!"

"Amen," I said, completely stunned. Mrs. Brandywoth, it seemed, was another complete loon.

The lady of the house sat down. "Are you a Christian?"

"Well, I consider myself a spiritual person."

"I'll take that as a no," she said.

"Well, if you must …"

"The Lord sent you here—you do know that?"

"Yes, I'm sure he did." The humble pie wasn't very good, but so far it didn't taste rank, and I could always throw up when I got back to the Inn, so I went along with Christian-play-time for now.

"We must be thankful for all He's given us, and thankful for your safe journey here … and back. You do want to have a safe journey back, don't you?"

"I was planning on it."

She brightened considerably. "Good! Now that we've gotten that out of the way …"

"Excuse me, Mrs. Brandyworth … may I call you Sofie?"

"No you may not," she responded, pouring more coffee.

"Oh. Okay. Mrs. Brandyworth, I was told you have seventeen children."

"You are correct, Mr. McCrae. Seventeen *glorious* children ranging from age seven to fifteen."

"My, that's quite a close range." I was trying for light conversation, if that was even possible when discussing seventeen children. "Just out of curiosity, where do they all sleep?"

"Why, in bunk beds, stacked three each."

"Three each? The bunk beds or the children?"

"Mr. McCrae, we only have so much room," she added, picking at her eggs. "Praise the Lord, they are all such *fine* children," she continued, shoving a sloppy mouthful of goo and a piece of bread into her most frontal orifice.

"I'm sure. Am I going to meet these fine children?" I asked.

She waited. I couldn't tell if she was pondering the question or if she had discovered a piece of fat from the sausage lodged between two teeth and was trying to decide whether or not to spit it out. "Probably not," she said, and scooped another mouthful of eggs into her eager mouth. She swallowed. "The Lord has seen fit that they go to visit my sister in Florida for a month or two. This happens each year and it gives them a chance to learn to appreciate what they have here, with me and the Reverend."

"Certainly gives you a break."

"Well, enough about my children, Mr. McCrae. You're here to talk about the cookbook and what plans I have for it."

"It was my understanding that it was the Junior League's cookbook and Mrs. Weems said …"

"Mrs. Weems!"

"I met with her the …"

Mrs. Brandyworth sighed heavily and set her fork down with disgust. "I wish I'd known. You know, Mr. McCrae, it says in the Bible that it is easier for a camel to pass through the eye of a needle than it is for a rich man to enter into heaven."

"Well, it would seem Mrs. Weems is a rich woman, not a man."

"Do not make light of the Good Book, Mr. McCrae. I know whereof I speak." Then she bellowed in the direction of the kitchen to the poor cook: "DELILAH, GET US SOME MORE COFFEE, AND STOP DRAGGING AROUND IF YOU WANT TO KEEP YOUR JOB!"

I listened, searching my conscience for something to say. Mrs. B's treatment of Delilah was not the most benevolent and her take on religion was already getting on my nerves. "You know," I said, cutting a sausage in half, "isn't it a bit non-Christian to be so, well, aggressive with Delilah?" I continued eating, hoping to show no real upset.

"The Bible doesn't say anything about being *nice*."

I sat in thought, not being able to remember the often-quoted and extensive tome that well, word-for-word. "You may be right."

"Of course I'm right," she snapped. "Now, let's get something straight. This cookbook is going to be done *my* way. *My* way, with God's help. And Delilah is just the cook. Mrs. Childers is our maid. Frankly, I'm not sure which one is lower. Oh, it doesn't matter. This cookbook is going to be dictated by God himself!"

"Then why am I here?"

"You are to be an instrument of God. There's a reason you're here in Chalybeate Springs."

I wanted to say, "You've got that right," but things were starting to get interesting with everyone I'd met so far and I didn't want to push my luck. "Okay. I'm listening," I said. Then to myself: "$50,000.00. You've got $50,000.00 so far."

"First of all, I want one of my recipes to be the *very* first thing in the book."

"Good," I thought. No arguing with Weems over that. She had fortunately had the good graces to offer that position up—she was looking better all the time.

"Next, I will *not* have that Godless woman, Mary-Ellen Killchrist, put anything into this book."

"Now, wait a minute," I said. "There's only five women in the Junior League and Mrs. Weems has already said that she didn't want Mrs. Childers's recipes in the book and ..."

"Mrs. Childers may not be high society, but she's a God-fearing woman. She and Delilah don't get along, but I just see that they're not here at the same time. That Killchrist woman is *not* God-fearing. She's not married and as far as I can tell, has dated every man on the planet."

"Well now, we've got a problem since Mrs. Weems doesn't want Mrs. Childers's recipes in the book, and you don't want Mary-Ellen Killchrist's in it."

"Mary-Ellen was a cheerleader, PromQueen, and Homecoming Queen. No woman of God would dare to participate in those activities."

"Okay, okay. Let's just calm down and see where we can go with this." Fortunately, about that time, Delilah came around and cleared the plates. I looked up at her. "You know, Delilah, that was an excellent breakfast."

Delilah said nothing but Mrs. B did: "Delilah is an excellent cook. Her specialty is stuffing."

"Oh, like dressing for a turkey?"

Mrs. Brandyworth laughed. "Oh no; *anything*. She makes stuffed ham, stuffed pork chops, stuffed shrimp. Turn her loose in the kitchen and she'll just stuff all day."

"Sounds filling," I said. "Maybe we should include some of her recipes in the book."

And ugly pause ensued.

"I think not," Mrs. Brandyworth intoned, and then after taking a sip of her coffee, addressed the cook, letting me know that my discussion of Delilah was at an end. "Thank you, Delilah. Now, if you will bring me my notebook, Mr. McCrae and I can get started." Then to me: "I've got some recipes written out and I think they're *just* the thing for this cookbook." She paused. "Are you a Christian, Mr. McCrae?"

"Uh, you already asked me that."

She became indignant. "I most certainly did not!"

"Uh, yes ... yes you did."

"Oh, well, it doesn't matter right now. Where is Delilah? As I was saying, I've got some ideas and I think they're ..."

"That's fine, but let me tell you what I've got in mind," I said, hoping to at least get a few pennies of my own into the project. "My way of thinking is this: I'll put together a binder and you can write down your recipes and whatnot. It's my understanding from Mrs. Weems that there should be a blurb after each recipe, you know, something about where each idea came from, how it was passed down, or some interesting fact about it or how it ties into Chalybeate Springs."

"That, Mr. McCrae, is the first thing you—and Mrs. Weems— have said that I agree with."

"Good, then why don't you show me what you've got, I'll get the binder started, and when it's all done, I'll go back in and add an introduction to each recipe—this, after all of you have finished with what you have put in each time."

I could see her thinking, wondering if it would work. "So we'd pass this around to each other?"

"Yes."

"Then everyone would be able to see my recipes. What if they try and steal them?"

"Mrs. Brandyworth, I can assure you, none of these women are going to do that. I'll oversee the entire process and make sure it all goes on the up-and-up. Like I said, after you all get through adding in your dishes and comments, I'll go back and do a small introduction to each one."

"And we'll all get to read this finished product before it gets published."

"Of course. But there's one thing."

"I knew it. What?" she asked, crossing her arms.

"If Mrs. Weems doesn't want Mrs. Childers in the book, and you don't want Mary-Ellen Killchrist in it, I have to wonder what the other women—the ones I haven't spoken with yet—are going to want. We can't have a Junior League Cookbook with just two contributors in it. I mean, five is a small enough number."

I waited. She didn't seem keen on the idea. "Look," I went on, "here's what I propose, to all of you: You just write down your recipes and once we get it all down on paper, we can make changes; delete things, change things around." Then I leaned over the table, for added effect. "We might even manage to make some *major* editing changes, if you know what I mean."

I could see her wheels turning. I started to speak but she stopped me with an upheld finger.

It was her turn now. She too leaned on the table. Her eyes narrowed. She was almost seductive. "You know, Mr. McCrae, we may not appear to have as much money as the Weemses do," and with this she looked around, making sure Delilah was out of earshot, "but we're better off than you might expect."

"I'm listening."

"Well, seventeen children. We have to clothe and feed them. Our house isn't exactly small."

"I have noticed that it is still one of the nicer homes in the Springs area."

"So you know where I'm going with this."

"Not totally sure, but go ahead. Not a lot surprises me," I said.

She waited, looking confused. "Are you a Christian?"

Now it was my turn to wait. "Mrs. Brandyworth, you've asked me that twice already. This will make the third time. Is there something …"

"Where was I?" she said.

"You were telling me that you didn't have as much money as the Weemses but that you and the Reverend were better off than most."

She licked her lips and glanced from side-to-side. The she remembered. "Oh, yes. Just how much has your publisher agreed to pay you for this … cookbook?"

I sighed heavily, as theatrically as I could. "Mrs. Brandyworth, I'd like to tell you that I'm receiving quite an advance, but the truth is I'll only get royalties, and I can tell you from writing for years, that isn't that much."

She put her finger to her lips and squinted. "How about ... if I were to make it worth your while?"

"Hmmm?"

"Like you said, the book could be written any which way, but in the end, only you and I would have to see it—if you know what I mean."

"And make certain editing changes," I added.

"Or take out certain people's recipes."

I wanted to jump on the opportunity but waited, playing it close to home. "And what might the impetus be for this—for *me*, I mean?"

She brushed off a few crumbs that remained on the glass-topped patio table and looked around. Then she looked me squarely in the face. "How does, oh, say, ten thousand dollars sound?"

I sat back. "I don't mean to be rude or presumptuous, but ...well, do you have, I mean, would you want to spend that kind of money?"

"Mr. McCrae, if it would get me what I want, I'd be willing to spend much more."

"Well then, Mrs. Brandyworth, I think we might just be able to work something out." It was odd (but good), this offering of money. I had to wonder why Mrs. Weems—the wealthiest woman in the town—had not done the same. Then again, perhaps she had, and I had simply missed it—or agreed to some other bizarre conditions. I couldn't be sure and recalling the conversation with Weems was like trying to imagine my own circumcision—something I neither could nor wanted to do.

Mrs. Brandyworth, smiled broadly across the table, smirking. Then I spoke. "Mrs. Brandyworth?" I said.

"How formal," she countered. "Sofie. Call me Sofie."

She paused.

I did also.

"I insist," she said, and that ended our conversation.

11

Psych-Beat Salinger

The conversation with the multi-faceted Mrs. Brandyworth was definitely food for thought. And the added attraction of $10,000 that she had given me didn't hurt either. I was smarting from Miss Henrid's trickery but the money she and Mrs. B had coughed up certainly took my mind off the pain. As Mrs. Brandyworth had also given me her first recipe, I decided to start my collection right then, taking out some old notes for another book I had worked on and using the binder for the purpose of the cookbook.

I opened the clips and took out the pages. And guess what fell out? Another note. "Psych-Beat Salinger," it read. Well, at least that made some sense. I gave up trying to figure out who was sending the messages, or why, and decided to add them to the beginnings of chapters and essays in my electronic collection of Chalybeate Springs ephemera.

But sitting in my room at the Inn reminded me too much of my last conversation with Henrid and her Joan Crawford imitation, and I wanted to get out and revive myself with some fresh air. I made my way down the carpeted stairs of the Inn, carrying my laptop and the binder, with the thought of being alone—someplace, anyplace—when an enormous waft of cigar smoke came over the banister. I landed on the last step and turned to see Salinger, puffing away.

"I appreciate the gesture," I started in, trying to head off another police car ride, "but I was looking forward to spending a bit of time alone."

"Suit yourself," he said. "Know where you're going?"

I thought for a moment. I didn't have any idea. "Didn't we pass a park the other day?"

"Yup. You remember where it is?"

"I'm pretty sure," I said, moving toward the door. Salinger blew a cloud of smoke in my direction as I reached for the knob. I was outside when he called after me.

"You get lost, you just holler real loud. Not that big a place, this Chalybeate."

"Boy, you're not kidding," I thought to myself as I took off in the direction opposite Main Street—the very area in which I thought the park was located.

After circling a few of the town's blocks (sturdy turn-of-the-century houses with magnificent plantings in the front yard and the occasional birdbath or reflective ball thrown in for good measure), I made the brilliant deduction that I was lost. The park had eluded me. It was still somewhat early so I wasn't worried. Besides, the town was so small that all you had to do was walk in one direction for ten minutes and you'd be on the edge of it; then you could circle your way around again.

I took off in another direction this time and recognized a few cast-iron fences and hollyhocks that swayed in front of a remodeled Victorian. It was then that I saw something familiar. In the distance, at the top of a small hill was a cluster of gigantic cedar trees. They stood out like Greek gods on Mount Olympus. It was the cemetery that I had seen Salinger stop at that first day, and I knew the park was just beyond.

I slowed my pace now that I had some bearings, and was just coming up to the edge of the eternal place of rest when I saw the sheriff's car parked about a block away.

"Damnit!" I said out loud. "I can't go anywhere without Bubba tailing me." It was bad enough that he and his fiancé had cooked up (how appropriate) a scheme to get me to this town under false pretenses, and that I was essentially trapped here without transportation of my own, in a place that was so small that the Junior League consisted of five women who had met only once, but to be constantly under surveillance was too much. I was getting ready to let off some steam, New York style, when I noticed that Salinger wasn't actually *in* the car. I looked around but he was nowhere to be found.

"Perhaps I'm overacting," I thought to myself as I walked up the other side of the cemetery. But before I could finish my peregrination, I stopped. There, on the same hill where I had seen the sheriff the first day, was the self-same object of my disgust. And in front of the same pink grave marker.

I quickly made myself invisible behind an enormous oleander and waited. Being slightly farther away this time than the last, I wasn't able to hear, but the man had his hat off and was mouthing something. He stood for only a moment or two, and then loped off down the path toward the gate that would lead him around to the opposite side of the graveyard—the one farthest away from me.

As he headed out, I took my cue and went north, careful not to be seen. The park was just two blocks away and I made it safely there without him noticing me. Once in the green oasis I finally felt at peace.

No Salinger, no Mrs. Weems, Brandyworth, Jecko, or Mr. Hastings. No one but me, the binder, and the laptop that would hold the recipes of a few peculiar ladies of the Springs area.

Sitting down on a park bench, I opened my computer, took out the binder, and reached inside the envelope that Mrs. Brandyworth had entrusted to me. I unfolded a piece of paper and read her first recipe. It wasn't anything too exciting, but it fit in perfectly with her demeanor, so I left it as is … or was, writing a short introduction to the "book" and another even shorter one for her recipe.

Forward by Jackson Tippett McCrae

The lovely ladies of Chalybeate Springs agreed to have me preside over a cookbook they wanted to create, and, knowing of my spreading fame as a writer, particularly in the South, they thought that I would be the perfect one to give advice and a guiding hand. The initial idea of the book was to raise money for such worthy causes as the Toys for Tiny Tots in nearby Tittusville, or the "Bring Religion to the less Sanctimonious" mission which was to minister to neighboring Scumpter County—a suggestion I evidently wrote about in my introductory letters—however, by the time we finish this joint venture, it may be decided that the funds should be directed toward other endeavors. But enough about the saga of how this little book came to be published. It's the recipes you want to see, so read on and enjoy.

Our first recipe in this tantalizing little cookbook is by the chairwoman of the Junior League in Chalybeate Springs—Mrs. Otis Brandyworth. (Her first name is Sofie.) As everyone in Chalybeate Springs knows, Mrs. Brandyworth is the wife of Reverend Otis, who has presided over the Bible Road Brandyworth Church of Christ for twenty-three glorious years. With seventeen children in the Brandyworth household, we figured Mrs. Brandyworth knew a thing or two about cooking, so it seemed proper to let her start off. Here's her first contribution—one of biblical proportions, I might add …

♦ LOAVES AND FISHES♦

17 cans of sardines
24 slices of white bread
2 sticks of butter
2 cups of milk
4 cups of grated cheese (or cheese food)
Salt
Pepper
12 eggs
5 cups of mustard
1 cup cooking sherry

Heat oven to 400° F. In the largest baking dish you can find, spread bread out and dot with one stick of butter. Add cheese to the top, then place sardines on top of this, covering evenly. Dot with the rest of the butter. Mix eggs, salt, pepper, mustard, and milk, cooking sherry, and pour over bread and fish. Cook one hour.

Just as Jesus fed the multitudes with only a few loaves and some fishes, you too can feed your hungry brood. All seventeen of my children love this quick and easy "after-church" recipe. If you like your dishes extra spicy, just add more mustard.

As I said, nothing earth-shattering, but it had her personal stamp all over it. I sat for a while longer in the park, enjoying the solitude and greenery. Gigantic weeping willows dipped their long strands into a placid lily-pad-filled pond, and graceful swans glided gently among the drooping branches. A family of geese noisily conversed in the distance, near a rose garden that appeared to be quite well cared for, and winding paths crisscrossed the park in almost every direction. It was one of the most beautiful spots I had ever seen, and probably the pride of Chalybeate Springs. I stayed as long as I could until my backside started to ache from the hard park bench; then I made my way out of Eden and down the sidewalk that led past the cemetery.

Just as I passed that place of permanent Chalybeatean interment, right about the spot where Salinger's car had been parked, it hit me: Twice I had seen the man at a particular gravestone—the one with the small urn. My first day, in the police car, he had stopped, saying something about a ritual. I had to wonder if he meant every now and then, or every day. I turned the corner (Salinger was now nowhere in sight), and walked around the iron fence surrounding the dead. Entering the main gate, I followed the path up the hill to where Salinger had been standing. Why I had not more closely noticed the layout and magnitude of this resting place before (other than the cursory glance I had given it that first day) was beyond me. Carved drapes, urns, cherubs, angels, and every knick-knack possible adorned monuments from the Victorian era. Going farther back, to the Puritans, only simple slabs ornamented the final resting places. Then there were the modern numbers: slick granite and marble rectangles with rough edges, smooth lettering, and even a picture or two embedded within glass and set into the stone. One older couple's read, "Together now finally in death." One had to wonder how well they had gotten along in life. Another was, "God called him away because HE needed him more than we." I wanted to gag, hoping that no one would put anything that corny on my grave. Then again, I had decided to be cremated, so the worst I could get was a bad urn.

I moved on. "Resting in heaven now," was the next quotation, and then, "You will be missed," capped off my travels throughout the land of the dead. "Well, duh," I thought, that's original—"You will be missed." I was hoping for something with imagination, you know, something such as, "Glad you're gone you sorry bastard," or a simple, "Finally!" but no such admissions of truth were to be found.

By that time I had arrived at the site where I had seen Salinger. The stone was a modern one, again with slick engraving, and as I said, a modest urn and some scrolling. Nothing too fancy but not as boring as some of the others. I leaned down to read the lettering. "Caged Marshals." While it didn't make much sense, I did have to admit to its originality. Finally, one I could appreciate. Then I saw the name on the stone—Dick Hunter—common as dirt and about as exciting ... and extremely unfortunate. I was positive his real name had been Richard. Surely no parents would have bestowed such a regrettable moniker as this on a child. I imagined tormented elementary school recesses where bewildered schoolmates searched for some way to humiliate the boy by twisting his name around so that it meant something horrible; totally frustrated that the work had already been done for them. A least a name like Waller could be turned into, "Pig go Waller in the mud," and some poor Jewish girl with Fineblatt as a last name offered myriad possibilities for social ruin. "You're a Fine Blatt," or "This is another

Fine Blatt you've gotten us into," could easily be cajoled from their tiny brains somewhere between isosceles triangles and Pocahontas saving John Smith.

But Dick Hunter? Everything you needed was there. One would have at least thought that he would have changed it himself as an adult, but then he had died at a relatively early age and may have actually been going through that particular process when death came calling.

So now part of the riddle had been solved: Salinger knew Dick Hunter and came here every day to pay his respects ... but who was Dick Hunter and why did Salinger care so much about him?

12

Aghast By Pencilers

"**S**helby was here, looking for you." It was the front desk man, Mr. Hastings, speaking to me as I entered the Inn. I started to ask how she had known where I was, but figured it out pretty quickly from previous conversations. Also, I didn't want to antagonize him too much since I'd learned earlier of his illness. I searched for visible signs of his demise, but, finding none, decided to take Salinger's advice and treat him as if nothing were wrong. "Left this here envelope for you," he said.

I took the offering and started to make my way upstairs, tearing into the thing on the way. I stopped at the first step, still within sight of the reception desk. Along with a small note on feminine paper, a recipe was enclosed in the letter. The note contained the following:

> Dearest Mr. McCray [sic]
>
> I'm so excited to here [sic] you are finally in the Springs area and am enclosing my first recipe for the cookbook. I hope you do not mind as I wood [sic] like to have mine be included on the first page and all. Your [sic] one of my favorite writers and I wold [sic] be honored to have you come to dinner some night soon so that we might get better antiquated [sic & sick, not to mention confusing] and go over some thing. I haave [Weem's speak?] grate [you get the idea] plans for the book. Enclosed is my phone number.
>
> Very truly yours,
>
> Mrs. Shelby Hatoon [sick to the point of death]

Oh, and yet another scrap of paper made a cameo appearance—one that couldn't have been more appropriate: "Aghast By Pencilers," it read, though in a different hand from that of Mrs. Hatton.

I looked up at the keeper of Inn. He was deep in thought over something, though I couldn't imagine what.

"Excuse me," I said in his direction, garnering no results. (Who else could I have been talking to?)

I tried again. "Excuse me," I said, making my way over to the front desk. "You said a Mrs. Hatton left this note?"

He looked up. "That's correct."

"And she *is* the librarian here in town."

"Has been for humpty-leven years."

"Just how well do you know her?" I asked, leaning slightly onto the linoleum top of the counter, one elbow pointed toward him.

"All my life," he said.

"So you'd know her handwriting," I went on.

"Absolutely."

"Then, would you look at this note, if you don't mind?" I thrust the paper in his direction—the one with Shelby's invitation. He took it and read it—for a good ten minutes, I assumed to try and count the mistakes. "That would be hers all right," he said, handing me back the paper.

"And her last name ... uh, this week ... is Hatton, right?"

"That it would be."

"All-righty then," I said, and proceeded upstairs, shaking my head.

When I got to my room, I read it again. I had learned years ago never to assume anything, but one thing I had always, well *assumed,* was that a librarian would have basic rudimentary knowledge of spelling and grammar.

"I'm so excited to *here*?" I thought, as I reread her note. And she had left out words and even made up a few: "haave" instead of "have." "Your" instead of "You're," and the woman had even misspelled her last name (as well as mine.) But then, considering how many she had gathered along the way and might add in the future, I suppose that wasn't the social gaffe it might be with any other "normal" (a word I was learning to redefine) person. I didn't want to be overly critical, but there was going to be some serious editing to do if her recipes were to make sense. I had to wonder if she had simply killed several of her husbands by mistake, by writing down the wrong information or simply misspelling some of the ingredients. "Arsenic" *could* look a lot like "aspic."

I set the note aside and pulled out my binder, placing her recipe right next to the first one from Mrs. Brandyworth. Here is what Mrs. Shelby D wrote, along with the introduction I added—just off the top of my head at that moment—and her postscript about why exactly, she was including this fascinating little gem in the collection. I have corrected her typos.

Mrs. Shelby Dipsey-Ewell-Adams-Tellerman-Hatton is the next fine and upstanding citizen of Chalybeate Springs to provide us with a recipe. Mrs. Dipsey (we'll call her for now ... how about plain old Mrs. D?) knows how to cook, what with having a husband (the latest one) who loves to eat. Mrs. Shelby D is the town librarian and claims to have read every cookbook in that particular institution, searching for the most delicious recipes and trying them out on Messieurs D, E, A, and T, before their untimely demises. Good books and good cooking—that's Mrs. D's motto and we couldn't agree more. Here's her first little ditty:

♦TUNA SALAD FOR ONE♦

1 can of tuna
1 boiled egg
1 tomato, sliced any way you like
2 tablespoons French dressing

Open can of tuna and drain. Chop hard-boiled egg and slice tomato. Spread over tuna and cover with French dressing.

I thought I'd offer up a dish from the deep. I learned to make this right after my last husband died. Being alone for seven hours before my next marriage and not needing to cook for more than one, I found that this recipe came in handy. Whether your husband is dead or not, you'll enjoy this lo-cal treat. It's infinitely healthier than bread and sardines! And my current husband, Mr. Hatton, will even eat *this* tuna dish from time to time.

Thankfully the thing was somewhat free of errors and I deduced that her introductory note had been something she'd dashed off in haste. After all, I had yet to meet her.

Since I knew where her house was and I had no desire to further involve Salinger, I brushed myself off and jogged downstairs to use the phone as none was in my room. Modernity was not an attribute that either the Inn or the town possessed. The only means of calling was via an ancient black wall-model that begrudgingly hung right next to the stairs of the Inn. It was an old circular-dial-it-yourself-and-let-your-finger-ride-around phone. Getting long distance was out of the question and one was lucky if a dial tone was heard at all, so spotty was the service.

I picked up the receiver and dialed. I let my fingers make the arduous journey around, remembering back to my childhood (or lack thereof) and what it had been like before the advent of push buttons. Finally the librarian answered. While Shelby tried to cajole me into dinner that evening, I insisted I had plans (I didn't) and begged to come right away as that particular time of day wouldn't entail consuming anything she had actually cooked. Her reputation preceded her and I wasn't about to be her next victim. We agreed to speak the next day about getting together on Monday, and I hung up, elated that I had yet another 24 hours to live.

The following day I phoned again. No one answered, and with Shelby evidently not owning an answering machine, I hung up. Then it dawned on me: She was at the library, the perfect place to meet since there would be no chance for her to try and feed me anything. I hastened over to the building which was located just two blocks away and not hard to find considering the large sign out front that boasted the announcement, "THE SHELBY D.E.A.T MEMORIAL LIBRARY—OVER FIFTY BOOKS!"

Stepping up to the desk I inquired about Mrs. Hatton. The woman I asked looked at me for a moment, questioned who I was, and when she heard the name, changed her demeanor from indifferent to more of the same.

"I'll get her," she said, and continued to stamp a series of books she was checking back in. I waited.

"When?" I finally asked, seeing that she wasn't moving. It wasn't so much that I was in a hurry to meet this next member of the Junior League, but rather that I didn't want to prolong my introduction to the point where lunch, tea, or dinner might be involved.

"When I'm done here," she said, having perfected the Chalybeate Springs method of speaking to people without actually looking at them.

"Couldn't you just call out to her or something?" I asked, seeing the clock hands move closer to lunch time. She stopped what she was doing and sighed heavily. Then she looked at me for what seemed like a good five minutes, and finally walked toward the back of the library.

"A McCrae somebody is here to see you," I heard her unceremoniously mutter. This was followed by what sounded like a herd of water buffalo stampeding after they've seen a pack of five thousand lions with rib cages showing. Within moments, Shelby came out to greet me, admonishing the assistant for her lackadaisical attitude and inattention to an actual breathing author.

"Mr. McCrae," she said, extending the proverbial graceful and overly jeweled arm long before she was anywhere within reach. "I can't tell you what a pleasure it is to meet you. I'm guessing you got my note?" I looked her over. She certainly was pretty—far prettier than most of the other women I had seen about town with the exception of Miss Henrid. It wasn't hard to see why so many men had fallen for her, even with her inability to spell and talent for collecting life insurance policies.

"Yes, I, uh, got your note … and your recipe," I said. "I was a little confused why you would include such a small item," I went on, as she ushered me into the back of the library where the offices were. I prayed the space didn't contain a kitchen.

"Well, that was just my first one. I've got so many more."

"I'm sure."

"And you mentioned Mrs. Weems's recipe, I thought, rather obliquely—'Healthier than bread and sardines.' How did you know about that?"

She ignored me.

"Now, why don't you have a seat and I'll get you something to drink," she offered.

"No! I'm fine," I said. "Really, I just had a gallon of iced tea and I'm full—couldn't hold another drop."

"Well, if you're sure."

"Quite."

She sat down across from me and her eyes dug into my flesh. "I just can't *tell* you how thrilled we all are that you volunteered to come down here and help us with this little-ole cookbook," she cooed. Why, it's just *precious* of you."

"I actually feel precious," I said, adjusting myself on the burlap-covered office chair. "You have no idea just how precious I feel at this moment."

"Oh, that first recipe of mine was just to, well (and here she put her hand to her mouth and feigned a giggle), whet, if you'll excuse the expression (I couldn't), your appetite." She then guffawed so heavily that I thought she'd fall out of her chair.

"Well, it certainly got my attention," I said, thinking that my publisher was going to hang me out of his thirty-story window if and when I ever got back to New York with the lackluster performance these women had shown so far concerning culinary expertise.

"I just can't wait to fill you in on what else I have. And, oh, I'm certain you'll want to be made aware of all there is to know about the town, and, well, being the librarian and having access to all the history, I can fill you in on just about everything."

"Great. I would like to know more about the natives of the place," I said.

She pulled a blank look. "Natives? Oh. Well, I'm sorry, but there haven't been any Indians here for over a hundred years, you see ..."

"I meant the townspeople," I said, trying to clarify a situation that shouldn't have required it.

"Oh, yes, that. Natives. Well, it just sounds so ... rustic."

"Hmmm."

"But if there's anything else I can fill you in on, you just let me know."

"Well, I've already met with Mrs. Weems (who seemed to understand the term "native," I thought, but didn't say—then again, I couldn't really tell), and Mrs. Brandyworth, and ..." but I stopped when I saw her facial expression go from genially stupid to hateful death-grip.

"I thought I would be the first on your list," she said, straightening up in her chair. After all, I *am* the town librarian and you, being a writer, might have shown a little more respect."

If she was Jeckyl before, she was certainly Hyde now. The transformation was immediate and unfortunate. I treaded carefully, cognizant of the fact that she was cocked and loaded.

"I'm ... sorry ... I didn't think that it was that important." I was trying to figure out how to escape from possible death. I hadn't even written to these women myself—Miss Henrid had—and now I had to backpedal. Anger was starting to replace any joy I had for the money Henrid and Brandyworth were giving me—$60,000 so far. So I swallowed hard, knowing I wanted, *needed* the money, and my publisher needed a book.

Evidently she read even more contrition into my demeanor than I had planned, for she softened. "I didn't mean to jump at you like that," she said. I thought of her list of dead husbands. It wasn't hard to imagine that more than one had died by leaving his toenail clippings on the bathroom floor or asking if she could turn down the volume on the television. Aren't librarians supposed to be meek, with glasses and boring lives? So far this one was bucking the trend.

I took a deep breath and decided to try again, attempting to connect with her on home ground. "You said you knew about the town," I began. "Why don't you fill me in on a little history of the place, who everyone is, what roles they play?"

I might as well have asked for the *Encyclopedia Britannica de la Chalybeatea Springnifica*. Evidently I had hit pay dirt when it came to stroking Shelby's ego as she immediately became a fountain of knowledge and gossip.

She sat up, all perky and pleasant once more. "Well, since you've met Weems and Brandyworth, I'll fill you in on those two. First off, Mrs. Weems and her husband have control over the entire town. Then, there's Mrs. Brandyworth. Now, I don't want to gossip or anything (she could have fooled me), but there's some *mighty* fishy things going on with her and certain other persons in that household."

I wanted to say, "You're not kidding, the first recipe had enough fish in it to fill an aquarium store," but I abstained.

"And then there's the Inn," she went on.

"I'm actually staying at the Inn, you know," but then realized my mistake as everyone knew everything about everyone and I was still waiting for her to ask about the roast beef.

"I know," she said, and I can bet Jecko overcooked that roast the other night, didn't he?"

Right on cue. "Well, I like it a little overdone and besides …"

"Now that Mrs. Brandyworth," she continued, as if I didn't exist, "well, she may be the chairwoman for the Junior League, but that's just because she was self-appointed. And Weems appointed herself President. Personally, you'd think that the town librarian would have gotten that job, but noooooooo. I don't think I have to tell you about small town politics," she went on.

"No, I'm pretty much getting a taste of it every minute," I said. "But I do have a question about Mrs. Weems, if it's not too personal."

"I'll do what I can."

"Has she had a stroke or something recently?" I asked, as gently as I could.

Shelby exploded with excitement. "Good God! Don't you know?" she asked, leaning forward. I obviously didn't. "The woman was born with no lips!" she screamed.

I thought back to my first meeting with the Mayor's wife. The face—Mrs. Weems's face—there *had* been something wrong with it.

The vision was becoming clearer. Her lipstick had been odd, but then, why wouldn't it have been?—it had literally been painted on.

"She was born that way?" I said.

"Treated horribly as a child. You can imagine how the kids tortured her."

"Sure enough," I said. "That would explain how uneven her speech was ... is," I went on. "Some words were okay, and some were really out of whack."

"Oh, that," Shelby said, obviously not as interested as before. She rummaged through some papers on her desk, attempting to placate my interest and get a modicum of work done at the same time. "That stupid woman and her husband went to Greenland six months ago and Weems stuck her tongue to a giant candy cane they had up for Christmas decoration in some town."

"I don't get it. What does that have to do with her speech impediment?"

Shelby looked at me as if I'd just admitted to Communism and this was 1950. "It was sixty below zero and the pole was metal," she said. "Took the tip of the stupid woman's tongue right off. She can get some words out okay by using the two new tips that she now has on each side. The middle is missing. Talk about speaking with forked tongue." Then she continued, as if this was common knowledge to everyone in the town. "Someone had sent her this Christmas card with Santa and his reindeers? And one of the reindeer had licked the pole and had gotten stuck. I guess Weems wanted to see if it would really happen. Now, who else have you met?"

"That's about it," I said, trying to get the image of Mrs. Weems's most important speaking tool stuck to a giant candy cane in Greenland out of my mind, "as far as the Junior League goes. I've met a Miss Henrid and Sheriff ..."

"Oh, my God! Those two? You poor thing!"

"I'm guessing you know them."

"Went to school with J.D. Salinger and ..."

"Wait a minute. His first two initials are J.D?" I asked, incredulous.

"Why yes? What's so unusual about that?"

I sat there thinking: "Okay. This woman is a librarian. She can't spell. And she has no idea who J.D. Salinger is." Just when I thought it couldn't possibly get any better, or worse, it did.

"John Dillinger and I go waaaay back," she said.

I sat in silence, slightly slumped down. For some reason totally beyond my grasp and that of the universe, Shelby D.E.A.T.H had enough insight to notice.

"Is there something wrong?" she asked.

"John Dillinger Salinger?" I asked

"Yes."

"Well, that certainly rolls off the tongue easily."

"Captain of the football team," she said. "He and I dated once, and mind you, only once. But, what's wrong? You look like you have a headache."

"I do Mrs. Hatton. I do have a headache. An awful one," I said, and rubbed my temples.

13

Shelby's Tear Pacing

The soda bottle was unopened and the aspirins came in a sealed packet, so I felt reasonably safe when Shelby offered them to me.

"I get these migraines too," she said, sitting back down.

I sniffed the rim of the soda bottle after opening it, but realized that myriad poisons have no smell or taste. It didn't matter; my head was throbbing. I knew I would gain fodder for a novel, but the process of extracting it from the cadre of characters masquerading as people in Chalybeate Springs was already taking its toll, and I had been here only two days.

"It's just a lot to take in," I said, after swallowing the aspirins and washing them down with the soda. "You were telling me about Sheriff Salinger. John D—captain of the football team. All that."

"Right. Well, we did date, but it just didn't work out. He might have been a star athlete, but he was, well, you know …"

"No, I don't know. He was what?"

She sighed. "Among other things, he was an absolute control freak. I just couldn't deal with it." I thought about Salinger's current craze for following me around, insisting on driving me to every location, and I had to agree with her on that point.

"That's why he became a police officer, and then the sheriff."

"*Of these here parts*," I said, trying out my best Western accent. It was lost on poor Shelby.

"Exactly right. He did go off for a time. I don't remember all of it. Was either Nashville or Mobile, or maybe it was, well, I can't remember. Even went to New York for a couple of months once. Came back different, if you know what I mean."

"No, I don't. But you say he grew up here?"

"All of his life. If you can call it that."

I shrugged my shoulders, shook my head and widened my eyes—a gesture in most cultures that says "No, I have no idea."

"Are you all right, Mr. McCrae," Shelby asked.

"I was trying to tell you that you could go on, you know, explain Salinger to me."

"Oh, okey-dokey. Nice enough guy, most of the time, but his family was not wealthy and some of the people in town took advantage of them—you know how that can be."

"I'm beginning to understand."

"Weems, the husband, got him that job as sheriff-slash-police officer, firefighter, undertaker, and whatnot."

"Wait a minute. I knew he was the sheriff of the county, the town's only law enforcement official, and he mentioned something about being a firefighter, but undertaker?"

"Creepy, huh?"

"Wouldn't that be a conflict of interest in most places? Not to mention slightly disgusting?"

Shelby pursed her lips and added a dramatic pause, "Mr. McCrae, I don't know if has occurred to you or not, but Chalybeate Springs is not exactly 'most places.'"

Her verbal arrow landed with a "Boiiiiiinnnngg!" completely out of character again from the sweet persona she had managed to maintain for the last few minutes. Robin Hood, this one, without the benefit of the rich-poor thing going on. I tried to edge her back onto the happy trail of cat scratching. "You were telling me about Salinger," I said, even though I had grown tired of his story—or lack thereof.

"Well, he was barred from the Brandyworth Church of Christ because of that incident with the football team when they all went over to that whorehouse in the state's capital? He claimed nothing happened, and the others never went in, so they *said*, but he was the one that took the brunt of it all."

"So that pretty much fixed him with Reverend Brandyworth."

"Yes. Then he got into some kind of dispute with Mrs. Wash Childers's husband, Bud—when that man was still alive—over a hunting license or something."

"Salinger likes to hunt?" I said.

"This is the South."

"Okay. He had a thing with the Childers clan. What next?" I said.

"How did you know they were in the Klan?" Shelby asked, wide-eyed.

I tried to think on my feet. "Doesn't everyone know?"

"Yes, I suppose it is common knowledge."

"You can continue," I said.

"Let's see," she mused, putting a finger to her lips for a moment—a calculated move to look more demure. But before she could finish that forced tableau, the phone rang.

"Hey, Honey," she said into the receiver with enough sweetness to kill a beginning type-two diabetic. "Well, I don't *know* what time I'll be home," she continued, her tone changing from pure cane sugar to more temperate molasses. She looked at me, rolled her eyes, then put her hand over the receiver and mouthed the word "Husband." I assumed she meant Hatton as she had been married to him when I came into the library and no new ceremony had taken place while I was there. Then again, she had gone out for soda and aspirin, so there might have been enough time. I casually searched the floor for signs of rice.

She continued, "I get off work *when* I get *done* here." Her tone was now dissonant; a Schoenberg twelve-tone matrix of angst. "WELL, FUCK YOU AND YOUR TEE-OFF TIME!" she screamed, and slammed the receiver down with such force that it actually split into two pieces.

I sat perfectly still, not sure where this was going and hoping her anger had been pointed toward Mr. Hatton's golf clubs and not *all* men. She closed her eyes, took a deep breath, and then changed back into the original version I had first met.

"Where were we?" she asked.

"I don't think I've actually ever seen anyone break a telephone," I said, forgetting for a moment that the slightest thing could set her off. (Where had *I* been?)

"This is some cheap shit the librarian who was here before me bought."

I wanted to ask what had happened to said librarian but could pretty much figure it out from the list of dead husbands and Shelby's temper.

"You and she didn't get along?" I said, attempting innocence, referring to the librarian.

"Doesn't matter now," she smirked. "She's dead."

"Oh." (Shock.)

"I was telling you about Salinger. Where were we?"

"The Childers family."

"Oh, right. That hunting dispute. Who else, who else?" she mused, looking up at the ceiling.

"I think there's one more person, besides yourself, in the Junior League—a Killchrist or something? Salinger have anything to do with her?"

"Now *that's* a story all in itself." She sat up straight, giggled slightly, and leaned forward. "Mary-Ellen Killchrist just thinks she's God's gift to mankind," and she slapped her hand down hard on the desk and looked satisfied with herself. "Homecoming Queen—it was fixed—cheerleading squad—that too—and now she's somehow finagled her way into becoming the economics teacher at the high school, *and* had the damn thing named after her!"

"What's all that got to do with Salinger?"

"Well, it all goes back to the night of the prom. J.D. was supposed to take *me* to the dance, but Mary-Ellen Killchrist told him she was pregnant with his child and wouldn't have an abortion unless he took *her*. And she was the Queen—the PromQueen, so she did have some pull."

"Nice girl."

"Oh, but there's more bad blood than that between the two—between Mary-Ellen and J.D. A couple of years ago, shortly after I lost my … (she counted on her fingers for a moment), third husband." She sat still, thinking. "Yes, it was the third—that deputy Charles Adams. It was sometime after that, when Mary-Ellen's brother disappeared, which, if you ask me, was no great loss."

"Any reason?" I asked, knowing full well that even if there wasn't one, Shelby would come up with something.

"A bad lot all around. Harry Killchrist dropped out of high school and robbed a liquor store over in Titusville. Mixed up in drugs and everything else you can imagine. Moonshiner. Rum-running. Frankly, nobody was surprised when he came up missing, but Mary-Ellen insisted that J.D. hadn't done enough to find his body so that there could be a funeral, closure, that sort of thing. They both *say* they're over it. But I don't know."

So Salinger seemed to have a beef with more than one person on the Junior League: Brandyworth because he'd caused Salinger's exclusion from the church, Weems because he was Salinger's employer, Mary-Ellen Killchrist because she tried to trick him with a false pregnancy and Salinger had lost her brother. Then Mrs. Wash Childers because of a dispute he had with her husband over a hunting license.

It was becoming clear on another level entirely why I had been asked here. Miss Henrid had initiated this cookbook idea because she wanted into the Junior League, but there were secondary motives accompanying this, namely, that Salinger had something up his sleeve when it came to these women (or their husbands)—some unresolved issues. I was becoming more wary with each moment but the money *was* rolling in. I couldn't wait to see what the town's librarian—Shelby—was going to come up with to bribe me.

"I've got it now that Salinger is not on the best of terms with some of the town ..."

"Some of the town? Try *all* of it," she jumped in.

"Oh, I didn't know it was everyone."

"Well, there aren't that many," Shelby countered. "Still, he's mad at most, and the majority of the townspeople don't care for him since he won the Chalybeate chili cook-off, or the CCC as it's known around here, for the past five years." She paused, reflecting on something.

"What?" I said, seeing her expression change.

"Look, Mr. McCrae, like I said, there are not a lot of people who like Salinger, but we do feel sorry for him."

"Why? What's there to feel sorry for?" As far as I could tell the man was excessively jovial and a bit too aggressive for my taste—he didn't seem that scarred by the town's treatment. Then again, he was in law enforcement—a definite theme for those seeking power.

"It happened about the time of Mary-Ellen's brother's disappearance, this ... thing."

"To Salinger."

"He changed, but who could blame him? You see, at one time he wasn't the only law enforcement officer around here. There were three. Well, Salinger was the sheriff but he had two deputies—at different times."

"Right, you told me your ... third husband, Charles G. Adams I believe was his name; he was one. But who was the other?"

"This is the sad part. Salinger and his other partner were busting up a still over on the border of the county, when the man they were after shot at J.D. He missed and hit Salinger's partner, killing him. Hit him in the face and then somewhere else on the body. It was a mess. Closed casket and all."

"I'm sorry to hear about that, but Salinger doesn't seem to be terribly upset about it," I said.

"We all suspected the obvious," she went on.

"Obvious?" I said.

"Well, after that hunting incident with Mr. Childers, and them being the way they are—backward and all—we all assumed that Mrs. Childers's husband was the one operating the still—the one who shot Salinger's partner."

I let it all sink in. Yet another motive for Salinger to hate Mrs. Childers, and a more intense one than some dispute over a hunting license. Finally I looked up. "What was his partner's name—Salinger's partner's name?" I asked.

The answer made sense as I heard Shelby say it. Unlike Mrs. Weems and Mrs. Brandyworth, she had not offered me any money—any bribe—but she had given me much more: she had given me volumes of information and background on why I had been called to this place.

"Dick Hunter. That was the man," she said, a sadness coming over her. "He was Salinger's best friend in high school and (she seemed to choke up slightly), the one Salinger got to take *Yours Truly* to the prom in high school after that awful Mary-Ellen tricked him into dumping me."

"How unfortunate," I said.

She sighed again. "It was sad, his death and all."

"Oh ... I meant his name."

"Huh?"

"An unfortunate name if ever I've heard one," I pressed on. "Dick Hunter, you know?"

"I don't follow." Why, I do not know, but this surprised even me for a moment. As is always the case, I thought the tale ended there.

It didn't.

"So other than Mary-Ellen being a bit conniving, is there any reason I shouldn't pay her a visit?"

Shelby snorted and crossed her arms. "Mr. McCrae, you're going to have to wait on that one."

"I don't follow."

"She's laid up in bed for a while. Miss Brain-trust of Chalybeate High tried to pick up a rattlesnake the other day and she's recuperating, unfortunately quite nicely, from the bite. If you want, I'll take the binder with the recipes over to her."

"I'm thinking I'll just let you lovely ladies have it most of the time and when you're done I'll take it and edit it—you know, clean up the spelling and make a few adjustments."

"That sounds like a marvelous idea," she said, standing and indicating that our meeting was (thank God) over.

Then I caught up mentally. I might not have been a few thousand dollars richer in librarian dollars, but in my head I heard the sound I most liked as a writer: "Ka-ching!" and I knew I had something to follow.

14

Retyping Heals Scab

Salinger's pilgrimage each day to the cemetery now made sense. He would visit his best friend's grave to pay homage for the guilt he felt at not taking the bullet that was offered him by a moonshiner in the county. I couldn't blame him, and now *that* particular piece of the puzzle was in place. But I was sure there were items of interest not yet uncovered in the Springs area.

I was right.

Back at the Inn, I began to compile all the data I had garnered from Weems, Brandyworth, and especially the loquacious Shelby of library-land. She may not have been able to spell, but she certainly could talk. I had met only three of the five women, but from what I'd heard I could put off meeting the infamous Mrs. Childers and the blackmailing Mary-Ellen for a while. And the scraps of paper with cryptic messages continued, non-stop. Instead of alerting you to each one's appearance (it *can* get so annoying), for the sake of brevity I'll just include them at the top of each chapter. At this point, they make no sense to me, but hopefully by the time I'm through here, some headway will be made with regard to their strangeness.

Now, completely cut off from the outside world (the Inn had no Internet access and my cell phone languished in my New York apartment), I comforted myself with only my laptop and began typing. As I was finishing the sentence about the lack of Internet service, the cleaning woman rather unceremoniously entered my room.

Just a moment while I take care of this. She seems to be unaware that I'm working and I'm not ready to have my room done just yet...
....
....
....

Oh, dear. I accidentally left the end of a book touching one of the computer's keys and it seems to have gone its own way. Sorry about that.

Okay. I'm back now, having chastised the woman for her inability to use her knuckles properly on the door and announce herself. But it really should not have come as a surprise as, when I got up for those few moments, I had the most interesting conversation. I shall relate it to you now as you are not here at present (obviously) and it is integral to this story.

After I admonished her for interrupting me, she asked what was so important, and I, in my bashful New York fashion, told her—all about the Junior League and the cookbook and my plans here to help—the whole thing. Her head almost blew off.

"Ain't nobody told me about it!" she said angrily.

"And why would they have, my good woman," I replied, using my best George Sanders accent.

"Well, I'm *on* the durn thing."

"What durn thing?" I asked.

"The Junior League."

Math was never my forte, but it wasn't hard to figure out that this was not a former Homecoming Queen or head cheerleader, much less a home economics teacher at the local high school. A stretch more and I remembered that the illustrious Mrs. Childers was housekeeper to the other four women. It only made sense that she was also the Inn's maid.

"You must be Mrs. Childers," I said, extending my hand. Hers remained firmly under a bundle of dirty laundry (I suppose I should be thankful) and her demeanor was hard—country-like.

"How comes you to be here and I not knowed anythin' about it?" she asked as her eyes squinted almost completely shut. The woman could have been a stand-in for Granny on *The Beverly Hillbillies,* except her disposition was slightly less pleasant. I looked over her shoulder at the now-opened door.

"What you a-lookin' for?" she asked.

"I was wondering where Jethro Bodine and Elly May were," I said. The comment sailed over her head at about the same altitude as one of NASA's satellites.

"My kids is all in jail she said, and ain't none of them named Jethro."

"I see."

"You want I should clean your room or-a-come back?"

"Well, I'm sort of busy right now, so if you could go clean some of the other rooms and come back later, that would be great." I added a smile, even though I didn't feel up to it. If what Shelby had told me was true—about Childers's husband allegedly killing Salinger's partner—then I didn't want to get a rise out of her (the possibilities of death by mop bucket did not thrill me, thinking of the headlines in the *New York Times* ... if any.)

"Can't do that," she responded to my request that she clean the other rooms.

"The reason being?"

"This here's the only room the Inn's got," she said.

"Oh. I see. Well, then."

"You want I should come back? And you ain't answered my question 'bout why you ain't contacted me since I's on the Junior League."

I remembered that Miss Henrid had sent the women of the League a letter, forging my name, and was about to remind Granny of this when it occurred to me that Mrs. Childers was the one person no one wanted to associate with. After meeting her, I was somewhat in agreement—evidently Henrid had left her off the mailing list.

"I was coming over to see you later today," I lied, stalling for time to get out of the situation.

"Didn't even knowd you's here," she went on. "That old cow Weems and that she-dog Brandysnoot don't tell me shit."

"Indeed."

"You met that whore Mary-Ellen yet?"

"No, I can't say I've had the …"

"Shit, boy, she'll try and get in yur pants faster than a duck on a June bug."

"That so?"

"And that Shelby bitch over at the ly-berry is got somethin' again' me I can't figger out."

"I did speak with her and …"

"She talk about me?"

"Actually," I said, scratching the back of my head, "I don't believe your name came up at all."

"Bitch. That's what that one is. I can tell you a few things."

"I'll bet." She stood and eyed me from head to toe for what seemed like an eternity. Then she spoke again, a little more at ease.

"You said somethin', 'bout a cookbook."

"I'm collecting recipes for the Junior League version of that much sought-after compilation of ink and paper. It's going to be published and hopefully the money will go to some charity or good cause."

"Shit, ain't no good causes 'round here," she spat out. "You talked to everybody but me, is that right?"

"Well, we are conversing now, in case you didn't notice."

"I suppose my cookin's not good enough for them bitches," she added, leaning forward and squinting more—it was a wonder she could see at all by this time.

Waiting a good minute, I collected myself: "Mrs. Childers, if you dislike these women in the Junior League, then why, may I ask, are you in it with them?"

Having perfected her Chalybeate gestation period for just the right amount of time, she answered: "Just to *piss them off*," and with that she dropped her bundle of sheets onto the floor. I too waited, wondering first of all what she had to be so angry about, and secondly, why if there was only my room to change, had she come bearing a bundle of dirty sheets. I had to ask at least one of the questions.

"Mrs. Childers, if there's only my room to clean, why did you come in carrying a bundle of dirty sheets?" (You knew that was going to be the one.)

Her answer was simple enough. "To change yur bed with 'em."

"So, you were going to take the dirty sheets off my bed, and replace them with more dirty ones," I said.

"Guess so."

"This doesn't strike you as odd?" I asked.

She pulled a blank look. "Never mind," I said. "I really need to get back to work on this book—you know, writing down the information I've gathered and try to get it into some format for my editor, so you can just leave the sheets on the bed for now."

"I've got to git you my recipes fur the book, anyway," she said as she sloughed out of the room like dead skin off a snake. Then she stuck her head back in the doorway and added, "I'll write 'em down fur you, one at a time."

My first thought was, "You can write?" but I said nothing. "Just bring me the first one," I said. "After that I'm going to let you ladies pass around a binder and you can add what you want. I'm writing a small introduction for each one, oh, and we'll want something after each entry—you know, some tidbit on where you got the recipe; if it came handed down through the family—that sort of thing."

She nodded and left. While she wasn't the most genial creature, I knew people from the country, from my youth, and I imagined her recipes to be filled with good old-fashioned homemade ingredients, farm-fresh and mouth-watering. Images of pies cooling on the window sill, fried chicken, home-grown tomatoes and onions, and delicious desserts filled my head. I couldn't imagine that Weems or Brandyworth were going to have anything really edible. I'd seen the recipe

Brandyworth had offered—her holier-than-thou-concoction—and the one I'd gotten from Shelby was about as exciting as watching paint dry. Surely Mrs. Childers would be the one bright spot in the dark firmament that was Chalybeate Springs cooking. And, as it turned out, she was—just not in the way I had imagined.

15

Rebating Class Hype

Foods With Local Color

This recipe was donated by Mrs. Helen Weems, wife of the town's beloved mayor, Wally Weems. Wally's great-grandfather (Wilfred Wormwood Weems) was a direct descendent of one of the very people who founded Chalybeate Springs. We don't think this recipe is quite that old, but it's sure to add some flavor to your next gathering of movie stars! (Mrs. Weems made me put that in.) The Weems family likes to travel a lot—when they're not spending time at their beloved Weems Town Hall—and it shows.

◆CHEESE LOG◆

½ pound of any sharp Cheddar cheese
½ pound of hoop cheese
1 packet of cream cheese
½ cup dry sherry
3 small shallots, grated and lightly toasted
1 teaspoon garlic salt
Dash of cayenne pepper
½ cup mayonnaise
1 tablespoon paprika
1 cup chopped walnuts

I'm going to break this current fish trend with something new. Here goes: Mix ingredients in a large bowl. Add more or less mayonnaise depending on the consistency you want. Form mixture into a log. Roll in nuts, wrap in waxed paper and chill for twenty-four hours.

I simply love this great party treat. The last time we traveled through Europe on our way to China and Taiwan, we brought some of this along to share with the "natives." Many of them became sick but we wrote it off as food being so different from what they were used to.

On our way back home, we stopped in Hawaii and saw a VERY famous movie star in a restaurant. My husband insisted I go over and offer her some of the cheese log, and, having a few remaining bits in my purse, I approached the mega-star. While the actress didn't get to sample my wares, the Honolulu police enjoyed it at the station. "Book 'em, Danno!"

This recipe was given to us by Mary-Ellen Killchrist, of 46 Farmsway Road, out near the lake. We especially wanted to include it as Mary-Ellen is recovering from her run-in with a rather nasty rattlesnake that appeared one day in her backyard. Mary-Ellen thought the poor reptile was too "pretty" to get rid of, so she picked it up and brought it into the house. Her boyfriend came over just in the nick of time—her breathing was shallow and she had suffered quite a bit of tissue damage. Get well soon, Mary-Ellen. You need to get back to teaching that home economics course at the local high school.

♦HORS D'OEUVRE DU SERPENT—A HOMECOMING-QUEEN TREAT!♦

1 rattlesnake, killed
3 cloves of garlic
1 can of chicken broth
Salt & pepper
Half a stick of butter

Take one large rattlesnake (after your boyfriend has killed it with his putting iron when he comes in from school—careful not to damage the head ... of the snake). Skin and cut into sections about an inch wide. Gently sauté over low heat, using a half stick of butter. Caution! Do not overcook the rattlesnake meat just yet! Place browned pieces in shallow baking dish and cover with the three crushed cloves of garlic, salt and pepper, and chicken broth. Cook for three hours until you're sure the thing is dead. Serve pieces on Ritz crackers with melted cheese. Yuuuuu-ummmm!

This recipe was especially easy since I already had the snake. I'm sure any other reptile would do, but revenge is a taste I enjoy cooked to death! Be sure to remove the head and use as a centerpiece on your tray, surrounding it with the crackers and the snake meat. A definite conversation starter.

Mrs. Wash Childers is next on our list. An unusual addition to any Junior League roster, Mrs. Childers "keeps house" for Mrs. Helen Weems, Mrs. Brandyworth, Shelby, and even the youthful Mary-Ellen. It seems that her expertise as a household technician has made her invaluable to the high society matrons of Chalybeate Springs, and they have seen fit to include her in their group—a benevolent gesture if ever there was one. Mrs. Wash Childers's claim to fame is that she's the only white housekeeper within seventy-five miles of the Springs.

◆CHICKEN-FRIED QUAIL◆

1 quail
Fat
Spices
Flour
Cornmeal

Now, here's what you've got to do. Split that there quail into pieces and clean it good. Put it in a shallow pan of salt and roll that thing around. Let it stand in the icebox for five hours, all salty-like. Then you want to heat a large skillet with the fat in it. Roll that there quail in the flour and spices and fry till it's good and brown.

This is the best darn thing you'll ever set your teeth into. If you don't eat quail, try this here recipe with squirrel. My late husband "Bud" liked this fixed for him early in the morning afore he went a traipsen' out to go huntin'. "Never hunt on an empty stomach," he'd always say, and it seems like good advice to me.

Evidently the route of Mr. Binder was not a straight line, for somehow it wandered back to Reverend Brandyworth's wife, then Shelby.

♦LOAVES AND FISHES♦

17 cans of sardines
24 slices of white bread
2 sticks of butter
2 cups of milk
4 cups of grated cheese (or cheese food)
Salt
Pepper
12 eggs
5 cups of mustard
1 cup cooking sherry

Heat oven to 400° F. In the largest baking dish you can find, spread bread out and dot with one stick of butter. Add cheese to the top, then place sardines on top of this, covering evenly. Dot with the rest of the butter. Mix eggs, salt, pepper, mustard, and milk, cooking sherry, and pour over bread and fish. Cook one hour.

Just as Jesus fed the multitudes with only a few loaves and some fishes, you too can feed your hungry brood. All seventeen of my children love this quick and easy "after-church" recipe. If you like your dishes extra spicy, just add more mustard.

Shelby adds her comments/recipe:

♦ALZHEIMER'S SPECIAL♦

1 horrible recipe … again
1 bad case of forgetfulness

Mix ingredients well and write out EXACTLY the same as before.

You just gave us this recipe. Take your medication!

I sent the recipe collection back out, the binder going to Mrs. Weems first. While it was passed around, I needed to find something to occupy my time. Chalybeate Springs wasn't exactly the entertainment capital of the universe, and as there was no Internet access, no television or movie theater, and I had no personal access to transportation other than that provided by Security & Co., I decided to visit the library and do some research on the area. Shelby was most helpful, pointing me in exactly the direction she most wanted me to go—indirectly steering me to the locations she most wanted to keep me clear of via her attempted sabotage. I simply looked in every location except the one she suggested.

With the help of the manner-less assistant I had first encountered upon entering that great institution and repository of literature (I was later to find out that she was the niece of the Weemses and therefore predisposed to detest Shelby as much as the rest of Chalybeate Springs), I was able to find numerous old newspaper articles and information about the inhabitants of the town. The first thing I came upon was the article about Sheriff Salinger and the unfortunate incident where his sidekick, Dick Hunter, was killed.

>   Chalybeate Springs's own Dick Hunter
> was   fatally   shot   yesterday   while
> attempting to make an arrest in the
> eastern-most part of the county. Sheriff
> Salinger and Deputy Hunter were attempting
> to apprehend a suspect as he was trying to
> cover   his   homemade   still   with   pine
> branches. The moonshiner, while resisting
> arrest, shot at Salinger, missing and
> killing Hunter instead. The suspect then
> fled on foot and has not been found since.
> Sheriff Salinger filed a full report with
> Mayor Weems at the Town Hall and the
> matter has since been considered closed,
> but anyone knowing the whereabouts of said
> moonshiner   should   contact   Sheriff
> Salinger. A reward of $10.50 has been
> posted for his capture.

Having found verification on Salinger and Hunter's story, I went on to the rest of that day's paper. It made for equally fascinating insight into the workings (or not) of the minds of the Chalybeate folk.

>   Item: Pig found on the Roger Satchel
> farm Tuesday. Pinkish with black spots.

Answers to the name of "Quagmire." If not claimed by Friday, will be eaten.

And another:

> This year's Fourth of July Chalybeate chili cook-off, or CCC as it is affectionately known, will be held as usual in the town's park, just left of the small pond. All residents are reminded that the swans in the pond are strictly for visual purposes and do not make good eating.

I read on:

> Whoever has stolen the mailbox of Easter Wilcox will kindly replace it. She is expecting a letter from her son who is stationed in Ty-wan [sic.]

Then, in another earlier edition of the *Times*, this item:

> Mrs. Charles Adams, formerly known as Shelby Dipsey-Ewell, is once again a widow. Mr. Adams died of what Sheriff Salinger termed "suspicious causes," though the sheriff could provide no further information on the matter. Mrs. Shelby Dipsey-Ewell-Adams plans to marry Mr. Sigfried Tellerman of nearby Titusville this next Sunday. Mrs. Dipsey-Ewell-Adams is a long-time resident of the Springs area and head librarian of this community's esteemed institution. Mr. Tellerman is the son of the late Tristan and Isolda Tellerman [another unfortunate combination of names in my opinion], both of Titusville. The wedding ceremony will be held at Chalybeate Springs's only church, the Brandyworth Church of Christ. A reception will follow at the Inn. Guests are reminded not to wear white as they did at the wedding of Miss Gladys Stoats to her brother, Mr. Billy Stoats, back in May.

I found another copy of the *Times*—this one from several years earlier:

> The contest to rename Main Street is still open. So far the anonymous entries include, "Weems Way," "Brandyworth Road," "Dipsey Circle," (even though the street is entirely straight and only one block long), and "Salinger Row."

Chalybeate, it seems, was short on a lot of things, but ego wasn't one of them.

And then:

> A neighboring county man was decapitated accidentally when a chainsaw his brother was using slipped out of the brother's hand and severed the man's head. Authorities say that no foul play was suspected.

Then another familiar name—this in an edition only two weeks old:

> The Brandyworths were visited last week by two men in an FBI car. While no one knows anything official, it's assumed that there was some problem with one of their seventeen children while said children were away in Florida, and that the good officers of the government had solved whatever problem occurred. The Brandyworths, being the most God-fearing of all people, have nothing to worry about with the Lord on their side.

It ended with this:

> Have an item you'd like to see in the *Chalybeate Springs Times*? Then write to us or give us a call! We're always looking for interesting stories.

"Well," I thought, "there shouldn't be any shortage of fascinating items from *this* area." It was then that I saw that day's version of the *Times*. There, on the front page, was an enormous headline reading CHALYBEATE SPRINGS VISITED BY FAMOUS AUTHOR. The attached article went on to say how much I had praised the area for its beauty and intelligent residents, and how welcome they were making me feel. It also added that I was donating all proceeds from the sale of the cookbook to the town, and possibly even moving to the Springs area.

"And I thought *I* wrote fiction," I said to myself.

16

Shelby's Carnage Tip

Simple math, accompanied by the so-far quality of the cookbook and recipes, didn't exactly have me throwing a party as far as monetary issues were concerned. I calculated an approximate cost, the number of residents in the town (who else would buy it?), and the recipes themselves, and was left with a not-so-pretty number. Something would have to change considerably if I was going to achieve the goal for the ladies of Chalybeate, realize *my* objective (read: keep the money), and offer something up to the publishing world. So far I was getting $50,000 from Miss Henrid ($25,000 of that most recently delivered in cash and carried with me at all times in my laptop case), $10,000 from Mrs. Brandyworth, and not much else but gossip from the rest.

I didn't expect anything from Childers—she could barely clothe and feed herself. And I had yet to meet Mary-Ellen since she had been the victim of a bad reptilian encounter. I wasn't holding out that the former Homecoming Queen would have several thousand dollars lying around for the purpose of bribing an author, so I counted her out. That left me with a total of $60,000 so far. Not bad, and certainly enough to pay my expenses at the Inn. So while I was comfortable enough financially for the time being, I did need more dirt on those who called themselves Chalybeatens. The name sounded vaguely downtrodden or even slightly masturbatory, but that was what they wanted, and as long as I wasn't a permanent resident, I didn't care.

Even the town's café (the one and only) sported the usage of the word: "Welcome to the place where Chalybeatens LOVE to eat!" it proclaimed on its grease-stained paper menus. I had found it (both the café and the menu) on the third day after a steady diet of the same thing for breakfast and dinner. Jecko, it seems, while having quite the reputation for being a gourmet cook, would fix only two menus for the Inn. Something about a grudge was mumbled but I didn't care. I just wanted something different to eat.

Now, the Chalybeate Springs Café did not have the greatest food, but they did at least offer exotic items such as cured meats, pickles, and bread. Strange though, I never once saw Salinger, Weems, Brandyworth, or any of the others I had become acquainted with in the town eat there.

But even the food at the café became a bit of a bore. What to do? And after seeing some of the recipes in the book so far, I wasn't exactly eager to become the guest of honor at one of the Junior League women's table.

As I sat in the small restaurant, picking at my ham on rye (not to be confused with *Catcher in the* …), I ruminated over the next set of recipes the ladies had offered up. What little appetite I had quickly quieted down. Here. You read the thing:

Hearty Fare

Helen Weems, the Mayor's wife, has worked for years on charity events and church socials, and has almost always had the assistance of Rastus "Jecko" Washington who is the chef at the Chalybeate Springs Inn, just off Main Street. Rastus, or "Jecko," as he's known to the locals (some just call him "The great big Negro"), is said to be one of the best chefs around and Helen has worked with him on many a Chalybeate function. While Jecko's repertoire is purposely limited at the Inn, he is an excellent cook and you'll be delighted to share in this bounty of knowledge offered up to a very select few. Below is a recipe he has made many times (though I have yet to taste it). It comes to us via Mrs. Weems.

♦CHERRY DELIGHT WITH BIG NUTS♦

1 can of red cherries, pitted
2 tablespoons lemon juice
1 can condensed milk
1 cup whipped cream
 1 ½ cups graham crackers
1 cup walnuts, chopped

Place the can of cherries in the refrigerator over night. Drain cherries next day. Mix lemon juice, condensed milk and cherries together. Beat cream until peaks form. Fold whipped cream into cherry mixture. Mash graham crackers into pie pan. Save ¼ cup of the crumbs for the top. Pour in filling on top of pie base. Add remaining crumbs to top and then cover that with the crushed nuts. Chill overnight.

Let's just try and pretend that no one would actually eat a quail. I'm not even sure I'd know what one looked like, but thank you anyway, Mrs. Childers, for that lovely recipe. Hopefully this Cherry Delight will take the taste of a dead bird out of your mouth. By the way, when you come by to clean this Friday, would you mind picking up some toilet bowl cleaner? We're running low.

Mrs. Brandyworth, our devoted Reverend's wife, is back once again with an entry. Many of you know that the Brandyworths love children—that's why they have seventeen. So here's a recipe that will feed those hungry mouths along with Mom and Dad. This one is sure to satisfy any church-going bunch.

♦MOTHER BRANDYWORTH'S MEATLOAF FOR NINETEEN♦

12 pounds of ground chuck
1 onion (Chalybeate size)
1 bell pepper, green (… again, the size…)
1 large bottle of catsup
2 cups cooking sherry or plain gin
½ cup vinegar
3 tablespoons of salt
2 tablespoons of pepper
1 dozen eggs
1 loaf of white bread

Mix ingredients in large receptacle—a small bathtub works wonders for this! (Note: clean bathtub first—Mrs. Childers obviously never does.) Mold meat concoction into several pans and cook each pan for exactly one and one half hours or until top is crusty. Serve with catsup and a nice salad. A lovely meal after church.

On another note, regarding Mary-Ellen Killchrist and her unfortunate run-in with the snake, she's obviously not a God-fearing woman or she wouldn't have been bitten. We handle snakes every Sunday with only seven or eight casualties each week, even though I know other Church of Christs don't do this. And Helen, you're playing with fire, and I'm not talking about Jecko's

100

famous Cherries Jubilee. You know what the Bible says about this sort of thing.

Next, Mrs. Weems (mayor's wife and friend of "Jecko") again, with a special concoction that she says is bound to get the message across.

♦SHUT MY MOUTH 'TATER SALAD♦

4 baking potatoes, cleaned and scrubbed (not from the Springs area)
1 cup pickle relish
1 very small Chalybeate onion, chopped
1 cup mayonnaise
Salt
Pepper
2 tablespoons vinegar

Peel and cut up potatoes. Drop into boiling water with some salt. When soft, take off stove and allow to cool. Drain. Dice onion and mix with relish, mayonnaise, vinegar, salt, pepper, and add potatoes. Mash together until consistency is desired.

Then mind your own business.

Our next entry comes from our dear Mrs. Wash Childers. It's a perfect dish for any season and guaranteed to put a bounce in your step. Have at it, Mrs. Childers. (Note: guest author has not attempted to correct any of the colloquial and/or provincial color that some of these fair ladies use—it only seems to add to the uniqueness of the dishes. One exception has been a few typos of Mrs. Shelby. Other than that, any mistakes and alcohol additions belong to the lady providing the recipe.)

♦ROAD-KILL SOU-FLAY♦

Possum, raccoon, large squirrel, or even small dog
¼ cup butter
¼ cup flour

1 cup milk
1 cup grated cheese (It don't matter which kind—this is road-kill)
3 eggs, separated
1 teaspoon salt
½ teaspoon cayenne pepper
One can cream of mushroom soup

Strip and clean the darn animal. Dee-bone with a sharp knife. Discard that there head (if any). Heat your oven to about four hunert degrees. Melt butter in a pan and add flour and cook jest a bit. Remove the pan from the heat. Add milk, a little at a time and stir jest a bit mo. Add animal parts, spices. Add cheese, then soup. Beat them egg whites and fold into that there mixture. Pour into greased-up old casserole and bake for 45 minutes.

Try to find road-kill that's been hit and thrown to the side. My late husband died while trying to scrape up a possum—the thing's head had been completely squashed. Big 'ole eighteen-wheeler just leveled him (husband, and possum too). Use a flat shovel to be sure and get up all the carcass (possum, not husband). This recipe goes *real* good with some moonshine and a *Hee-Haw* rerun.

Well, it was only a matter of time before Mary-Ellen Killchrist came up with something again. This one seems perfect for football season, which, as everyone knows, is an institution in the South. As many will remember, Mary-Ellen was high school Homecoming Queen for seven years in a row at Chalybeate Springs High before becoming home economics teacher and part-time supervisor for the cheerleading squad. Really, she elevated the position of Homecoming Queen to an art, and she wants everyone to know she appreciates their vote. Three cheers for Ms. Mary-Ellen! [Again, I was forced to add that and the exclamation point.] Did we mention that she was also head cheerleader for the Killchrist High School way back when? But you knew that already, didn't you?

♦PORK CHOP DE-LIGHT (WILL FEED ENTIRE FOOT-BALL TEAM)♦

200 prime-cut pork chops (you may want to feed the opposing team and some of the fans too)
1 case of chicken broth
A bunch of pots and pans
Something to heat everything with
Enough aluminum foil to cover a football field

You'll want to put these pork chops in the various pans and season with salt and pepper (I forget that part sometimes). Cover chops with just enough chicken broth and then cover the pots and pans with the foil. Start cooking these pre-game, and they'll be ready by the time your team wins! Goooooooooooooo Chalybeate!

Mrs. Brandyworth—you all remember her. Here she is with her latest entry, designed to be either eaten, or for those with a religious bent, simply burnt and left as an offering.

♦LAMB OF GOD♦

1 lamb, whole
16 cloves of garlic
2 sticks of butter
Various spices
Outdoor cooking pit
Fifth of bourbon
Soak lamb in bourbon, spices, and melted butter. Stuff insides with garlic. Place over open fire until the thing is burned to a crisp (usually four hours).

I came up with this recipe several weeks ago while praying in my bedroom. Sensing that it was my duty to enlighten others in the way of the Good Book, I sought out some Scriptures and the end result was this lamb. If you don't fancy eating it after it's done, simply put it back on the fire and burn it some more. If possible, you may want to build a stone altar in your backyard and burn it there. If the neighbors complain, simply show them one of the many passages in the Bible where it says to sacrifice burnt offerings to the LORD. That should shut them up. By the way, speaking of church, I was not able to see Reverend Brandyworth preach this last Sunday because of someone's large hair-do. Uh, that would be you, Helen. I realize we all want to look our best for the LORD, but three feet high is a bit much for a hairstyle in this day and age. Since Reverend Brandyworth's lesson was on the burning bush, I was tempted to set fire to the thing. Next time you come into the house of the LORD, might I suggest you tone it down a little? And as for Mary-Ellen, it's about time you and the entire town realized that football is the work of the devil. It says in Leviticus 11:8, that if you touch the skin of a dead pig, you are unclean. You may wear gloves to play football, but just make sure they're of a man-made material. Also, no pork rinds! PRAISE the LORD!

As the saying goes in the South, "You can't have a party without a pig," and Southerners dearly love pork—despite the warnings of Leviticus—so it's only natural that we'd have a multitude of recipes for this hefty little animal. We've already had one recipe for this delicious beast, and so here's a second. Mrs. Shelby Dipsey-Ewell-Adams-Tellerman-Hatton provided us with our next dish and it's a hum-dinger. She says she would make this for her ... fourth husband, and that he enjoyed it very much. Shelby claims that if you want to keep a man at home, pork chops are the way to go. What could be more delicious than these chops made with lots of garlic? Here's the concoction:

♦SHELBY'S KEEP-THE-OTHER-WOMEN-AWAY PORK CHOPS WITH WILD RICE♦

1 box of wild rice
2 ½ cups water
4 pork chops
1 can of cream of anything soup
½ cup milk
Salt to taste
42 cloves of garlic, crushed
Pepper to taste

½ teaspoon celery seed
½ teaspoon paprika
½ teaspoon sage

Combine the rice and water in large casserole dish. Make sure rice is adequately covered with water. Mix salt, pepper, paprika, celery seed, and sage in bowl and rub onto pork chops. Arrange pork chops on top of rice. Cover with garlic cloves after crushing, beating, hitting them with hammer, and grinding them into a fine pulp. Bake all of this at 350 degrees in covered dish for 1 ½ hours. Remove from oven. Combine soup and milk and pour over casserole. Put back in oven without the cover and bake until soup begins to bubble.

All my husbands loved this dish. But Siegfried—the fourth—swore by it. It was so unfortunate that he succumbed to food poisoning, but the doctors at University Hospital in the state's capital did everything they could. When you make this dish, please do so in poor Siegfried's memory. My current husband, Mr. Hatton, has been enjoying this tasty pork treat for several months now!

Helen Weems is back, this time with her well-known Red Velvet Cake. We understand that Mrs. Weems spent countless hours at the Chalybeate Inn, working under the tutelage of "Jecko," the cook for that institution, when she wasn't being a good wife to the Mayor or re-decorating the Weems Town Hall (her pride and joy). That is, until the unfortunate incident that got Jecko fired. But let's not dwell on that. Mrs. Weems came away unscathed for the most part and this pretty cake is bound to make even the most dire occasion festive.

◆RED VELVET CAKE◆

1 box yellow cake mix
3 large eggs
1 cup water
½ cup cooking oil
14 bottles red food coloring
½ cup cocoa, unsweetened

1 package instant vanilla pudding

4 eight-ounce packages cream cheese, softened
1 cup margarine
1 ½ cup confectioner's sugar
1 tablespoon vanilla extract

Combine cake mix, pudding mix, and cocoa in mixing bowl. Add water, eggs, food coloring, and oil. Beat on low for two minutes, then on high for two. Grease two nine-inch baking dishes and then flour them. Pour batter into pans. Bake in oven at 350 degrees for thirty minutes or until done. For the icing, combine cream cheese, margarine, sugar and vanilla extract in bowl until soft. Ice cake.

I've found that this delicious dessert goes great with an after-dinner wine or (if you're Mrs. Brandyworth) a fifth of Jack Daniels. You can't go wrong with this pretty and appetizing dessert—regardless of how high your hair is.

This special entry makes its way to us from Mrs. Brandyworth. It pretty much speaks for itself. Evidently Leviticus says it's wrong to touch the skin of a pig, but eating the darn thing or any portion thereof is up for grabs. Hypocrisy is dish evidently served well in the Springs area.

◆PRAISE THE LARD! (LARD PATTIES WITH FLOUR)◆

Six cups hardened lard
Five tablespoons salt
One cup flour

Mash all elements into small balls and press flat with your hand. Fry for five seconds—no more—or else the lard will melt and you'll have a mess. Use leftovers as a facial cream.

I like to cook just about anything using lard—it's like manna from pigs. You can't go wrong with this savory essence and it's sure to add flavor to even the blandest of dishes. Also makes a wonderful hand cream. Special note: Plan to have the hospital over in Bugger Holler on speed dial if you have too many of these. You can visit Helen Weems while you're there—after her hair has been set ablaze. PRAISE GOD!

Mrs. Shelby D (let's just leave off the rest) is next and she's provided us with a wonderful dessert that can be whipped up in a jiffy. Here it is for those who love chocolate. Not exactly politically correct, but then, what is nowadays? She served it at the last library board meeting that she presided over. (Mark Twain's *Huckeberry Finn* will NOT be banned, by the way).

◆CHOCOLATE NIGGER TOES◆

1 can of Brazil nuts
Several chocolate bars
½ stick of butter
Baking pan

Melt butter and chocolate in double boiler until soft. With a small pair of tongs, dip Brazil nuts, whole, into chocolate and set on baking pan to cool.

This quick and easy recipe will surely delight everyone, especially Mrs. Helen Weems, who seems already to have a taste for the *exotic*. Helen, we noticed that lovely picture of you in the *Chalybeate Springs Times*, with Jecko standing so close "behind." But my question is this: "Why was he grinning so big?" Honey, the only thing missing was the little jockey suit and a lantern.

What would we do without Mrs. Childers and her colorful down-home cooking? We'd surely be *poorer* for it and so here's one of her favorites. What with all that house cleaning, who has time to go out shopping for new ingredients? She couldn't come up with a name, so I created one for this unusual bit of fare.

♦WHITE TRASH MEDLEY♦

Lime Jello
Leftover beef fat
Anything you have in the icebox you want to throw out
Old noodles
Pudding
1 can of beer
Old suppositories (only if past expiration date)
Breast milk
1 loaf of bread
Cream of asparagus soup
Cream of broccoli soup
Cream of bean soup
Cream of celery soup
Cream of mushroom soup

Mix all these here ingredients well and mash 'em down into wash tub. Heat over that there garbage you is burnin' in your backyard for two whole days. Make sure you cover this stuff with a large piece of tin as them dogs will surely want to get at it.

My late husband enjoyed this 'un, and I made it fur my two children before Sheriff Salinger carted them off to the jailhouse for armed robbery. The whole family kin enjoy this anytime of year and the cleanup is a snap. Bone-appa-teat!

Our next foray into the land of food comes from Helen Weems. She asked if she could submit a wonderful pot roast that she once had at the home of Mrs. Dipsey-Ewell-Adams-Tellerman-Hatton. The Weemses are one of Chalybeate's oldest families and Helen has won the Chalybeate Best Beehive Hair-do Contest over twenty-five times. She even had the contest hosted in the new parlor of the Weems Town Hall, complete with a tour of the changes she had made to the structure (the Town Hall, not her hair). Mrs. Shelby D and current husband gave a housewarming party for twenty of her *closest* friends when they moved into their new home, and evidently this is where Helen tasted this wonderful beef selection. Sounds like she may have a "beef" of her own.

◆MRS. SHELBY'S POT ROAST (AS TOLD BY HELEN WEEMS)◆

1 frozen pot roast
Assorted husbands

Hit first husband over the head with frozen meat (Darnell Dipsey). Marry second husband (Frank M. Ewell). Fix pot roast used to kill first husband, season with arsenic, serve to second hubby. Bury second husband. Keep a modicum of the pot roast, just in case the next marriage doesn't work out. Marry deputy that comes to investigate (Charles G. Adams). When he decides to give you a black eye one Saturday night, take your famous Arsenic Pot Roast out of the freezer and heat on high. Claim that the coincidence is uncanny and sleep with the country coroner to cover the whole thing up. Marry Siegfried Tellerman (county coroner). Kill him by serving White Trash Medley (see recipe from Mrs. Wash Childers) when he discovers your secret. Send copy of this cookbook to a Mr. Hatton, marked "confidential."

This just in from Mary-Ellen Killchrist.

♦WHY ARE Y'ALL SO MEAN?♦

What is going *on?* I can't concentrate on grading all these brownies that my home economics class made if y'all don't settle down.

I don't have a recipe right now. I just don't want to be left out! Gooooooo Chalybeate Tigers!!!!!!!

Mrs. Shelby Dipsey-Ewell-Adams-Tellerman-Hatton contributed the next dish. It's a festive casserole that will serve one or twenty. We asked for something really unusual and, well, we got it. Oh, and by the way, our condolences, Shelby. We know the late Mr. Hatton would have enjoyed this one as well. See you at the funeral. I'm guessing that 3:30 means p.m. and not sometime in the morning. P.S. I didn't bring anything black to wear, so I'm hoping the double-breasted navy blazer will do in a pinch.

♦REVENGE CASSEROLE♦

1 old cow, preferably nouveau riche
Hate
Libel
Slander
No lips
400 lbs of inflated self-worth
Bad breath
Pieces of tongue missing
Enough blond hair color to make the entire country of Pakistan look like Marilyn Monroe

Take one pretentious, beehive-haired, orthopedic-shoe-wearing country bumpkin bitch. Sauté in hate for at least forty years. Cover with a generous helping of "no-sex marriage" to a husband who probably has a penis the size of a Vienna sausage. Baste in low self-esteem for a lifetime and add a generous helping of libel. Serve cold.

Helen Weems is next. Let's hear from the Mayor's wife ... once again. Many of you may remember the recent confrontation ...

♦I'M THIRTY-FIVE IF I'M A DAY AND DON'T HAVE TO LIVE OFF MY HUSBAND'S INSURANCE MONEY MEDLEY—SERVES FIVE ... SO FAR♦

The ingredients and instructions on this one are simple: Never work a *real* day in your life. Learn how to be a whore-doggie in high school. Marry more times than Elizabeth Taylor and end up owning half the town. Make sure last husband owns car dealership (because just about everyone else in town is dead and you like a change of pace). Price-gouge all the residents of Chalybeate so that there's no money left to do anything with, all because they pay you *squat* for being the head librarian. Lie, cheat, steal, and work the nerves of every women in town who is worried about THEIR husbands being snatched up by THE BLACK WIDOW. Pray to God that lightening will strike where's it's most deserved.

Mrs. Brandyworth ties up this latest list of entries with a recipe I'm sure you'll all want to try.

♦DOO-DOO BARLEY CAKES♦

17 lbs human excrement (this is really the key)
13 eggs
4 cups flour
7 very strong Martinis
5 cups barley

Mix flour, barley, and eggs in large bowl. Take approximately 17 lbs of the excrement and mix in well. (Note: Since Delilah will not make this particular recipe, I do it myself.) After mixing ingredients, mash into small hamburger-sized patties. Bake at 400 degrees until golden brown.

It says in Ezekiel 4:12 "And thou shalt eat it as barley cakes, and thou shall bake it with dung that cometh out

111

of man, in their sight." (Another note: Cow's dung *may* be substituted for this, though I'm not sure—Ezekiel 4:15 is not clear on this point. It's not apparent if God is speaking here or not).

17

Ascribe G(h)astly Pen

I felt it necessary to intervene, if for nothing else, the safety of the town. I put pen to paper in the hope of quelling a major storm. While I wrote, the reason occurred to me for the plethora of porcine recipes (okay, there were only a couple so far) that dotted the book's landscape. Upon arriving at the new landing strip, Salinger had said that the area was a one-time pig farm. Evidently something needed to be done with all that pork, so the ladies were putting it to good use. While their industriousness was commendable, their mood swings and eye-scratching were getting in the way of the (very) rough draft. And Brandyworth's latest religious addition was way over the top—not that anyone was actually ever going to make it. No wonder her seventeen children relished the idea of visiting relatives in Florida.

Each and every woman was becoming more spiteful, and the slings and arrows were directed in every direction—as if they had been delivered by an archery expert with an advancing case of Parkinson's disease. I tried to smooth the ruffled feathers of the brood of hens known as the Junior League, begging them for cooperation. A note, included in the binder, was sent out to each of them. This is what it said:

> Now ladies, let's all just calm down. I feel I have to say something at this point. Let's remember why we're all here: We're here for a good cause and I'm sure our readers appreciate the multitude of recipes for pig and the other goodies we've come up with. Let's take a break here so that I can interject a little history about the town for those who are unfamiliar with the area. It'll give us all a chance to cool off.

I then went to work on some "Chalybeate lore," if you will, thinking that adding a few regional touches (besides the succulent and scrumptious dishes) was just the thing for this book. Here's what I came up with:

> If you look up "Chalybeate" in the dictionary, you will see that it has something to do with iron, most specifically, water impregnated (sounds like "original sin," don't you think?)

with that mineral. The town of Chalybeate was founded around an iron-rich spring that was said to be a cure for mental illness. Now, whether or not this is true, I don't know. But having spent several hours at the Chalybeate Library researching the stacks (a special thanks to Mrs. Shelby for her help), I can only say that it seems Chalybeate was a sort of Mecca for the mentally ill in the early nineteenth century. It goes without saying that the descendents of those early settlers still live in the area.

The jury is still out on the actual merits of the waters that the spring brings forth each day, but one thing is certain: Chalybeate Springs has grown to a thriving metropolis of over 300 individuals, and each and every one is totally unique. For those interested in times gone by, the Historical Society at 2 Main Street has an actual piece of wood that is supposedly from the very first structure to occupy land in the town. Also on display is a sleeve of a Confederate general's jacket, a cigar butt that once belonged to Harold Jessup (the town's accountant in 1856) and an old shoe. The hours for the Historical Society are 11:00 a.m. to 12:34 p.m., Monday through Wednesday, and 4:00 p.m. to 6:00 p.m. on Saturday. They are closed Thursday, Friday, and on Sunday in order to worship the Lord. Of additional interest are the courthouse, where Mayor Weems works, the Killchrist High School that M.E. Killchrist attended and now teaches at, and the historic Chalybeate Springs Inn, which has stood on the same spot since 1957. For more information, contact Mrs. Shelby D at the library.

The funeral for Shelby's last husband was short and sweet, with a lot of eye-rolling and Reverend Brandyworth getting in a few potshots at divorce and remarriage. Virtually no one spoke to anyone else, and while the funeral routine was getting to be old hat in the Spring's area—at least for Shelby—you could tell that a few of the Junior League were becoming irate at the number of available men disappearing. After all, there were jobs to be done, and now that the used-car dealership was closed, where were they to go for a trade-in? Cars, not husbands.

I sent the binder back out, but in the meantime I received a note from Mary-Ellen Killchrist, alerting me to the fact that she would like to have me over for dinner. She had recovered from her bout with the snake and was evidently feeling much better. As she was the only one I had yet to meet, I accepted the invitation. Unfortunately, she lived somewhat on the outskirts of town (where rattlesnake populations are at a premium) and it was necessary to have Sherriff Salinger drive me over. I hadn't spoken to either him or Miss Henrid for a while, and thinking that I might fit more of the puzzle together by conversing with the Keeper of the Peace, told Mr. Hastings at the front desk of my need for transportation. That evening, Salinger appeared, but he wasn't wearing his uniform. Instead, he was clad in a pair of plebian dungarees and a tee-shirt—gray with small red lettering over the left nipple that read, "Fuck All Y'all."

"Classy," I thought to myself. His thinning hair was slicked back and he was wearing a minimum of seven gallons of some (and I use this term with much hesitation) cologne.

"Ready to go?" he asked, as he opened the back door of the car for me. It hit me again: I was *always* riding in the back. If I was such a free person, why didn't he let me ride up front?

I couldn't hold back. Standing next to the car, on the driver's side with the door opened, I asked. "Not that it really matters that much or anything, but why do I always have to ride in the back of the car? It's like I'm a criminal or something," I said, laughing to show that I was more curious than upset by the seating arrangement.

Salinger also laughed it off. "Well, son, you never know, before you get out of here, you just might be," he said, and put his hand on my head with more than the needed pressure, just the way I had seen police do to perps when they were mashing them into the back of other patrol cars—something about wanting to protect them from getting injured on the way to a jail cell where they would undoubtedly be knifed, robbed, or raped (if not all three) within the first three hours of incarceration.

Salinger had easily evaded the question, and I was still in the back. He saddled in and shut the door, turning slightly to the partition. "You see now, you're the town's guest and I get to chauffeur you around. How would it look if I let you up front? It would look like you're just a buddy and we want everyone to know how special you is to the town."

I wasn't buying his brand of patronizing. After a few minutes of traveling, I decided to ask him a question. "Why are you out of uniform?" I began. "And what's with taking a bath in a tub of flowers and a new hairstyle?"

"The cologne is *British Sterling*," he said, and I'm invited to dinner too at Mary-Ellen's."

"They were out of *Brute*?" I asked, hoping he wouldn't pick up on the fact that I was making fun of his body-odor-masking choice.

"That and *Old Spice*," he said, totally unfazed.

"So, what does Miss Henrid, or should I say, the future Mrs. Salinger, think of your outing?"

"Just between you and me, it's our little secret."

"She won't be jealous?" I asked.

"Boy, howdy, man, let me tell you, them eyes of hurn would pop outa her skull if she knew."

"How come?" I asked. "I mean, you're taking me—how else would I get there? And not much can happen if I'm around."

"Still, that is one jealous woman I've got. Let's just keep this little visit between the two of us, if you don't mind. What say a nice hundred dollar bill to keep your mouth shut," Salinger said, and held up the item he had just described.

"That works for me," I said, thinking that perhaps the residents of Chalybeate Springs were not as poor as they let on. Where was all this money coming from?

As Salinger drove, he managed to fold the bill several times length-wise. At the stoplight just on the edge of town he stuck the bill through one of the holes in the mesh.

"Our secret," he reiterated, and I nodded. Between Weems, Brandyworth, and the sheriff, I might not come out so bad after all.

"And I've got one more thing I'd like to talk to you about," he said as we left Main Street and turned onto a two-lane highway.

"Okay."

"The Fourth of July is coming up and my way of thinking is this: You're down here to do this cookbook, what with these ladies and all, and it's already June. So why not just prolong the stay a bit and be the judge of the chili cook-off contest."

"You wouldn't by any chance have a vested interest in winning, would you?"

"Now, what makes you say a thing like that? You know, if I wasn't a true Southern gentleman, I'd take offense at a remark like that." He was pretending hurt, but he was one of the worst actors I'd ever encountered.

"I didn't mean anything by it," I said, looking out the window as the hot, dry cotton fields whizzed past. We turned onto another new road and then down an even smaller lane.

"Oh, don't you go worrin' about that. I know you'd be fair and impartial. All I'm sayin' is that we need someone to judge the contest, and you, what with bein' an outsider and all, would be the most uninfluenced one to make the call of who's got the best durn chili in Chalybeate."

"I understand that you won for the last five years. Isn't that enough for you?"

"Son, that was the first five in ten that I'd won, and let me tell you, it felt like sunshine on a dog's butt."

"I'll try and imagine that."

"Sure enough. Them uppity crusts of the town has looked down on me for so long a time and that felt *good*—to show them that I could win something." He was beaming, remembering his former glory. It was a little sad, this preoccupation with winning a chili cook-off in a town so small, but then, I guess that was their equivalent of the lottery.

"But you won fairly these last years. At least that's what I heard," I said, as the car pulled to a stop in front of the house. The abode was more reminiscent of something in the low country of the Carolinas—built up so that the true living space was an entire story off the ground—in case of flooding. It wasn't large by any means, but it looked comfortable from the outside with wide railings and at least six enormous fans strategically hung from the porch ceiling. They turned lazily in the summer heat.

We exited the car and Salinger stood looking at the house, his usual squint and reserve showing. "Just because I won so much recently don't mean I'll do it again," he said.

"Aren't you using the same recipe?" I asked, as we walked toward the house.

"Same one. I hope."

I thought for a moment. Putting things together about the townspeople was becoming not only a hobby but a necessity in a place with little access to the outside world. "You wouldn't by any chance want to get your recipe into that cookbook that I'm overseeing?" I asked. We were mounting the steps now to the second floor.

"No intention at all."

"How about sneaking it in via the lovely Miss Henrid?"

He stopped on the second step from the top and looked at me, a wry, impish smirk coming across his face. "Now, what makes you think I'd do a sleazy thing like that?" he asked.

"Sheriff," I said, as we both approached the door and he rang the bell, "I don't know what I could have been thinking."

18

Cigar's Sylph Beaten

Mary-Ellen answered the door with an oven mitt, a squeal, and not a lot more. She was wearing a halter top and a pair of shorts that had evidently been spray-painted on. Her shoes were those high-heel wedge sandals with up-the-leg Roman-like straps and she completed her look with a perfect tan, hair color found only in a bottle, and teeth that, if reflecting the sun, would have easily melted titanium. Unlike most homecoming queens, who after fifteen or twenty years triple their weight and lose any semblance of beauty, Mary-Ellen's physical appearance had remained intact.

"Y'all come on in," she giggled, as she held the screen-door open. Salinger went in first, miming taking off his cap, even though he had worn none (a habit I deduced from years of polite police work), and I followed, nodding my head.

"You must be the author," Mary-Ellen cooed in my direction after giving Salinger a full body hug (none for me).

"Guilty."

"Did you get the recipes I sent?"

"I did, and thank you."

"I'm sorry we don't have any more snake," she said, ushering us into an open-planned living space where dining room, kitchen, and living quarters all vied for equal attention.

"Y'all sit down and make yourselves at home. J.D., I'm guessing you'll have a Bud," she said.

"Right-O," Salinger answered, now sitting on the oversized and comfortable furniture. He gestured an index finger salute in her direction and she smiled.

"And for you?" she asked.

"What have you got?"

"Coke, Pepsi, Scotch, vodka, Budweiser, some special stuff, you name it."

"Special stuff?"

Salinger and the Barbie-doll-come-to-life exchanged glances. I got the hint.

"I'll take a Scotch," I said.

"Dewars okay?"

"Close enough."

When my drink had been presented, she sat down on the sofa next to Salinger, bringing her legs up to one side and leaning in toward him. With her hair, outfit (of lack thereof), and attitude, she could easily have been a pinup girl for Playboy. She wound a few strands of Salinger's greasy hair around her finger and addressed him.

"Does the illustrious Miss Henrid know you're here?"

"No she does not," Salinger answered, looking straight at me—a gesture I interpreted as a reminder of the hundred dollar bill he had given away earlier. "And you're not going to say anything." While the last comment was addressed to Mary-Ellen, verbally, it was pointed in my general direction.

Mary-Ellen got up. "Poo. I don't know why you fool with her anyway. That damn Yankee."

"Yankee?" I said. "I thought she was from the southern part of the state."

Mary-Ellen walked toward the stove where dinner was simmering. I hated to think it might contain her latest run-in with a local reptile. "Well, she *claims* to be, but she was in New York for a while, and even lived there at some point."

"Lived there?" I said.

Salinger jumped in. "Now let's just leave Tuck out of this, if you please." He took a slug of his beer and scratched himself.

"Tuck," said Mary-Ellen defiantly, lifting the lid off of one of the harvest-gold-colored pots (it was a matching set). "That's her nickname. For Tuckahoe, New York. If that's not Yankee, I don't know what is."

"Now don't go gettin' all jealous, M.E.," Salinger said. "She's a fine woman."

I wanted to add, "Who never tried to trick you with a false pregnancy the way Prom Queen here did," but held my tongue. It did appear odd to me that Salinger would want to have dinner with Mary-Ellen, especially after what she had done to him at the senior prom with her trickery and with her feelings of abandonment when it came to Salinger looking (or not) for her missing brother. But then, this was a very small place, and if everyone held grudges for a long time, it would also be a very lonely one.

"I don't know, J.D." Mary-Ellen continued, stirring some concoction. The steam rose up in her face and she fanned it away and then tried to adjust her hair. From the look of it, enough spray had been used to completely deplete the world's lacquer supply. The steam didn't stand a chance. "Seems to me there's something not right about her. She's different from the rest of us."

"Honey, now you know there ain't nobody else in the world like us folks from Chalybeate."

"That's for sure," I said, and they both looked at me askance.

"I mean, these are some of the nicest people I've met," I added, trying to cover my tracks. The Scotch was hitting me and my tongue was loosening. Not a good thing with volatile materials around such as Chalybeate cooking, sheriffs, old girlfriends, and the information I had gleaned from the four women of the Junior League so far. Plus, the cookbook was turning out to offer new glimpses into what was really going on in the town—glimpses that couldn't be wheedled out of the matrons, caretakers of books, maids, or the overly pious by simple conversation. The cookbook was quickly becoming these women's way of venting frustrations and long-festering feuds and I wasn't about to stand in the way. I might be good at coming up with a story, but the things emanating from their pens (and kitchens) far outdid anything I could make up. I was interested to see what Mary-Ellen might pull out of the hat, knowing the female penchant for gossip, and with Salinger there and drinks flowing, there was no telling what might pop out.

"Might I inquire as to what you've cooked for this evening's dinner?" I asked. I hoped the word had gotten out among the snake population that Mary-Ellen was, if nothing else, creative with their species.

"It's called Moonlight Surprise," she said, and offered no further explanation.

"I'm guessing this has something to do with the moon?"

She took a sip of her drink—a Harvey Wallbanger (I know, I saw her make it)—and answered: "Not really." She had one of those minutely-thin straws that get stuck in mixed drinks, not meant for imbibing, and as she tried to suck the liquid into the small tube her cheeks began to sink in and her face turned the color of blood.

"Honey, why don't you just sip it out of the glass," Salinger offered, seeing her difficulty with the straw. "Them things ain't made to really drink through."

Mary-Ellen shrugged and shuffled back to the stove to check on the "Moonlight Surprise."

"I figure that we'll eat in the living room area," she said, indicating the large four-by-four square foot table that was the center of attention in the middle of sofa-land.

As she stirred and tasted—whatever it was—I competed for her attention by trying to garner more information on the town and the other ladies. "So, how do you feel about the Junior League?" I was trying to sound nonchalant.

"Okay, I guess. I think it's *real* nice of you to have written me that letter asking to come and help." I shot Salinger a look and he just shrugged.

"This recipe I'm making tonight is going straight in the book. I've already written it down for you so you can just take it with you and stick it in with the others. Was real nice of Mrs. Childers to bring the binder over to me so I could add my two cents' worth." She paused and looked sad for a moment. I hoped it wasn't because of the way the dish was turning out.

"You know, frankly, I don't understand some of those nasty comments these women have said."

"Oh, you noticed," I added, and took a sip of Scotch.

"Um-hm. I just try to be nice to everyone," she ladled on, then changed her facial features to look purposely mean, "until somebody really pisses me off."

I wanted to say, "Honey, that's not going to be long, judging by the way things are going," but sat silent for the moment.

"Do you know these women well?" I asked.

"Hmmm. Some. Weems is snotty. And Shelby and I don't speak—at all. And Brandyworth—she's the worst."

"How so?"

"Treats her cook Delilah awful!"

"So you're not the prejudiced type, as most are in this town?" I asked.

"Oh, yes, by all means, I am! But Delilah used to work for our family when I was a kid. She practically raised my brother Harry. Used to bathe him when he was a little thing. Hell, she did everything except breast-feed him." She paused. "You know, she may have done that too. And Brandyworth, well, she's that 'A' word."

"Asshole?" I asked.

Mary-Ellen made a face—as though she'd just hit a skunk on the highway. "No," she said. "Alzheimer's. They say she's in the early stages, so she comes and goes."

Mary Ellen focused her attention on her cooking and held the wooden spoon up, tasting the evening's dinner. "Ummmm-mmm! That sure is tasty," she said. I imagined some horrible concoction—something like Elly May Clampett might have made—something inedible by even Paw and Jethro. I couldn't help but recall the blond-haired girl in the show with her accent and bare midriff showing. But the kitchen area was clean enough, and Mary-Ellen appeared to be an excellent housekeeper and to know her way around vintage 1970s cookware, so snake or not, I waited for her to serve the prized meal.

I didn't have to wait long. Within a few minutes she had scooped out the harvest-gold pot's contents onto an enormous platter that I had seen before she covered it up (Santa Claus with his sleigh and twelve reindeer, even though this was June). She presented the dish with such relish that I felt a forced "My, this certainly does look good," coming on, even though I had yet to figure out what the food was. Something crumbly and dark topped off a noodle-and-meat-like combination, and the whole thing was surrounded by what looked like vanilla wafers, the most unfortunate part of the thing being, that's exactly what they were. I include the recipe here for those who are tired of roast beef and diner food, along with Mary-Ellen's fascinating tale of how she came upon this little gem.

♦MOONLIGHT SURPRISE♦

1 large bag of noodles, cooked till slimy
1 pound of hamburger meat, browned in skillet and seasoned with sugar
3 large pickles, finely chopped
1 stick of butter
1 jar of peanut butter
5 large moon-pies (this is where the name comes from)
1 box of vanilla wafers

Brown meat with sugar. Then boil noodles. Combine in Teflon pot. Note: don't worry if some of the Teflon has come off of the sides as this will only add to the texture of the dish and give it another dimension. Combine peanut butter, pickles, butter stick, and meat and noodles. Let simmer for one hour. When done, put onto large platter and top with crumbled moon-pies. Then, surround with vanilla wafers.

I discovered this recipe purely by accident one day when I had forgotten to go to the grocery store. I was experimenting while recuperating from a woodland accident and still on pain medication. I found this to be

---

one of the most excellent dishes, though for some reason it doesn't have as much appeal for me as it did when I first made it. Nevertheless, give it a try and see if your man stays at home!

On the ride back to town, Salinger and I sat mostly in silence. "Gonna take another route back into town," he said, and swung the car down an even smaller road than the one we had come in on. The moon played hide-and-seek with some clouds, only occasionally illuminating the landscape. "A perfect night for an imperfect dish" I thought to myself.

"Man, that rattlesnake poison will sure do a number on a body," he said, and turned on the radio. A twang-filled country song came over the airwaves, static-covered and decades old. The station had to be a good two hundred miles away. I assumed Salinger's last comment was in reference to Mary-Ellen's most recent trip into snakebite-land and the recipe she had just served. I wasn't sure what Salinger thought about the Prom Queen-slash Homecoming Queen's newest dish as the residents of Chalybeate Springs had yet to display an appreciation for haute cuisine, so I didn't say anything.

Then he asked.

"What did you think of it?" Here it was. I saw how chummy he had been with Mary-Ellen and I knew he was a control freak. Praise sweet Jesus that, at the moment he asked, we drove by the most enormous plantation house I'd ever seen. The moon, which had been blackened by the clouds, broke free from its heavenly prison and shone full force onto the land that sprawled beside the road, illuminating the mansion with an eerie quality.

The house was shuttered up, but its former beauty and size could not be masked by age or lack of upkeep. It sported enormous columns, each at least four feet thick, and ancient live oaks splayed out on all sides—a regular Southern Gothic experience with no one left to tell its story. A rutted-out drive led up to the place and an old woman in a mule cart jostled toward the house, her whiteness reflected by the moon. Before I knew it, we had gone past the plantation and I was still trying to regain my composure. No one in town had mentioned the house yet—that I could remember—and it could easily have been the central attraction of Chalybeate.

"My God, that was fantastic!" I said, speaking about the stately residence.

Salinger chuckled to himself.

"My friend, I'm glad you liked it. Personally I thought them 'nilla wafers was a bit much, but other than that I coulda eat it all night."

"Moonlight Surprise" that evening hadn't been the substandard fare Mary-Ellen had served, but rather the romantically lit, two-century-old plantation I had just seen. While Mary-Ellen's dish had been inedible, its name had surely been prophetic.

19

Rentable Cash Gipsy

Starting my day off with yet another lovely note handed to me as I jostled myself to the bottom of the Inn's stairs (laptop in tow) and found no sign of Salinger in sight, I yawned, took the envelope, and headed toward the door. I stopped before reaching the entryway, turning to the front desk man.

"By the way, what happened to Jecko? I understand you let him go."

"Boy got above his station, let's just say," he answered.

"Boy," I thought. At least we had progressed from 1850 with the "N" word to 1912 with "boy." If I kept at it, I could get Mr. Hastings to actually consider the term "colored." I had to say something. "You know, nowadays, it's customary to be a tad more politically correct in other parts of the country."

He paused and looked up. No malice, no joy, no … anything. "We ain't in another part of the country."

"I'm just saying, you might consider using something a little less offensive."

"Why?" he asked, "that Negro (he pronounced it knee-gra) ain't here anymore."

I sighed heavily and opened the door, thankful that Mr. Hastings had at least made it to 1925. "After all," I said to myself, "tomorrow is another day," and jauntily sailed up the sidewalk toward swans and weeping willows.

Since no breakfast had been served, I decided to take the morning and relax in the park. It was one of the few places that seemed unmolested by the townspeople. Who did the upkeep, I had no idea, but it was restful and just the place to do some writing.

Turning the corner I saw a familiar but unwelcome sight: Salinger's police car. Moving cautiously now, around the corner and behind the same giant swath of oleander bushes I had hidden behind last time, I made my way next to the cast-iron fence. I could see him approaching the gate on the other side of the cemetery, just as he had done that first day and then the second time I had seen him there. This was his third trip to the land of the dead that I had witnessed, so it was indeed a ritual—or a bad habit.

While the prospect of chatting him up was not first on my list, I was curious as to what all the fuss was about. By now I had found out that his best friend in high school and one-time police partner was buried there. Shelby, and a few others in town, had intimated that the two were as close as close could be—without arousing suspicion. While there wasn't anything said outright, there were those who inflected their voices or raised their eyebrows in some way—a sort of "You know—that kind of friendship Skipper and Brick had in *Cat on a Hot Tin Roof* kind of way?" Frankly, I couldn't see it. Salinger was a beefy brute who chewed tobacco, smoked cigars, and swaggered to the max. Plus, he was pretty chummy with Mary-Ellen and betrothed to Miss Henrid.

These thoughts shuffled about in my brain as I backtracked around the perimeter of the fence, well out of Salinger's sight. I was coming up behind him, only six feet away by the time he was approaching the tombstone, and was thinking of shouting "Boo!" or some other totally unoriginal item, when something stopped me. Maybe it was his gait, or perhaps his demeanor, but up close, even from behind, he had changed. He was not the jovial Salinger I had been used to seeing.

At first, I couldn't believe that he hadn't heard me sneaking up on him. Then I remembered his one deaf ear and realized he was completely unaware that he had company. I was caught now, half afraid to speak to him and scare him out of his wits, and half afraid to have him think I was spying on him (which I was).

Just as he got to the pink monument, he removed his hat and waited a second or two. I stood perfectly still, terrified that he would turn and see me. And while I was uneasy to the point of distraction, I wasn't about to move. It was then that I truly became confused, for Salinger let out a string of epithets that would have curled even some New Yorkers' ears.

"You filthy pig-shit bastard," he said to the grave. "I hope you rot in hell for rest of your mother-fuckin' days. You Godless fool. You have no idea how much you fucked everything up. I hope they feed you nothin' but shit in hell."

By now I was frozen. Salinger's words were so hate-tinged, so rancid and acrid, that if he turned and saw me, he might focus some of that anger my way. He was wound tight. As quickly and quietly as I could, I made three large strides away from him and ducked behind the most enormous oak I could find—it couldn't have been better placed. Right before I brought myself around the side where I was completely invisible, I saw Salinger work up the largest wad of spit known to mankind, and hawk the thing straight at the marker. It hit the "H" in "Hunter," and slowly ran down.

I stayed behind the tree for a good ten minutes after I had heard him leave, my laptop clutched to my chest, praying that he was gone. After a while, I ventured around the massive trunk and saw that he had indeed left. Breathing a sigh of relief, I gingerly made my way out of the cemetery, hoping Salinger wasn't circling the place.

With no sheriff in sight, I walked quickly up the side of the cemetery and entered the park. All was deserted and I didn't fully feel safe until I had sat for a good twenty minutes and taken in the drooping willows, the swans gliding by like some Wagnerian production of "Lohengrin," and the gentle breezes that filtered through long-ago-bloomed azaleas.

Finally, I summoned the courage to open the letter that the front desk man had given me. I had forgotten about it until I opened my laptop case.

Here is what it said:

Dear Mr. McCrae,

I cannot tell you how disappointed I am in you and this writing endeavor you call *The Chalybeate Springs Junior League Cookbook*. It was my understanding that this was to be a socially acceptable contribution to the hospitality and culinary artistic possibilities that the South has long offered and will, hopefully, continue to offer.

It was also my understanding that Mrs. Childers was to be left out of this book altogether, and I can't say that I appreciate certain individuals making off-color, if you will pardon the pun, references to my alliances with certain cooks of the town, not to mention my hairstyle and other problems. And we won't even discuss Ezekiel 4:12 right now. Suffice it to say that dinner at the Brandyworths' has been marked off my calendar.

I do hope that the enclosed check for $17,548.35 will help to change your mind.

I immediately searched the envelope—a child at his birthday party caring nothing for Great Aunt Bertha's card but everything for the money inside. Sure enough, there was a light blue check for the aforementioned amount.

She went on.

I don't think I have to tell you that my husband, Mr. Weems, is a most important man in town and has pull in and over a multitude of individuals. I don't want this to sound threatening, but I must convey to you my great disappointment in the book so far.

Best,

Mrs. Helen Weems

So she had finally come around. And how funny that she, the allegedly most wealthy of the lot, had come up with an amount so unworthy of her. And what an amount—$17,548.35? Where the hell had *that* come from? Thirty-five cents? What was she—on a budget? Could I have actually gotten her to round the check off to $17,549.00 if I had pressed the issue? I didn't know whether to laugh, cry, or feel sorry for her. True, she was a mess with her speech problems and inflated sense of self-worth, but she was the only one who had offered decent recipes so far. Still, I couldn't see throwing Mrs. Childers out— her contributions, while disgusting and inedible, were at least food (pardon) for thought. And they did come from the heart (and kidneys, liver, and just about every other organ).

Then there was Mrs. Brandyworth. I wasn't in love with the woman, but her sanctimonious mega-dishes would be something my publisher might take a shine to. Each one of these women had their own distinctive brand of cooking—mind you, nothing you would actually want to eat—but they were amusing in their own fashions.

I thought for a moment. Here is what I would do: I would write to Mrs. Weems, a note explaining that I would continue to let each of the women add whatever they wanted. Then, she and I would sit down—this, because of her generous offer of money—and edit out all the offending tidbits and parts she found unacceptable—the same deal I had made with Brandyworth. The only thing I'd leave out was a cheesy finger to the lips and a "Shhhh—our little secret" with a wink. Mrs. Weems was, after all, the matron of the community and the President of the League. So I wrote a note (again, trying not to gag), and hoped it would placate her for the time being.

Of course I had no intention of actually editing any of the recipes or comments out; if anything, I would egg the participants on. They weren't the most likable bunch of ladies and while I needed them, or rather their money, *they* were salivating for the fame and fortune (in their minds) that the book would bring. Evidently they were not familiar with activities like printing, shipping, marketing, advertising, and a host of other ills that eat into profits, and were laboring under the assumption that they would actually make some money and become known outside the tiny hamlet of C. Springs. For the time being, I let them think just that. Work on the cookbook continued, but in the meantime I wanted to find out more about Salinger and his love-turned-hate for his best friend, Dick Hunter.

20

Absence Plays Right

The binder arrived back at the Inn, dropped off by one of the female brood. I had no idea who the culprit was and didn't ask the overly-friendly (read: sarcasm) Mr. Hastings at the front desk.

Since Jecko's departure, the Chalybeate Springs Café had been nice enough to send me over a Styrofoam container (I marveled that such a modern element existed in the town), full of whatever leftovers they had that day. I couldn't complain after the short but steady diet of bacon and eggs in the morning, and nothing but roast beef at night. My insides were begging for variety. I took the container from the café and the binder to my room, thinking of the limited food possibilities in a town whose cookbook I was helping write.

While in no hurry to be invited back to Mary-Ellen's, an invitation to Mrs. Childers's would have sent me into a tailspin as to how to extricate myself from *that* situation. Dinner with Mrs. Weems— even if she had offered—would not be a good idea as conversation would have to be entered into at some point during the meal, and the thought of translating her babble-speak was about as appealing as one of Mrs. Childers's recipes. If I dined with the Brandyworths, God would be the main dish, and right now I didn't think I could stomach that, or at least their brand of it. That left Shelby Dipsey-Ewell-Adams-Tellerman-Hatton, and at present, even feeling as low as I did, death wasn't something I looked forward to. Then again, I had been here only a few weeks.

"Give it time," I said to myself, and was ruminating about what the café might have sent over, when there was a knock at the door. It was Mr. Friendly himself—the front desk man, hand-delivering a note that he had forgotten to include with the take-out and so-far-completed cookbook. I worried about what his throngs of imaginary guests would do without him for the nanosecond it took to bring up the correspondence. Thanking him and setting the binder and food container down, I opened the letter and read.

My dear Mr. McCrae, would you please give me the pleasure of your company tomorrow night, if you do not already have other plans.

The short note was signed by Miss Henrid. I thought about dinner at Mary-Ellen's and what *that* had been like. Evidently attractiveness and cooking ability didn't go hand-in-hand. But then, if a female in Chalybeate possessed one or the other, she could usually catch a man—it didn't necessarily take both. Oh, the two together could guarantee success when husband-hunting was in season, but one attribute would do nicely for most men. And here lay my trepidation about accepting the invitation. Miss Henrid was by far one of the prettier specimens in this museum that was Chalybeate Springs, and her Colt .45 gingerbread had been delicious, but she had yet to offer up even one recipe for the book. Then again, her goal, as she had expressed it to me so unashamedly, was to *enter* the Junior League, not to be in this particular literary endeavor.

I opened the carry-out container from the café and took stock of its contents. Collard greens and mashed potatoes. While I enjoyed both, the food was cold, and as there wasn't a microwave within six thousand miles, I ate it anyway, using the plastic fork which had been provided—again marveling at the fact that someone in the town actually had gone to the trouble to procure such an exotic item.

After finishing the food, I dashed off a note to Henrid, telling her that I would be more than willing to come for dinner. Then I took the correspondence downstairs, and requested that Mr. Hastings find a way of having it delivered. He stared at the envelope (I could see his ire at the fact that I had sealed it—Chalybeate was short on entertainment), and frowned.

"Have to take it over myself," he said.

I wanted to say, "If you hadn't fired Jecko's ass, perhaps he'd have been able to do it," but held back. Having witnessed the townspeople's knack for uncomfortable silences, and studying the technique in my spare time, I said nothing (a difficult feat for me if ever there was one). He got the message and offered to "run it over" after the Inn closed. I'm guessing he meant "deliver" it since he owned no car to my knowledge, though from what I had experienced so far, seeing him back over my envelope and then put his imaginary car in drive to completely flatten the note wouldn't have been that much out of character.

"Expecting a tour bus later tonight?" I asked, irritated at his hesitation in doing a menial task, remembering that I was the *sole* guest in the *sole* room.

Now it was his turn. He studied the envelope again. Why, I have no idea. "Nope," he said, and with that I made my way back upstairs to get some sleep.

The next day broke with a thunderbolt only slightly smaller than a nuclear explosion. Zeus himself could not have done a better job if he had batter-rammed the door to my room. This spectacular feat of nature was followed by rain pelting the windows so hard that I thought the glass would shatter. I sat straight up in bed. A tazer to my groin area would have been less jolting.

"Jesus fuc …" I started to say, my heart racing, and threw back the covers. Making my way to the window I looked into the street. A small flash flood was happening and trees swayed in a wind of hurricane-like proportions.

After a few minutes I calmed myself, remembering the immense percussion section and light show that the South could offer when it stormed. Living in New York for so many years had somewhat sheltered me from the immediacy of storms such as this. Solid apartment buildings with thirty floors on top of mine, and a penchant for sleeping through sirens, murders, and all-night parties next door had given my system immunity to noises that would have bestowed upon the average American a prompt heart attack. But the last few days I had spent in Chalybeate had easily erased that resistance and the thunder and lightening that was now assaulting the town took me by surprise and sent waves of adrenalin flowing.

"No morning in the park," I said, as I got back into bed and pulled the covers up. With nothing else to do, I got out Mr. Laptop and set to writing, making notes on the recipes, the town, and what I had experienced. I also had time to decide what I was going to do with all the information so far gathered, and what it was all going to mean for the final book. The only other thing to do was go over what new recipes the lovely ladies of the Junior League had written down. The women had taken my advice and attempted to bury the hatchet—or so it would seem, for a while. A short while. Here is what followed, along with my introduction to each item.

> When things start to heat up, I suggest cooling off with one of Helen Weems's holiday drinks. Helen, you may all remember, has the distinction of having the tallest hair in five counties. Several months ago, after her tongue was operated on, she

133

claims this punch helped her get well. We have to listen to what she says. After all, she's the mayor's wife.

♦COLONEL WILFRED WORMWOOD WEEMS'S "WAR OF NORTHERN AGGRESSION" PUNCH♦

1 can of frozen orange juice
1 can of frozen lime juice
1 can of frozen pineapple juice
1 small jar of maraschino cherries
7 cans of ginger ale
1 pint of vanilla ice cream
1 bottle of champagne

Mix all ingredients together in large Waterford crystal punchbowl that Governor Brewster gave you last year. Serve with your best china and silver for that special occasion when you invite only the wealthiest people in town. I found this punch to be a great icebreaker for discussing [!] the many reasons the South actually lost the war with the North. For a special treat, show everyone the latest diamond necklace that your husband ordered for you from New York—it'll go expertly with the crystal!

Mrs. Otis Brandyworth is next with this celestial concoction of unearthly delights. We hope you enjoy it as much as others did at the last social picnic the church had. We know her husband, the Reverend Brandyworth, had second helpings. And all seventeen of her children seem to like it (so they tell me). Praise God.

♦MANNA FROM HEAVEN (SERVES MY ENTIRE FAMILY OR THE CONGREGATION OF THE CHURCH)♦

6 angel food cakes
3 pounds of Communion crackers
1 gallon Communion wine
Whipped cream
6 packages of Vanilla pudding—instant (add milk)
Enough holy water for the whole town

Begin by layering the bottom of a large cafeteria-style pan with the communion crackers. Crush slightly. Break up the angel food cakes into large pieces and place on top. Pour the communion wine over the pan until all is absorbed. Prepare vanilla pudding and layer over cake. Whip the cream and spread over cake. Sprinkle generously with holy water. Pray.

Everyone should love this delicious dessert. If you don't, your place in hell is secure. Only a non-Christian heathen would refuse to eat this wonderful food of the Lord! I'll bet the Jews won't even go near this! Praise his Holy NAME! P.S. if you don't have Communion wine you may substitute a mixture of vodka, gin, rum, and tequila. Oh, go ahead—it'll be fun!

Mrs. Wash Childers is up to her old tricks again, this time with a tasty dish that can be made as a result of a hunting accident.

♦EASY-BAKE BIRD-DOG STEW♦

1 bird dog that has been killed in a hunting accident
Salt
Pepper
Paprika
6 medium sized potatoes (not from Chalybeate)
1 white boiled onion (if from the area)
1 carrot, quartered (12, if not from the Springs)
1 can cream of mushroom soup.

Clean bird dog of all that there buckshot. Remove genitals and dodie-hole. Set these aside. Cut dog into bite-size pieces and season with salt, pepper, and paprika (the paprika is the real secret in this recipe). Place meat in Dutch oven and cover with them vegetables and soup. Place skinned tail on top to make it look purty. Cook for five hours. This is an easy dish that every cook dreams about.

Mrs. Brandyworth is back, this time with a soul-saving dish that's guaranteed to give you a bad case of déjà vu … all over again.

♦DOO-DOO BARLEY CAKES♦

17 lbs human excrement (this is really the key)
13 eggs
4 cups flour
7 very strong Martinis
5 cups barley

Mix flour, barley, and eggs in large bowl. Take approximately 17 lbs of the excrement and mix in well. (Note: Since Delilah will not make this particular recipe, I do it myself.) After mixing ingredients, mash into small hamburger-sized patties. Bake at 400 degrees until golden brown.

It says in Ezekiel 4:12 "And thou shalt eat it as barley cakes, and thou shall bake it with dung that cometh out of man, in their sight." (Another note: Cow's dung *may* be substituted for this, though I'm not sure—Ezekiel 4:15 is not clear on this point. It's not apparent if God is speaking here or not).

And now, something from our town's librarian, Mrs. Shelby. She claims she did a good amount of research on this, asking around town for helpful hints on how to prepare it. Let's see what she's come up with, shall we? It's dedicated to Mrs. Weems.

♦BACKDOOR PIE♦

1 cup sugar
3 eggs
¾ cups flour
½ cup butter, slightly melted (salted)
1 tablespoon vanilla
2 big black nuts
As much chocolate as you can find

Combine all ingredients in a secluded kitchen. Put in greased pie hole … I mean plate. Bake until steamy (usually seven to ten minutes, depending on how much energy the cook has). Serve with a very WHITE topping of meringue, or better yet, whipped cream. Note: an additional person may be needed to *whip* the cream till frothy.

This "fudge" pie is a favorite of those who like "light on dark," if you know what I mean. I hear though the grapevine that this is Helen Weems's favorite pie—it is, after all, chocolate. It seems that she learned it from Jecko when they were working quite closely at the Chalybeate Springs Inn, preparing for a charity event. He would stand behind her and "instruct" her as to how to prepare this lovely dessert. Evidently, most recently, someone else at the Inn observed this "close" instruction and terminated Jecko. We're pretty opened-minded in the South about some things, but we take our pies VERY seriously. (Note to Mrs. Brandyworth: You already gave us that "Doo-Doo" recipe.) Will somebody put her in a straightjacket, please!

Helen Weems here responding to Mrs. Shelby D.

♦SOUR CREAM DIP♦

1 container of sour cream (very sour, if you know what I mean)
1 packet of French onion soup mix
1 year's worth of spelling lessons

Mix all ingredients and chill for at least two hours before serving. Goes well with "crackers" (who can't spell) or raw vegetables. If your guests don't like it, tell them to find someone else to pick on. Best eaten while re-shelving books.

It was clear that the women had it in for each other. For the most part it was Mrs. Weems and her trysts with Jecko that were causing the disturbance, and Shelby was letting it go with the politeness of an amphetamine-injected pit-bull.

The women had done their homework.

21

Archangels Bite Spy

"**L**adies! Let's move on, shall we?" I wrote below the last recipe after sending the growing collection of food preparation instructions out. I wanted to introduce each one with a bit of background, but, given the amount of information the women were adding, especially at the end of the recipes, my help wasn't really needed.

Local Foods

How about a lovely soup from Mrs. Wash Childers of Punta Lane? We have here what Mrs. Childers calls her "Sunday Go-To-Meeting-After" dinner and we're sure some of you will want to try it out just as soon as you can get over to the Piggley-Wiggley in Swillville and get a fresh pig snout—or find one left by the road near the airstrip.

♦PIG SNOUT SOUP♦

1 meaty pig snout, cleaned
1 medium raccoon
2 onions (Chalybeate sized)
Salt & pepper
Chicken feet
1 can cream of mushroom soup

Strip and clean raccoon after hitting in head with rubber hammer. Boil for two days in large pot, adding chicken feet on the second day. Salt & pepper to taste. Strain into another pot, discarding the chicken feet and raccoon carcass. Place pig snout and chopped onions into soup and continue to cook, covered, for four to six hours. Feeds ten.

This makes a lovely dish that you can put in Tupperware and take down to the county jail to feed your kids.

This just in from Miss Mary-Ellen, interjected right after Mrs. Childers's latest.

♦WHAT ARE Y'ALL TALKIN' ABOUT? WILL SOME-BODY FILL ME IN?♦

Mrs. Brandyworth added this little gem. We hope all will take heed of her message.

♦VEGETABLE DO-NOT♦

1 pound of fresh peas
4 ears of fresh corn
Some pig fat
Salt and pepper
1 gallon of gin

Note: Do NOT use store-bought canned vegetables for this. You'll want to shuck the corn and clean thoroughly. Also, shell the peas. Wash everything well and put into separate pots on the stove, adding the fat, salt, and pepper. Boil until tender and enjoy. If you use vegetables from the area, this will serve eighty to ninety people. If not, it will serve about four.

Many of you may be asking yourselves why no store-bought canned vegetables? The reason is this: Leviticus 19:19 states quite clearly that you shall not plant two different crops in the same field. If this is done, the entire town must gather and stone the farmer who did this. I happen to know Old Man Epperson out on Highway 65, and he has a good three feet of trees between his peas and corn fields. This qualifies him to escape the stoning. He also uses Sheriff Salinger's homemade fertilizer, as we all do, so you know his vegetables are high quality. Now, if you buy your vegetables in cans or from the market, you have NO WAY of knowing if they were grown in the same field. We MUST follow the LORD'S WORD and make sure everything is done according to HIS plan. I might add that I noticed Mary-Ellen Killchrist

139

the other day wearing that little tangerine number that was hanging in the window of the Snooty Fox Dress Shoppe. Mary-Ellen, I looked at the tag on it before you bought it, and it said, "80% polyester and 20% cotton," thereby making it a sin to wear. In Leviticus 19:19 again, it says that you can't wear two different kinds of thread together. CAST OFF that demon garment now and repent! As far as Helen Weems goes (Helen, are you listening?) the Bible clearly states two things that you need to be aware of. First, the races shall not mix (Joshua 23:12, Deuteronomy 7:3) and secondly, you *may* own slaves if they are from a nation other than your own (Leviticus 25:44) So technically Jecko should still be in bondage. Perhaps we could fix him up with Delilah? And then we could change his name to "Sampson."

Mary Ellen Killchrist offers us this treat from her past.

♦I HEARD IT THROUGH THE GRAPEVINE♦

1 half gallon of grape juice
2 packets of unflavored gelatin
2 small cans of fruit cocktail

Heat the grape juice until hot. Pour over the gelatin in plastic bowl. Let stand for thirty minutes in the refrigerator. Add fruit to mixture and stir. Continue to chill overnight.

I made this treat for one of the dishes we were to bring to the reopening of the Chalybeate Killchrist High School Gym after its remodeling. They asked ME to be the master of ceremonies and I couldn't refuse. Chalybeate High is where I have my fondest memories!

While this recipe has been in my family for months now, I'm getting worried about mixing canned items with those in a bottle. Also, I know the Bible says many things about cloven-hoofed animals, and especially the pig, and someone told me that it was a sin to eat Jello. Is this true? And I don't actually play football, but my boyfriend does—he's on the high school team. Does this mean he's going to hell for touching the dead pig's skin? On another note, based on what I heard about Helen Weems, *she's* the one in bondage, not Jecko. Or maybe I got it confused. Also, does it say anything in the Bible about a thirty-five-year-old woman dating a fifteen-year-old boy? I hope not. I've looked, but I can't find it anywhere. And Jeffrey is just doing my yard when he comes over every day, not anything else. Y'all just print my recipe and leave the other stuff out. Isn't this fun?

Mrs. Weems is back, this time with a concoction entitled ...

◆SECOND THOUGHT STEW... (A "MARRIAGE" OF MANY ELEMENTS)◆

1 rumor that should not be repeated
1 black widow spider
1 husband who should have read the note I sent (too late now)
1 job that you're not good at
1 famous author who you've wrapped around your little finger

This dish is best for those who are jealous, hateful, and like stir the pot when it really doesn't need it. It's best if you "spread" your gossip on your hateful self and not on others and try and not to influence a certain *visiting* person who is evidently not interested in the "greenery" that Chalybeate Springs has to offer.

I set the binder down. It was clear that the problems brewing—both literally and figuratively—were not going to disappear overnight. And I was now being brought into the equation. I had seen these women's leanings toward the land of retribution and I could imagine how ugly things could get. The binder had been passed around already and every one of them had read this. I took a deep breath and continued, realizing that every one of Mrs. Brandyworth's recipes would have more and more liquor added, and Mrs. Childers would never make anything without a can of cream of mushroom soup.

Mrs. Brandyworth, again. Obviously feeling quite fine on the day she submitted this one. What can I say?

♦JESUS LOVES PEAS, THIS I KNOW♦

17 lbs of peas
1 small onion (if it's from Chalybeate)
5 pounds of butter
2 gallons of vodka
Salt and pepper to taste

Empty all the contents into the biggest pot you have. Dump in the onions, butter, vodka, and salt and pepper to taste. Cook on high until steam comes off. Simmer for an hour and serve. Note: Occasionally the vodka will catch fire if you cook with it, so you might want to add it later. Hell, just drink it beforehand and you won't give a shit.

Thankfully this was the last entry in the collection, so far. I set the thing down in my lap, realizing now that the thunderstorm had stopped. While the sun wasn't exactly shining, the rain had ceased to pelt the windows, and the street outside was beginning to come to life. It seemed that the day would turn out all right after all. That is, until I heard the loud wail of a siren in the distance.

It came closer—the siren—passing directly beneath my window. I pulled on a pair of pants and a shirt and pounded my way downstairs to the front desk. No one was there but the door was wide open. Finding my way outside, onto the sidewalk, I could see the flames a block away.

"Church's going up like a tinder box." It was Mr. Hastings. Frankly, I didn't need his bit of information to tell me this, but it was the first time any real emotion had registered at all with him and I couldn't complain. "My guess is lightening struck it. Shame, too," he continued.

As Salinger was not only sheriff, but fire department and undertaker as well for the town, I wasn't enjoying the proposition that anyone or anything would save the flaming structure—Jack of all trades; master of none. The conflagration was now immense and black smoke billowed up into the morning sky—a black ink bleeding into water. Its acrid stench began to fill Main Street and by now throngs of pajama-clad Chalybeatens and early risers, fully-clothed, stood and watched as the roof of the church caved in. It thundered down, and as it crashed, stirred the burning building to a higher level of destruction.

It was at that moment—the moment the roof caved in—that I caught sight of her: Mrs. Brandyworth. She was wearing a housecoat (I assumed nothing was underneath), and a pair of pink bedroom slippers made to look like bunnies. (Discuss amongst yourselves.) Crying and heaving up and down with assorted sound effects, in the arms of her husband, the Reverend, she appeared to be completely destroyed. If not, she was doing an excellent imitation.

22

Nip Beastly Charges

By ten o'clock the fire was completely out. It had not been doused, as Salinger had no real equipment for said purpose, but rather had blazed until almost nothing was left. One wall was partially standing, and a sink and water fountain cowered near the middle of the rubble as if to say, "This is what we've come to?" Practically everything else was unrecognizable. Fortunately, the fire had not spread to any nearby structures, so the rest of the town had been saved—a result of the massive amount of water that that morning's rainstorm had delivered. I returned to my room to collect what was left of my thoughts.

I vacillated between angst and suspense thinking about the binder's next journey. It was like throwing a boomerang at this point: You knew it was going away from you, but you also knew it would return, and if you were caught off guard you might easily be hit between the eyes. My idea was to get it to Mrs. Childers A.S.A.P., and the fact that she was due to clean my room today would make the chore easier. But by eleven o'clock, she hadn't arrived. I went downstairs to inquire and was told that Childers wouldn't be in as she had an emergency at home. (What, another bird-dog had gotten in the way of a gun?)

Sighing heavily at the thought of waiting a day to get her the collection of yet-to-be cookbook items, I considered who else I might pass the thing off to. Brandyworth was too traumatized from the morning's events and Shelby was probably too busy husband-hunting. Mary-Ellen was an option, but her recipes weren't exactly the most exciting. I considered Mrs. Weems, but I didn't feel like becoming a novice at the United Nations trying to decipher a new alphabet that hadn't yet been discovered in this universe. Mrs. Childers, while not exactly the most desirable of the clan, was the only one I had yet to visit. My thoughts went back to her.

I was still on the stairs contemplating the possibilities when Salinger blew in. He had collected himself and was somewhat put together despite the fire, but Hastings was the first to speak.

"Was it that lightening, like I said?" he inquired of the sheriff.

"Hell no," Salinger shot back, angrily. "Two friggin' cans of kerosene was found inside the damn place." He was steaming, close to what I had seen that day in the cemetery when he thought no one was looking. "Arson, pure and simple," he continued.

"Arson?" Hastings said. "Who in tarnation would do a thing like that?"

I paused. What, exactly, did "tarnation" mean? And did anyone still use it outside of a bad sitcom or *Hee-Haw* rerun?

"We'll get who did it," Salinger went on. "Reverend is pissed off big time. And poor Mrs. Brandyworth has been babbling and praying all morning."

"What's new?" I thought to myself. Just then Salinger saw me on the stairs.

"You gettin' an earful?" he asked.

"It got me out of bed too, you know."

"Is that right?" he asked, hands on hips. "And can you prove you was here when it began?"

"You've got to be kidding. I came here to help with a cookbook, not burn down the only church in town."

Salinger squinted and gave me a twenty-second look. It was a most uncomfortable silence.

"No need to finger him," Hastings said. "I seen him come out right after it happened. Looked like death warmed over. Musta just gotten up."

"Thanks for the alibi," I said, rolling my eyes, "and the fashion critique."

Salinger rejoined the party: "Well, somebody's got to pay for this. If I don't catch who did it, Brandyworth will have my ass on a platter." He paused, looked at Hastings, then at me. "And that will be *one* recipe you won't want in your book, Junior League or not."

I tried to picture his buttocks surrounded by candied apple rings, wilting lettuce, and large sprigs of parsley. It just didn't work for me.

Not wanting to press my luck, but knowing that I needed to get someplace, I thought of asking Salinger for a ride out to the Childers place. While most of the ladies were within walking distance— the exception so far being Mary-Ellen—Mrs. Childers was also a bit of a ways out. I was about to inquire but stopped.

"What?" It was Salinger, seeing me hesitate.

"Nothing."

"No, you was gonna say somthin'. What?"

"I need to get out to Mrs. Childers's place," I said, "but you don't have to …"

"Lord, God-a-mighty, the only house of worship has just ..."

"Brandyworth Church of Christ," I corrected.

"...burned to the ground and you need a recipe for possum soup."

"I was just going to say that you don't have to ..."

"Well, ain't that some idea of a priority," he went on, completely flabbergasted.

I was getting fed up. "Look, just forget it. I'll do it some other time. Or you can run the binder out there—I don't care," I said, and started up the stairs.

"No, hold on there," Salinger called after me. His tone had changed. Evidently he remembered that this cookbook idea was Miss Henrid's and not mine, and the few seconds he had to think about an evening without sex hit a nerve. I couldn't resist the opportunity.

"Oh, I get it. Afraid you'll be in the doghouse if you don't comply?" I said. I was in no mood for his antics and simply let it out.

"Now don't be gettin' all smart-alecky with me, city-boy. I can get poontang any time I needs it."

"Oh, really?" I said, coming down the stairs. "And I suppose you don't mind me telling Tuck you said that?" Salinger and Hastings exchanged uneasy glances. While they did so I internally nauseated myself with the possible origins of the word "poontang."

Salinger's color changed. "Now listen here," he started, testosterone going full steam ahead.

But I'd had it. Too much roast beef, then none, café food, invitations I had to dodge, mute African-Americans, speech-impaired matrons, and blonde idiots that served rattlesnake as if it were something from the best restaurant in New York, plus a woman who thought she was God's gift (literally) to The Maker Himself, and a librarian who couldn't spell, all came together in my mind and I exploded.

"No, *you* listen," I began. "I'm sorry about the house of worship, church, whatever, but *you* can answer to Miss Henrid if you don't like what *I'm* doing."

I knew I had him by his family jewels. He knew it too. And they weren't exactly small diamonds and rubies either. I mentally wrapped my hands around them and squeezed.

He flinched.

I saw it.

He knew I saw it.

I knew he knew I saw it.

He sighed heavily and scratched his gut. "When you need to go?" he asked, his tone muted and accepting.

"Ten minutes," I said, and went upstairs to change.

23

Basic Greenly Paths

The ride out to Mrs. Childers's place was not without ceremony. Salinger made a production of holding the door open for me, which added a nonverbal patronizing element to the trip. I tried, as best I could, to smooth his ruffled feathers.

"Who do you think did this?" I asked. He knew I was talking about the church burning. "Other than me," I said.

"Look now, you can't blame me for jumping on you like that. You *is* the new guy in town and all."

"So, now that Hastings bailed me out, who do you suspect?"

"Funny you should ask," he said.

"Why?"

" 'Cause we's headed right over there."

"Mrs. Childers?" The theory of her setting the fire had never occurred to me.

"What gives you that idea?" I asked.

"Well sir, she burned down her house five times … in a seven-year period."

"First of all, she burned down her *own* house, if what you say is true," I said, putting the unbelievable unbelievability of those events aside for a moment, "and secondly, why would she burn down the church?"

"Pyromaniac if you ask me," was Salinger's reply. He turned to look at a bent-over woman selling tomatoes on the side of the road. The breeze his speeding car created caught her large straw sun hat and she was forced to hold onto it with one hand.

"Them suckers is big as basketballs. My doin'," he said.

"What do you have to do with her tomatoes?" I asked, turning around to see the woman and her large wares as they faded in the distance. The two-lane highway receded like a bad hairline and she became a small moving speck in the distance.

"Give her the fertilizer for 'em," he said. He looked in the mirror and ran his large hand over his face. "Forgot to shave this mornin'," he said, adding to the loosely held-together conversation we were having.

"Back to Childers though," I said.

"Yes sir-eee, people pays good money for that bonemeal and fertilizer I've got. You come out to the house sometime and I'll show you my setup. Let that stuff set up for months before it's ready so as not to burn the plants. You know about farming?" he asked the mirror.

"Not a blessed thing," I said, and slumped in the seat. There was some silence as we rode the double-barreled highway out of town and turned onto a dirt road.

"She lives in the nice part, huh?" I said as the landscape deteriorated dramatically. Where there had once been lush strips of oak and hickory, and acres of neatly-ploughed cotton and soybeans, there were now only broken fences, trash heaps, and fields of rotting tree stumps and debris.

"Town dump," Salinger said, to no one in particular, easily turning the wheel so that the car bumped off of the dirt road and onto a gully-ridden drive that led up to a small trailer.

"No cliché here," I thought. I noticed it was one of those stainless steel jobs, rounded on the upper corners—a real 1950s type. The windows had rusted screens in them and the proverbial car-up-on-blocks sat to one side in the front yard—a 1967 Impala with no doors and little paint left on the body. Chickens scampered in and out of the vehicle, and a hound dog snoozed underneath the temporary structure in an attempt to escape the heat that was already building. Nearer the trailer sat several large bales of hay—sagging and beginning to rot.

"You want to just drop off that booklet, or you planning to stay?" Salinger asked.

"Oh, I thought I'd get a sample of her cooking," I said.

"Suit yourself."

"I was making a joke."

The sheriff got out of the car and picked at a piece of straw that was sticking out of the bales that sat to the right of the rain-stripped and muddy drive. He pulled a single straw from the group and chewed on it, giving him the immediate appearance of the Southern redneck that he was.

"Got a few questions I want to ask," he said as he approached the door, and then banged his fist against the metal.

While the trailer couldn't have been more than twenty square feet, it took Mrs. Childers more than three minutes to answer the door. We knew she was a home by the sounds emanating from the metal box, but she offered no "Just a minute" or any other explanation. We waited. I looked around, realizing that the term "dirt poor" meant you were so poor that all you had was dirt. Evidently this was where Mrs.

Childers brought all the filth she cleaned out of other people's houses. Looking around I noticed an outhouse (still in use), a propane tank the size of a bus, and a wagon with mule. The mule and cart (in proper order) were evidently her only mode of transportation. I had seen them "parked" around the back of the feed and grain store on the days she was in town to clean at the Inn, but hadn't made the connection that it was her only way of getting around. Then I remembered the same transportation being driven by a ghostly-white woman the night of Mary-Ellen's dinner. The cart and driver had been making their way up to the moonlit and eerie plantation I had seen.

Finally she came to the door.

"Yep"

"Mrs. Childers," Salinger sang out, his chest puffed up and one hand scratching his ear, "this here Mr. McCrae wanted to bring you the binder out since you was not going to be at the Inn today."

"Well … all right then," she said. Her voice was a muted horn, tinny and far-off, made softer by the metal skin of the trailer. She finally opened the door so that I could reach around the portly sheriff and hand her the book.

"And I got a few questions if you don't mind," he went on, removing his hat. The sun was now getting quite hot and within a moment or two, Salinger replaced his headgear. Mrs. Childers came outside and stood with her hands on her hips. "Said you wasn't at the Inn today," Salinger offered up. "That you wasn't feeling well," he went on. "Look all right to me now."

"Was down with the rheumatism," she said believably. "What's it got to do with you?"

"Church of Christ was burned down this mornin'," the sheriff continued. He looked away at the fields surrounding her trailer and then back at her.

"Don't know nuttin' about that," Mrs. Childers said, squinting in the bright sunlight and turning to look at her chickens as they came and went through the Impala.

Salinger pressed on. "It's just that I know your knack for burning things down and thought you might be involved."

I couldn't believe his straightforwardness—or stupidity. Nothing like coming right out with it. But just when I thought he had won the prize, she one-upped him.

"Didn't burn down no church," she said. Was raining this morning and I wouldn't go out in that there mule cart and get wet." Her honesty was overwhelming.

She continued. " 'Sides, I only burned down my house five times for the insurance money. Wouldn't have gotten nuttin' fur the church." (And you thought Saran Wrap was transparent.) "Seems to me that lightening probably done it," she finished. Well, at least she was rational.

"I'd have thought so too," Salinger said. " 'Cept there was two cans of kerosene found at the scene of the crime. That blaze was deliberately set, Mrs. Childers."

It was the old woman's turn now. Just when I thought it couldn't get any better—this repartee between Bubba Law and the First Lady of White Trash—she came out with another gem. "Twernt me," she said, and shooed a chicken away from her hairy calves and dirty bedroom shoe (she was wearing only one). She waited, hoping Salinger would know why.

He didn't.

"I only use that paint thinner crap," she said. "Had a lot of it left over when Bud was still paintin' houses. Burns real good. Twernt me." And with that, Salinger seemed satisfied.

He scratched again; something he was good at. "Mind if I take a look around?" he asked, moving without her permission to the side of the trailer.

"Suit yourself," Childers said, and she and the binder disappeared back into the small box.

I followed Salinger to the rear of the trailer. In back, a dead-brown field stretched out for miles, obviously not used for some time. But immediately behind the small non-stationary abode that Childers lived in was a patch of green to rival anything seen in town. Cucumbers the size of submarines nestled next to eggplants that were so large they could have had their own gravitational pull. Tomatoes rivaled those I had seen only a few minutes before being sold next to the highway. Not those pathetic waxy pink things in New York grocery stores, but big, beefy, succulent red ones with sculptured, almost urn-like-handle welts that turned up and over, only stopping where the vine met the fruit.

"Jesus," I said, "talk about a green thumb."

Salinger looked at me and grinned as if he'd just been given a year's free membership to the world's largest whorehouse. He bent down to inspect a summer squash that needed its own zip code. "That's my fertilizer," he said, his beefy sausage fingers caressing the vegetable; tenderness from a man who probably couldn't even spell the word.

"Since when did you go into *that* business?" I asked. "The lady on the road, and Mrs. Childers too—they're customers of yours? My God, man, you're the law enforcement department, the fire department (I wanted to add, though not a very good one), and *now* you sell fertilizer? Who do you supply it to? Just friends, or everyone?"

"The whole town," he said, standing up and scratching once more. I had to imagine he had scabies, or something worse. (Is there a worse thing?) He went on: "Didn't you notice all that greenery at the Weems house; those azaleas over at the Brandyworth place?"

"You did that?"

"Not me personally, but my fertilizer did."

"Damn," I said, impressed for the first time by something Chalybeate had on the rest of the world. "If you could bottle this stuff, you'd make a fortune."

The sheriff walked back around the trailer toward the car. "Believe me, there's been times when I've thought about it."

"Seriously," I said, "if the size and quality of these vegetables are any indication of what your stuff does, you've got a gold mine on your hands."

He seemed to ignore me, or maybe he was thinking of my proposition. Perhaps he didn't need the money. I couldn't be sure. Certainly Tuck Henrid had a bundle, and I couldn't figure out where she'd come up with it. I had a pretty good job as a writer and lived well enough in the city, but I would be hard-pressed to hand over a total of $50,000 to just anyone, especially for a chance to join a two-bit Junior League in a town of three hundred. Maybe Salinger and she had cooked up some other scheme. Or maybe they were already selling their fertilizer on a bigger market. They were certainly selling the stuff in the town, but how much could they be making from those few people? Something didn't make sense, but then this was Chalybeate Springs and I was learning quickly that what looked like one thing was often something else entirely.

Salinger brought me out of my reverie as we headed back to town. "Oh, forgot to tell you. Dinner's been cancelled tonight over at Henrid's."

"Did she tell you?"

He paused; looked out the window. "Nope. I just found out you's goin' and I put a stop to it."

"But why?" I asked, sitting up and leaning forward.

Salinger waited again, so long this time that I thought he wasn't going to answer. I had my heart set on the meal and he was getting in the way. Finally he let it out: "You know ... you ask a hell of a lot of questions," and with that we drove back to town in silence.

24

Rich Typeable Snags

While the next batch of recipes was being concocted and making the rounds, I settled in at the library for a little more research. Passing Shelby at the front desk (she smelled slightly of smoke, but who didn't?) I asked to see some more of the newspapers they had on file. No microfilm here—just boxes of the real thing, yellowed and smudged. While the early history of the town interested me, I was more concerned at this point with finding out what made the ladies of the Junior League, and Salinger, tick.

Digging in after Shelby had dispassionately plopped down a weather-beaten box and shown me to a room in the back, I began to read and make notes. I knew things were laid-back in C. Springs, but I had no idea it extended to the filing system. Newspapers from yesterday were in with some from 1960. One proclaiming Nixon's resignation—six months later than it actually happened—was behind a copy from 1857. I finally gave up chronologically tracking the cadre of unique individuals, at least momentarily, and looked at whatever popped up first. September 3, 1996, was the first paper that came out of the box. It was a mélange of the usual down-home just-around-the-corner gossip and some actual news, heavy on the first item.

> The *Times* would like to thank Miss Betsy Firth of Slap-Tick Road for the thirty-inch beet that she brought in. It weighed a whopping eight pounds and was promptly eaten at the church social this past Friday night. This is the largest beet ever recorded in Chalybeate Springs history (perhaps we should consider re-spelling the town's name "ChalyBEET"?).

There was a picture of the proud owner with beet in front, grinning from ear to ear (the owner, not the beet). Nineteen ninety-six: Salinger would have been around then, though much younger. He'd evidently been in the fertilizer business for longer than I knew.

Next item:

> Mrs. Dix Shelton of Country Grove was seen in town last Monday with a new hat. The fine specimen was yellow with a small and tasteful arrangement of baby's breath and daffodils on one side. Mrs. Shelton claimed that she purchased the hat on a recent trip to see her nephew in Pisgah Hills and that the visit was most enjoyable.

Right next to this was ...

> A cow's head was found on Park Road yesterday. The owners may claim it by visiting the office of the *Chalybeate Springs Times* sometime before next Tuesday.

Then ...

> We wish Percy Abel Hastings, of the Chalybeate Springs Inn, would smile more when we pass him on the street. It would certainly improve all our moods if he did.

Finally ...

> Phil Kinderson has been missing since last Monday. Anyone knowing his whereabouts is asked to contact either the *Times* or Sheriff J.D. Salinger. All information will be kept confidential. Kinderson had no living relatives and there has been no reward posted. A quiet man who kept to himself, Mr. Kinderson was a farmer and a student of the Bible.

I ventured on to the next paper, this one more recent—from last year.

> This year's chili cook-off will be held at the town's park, with Reverand Brandyworth presiding over the judging. Mrs. Brandyworth will not be entering her recipe, as it was felt by the *Times* that a

conflict of interest would be raised. Applications for entry to the contest must be handed in by three o'clock this Saturday. After that, none will be accepted. Please write your name, address, and phone number (if any) on a three-by-five postcard also. Everyone is reminded that each entrant is responsible for his or her own setup and takedown, and signing of the insurance waiver. And remember, no two-person teams! Only one chef per chili recipe! We're not going to say this again, though it doesn't seem to matter, as Sheriff Salinger wins hands-down every year. Will somebody please take this man on?!?

The next page covered even more exciting events ...

Alex Henderson, of Knotty Pine Lane, was arrested Saturday for public drunkenness and indecent exposure. Henderson was found naked and tied to the large oak tree in the cemetery. He pleaded not guilty, stating that two men dressed as sheep had concocted the scheme and lured him into said cemetery with the promise of ten gold bars. He is currently being evaluated at Bernadaud State Mental Facility in Toketsville until the trial.

Right next to ...

Fire destroyed the home of Mrs. Wash Childers last night. Childers escaped unharmed and is now staying with a relative in town. The upset didn't deter Childers from her daily routine of making the rounds to Mrs. Weems's and Mrs. Brandyworth's house for cleaning purposes.

Then ...

We have a newcomer in our midst and we should do everything possible to make this lady welcome. Her name is Tuck Henrid and she hails from the southern-most part of the state. Tuck, so named because of the place of her birth--Tuckahoe, New

York, as she tells it--is just as much a Southerner as the rest of us. She claims that her parents were visiting that Yankee town when her mother's water broke. We can't blame her for where she was born, and the parents evidently whisked her immediately back to the safe confines of the South, where corn bread and collard greens are the accepted fare. Local menfolk take note: Miss Henrid is an excellent cook (we're told) and quite a looker!

Evidently this was a larger "local" issue than usual, for actual news items about the rest of the world had barely made their way into the pages along with this gem:

Retraction: We're sorry to report that the *Times* stated that Miss Betsy Firth of Slap-Tick Road held the record for the largest beet ever recorded--for the thirty-inch specimen that she brought in a while back. We were sent a note from Mrs. Mary-Ellen Killchrist who stated that her aunt, Beulah Wilcox, held that record with *her* beet weighing ten pounds and measuring forty inches, five years ago. We went back and looked, and sure enough, there it was, right in our own paper. We apologize to Mrs. Wilcox and Mary-Ellen, and promise not to let this sort of thing happen again.

Various other issues threw light on socials, gatherings, births, and deaths. There seemed to be an inordinate amount of news relating to oversized vegetables, and also missing persons who were never found. The final entry I looked at was from a paper that had been published the week before I arrived. It contained only two items that interested me:

FAMOUS AUTHOR TO VISIT TOWN NEXT WEEK was the headline. Followed by this:

Mr. Jackson Tippett McCrae (no relation to the Tippetts of Springfield, that we know of), will be in town next week. The kind Mr. McCrae offered his services to the Junior League, to help put together their cookbook. Mr. McCrae, while hailing most recently from New York City, is a born Southerner who will find our hospitality and ways easy to fall back into, we hope. McCrae is the author of several other books, one in particular on Southern homes and gardens, and we're sure he will enjoy himself during his stay here. Ladies, get those beauty parlor appointments lined up--we hear the dashing McCrae is a bachelor!

Evidently Mrs. Childers had not seen this issue or wasn't a regular paying customer of the *Times*, for she had informed me that she knew nothing of my visit. Either that, or she was lying. It didn't matter. I found her recipes, though disgusting, the most interesting of the lot. The other item that caught my attention was this next one as it was loosely connected to my visit.

Notice: Chalybeate Spring's population has shown a drastic decrease over the past five years. Accountants and census takers allow that the majority of the decrease is due to the inordinate number of missing persons--thirty-nine in the last few years. While Sheriff Salinger has been on each and every case, he has not been able to determine that the crimes (if any) are related. Some folks have speculated that many of the missing simply gave up and moved due to the bad economy and present world conditions. All we know is that this disturbing trend needs to be reversed. The population has gone from 347 five years ago, to 308. With Mr. McCrae's visit here next week, the population will be a good and healthy 309 for the remainder of his stay.

25

Sly Breathing Space

The cookbook continued, returning like a bad case of indigestion. Here it is.

Things That Need to be Heated

This next recipe is a real breath of fresh air. It comes to us by way of Mrs. Wash Childers and some of us are extremely grateful.

♦NO-FART FRANK 'N BEANS♦

1 package hotdogs
2 cans of pork 'n beans
1 small red onion (if from this area, use only a small corner)
1 can cream of mushroom soup

Cut them franks into small pieces and brown in skillet. Add beans and then dice one piece of a small red onion. Add soup. The red onion is the secret—it will keep the gas down and you won't be waking up in the middle of the night, wondering why them motorcycles keeps a-racin' up and down yur street. Cletus, my oldest boy—named after my late brother—really swears by this one, as do all the inmates in the Chalybeate County Prison.

I read on. Evidently something was cooking besides the recipes in the book. Because I had admonished each of the ladies in private about the lack of vegetable dishes so far, they were now coming to my aid. "Why," I had pleaded, "if Chalybeate Springs has the biggest and best produce in the land, are you focusing on pig recipes?" Their response was overwhelming. I actually had no idea you could do so much with the legume family.

This requested addition to our culinary delight-on-paper comes by way of Mary-Ellen Killchrist. Why, with all the vast array of mammoth vegetables in tow, she has chosen store-bought and frozen string beans, is beyond my comprehension, but here it is nevertheless.

♦STRING BEAN CASSEROLE♦

1 packet of frozen string beans
8 crackers
1 can any kind of soup
1 tablespoon of flour
Salt and pepper
Butter

Grease one medium-sized cooking pan. Note: scoop butter or grease out with waxed paper so that you don't have to touch it (this, if you have hired help who is not white). Put frozen string beans in. You can simply open the end and pour them in, again, so you don't have to touch anything. Mix in soup. Stir in flour. Crumble the crackers on top (use rubber gloves). Bake for one hour at 375 degrees.

This recipe is easy to fix and is totally sanitary. The most attractive feature of this dish is that you can have anyone prepare it, so you don't have to worry about coloreds. How Helen Weems manages to eat anything that a black person touches is beyond me.

Well, that was subtle. I read on.

Mrs. Weems (shock) is next on our list.

♦THE LOVE THAT DARE NOT SPEAK ITS NAME CASSEROLE♦

12 summer squash (or, if you're from Chalybeate Springs, 1 will do the job)
3 small onions (again, if from the Springs area, use only a third of 1 onion)

1 bell pepper (do I need to add that you make the adjustment if you're local?)
2 cups of diced ham (this is the same anywhere as our pigs are the same size as most people's)
Butter
2 medium-sized eggs (our chickens are nothing special, so just do what you always do)
Salt and pepper

Cut squash, onion, and bell pepper into small pieces. Blanch in hot water. Remove and drain. Grease cooking dish with butter (you can use your hands and, by the way, Jecko's hands are *always* clean). In another bowl, mix vegetables together with cut-up ham. Mix together salt and pepper and the slightly-beaten eggs. Put this concoction into the cooking pan and mash down until flat. For extra flavor and texture, you may add grated cheese on top. Whatever you do, don't *burn* this dish as it will ruin the flavors (and your life).

Mrs. Shelby D, as we've come to call her, is our next Junior Leaguer with her rendition of a dish that's best prepared over an open flame. She dedicates it to both Mrs. Weems and Mrs. Brandyworth.

♦BBQ'D VEGGIES♦

1 bell pepper
1 zuchini
1 onion
1 squash
1 eggplant

(Note: this dish serves twenty to thirty individuals, easily—about twice the size of the former Brandyworth Church of Christ's congregation.)

Cut vegetables into thin strips. Heat grill to at least 400 degrees (I leave the lid up so I can see the flames) and place strips on rack. Cook well (I like mine slightly burned and crisp) and serve on a decorative platter—one that doesn't have a picture of Jesus on it. On another note, personally I wouldn't let a Negro touch my food either. And has anyone seen Jecko lately? I hear he's been smoking and carelessly throwing away the match before he blows it out. Wasn't he at the Church of Christ the other day, poking around? Why wasn't he over at the black church? Oh, yeah, Chalybeate Springs doesn't have one. I forgot.

Mrs. Brandyworth adds her bit here, along with a helpful household hint. Is it just me, or …?

Helpful hint when having others prepare your food: I make Delilah wear rubber gloves ALL THE TIME as I believe it says something in the BIBLE about touching others' food items, though I could not find this right now. That should fix the problem.

DOO-DOO BARLEY CAKES

17 lbs human excrement (this is really the key)
13 eggs
4 cups flour
7 very strong Martinis
5 cups barley

Mix flour, barley, and eggs in large bowl. Take approximately 17 lbs of the excrement and mix in well. (Note: Since Delilah will not make this particular recipe, I do it myself.) After mixing ingredients, mash into small hamburger-sized patties. Bake at 400 degrees until golden brown.

It says in Ezekiel 4:12 "And thou shalt eat it as barley cakes, and thou shall bake it with dung that cometh out of man, in their sight." (Another note: Cow's dung *may* be substituted for this, though I'm not sure—Ezekiel 4:15 is not clear on this point. It's not apparent if God is speaking here or not.)

This was the last entry in this batch. Mrs. Brandyworth's Alzheimer's was evidently getting worse as her "Doo-Doo" recipe was now making a regular appearance. I breathed a sigh of relief that I could take a break from the epicurean ramblings of the ladies and headed over to the library to do some more research. Just as I was a few feet from the entrance, a pretty woman stopped me. It was only after I had shielded my eyes from the glare of the sun that I could see it was Miss Tuck Henrid.

"I am soooo glad I caught you," she said. She was wearing a light and frilly pale-blue-and-white sun dress, the usual too-large Minnie Mouse shoes (white), gloves (white), and a small pale-blue hat with a tiny veil. It was all very out-of-date yet perfect in appearance, especially for *this* town. She glanced uneasily across the street at the ruins of the church and then took my arm, steering me down the sidewalk.

"I need to speak with you, and it's probably better if we're not seen together too much." She looked around again. "This one time won't matter—they'll just think I'm sugaring up to you because you're a famous author and all, but if you could come over for dinner Thursday night, I would very much appreciate it."

About that time, a Chalybeaten I didn't know walked past, and Miss Henrid straightened up, completely changing her demeanor. "Yes, yes, we're so *glad* to have you in our *town* and I'm so glad to finally *meet* you," she said.

A consummate actress she was not.

"I do wish you the best of luck Mr. . . ?" she continued, feigning ignorance at my name.

"McCrae," I say, playing along until the townsperson had waddled off around the corner.

"Dinner would be fine," I said, resuming our previous, real conversation—thinking that a change of pace would be most welcome, and remembering her excellent, though somewhat unorthodox, gingerbread cookies. At least she could use a stove properly. And while her dress was odd, for the look *she* was attempting, it was just about perfect. She could have stepped right out of a squeaky-clean 1950s sitcom. I imagined her baking cakes while wearing heels and a strand of pearls.

"You know, I didn't come the other night because ..."

"I know. Salinger," she said, once again glancing around nervously. "He won't find out this time. He just gets *so* jealous."

"What time?" I asked. "For dinner, I mean."

She looked around again. "Seven prompt, if you don't mind." And just as she was walking away, she turned and added, "And whatever you do, don't tell Salinger you're coming."

"What's he so worried about?" I asked, still shielding my eyes from the sun.

She was a good twenty feet away now. "Don't ask questions," she yelled. "Just come."

I shrugged and backtracked to the library. Henrid's behavior was odd, but nothing when compared to the rest of the town. By their standards she was the benchmark for upstanding and they were at the opposite end of the spectrum. It was becoming clear why she had been denied entrance to the Junior League and why the entire town had so shunned her: she was the only one with any sense of style and manners, and she didn't have some horribly odd attribute or six-inch claws that she was using on every other female. Why someone with her sweet disposition—the bribery and forgery aside—would want to be in *this* Junior League, was beyond me.

I tugged at the library door and made my way in. Shelby had evidently been expecting me as the boxes of newspapers were stacked in the back room, awaiting my perusal. In addition she had added cartons of other ephemera: articles that had never made it to print in the paper, some legal documents, and even the past list of Chalybeate chili cook-off contestants and the results from that endeavor. I had requested this particular item—the list—as I had been asked (read: told) to judge this year's competition. It wasn't too hard to figure out that Salinger was going to bribe me or perform some illegal act to gain first place once again, but I had decided to actually get a taste of at least some of the town's cooking that didn't include bird-dog recipes, Jecko's limited Inn concoctions, the town's café fare, or anything remotely resembling the recipes from the Junior League, and so I acquiesced.

I sat down and started in on the list of past participants, where the cook-offs had been held, and who had been on the decoration committees. I wasn't looking for anything in particular, but one name in particular jumped out. Then another. There was some connection but I couldn't wrap my mind around what it was. Something said to look more closely. And I did.

26

Perishable NYC Stag

Harry Killchrist, brother to Mary-Ellen, was the name that popped up. I couldn't decide which was worse—having been the woman's brother or now having your picture on the back of a milk carton. My money was on the former, but the fact was, he had never been found. And it was that name, along with another on the list, Phil Kinderson, that caused me to go back and flip through countless papers and news items until I found the article I had seen before. This one:

> Phil Kinderson has been missing since last Monday. Anyone knowing his whereabouts is asked to contact either the *Times* or Sheriff J.D. Salinger. All information will be kept confidential. Kinderson had no living relatives and there has been no reward posted. A quiet man who kept to himself, Mr. Kinderson was a farmer and a student of the Bible.

I looked at the list of contestants who had at one time entered the competition—the very one Salinger always won. I wrote them down and scratched my way through the boxes Shelby had put out, certain that she was unaware that they contained some link, some ... something. I wasn't sure what it was, but I would find out. With the list completed, it read this way, in no particular order:

Harry Killchrist
Phil Kinderson
Paul Murphy
Baddah Shelkins
Ordine Bowling
Fatty Sherrillmire
Gladys Gallonheimer
Shelby Hatton (using only the *last* husband's name)
Helen Weems
Mrs. Otis Brandyworth
Mary-Ellen Killchrist
Mrs. Wash Childers

Maybe it was just me, but something looked odd. I spent the next four hours scouring each and every *Chalybeate Springs Times* I could find. Since the paper was small, it didn't take long. By now I had determined a pattern and it wasn't pretty.

Amongst the down-home attention-calling to events such as, "PIG FOUND ON OLD MOTAS ROAD" and "SUMMER SQUASH SAID TO RESEMBLE THEODORE ROOSEVELT—NOW ON DISPLAY AT THE WEEMS TOWN HALL," were mentions of missing persons. In addition to Phil Kinderson and Harry Killchrist, Paul Murphy, Baddah Shelkins, and Ordine Bowling had been misplaced in the last five years—the very same five years that Salinger had won the competition.

Fatty Sherrillmire and Gladys Gallonheimer seemed safe as they were not listed in any paper, and the rest of the gang—the Junior League—were still intact. One had to wonder at the coincidence, that so many who had tried to vie for the blue ribbon against Salinger in the past had disappeared from the face of the earth. Were their recipes any good, or was this just a quirk of fate?

I got up to take a break from my findings and snagged Shelby, who was always one for a chat. After a few moments of nondescript banter, I broached the subject of Gladys and Fatty.

"Do you know a Fatty Sherrillmire, by any chance?" I asked, but before I got the complete name out, she had turned angry. I saw her reaction and winced.

"What?" I asked.

Shelby waited. "Sad case," she said. "A wife and three kids and the man just ran off without any reason. Just up and left, and the youngest boy only one year old. Tragic, really."

"How do you know he just 'left'?" I asked.

"Well, what else would have happened to him?"

I wanted to marvel at her innocence, especially since she had experienced so many husbands die on her watch, and had probably helped the process along. I continued. "Did he ever write or call or … anything? You know, let them know where he was?"

"No. He was just never heard from again. What else could have happened?"

"How about a Gladys Gallonheimer?" I asked, ascertaining now that Fatty had probably met the same fate as most of the other members on the list, sans the Junior League.

Shelby paused and thought. She looked up at the ceiling. "Gladys Gallonheimer, Gladys Gallonheimer, Gallonheimer," she repeated. "Ummm, hold on just a minute, let me ask," and she got up and stuck her head around the corner. "Hey," she yelled to the assistant I had first seen when I came to the library, "You ever heard of a Gladys Gallonheimer?" she queried. There was a pause, but, knowing the individual Shelby was addressing, it came out of arrogance and not thought.

"You remembeeeeeeeer," the girl said snottily to Shelby, coloring the word "remember" enough to make it resemble a LeRoy Neiman sports painting and dragging it out long enough to be its own sentence. "That old woman who disappeared three years ago, the day before the chili cook-off."

I felt the hairs on the back of my neck stand up. That made it official—all the individuals on the list with the exception of the ones I knew at present had disappeared. Not that inhabitants of a town who possess names like Fatty and Gallonheimer deserved to live anyway, but their families and friends at least warranted some closure. And the good (I'm being benevolent here) people (again) of Chalybeate Springs shouldn't have been deprived of the chance to fairly judge a chili cook-off contest (my real concern, you can imagine). These people had conveniently vanished from the face of the earth before they could enter their recipes for judging. This was no coincidence.

Shelby brought her head back inside the office. "Gladys Gallonheimer disappeared ..." she started to say, but I cut her off.

"Yes, I know."

"Then why did you ask?"

"No, I mean I just heard your assistant say," I said, not wanting to die in the back room of a small town library (isn't that redundant?).

"Oh." She sat down. "Why do you want to know?" Then she laughed. "Seems like you're writing a mystery novel or something."

"I hadn't planned to," I said, shaking my head. "And you know that that's not my style."

She looked at me blankly.

I continued: "You've read what I've written, my first three books. You know I don't write novels of that sort."

Again the look. I paused. So did she. I paused some more.

"You haven't read any of my work ... have you." I said, cringing in my seat, making a statement out of the words and not a question.

Shelby didn't say anything again but managed a forced smile and tilted head as her eyes said a great big "I'm sorry."

I sat for a moment, thinking, looking around the room, out the window, down at my feet, then up. "You don't even have any copies of my books in this library, do you?" I said.

Again, there was silence, but, with the demeanor of a doctor telling the patient that he isn't going to live, with as much facial sorrow and sympathy as she could muster, she shook her head "No," and looked down at her hands which were now folded in her lap.

27

Beneath Classy Grip

The next morning, a note was brought upstairs by way of Mr. Hastings. It was accompanied by a copy of that day's *Chalybeate Springs Times* and a bill for my stay so far. I imagined the free copy of the *Times* was a way of softening the blow ... that is until I saw that the bill's itemized list included the paper. I opened the note that had also arrived. It was from Mrs. Weems and was a rather formal though short-noticed invitation to dine at her home that evening.

The note listed the guests who were to attend: myself, Shelby, Mrs. Brandyworth, and Mary-Ellen Killchrist. The time we were expected to partake of the sumptuous dishes was six o'clock exactly, and she had indicated that if any of us wanted to mingle or have cocktails, that we needed to come before that time. Mrs. Wash Childers was not mentioned and a postscript was included, saying that the lady of the house would prepare the entire meal herself to show Mr. McCrae and all of the most important people in the Springs area what a real dinner party was like. She added that she hoped I would include the evening's food items in the book. So now I had an invitation from Weems *and* Henrid; Weems being first on my list.

I stuffed the invitation back into its envelope and shuddered at the prospect of an evening's conversation with a woman who had no lips and only a partial tongue. At one point in my stay, just to test the water and see how bad things could get with regard to the absurdity of her speech, I had presented her with a copy of Lewis Carroll's "Jabberwocky," asking her to read it out loud for me. I fully expected the end result to be a complete and phonetically correct version of "Old MacDonald." What came out instead was a word-for-word account, exactly as it had been written and meant to be heard. So much for logic. So I somewhat placated myself with the fact that, Shelby, Mrs. B, and Mary-Ellen would be in attendance, hopefully upholding their end of the evening's festivities so that I would only have to make yummy sounds and occasionally say things such as "My, this *is* delicious," pretending to be so entranced by the quality of the food (if it indeed *was* any good) that I didn't have time to ask any questions or, God forbid, have Mrs. Weems shoot any my way. It wasn't lost on me that Weems was trying to make friends with the rest of the women, sensing their disapproval of whatever she was doing. It hadn't been too hard to figure out that she and Jecko had played doctor at some point, but since I hadn't seen it with my own eyes, I wasn't laying down any judgments. And it really didn't matter to me—what she did in her spare time was *her* business.

The rest of that day I took it easy, lying about the room, going for a walk, and just generally taking care of odds and ends; you know, adding recipes into my laptop computer, making some fine adjustments on the articles I had been writing on the town, and taking notes on what I'd read in the newspapers at the library.

It was when I was putting in the last newspaper notes that I had gleaned from the aged and yellowed collection that I turned to today's issue—the very one Hastings had brought up along with my bill. On the front page, alongside the real news that was happening in the outside world, was an item of special interest. "BRANDYWORTH HOUSEHOLD UNDER INVESTIGATION FOR ALLEGED CHILD ENDANGERMENT," it said, and went on to explain briefly that the couple's children had gotten into some trouble in Florida while staying with "relatives" in that state. The paper did not go into details regarding the tribulations of the youths, though it hinted at something no worse than underage drinking or possible curfew violations. After all, the Brandyworths were strict Church of Christ members and their children (all of whom I had yet to lay eyes on) were supposed to be model Christians. The article was written by someone who had chosen to sign only their initials: T.D.

As the day wore on, dinner time approached. I readied myself with the few presentable clothes I had brought, having aired them out. I attempted to steam the wrinkles from my blazer by placing it on a hanger in the bathroom while I ran a hot shower. Now, as put together as possible, and with a slightly damp jacket, I found my way to the sidewalk and proceeded to Helen Weems's house, taking the binder with me as Mrs. Weems had requested, so that she could be the next in line to add an entry.

Everything at the enormous house was virtually the same as the first day I arrived in town. Mrs. Weems answered the door wearing a lovely evening gown and extra-large earrings. They somehow visually balanced the enormous ring she wore on her finger. She ushered me into the living room and I acknowledged Shelby and Mary-Ellen who were each holding a glass of white wine and dressed to the nines. I set the binder containing the recipes down on an end table and indicated to Mrs. Weems that it was now her baby. She nodded in return.

"Evening, ladies," I said, as an overly-pompous and more than overweight butler passed around a large silver tray with assorted hors d'oeuvres. "You make these?" I asked in Mrs. Weems's direction, taking one of the stuffed shrimp with dill and popping it into my mouth. I swear I saw Mary-Ellen and Shelby titter. They probably felt a sense of relief at being saved from having to figure out what the woman said.

"I made eh-ery-hing, Mr. Mah-Tay," Mrs. Weems responded.

"I'm certainly including these in the book," I said, wiping my hands on a small paper napkin that had been served with the shrimp. "Might I ask where Mr. Weems is this evening?" I had decided to brave the translation process again, figuring that, if it became really unbearable, I would excuse myself early. Besides, perhaps Mary-Ellen and Shelby were better at Weems-speak than I was and might jump in if things got really bad. But my hopes were quickly dashed as they once again giggled at my question and turned away, fingers to noses and hairstyles shaking with laughter.

Mrs. Weems took me by the arm and led me out through a set of French doors and onto a flagstone terrace. Small candles lined a stone balustrade and tastefully hung lanterns punctuated the space. "Det noh dawk abouh mitah Weem."

"Let's not talk about Mr. Weems?"

"Wite."

I was momentarily disappointed. I hadn't counted on being the only man at the function, and I hadn't had the pleasure of meeting the mayor. "Just myself and four women," I thought, looking downward for a moment, disappointed. Mrs. Weems evidently thought I was looking at the enormous ring on her hand and proceeded to read me like the open book she assumed I was.

"I tee you-a wooking ah my wing."

"You're ring, yes," I said, even though I hadn't been. "It's quite large and ... well, aren't you afraid of someone trying to take it?"

"Not ooh whoh-wee," she said. "I ave a petal pace I-ide it."

"You have a special place you hide it? I'm sorry, I don't understand," I said, hoping she knew that I meant "I can't imagine where you hide it" as opposed to "I can't understand a frickin' thing you're saying."

"Dis is a copy. De o-wiginial is in a wewwy petal pace."

"This is a copy? The original is in a very special place?" I said as much as asked.

"Wess."

"Oh, good," I responded. "So you wear the copy at all times and keep the real one hidden."

"Wess."

I envisioned a house safe, behind one of the Renoirs or other expensive paintings that lined the walls. A safe stuffed with money, Mrs. Weems's other jewels, and wills and codicils. I was about to let the subject drop but Mrs. Weems thought the topic most interesting and didn't let it go.

"You-ah neb-eh guess where," she said, pulling me closer out of earshot to the others.

"I'd never guess where?"

"Hmm."

I looked into the opulent living room from where we were standing. "I would suppose a wall safe of sorts? Or perhaps a strong-box somewhere."

"Too bo-wing."

"Too boring? Well, then, where?"

Mrs. Weems smiled slyly and pulled me closer. "Is a pace you wood neb-ber e-pect."

The alcohol she had consumed had loosened her tongue (or what was left of it) to considerable proportions. Ordinarily a woman of her standing and good (ahem) taste would never confide in someone she hardly knew. But then, she had been drinking and I surmised that she had probably deduced that, by letting me in on one of her most intimate secrets, we would "bond" and she'd somehow come out on top with regard to the cookbook. Add to this the fact that most Southerners append syllables to words that need only one (the word "did" can become "deeee-aaa-uuuu-ddddd-uuu-hhhh" with little or no help), and it's a wonder I was able to extrapolate what Weems was saying at all from her *tromp l'oeil* painted orifice. And while I was most often able to manage the true meaning of her words, from time-to-time she would come out with something so horribly deformed that it should have been placed in a glass jar at the circus. "Eeeh-badahwann-teef comme da sisafus de-wwep!" might have been anything from "My tampon needs changing" to "The Gettysburg Address" recited backwards and in pig Latin. I did the best I could.

"I'd never expect? You hide the original in a place I'd never expect?"

"Hmm."

"Are you going to tell me?"

She waited demurely, smiled, and then rolled her eyes.

172

"If you-ah wewwy good boy," she said, and started to lead me back into the room where Mrs. Brandyworth had just arrived. But just before we reentered through the French doors, she pulled me closer and whispered the answer into my ear.

"I ide ith in my bu-bi-nuh."

I thought for a moment, trying to arrange the sounds into letters, the letters into sounds. Then it came to me. "Oh, I said, an ironic smile coming across my face as I viewed Mrs. Brandyworth inside the house (that also helped with the realization). "In your *Bible*," I mused to myself, "In your *Bible*," and said nothing, though I secretly pictured her carving out passages from Genesis, Leviticus, and Timothy in an attempt to create a secure resting place for her priceless valuables. As far as I knew, Mrs. Weems was not the religious person Brandyworth was, and didn't hold The Good Book in the same high esteem as *that* zealous student of religion, but she, like almost everyone in the South, at least owned a copy of the dictation God had supposedly given to man.

Mrs. Weems looked up at me as if to say, "Good, we share a secret now—I can trust you, and you can do a favor for *me*."

While the ever-religious Mrs. Brandyworth had been late for the cocktail hour at the Weemses' home, she had evidently managed one at some other locale, for she was barely able to stand, competing furiously with Mrs. Weems for Most Inebriated. The race was neck-and-neck.

"Mrs. Weems," Mrs. Brandyworth started in, "I certainly hope …uh you do *not* plan to *hog* Mr. McCrae all *ev-e-ning*. We alllll want a *piece* of him . . uh, [burp—hand to mouth—stagger slightly]," she went on, and let out a little laugh. She was within inches of becoming a pickle.

"You come sit by me, honey," Mary-Ellen cooed in my ear, and grabbed me by the arm. "She's drunk as a skunk. Just don't light a match too close to her or we'll all go up in flames." Shelby shot us both a pair of daggers from her eyes and I had to wonder where she had been hiding *that* green-eyed monster up until now. The four of us instinctively made our way into the dining room. Then the titanic grandfather clock in the hall chimed six and, just as planned, dinner was announced. Chalybeatens were, above all, punctual.

As Mrs. Weems whisked herself into the kitchen, I had to wonder at her sense of timing. Just a few moments before she had been schmoozing with me on the terrace. If I had been cooking for five I'd have been a nervous wreck, juggling pots and pans, sampling sauces, making sure everything was just right. And I wouldn't have been wearing an evening dress to prepare it either (for reasons other than the fact that I might get it dirty). She sported no apron and yet had remained pristine. Amazement was in the air as the swinging door that led from the kitchen to the dining room flew open and in walked our hostess with an enormous tray on which sat a most decorative tureen.

"Oh, dear," she said, finally realizing the problematical elements of serving, and looked around, caught off guard.

"Why not just let the butler help," I said, seeing the man standing by, not doing much of anything else. He was straight out of an old black-and-white movie; a sort of *My Man Godfrey* type; stoic and taciturn—very William Powell.

At this point, Mrs. Brandyworth, Mary-Ellen, and Shelby giggled hysterically, though *sotto-voce*.

"What? Was it something I said?"

"Private joke," Mary-Ellen whispered, and touched my arm.

"Exc-e-went decision," Mrs. Weems announced, and then to the butler, "Tames, will you epp me wid dis?"

"My pleasure, Madame," the man answered, bowing slightly in his white tie and tails. Evidently he had gone to school for the purpose of learning Weemian, for he understood her request at once while I had to use substitute letters and fifth grade phonetics to get the translation just right. The butler (James—he now had a name) held the large silver platter while Mrs. Weems ladled out the soup, careful not to spill any on the sides of her Spode dinnerware. The table looked as if it had just emerged from the pages of a professional magazine on Southern homes (We had yet to sit down.) The finest crystal and silver cutlery—every small knife, fork, and spoon known to mankind—covered the eating surface. The linen was stark white with not a crease to be found, and the arrangements of roses—pinks, yellows, deep reds, and even purples—graced the table in three enormous silver epergnes.

"Air-wee body have dehr own name cauds," she said, and we all looked at each other. Then James spoke.

"Madame says that everyone has their own name cards," he recited, and white-glove-motioned for us all to sit. We indeed had been positioned according to the matron's request. I was directly to her right (as is customary for Royalty), and Mrs. Brandyworth, because of her social-albeit-drunken condition, was positioned directly to Mrs. Weems's left. Mary-Ellen was next to me, and Shelby next to Mrs. Brandyworth. While the table could have been fitted with leaves so that it served sixty, it was in reduced form and we were quite cozy. The only problem was the enormous epergnes which blocked anyone from conversing without having to peer through the silver ornate arms and flora that perched on those fine limbs.

"My, everything looks just about perfect." It was Shelby, commenting on the setting as she gently moved a series of wine glasses around.

"I tow wan-ed eb-e-tin to ee urfek."

"She so wanted everything to be perfect," I said, and then realized I might have insulted her. I would try and keep my mouth shut.

As the soup was now in everyone's bowl, we all prepared to partake, soup spoons poised and ready.

"Waaiiiitt!" It was Mrs. Brandyworth. "Wait, you Godless heathens!" she hissed, standing up and knocking her chair over. She gazed around the table, sneering at everyone, staggering; then began to sit back down, more from gravity than her own accord. James caught her with the seat of the chair just in time. "Oh, fuck it," she continued, let's just eat," and with that we all made our way from soup to salad without much excitement.

It was only after the first two courses were finished and the main course was halfway through that the arrows started to fly. Evidently Mrs. Brandyworth had been so hammered (and ashamed of recent events) that she had kept to herself. By now, the cocktails and wine were doing a number on Mary-Ellen and Shelby, and Mrs. Weems wasn't exactly feeling any pain either.

Poor Mrs. Brandyworth: Thinking that she would introduce some innocuous bit of conversation into the evening, she began a story that led her in the exact opposite direction she so desired.

"You know," she said, dropping a fork full of pea salad (it was a side dish—cold, with mayonnaise, egg, and bacon—actually quite good) into her lap, then retrieving the glop with her hands, "my cousin lives in Florida and was telling me the other day that they have this heron that can ring doorbells." She paused to stuff the glop of pea salad into her mouth with one hand, completely ignoring the fork. Everyone, either enthralled, drunk, or both, sat and waited. Besides, what would you have followed *that* statement with? After licking her fingers, she continued.

"They all have those doorbells that light up, you know," she went on, "and evidently the bird was fascinated by one, and pressed it with its beak." She was now making an attempt at the beef Stroganoff, but the noodles kept slipping from the eating implement and she seemed confused. "I guess someone fed it once," she said, twirling the noodles spaghetti style, "and the poor thing associated food with those doorbells." For a while no one said anything as we were completely taken in by her attempt to simply get the food to her mouth.

Then I chimed in, hoping to keep her from feeling left out: "You know, some people say Florida is God's waiting room, but I prefer to think of it as his consignment shop with a no-return policy, even though nothing is for sale and most items are waiting to be marked 'out of stock.' "

No one said a word. Everyone looked at me, then Mrs. Brandyworth continued as if I didn't exist.

"They say that it keeps half the neighborhood up at night [slight burp, crossing of eyes, a delicate sway and then a regaining of equilibrium], ringing and ringing and ringing." She finally managed the noodles and a collective gasp went up. There was a dramatic pause, as if she expected some comment. She got one, but it was probably not the kind she was looking for.

"Speaking of Florida," Mary-Ellen started in, a bit tipsy now herself, "how *are* your children?"

Mrs. Brandyworth immediately choked on the mouthful she was attempting to swallow, and Mrs. Weems began to beat her about the back—a little harder than was actually necessary.

28

Secret Play Bashing

Now that we had polished off the appetizers, soup, salad, and main course, we waited for the dessert. As promised, Mrs. Weems once again insisted on serving with the help of James, or "Tames" as he was quickly becoming known.

"Dit pink ah-tic foout sa-wid is de-wishous" she said. "At weast I tink tow."

"Pink arctic fruit salad," I said, for the benefit of those not used to her since her run-in with that metal pole in Greenland.

Having evaded the Florida question, Mrs. Brandyworth was now snoring comfortably, her head slightly back, with a long string of drool coming from the right side of her mouth.

Shelby was becoming more acidic by the moment (my guess was the lack of a new husband to kill), and Mary-Ellen was jovial and totally ignorant, a combination that I've found works well on many blondes.

Eager to steer the conversation in a direction that would best suit my purposes, I brought up the topic of Tuck Henrid. "Do any of you know this Tuck Henrid woman?" I asked, as my fork dug into the pink concoction that had now been served up. It was a mixture of cranberries, Jello, whipped cream, small marshmallows, and pineapple.

"Wouldn't go near her if you paid me," said Shelby, putting her fork down as if she'd just lost her appetite.

"Because?" I said

"Because she's not from here, number one, and number two, she's very odd."

"Odd in what way?" I asked.

"I don't know." She paused. "She's a Yankee, you know."

"She is not," Mary-Ellen chimed in, her mouth full. She had mashed the dessert to one side of her mouth and her left cheek was bulging out. I found her defense of Miss Henrid ironic since she had made the very same comment the night she'd invited me and Salinger to dinner.

"Well she was born in Tuckahoe—that's how she got her name," Shelby went on. Mrs. Brandyworth snored loudly next to Mrs. Weems.

"I tay tee de-ters a tante," said Mrs. Weems, and Shelby and Mary-Ellen looked around the two epergnes at each other.

"Mrs. Weems thinks she deserves a chance," I said.

"She hasn't approached you or anything," Shelby said.

"No, I just heard some talk about her, that's all."

Mary-Ellen was the next to add her two cents. "What about that house she's trying to get?"

"What house?" I asked. I looked at Mrs. Weems and she rolled her eyes.

"Dig ole pan-tat-un."

Even I didn't get that one. There was a hesitation as we all waited. Finally, Mary-Ellen, after swallowing, filled us in.

"Big old plantation house, out close to me. Enormous thing," she said.

"Oh, that one," I said, remembering the ride back from her house the night she had made the "Moonlight Surprise." I shuddered again at the thought of eating meat surrounded by vanilla wafers. At least this Weems woman could cook. "I saw that house the night I came back from yo ..." but I stopped, realizing my mistake. If there was one thing I knew about Southern women, it was that they could be jealous over a man. The guy could be deaf, dumb, gay, pock-marked, blind in one eye, and have no feet, but if he was a man and showed *one* woman more attention than the others, he was doomed to a life of misery. He was also doomed to be the center of attention of those who had not received the aforementioned interest.

I was going to try and cover my tracks but it was too late. Shelby had seen the look on Mary-Ellen's face and made the connection.

"Been having a little extracurricular activity?" Shelby asked, and bit down hard onto the fork that had a chunk of frozen dessert on it.

I started to speak. "Well, I just ..."

Mary-Ellen jumped in to try and salvage what was left of the evening. "He just came out to bring me the binder," she said. "Salinger drove him out and then they left."

"Thought you and Salinger weren't on speaking terms," Shelby went on. Mrs. Weems simply watched the exchanges now—a front row seat at Wimbledon.

"We're okay," Mary-Ellen said, and sulked into her dessert.

"Since J.D. never did much to find your brother, I thought you'd still want to get even with him," Shelby went on. She was gathering steam; going in for the kill.

"J.D. and I have a history," Mary-Ellen retorted. "That is all. What's done is done."

Eager to steer things in another direction, I brought up the house they had just mentioned. I was enthusiastic not only to stop the ensuing catfight, but also to find out more about the residence and its history.

"There certainly seem to be a lot of great houses in the town," I said. "Yours, Mrs. Weems [she nodded politely, raising her glass], and a few others. Yours, Mrs. ..." but as I looked over at Mrs. Brandyworth I noticed that she was fast asleep; the comment would have been wasted. I went on. "Then there's that one you all were telling me about—that big plantation house. I'd like to hear more about that."

"Wouldn't we all," said Shelby, somewhat placated now that the conversation had turned from Salinger and Mary-Ellen back to domiciles.

"The oldest house in the county," Mary-Ellen added. "The old Yoke-Wacko-Hunter place."

"Hunter? Yoke? Wacko?"

"Brandis Hunter. Lived there for over eighty years. Before that it was his daddy's—Horace Bismirch Hunter, but it was originally built by Yoke-Wacko."

"Hunter, Hunter," I said, musing over the name, momentarily trying to put the unfortunate first and middle names of the man away for a moment.

"You-ah tink-ing of Ick Un-tuh," Mrs. Weems added.

"Dick Hunter," Mary-Ellen echoed.

"Where have I heard that ..."

"Best friends with Salinger way back ..."

Shelby interrupted: "Here we go again."

"I'm just *saying*," said Mary-Ellen. "The man asked and I was just *saying*."

"So Dick Hunter lived there? Before he died, I mean." I was thinking back now to the tombstone—the one Salinger had cursed at.

Mary-Ellen swallowed again. "Will somebody poke Brandyworth before she chokes on her own spit," she said. Mrs. Weems leaned over and gave Mrs. Brandyworth a shot in the ribs with the handle of a steak knife.

Nothing.

Mary-Ellen again: "As I was saying, Dick Hunter was best friends with Salinger way back in high school. Then he, the Hunter boy, became deputy, and that's when he got shot."

"By Mrs. Childers's husband," Shelby added, pushing away her dessert dish.

"We do not know that for a fact," Mary-Ellen retorted. "We have nothing to go on but speculation. Besides, some think another one of Childers's gang did it."

"Wait a minute," I said, eager to find out not only about the house, but also to quell the dispute between the two women. "Who owns the place now? And are you sure Salinger and Hunter were best friends?"

Shelby was the one to answer this time. "Place has been in probate since God knows when. Hunter's parents died a few years ago. They were a hundred if they were a day."

"She was ninety-eight and he was one hundred and two," Mary-Ellen responded. "Get your facts straight if you're going to tell things." She paused and went on. "And Hunter and Salinger were tiiiiiight," she said. "Tight as they come. Best friends. Why, that man cried for a month when Dick got himself shot. Like to have torn Salinger to pieces."

"Are you sure?" I said, remembering the curse at the cemetery.

Shelby jumped in. "That much I know. They were as close as you could get. Salinger was a mess at the funeral."

"He's not much better now when you bring the subject up," Mary Ellen chimed in.

At that moment, James, the butler, came to clear away the dessert dishes. "Should I take Mrs. Brandyworth's?" he asked Mrs. Weems snootily, and she shook her head "No," looking at the woman whose arms hung loosely by her sides and whose head was completely thrown back. "Noh jus wet. Tee mi-uh wan it waiter," she said.

"Yes, Madame," James responded, and Mary-Ellen and Shelby giggled again simultaneously.

"What is so funny?" I asked.

They both blushed and looked after James. Mary-Ellen kicked me under the table.

"What?" I said. "What?"

"You were asking about the house," Mary-Ellen continued, eager to get me off the reason she and Shelby had laughed at the butler. "We don't know who owns the thing now, but it's falling down. Needs a lot of work."

"Nothing was left of the family, after the parents died? And after Dick?" I asked.

"Not that we know of. When that Tuck woman first came to town, she looked at it," Mary-Ellen went on.

"Well, not officially," Shelby added. "They caught her on the property. She said she was interested, but *look* at her—she doesn't have that kind of money. And it would take a lot more of it to fix the place up."

I couldn't help but interject. "Yoke-Wacko?"

All faces turned to me. Mary-Ellen came to the rescue once again. "Yoke was his name. Wacko was just a nickname. Or so we gather—one of the first settlers in the area; dirt poor but made a fortune gambling."

"I'll bet," I said. Then the evening seemed to die down somewhat. Mrs. Weems, I noticed, had been extremely silent for most of the meal—especially now with our conversation about the old Yoke-Wacko-Hunter Plantation. She simply smiled and rested her chin on one upturned and cupped hand. I took her placation to mean that she had had enough to drink and eat, and that the dinner had gone as planned. And she hadn't seemed to be bothered by Mary-Ellen and Shelby's giggles, schoolgirl though they were.

"Eah ev-e-botee tati-fied?" ("Is everybody satisfied?"—no charge for that one), she asked, but before any of us could speak, there was a moan and then a slow movement coming from the other side of one of the rose-filled silver epergnes. Shelby, who was to the immediate right of Mrs. Brandyworth, was the first to catch the drift of what was about to happen, and Mrs. Weems, though aware, sat horrified and in wonder (and probably too drunk to do anything). The entire event took no more than five seconds—more than enough time for someone to respond and do something—but the shock of it and the actual performance overtook us all and we could only watch.

"Timmmmbeeeerrrrr!" Shelby sang out as Mrs. Brandyworth made a slow and even descent downward—a Japanese kamikaze plane heading straight for a pink American warship. Miraculously, the woman's weight managed to push her chair back slightly, and with perfect aim, she landed face-down, in the pink arctic fruit salad that James had not cleared away.

Shock set in for a full minute. We all looked at each other. Mrs. Weems was open-mouthed (lips or no). Shelby was unaffected. I could only think that I needed to save the mental picture for some future writing, which I have obviously done. (What? I'm a writer—I'm supposed to notice this stuff.)

Then Mary-Ellen spoke. "Will somebody lift up her head? That stuff is melted and she could drown."

Part III

"I'm not mad at you, I'm mad at the dirt!"—Faye Dunaway as Joan Crawford in *Mommie Dearest.*

29

Shelby's Giant Caper

While the binder made its rounds, things were brewing in the town. I know this because I was awakened a day later. It was either a bad case of déjà vu, or something else was on fire. As had happened previously, I was summoned from the land of sleep by the sound of Salinger's police siren. But this time it was still dark, right before dawn. An entire day had passed since the dinner at Mrs. Weems's house.

I got up and looked out the window. What shouldn't have come as a surprise did nevertheless. The Weems Town Hall—the tallest and oldest structure outside of a few homes in town—was lit up from the inside like a Halloween pumpkin. The building stood almost at a perfect forty-five degree angle from the Inn, so the eye-windows were clearly visible, glowing bright orange, with smoke pouring—teakettle-like—from the upper floor's eaves. I could hear glass breaking from the intense heat, and after a moment or two some internal beam collapsed with a thundering rip and thud. While the roof remained intact, it was obvious that everything inside was being destroyed. The outside of the building, since it was mostly brick, stayed put for the moment.

Salinger arrived once again, caught off guard. He pulled up right next to the Hall and got out, taking only a second to look up before throwing his hat toward the ground with such force that I thought it would actually dent the pavement. He sported his police jacket and not much else.

"Damn-nation to hell!" he shouted. "Bastards, the damn bastards!" He was ranting wildly but doing nothing about the blaze, pacing in his boxer shorts and a pair of wingtips. But what could he have done? There were no fire hydrants in the town and not even a bucket brigade.

By now a few shop owners had been roused, and the proprietors of the café and the beauty shop—the nearest places of business to the Hall—were attaching garden hoses to faucets at the front of their shops and running toward the conflagration.

"Give me that," Salinger shouted, as he took one of the hoses from a balding and elderly man. "You don't know shit," he continued, pointing the spray-nozzle toward a glowing window.

By this time, the other shop owner had pointed his equally puny spray in the direction of the fire, shooting his into another opening that belched black smoke and caustic stench.

For some time the two men continued to point and shoot their meager streams of water at the blaze, only occasionally veering off to other windows and toward the roof in an attempt to further distribute the water. But it was all for naught as the fire was now working on the main supports of the building and its collapse was inevitable.

While doom was in the cards, the men nevertheless stood there—two nozzles streaming useless water on an inferno of such immense proportions that even a real fire department with actual equipment would have had trouble dousing the incineration. Both Salinger and the other man looked like two Boy Scouts, pissing side-by-side on a camp fire gone wrong. I joined the growing crowd in the street, just in time to see Mrs. Weems in great distress.

"Ithe awa gone!" she sobbed, gripping the collar of her mink, pulling the coat closer around her even though the temperature outside was already ninety degrees and the air humid from the morning dew.

"There, there," a stern-faced man offered. Not the most original thing to say, but he seemed to be holding up rather well considering the circumstances. Then I noticed how familiar he looked—it was James, or "Tames" from the evening before last—the butler at the Weems dinner. But why was he here?

Salinger put down his hose and came over. "Sorry, Mayor," he said, addressing "James," but there's nothing we can do. It's purt much gone."

"Mayor?" I thought to myself. Doesn't he know who ..." and my mind began to do a play-back: Butler. Stoic. Giggling from Mary-Ellen and Shelby. Inside joke. It was adding up. "Might I ask where Mr. Weems is this evening?" I recalled saying. Her answer had been: "Det noh dawk abouh mitah Weem." ("Let's not talk about Mr. Weems.") And for good reason. While he might have been the all-powerful mayor—the man behind the curtain in *Oz*—he was strictly at Mrs. Weems's beck and call at home, forced to play butler when the occasion called for it. And everyone in town knew of the charade—everyone, that is, except me. I turned my attention to the couple, now in public, now mayor and wife. Mrs. Weems sobbed, inconsolable, fraught with anger and emotion: "I had juth we-deco-wated!" she drooled, and buried her face in her husband's pajama top.

It was then that something caught my eye. It may have actually been an intuition of sorts, or maybe even providence. I don't know, but

185

whatever caused it made me take stock of not only the fire, but everything that had happened to me since my arrival in the town. And the latest entries in the cookbook came foremost to mind as a part of this revelation also, for there, standing slightly apart from the crowd, fully dressed and showing absolutely no sign of remorse, was Shelby. While most Chalybeatens had come out in housecoats and pajamas, and even Salinger had arrived wearing only boxer shorts, socks with garters (it wasn't a bad look on him, if you're one for beefy calves at six in the morning), and a police jacket, Shelby was completely coiffed and looking well-rested. But the most unusual thing was that the library wouldn't be open for several hours and she was more than ready to start work. It was my opinion—and no one else seemed to notice—that she had been at work already—just not the type that had anything to do with books.

30

Racist Yelp Shebang!

Coming back inside from the fire, Mr. Hastings stopped me. "Package here for you," he said. "Marked 'confidential.'"

"What could this be?" I said out loud and tore into the brown paper wrapping. As soon as one corner was off, it became clear. The size and shape should have been a tip-off, but this morning was already off to a bad start and I was distracted. *The Chalybeate Springs Junior League Cookbook* I read on the outside—my own doing—a large-lettered cover I had made for the recipes. In an age of cell phones, the Internet, text messaging, and e-mail, Chalybeate Springs still favored pen and paper; still chose to communicate via the written word, and still favored hand delivery. Perhaps they were onto something.

"Thanks. I get it now," I said, and Hastings nodded. I took the newest recipes up to my room and read, getting up occasionally to see the progress of the fire as it burned itself out. Every now and then the morning was punctuated by a beam falling or wall slowly crumbling: exclamation points and parentheses from the land of arson—I'm assuming here.

While I was distressed about the town losing another building, I was more worried about myself. I knew that the person who would be most scrutinized would be Yours Truly. Sure enough, some time later, Salinger appeared at the Inn.

"McCrae, I want to talk to you," he said, after I had opened my door—a result of his meaty fist pounding so loudly that it shook the room.

"Why don't you bang a little louder?" I said. "People in Switzerland might not have heard you."

"I'm not worried about the rest of this country right now," he said. "I'm more concerned with who's been setting these fires. First the Church, and now the Town Hall."

I began to arrange some papers that I had been sifting through and spoke to him: "The Town Hall was being used as the church since that former institution was burned," I said. "Maybe the person who torched the church didn't want the meetings to continue." I looked up at him. "I know you're here because you think I had something to do with it."

"You *are* a smart one."

I looked him in the eye. "But how about this: Weren't you thrown out of that church? Denied membership?"

"I don't follow," he said.

"I'm not surprised." I was getting irritated at being the scapegoat for suspicious incidents in the town. Perhaps if Salinger had been more on top of affairs he would have seen this fire coming. But then, half the town had disappeared on his watch and he had not been able to solve any of those crimes, so why should this be any different?

"Is you sayin' that *I* burned it down?" he asked, a look of anger coming over his face.

"Well, you're looking at *me* and I had nothing to do with it. Everyone hates everyone else in this town," I continued. "It could be anyone."

"We didn't have this problem until you come," he went on.

"I'm here for a book, remember? Not to torch the place." While this was true, I had to admit that the festering wounds of the town, along with the cattiness and claw-sharpening of the ladies on each other, made for excellent fodder. It wasn't hard to figure out that someone associated with dinner a few nights before had done the Weems Town Hall in; it was just a matter of deducing "who."

"My money's on either Childers or Shelby," I said. "Not that I know anything official."

"Maybe you's just tryin' to throw me off the scent."

I turned to the man. "Sheriff Salinger, I am not a raccoon."

"No, but you's crafty like one. And I don't like it." The man was, if nothing else, eloquent.

"Have you questioned anyone else yet?" I asked.

"No, just you."

"How charming. What say you make the rounds with the ladies? After all, I was sound asleep."

"Kin you prove it?"

"If by that you mean, did I have a bed partner last night, the answer is 'No.'"

Salinger grunted and looked down at the floor. Then he looked up and crossed his arms. "Suppose you tell me what went on at that dinner over at the Weemses' the other night."

"Suppose I don't," I said.

"You tryin' to be difficult?"

"No," I said. "Look, ask away. I'll tell you whatever you want to know."

"Well, what did y'all talk about?"

"The usual town gossip," I said, thinking that I couldn't possibly let him in on the fact that he had been one of the hot conversation items. Then I thought of the booklet containing the recipes. While I had no desire to get anyone in trouble, I certainly wanted to extricate myself from Salinger's stare.

"Maybe this will help you out," I said, and handed him the three-inch-thick white ring binder that had been making the rounds just the day before. He took the amalgam of recipes from me and opened it. Here is what he saw, complete with the contributions I had scribbled that morning—the ones just before each recipe:

And now we have a complete dinner for those who can't seem to decide on what to serve. It comes from our very own mayor's wife, Helen Weems. She says she had a wonderful success with it a few nights ago when she invited myself, Mrs. Brandyworth, Miss Mary-Ellen Killchrist, and Mrs. Shelby to dinner. It's called …

◆NEGRO SURPRISE!◆

Cocktail hour: Stuffed shrimp with dill

First course: Cream of Tomato Soup

Second course: Iceberg lettuce with fresh cucumbers and a chunky blue cheese dressing

Main course: Beef Stroganoff (assorted breads and butter on the side)

Side dish: Cold baby pea salad with bacon crisps and egg

Dessert: Pink arctic frozen fruit salad

No need to go into the ingredients here as you can probably make them up as you go along. For a really successful dinner party, it's virtually impossible to do all the cooking AND entertain your guests. For this reason you should hire someone and supervise that person. And I can't emphasize this enough: KEEP YOUR GUESTS

OUT OF THE KITCHEN! Whatever you do, make sure they stay away from the food until it's time to eat. Then, here's where you come in. Quietly let the cook out the back and serve the meal yourself! Your guests will wonder how you did it. Let them think you're enjoying everything so much, that you're too busy playing "maid" to converse with them. Just sit there smugly until the very last bite is gone and announce that "Jecko," former chef from the Chalybeate Inn, just cooked EVERY BITE THEY ATE. Surprise! Or better yet, don't tell them *anything* and let them read about it as this collection of recipes makes the rounds! Yum--uuuuuum!

As the binder had made its way from home to home after this admission, it gathered no dust. It did, however, gain momentum as far as spite and retribution.

Our dear Christian, Mrs. Brandyworth, with her thoughts on that lovely dinner.

◆PINK-EYE, BROKEN NOSE, AND NASAL INFECTION DESSERT◆

1 horribly prepared pink thing for dessert, complete with something that looks like a pubic hair embedded in it
1 broken nose
1 bad case of pink-eye [the irony was not lost on me]
1 nasal infection
1 spiteful hostess
1 author who probably knew about this
47 Screwdrivers (the drink, not the tool)—before arriving
1 sinner woman who could have kept me from breaking my nose as she was sitting next to me. (I distinctly remember hearing something said about wood and trees a few moments before the accident.)
1 gossiping husband-hunter who probably had her hand under the table all night, feeling a certain author's thigh.

Take one evening that could have been lovely, invite three individuals who were probably in on the whole prank, and ruin a good dinner by having someone whose hands were no doubt dirty—HOW CAN YOU TELL???!!!!—

190

prepare the meal. Vomit up the dinner because you don't want it in your system and NOT because you had fifteen Scotches on top of the 47 screwdrivers. Hate everyone. Note: the Bible says NOTHING about having to *like* other people. While it does say "Love thy neighbor," this only applies to those living on either side of you, or directly across the street. As all of you live farther away than that, you DO NOT QUALIFY! My nose may never be its original shape, and my conjunctivitis is NOT clearing up anytime soon—even though I have prayed about it. In addition, I awoke this morning to find not ONE, but TWO small marshmallows which had emerged from my sinus cavities during the night and worked their way out of my head—by which route, I have no idea. If this town actually HAD an attorney, I would sue. P.S. I cannot control what my children do while they are away, and the contract that was recently reprinted in the *Chalybeate Springs Times* stating that "I hereby agree to the sale of my adopted children for the purposes of prostitution," is false and misleading. That quote was taken *entirely* out of context and I demand a retraction!

Mrs. Shelby DEATH adds her touch here. It evidently is a tribute not only to the evening we all spent together, but a reference to the Weemses' trip to Greenland several months ago and the unfortunate accident that left Mrs. Weems, how shall we say … changed. This recipe is a … (ahem) … mouthful.

◆COLD TONGUE SANDWICH (SERVED WITH A SIDE DISH OF SPITE)◆

1 ate-ful oad cow
1 autor ooh ith pob-a-wee teeping wid May-wee-Ehh-when
1 Tongue dat ith par-tu-ee mi-thing
1 bwee-ched bwond uth-ee ooh ith tying to get Mitah Mah-Tahy indo bay-ud
No wips a awe anywhere in tight
Eee-nuf mo-nee to buy any-ting

Dith weeth-a-pee peaks for ith-elf. My tug-esstion ith to wee-sign fom de Doon-uah Wee-geege tense ooh awe ah ate-full oad bee-uth.

Mary-Ellen weighs in …

♦TOO CHEAP TO AFFORD REAL HELP FOR DINNER (SERVES FOUR)♦

1 nosey author who is not doing his part to straighten out the rest of these women
1 *former* President of the Junior League
1 husband who is so P-whipped that he can't see straight (I can't actually write that "P" word)
1 totally jealous woman who has had more husbands than the town has skeletons in its closets
3 flower arrangement that are so large they take up the whole room
1 mediocre dinner that a dog would have turned up its nose at
1 new President (me) now that the Brandyworths are being investigated.
1 incident that made the entire evening worthwhile

Take one evening that is so loaded with possibilities for disaster that even the captain of the Titanic could have seen it coming. Overdress for the occasion (the hostess). Wear the same thing you've worn now for a week (the author). Dress like it's still 1980 (the woman whose been married five times … so far). Show up drunk and loud-mouthed (the preacher's wife), and mix all together. Oh, and I forgot the best part. Have your husband pretend to be the butler EVEN THOUGH WE'VE ALL SEEN HIM AT THE TOWN HALL! Serve with a generous helping of "Just how stupid do you think we is? [sic]" To finish off this horrible fiasco, have the cow-pimp of the seventeen child prostitutes fall face-down in the crappiest dessert ever made. Laugh your head off about it until it's your turn to write down a recipe and the book comes to you.

Mrs. Wash Childers with her comments ...

♦Y'ALL KIN ALL EAT SHIT AND DIE GHOUL-ASH (OR JUST EAT MRS. B'S DOO-DOO CAKES)♦

I'm just pissed off I wasn't invited. Y'all remember what I told each and every one of you's about how I'm treated. You know what I kin do.

This one was difficult. It could have been any number of individuals who had burned the Town Hall down. Certainly Mrs. Childers came to mind as she had been scratched from the invitation list at Mrs. Weems's "Negro Surprise dinner." And Mary-Ellen, Shelby, and Mrs. Brandyworth were worthy suspects as they had been tricked into eating food prepared by the one person they had for so long avoided—Jecko—not to mention their festering hatred for any and everything that didn't revolve around their own egos.

But what intrigued me most were the terse comments of Mrs. Childers. Not that she was a verbose individual anyway. Nevertheless the rather unveiled threat captivated me and I decided to pay her a visit. This would entail Salinger's help once again as her house was a bit out of town, but I had no other choice. While Weems, Brandyworth, Killchrist, and Shelby all had cars, I didn't think I could count on their hospitality right this minute. Plus, they all hated Childers, for what reason I didn't know. Then it hit me: Today was the day she was expected to clean my room. If I could get her to open up, I might strike gold. It was worth a shot. Besides, I wanted to know what made these people tick—I mean *really* tick—and Mrs. Childers might just be my entry to that off-off-off-off-off Broadway production. I prayed that the Weems Town Hall fire had not deterred her making her way to the Inn, and awaited her knock at the door—this time with great anticipation.

31

Richly Bent Passage

I've probably never jumped as high as I did when the knock came. I had been anticipating it all morning and I leapt to the room's door, slinging it open.

"Oh, I's sorry," a despondent Mrs. Childers said, "Thought you'd be out. Kin come back later if you like."

It was then that I noticed a large straw basket she was holding. It was covered with a red-and-white gingham checked cloth—very Little Red Riding Hood—very country-folk. But clean and neat— something I didn't normally associate with the woman.

"New sheets?" I said, seeing the basket, attempting an icebreaker and hoping for more than monosyllabic conversation (be careful what you wish for—you may get it).

"Nope. Thought you might like these," she said, and set the basket down, just inside the door. "Knowd how you probably would git tired of eatin' the same thing, not that we got much, and thought you'd like some fresh vegetables." With that she pulled the cloth from the basket and I looked down at the bounty she had brought. Tomatoes, onions, squash, cucumbers, and turnips lay side-by-side—scrubbed clean and gleaming. If the woman had presented me with Mars, Venus, Saturn, and Jupiter I could not have been more surprised (and the vegetables were about the same size).

I felt a pang, a twinge in my chest. So touched was I by this delivery that I almost started to cry. Here, I had thought of this woman only as some low-life joke, her recipes adding to the local color of a town that was already one step away from being an insane asylum. And now she was bringing me fresh produce from her garden. I had done nothing for her and she was showing kindness. It brought back memories of my youth: traveling to the country with my mother to visit people who lived in a simpler time and place.

"Won't you come in?" I said after I'd caught my breath. "I can't thank you enough for this." I took up the heavy basket and set it on the bed. "I really appreciate this." I gently picked each vegetable from its resting place and set it on the dresser and table top. Mrs. Childers stood by, saying nothing. I folded the crisp, clean covering and handed it to her with the basket. She took the lightened carrier and looked down.

"Is something the matter?" I asked, genuinely concerned. "Do you need me to leave so you can clean?"

"Nope. Ain't nothin' the matter ... really."

"Mrs. Childers," I said, bringing a chair from the desk and positioning it so that it was directly across from where I planned to sit—the foot of the bed, "would you like to sit down?" She looked around, hesitated, then closed the door. For a woman who had obviously endured a very hard life and wasn't one to mince words, she seemed almost fragile and lost.

"Please," I said, indicating the chair, seeing that she was hesitating.

"I'm not 'posed to," she said, but took a seat gingerly anyway.

"Are you upset because you weren't invited to the dinner party the other night?" I asked. While I had never held any ill will against Mrs. Childers, the simple act of bringing me something from her garden had uncovered a softness in me and I now wanted to know more about her—and what *she* knew about the town.

"Didn't matter much to me," she began. "Wouldn't have had nothin' to wear anyways. And probably wouldn't have enjoyed the food."

"You read what everyone wrote ... the recipes," I said.

"Don't take much to figure out that bunch." She seemed hurt. Her anger had been evident by her latest addition to the book.

I looked down at the floor. A soft breeze was blowing in from the open window and small-town street noises filtered up. Downtown Chalybeate Springs was probably the closest this woman had ever come to the term "civilized" and that was stretching it a bit.

"You work for them—the other ladies of the Junior League," I said. "You want to tell me about that?"

She sat silent, then looked at the wall above the bed, staring at nothing in particular.

"Mrs. Childers," I started again, adjusting myself on the bed, "I've spoken at length with all the women and I've spent a great deal of time at the library, looking at the history of the town. You're the only one I haven't spent any real time with. Well, Mrs. Brandyworth and I saw each other only a short while, but ..."

"Don't take much to figure *that* one out," she responded, her head up, her eyes defiant.

"Well, I know what the *Times* reported and there *has* been talk."

Evidently the mention of the woman's name was all that was needed. Mrs. Childers, who had been as mute as King Tut, suddenly came to life. "You know what she done, that Mrs. Brandyworth? I clean fur her fur *ten years*. Ten years, mind, and her and that Reverend, thinking they's so much betterin' everybody else. And them seventeen kids when they's home? Psssssh! Let me tell you, I thank the Lord they's not home that much—them kids, 'cause they treats me down-right awful too. But when they does come back ..." She stopped, staring into space again.

"What? When they come back, what?"

She hesitated. "Just ain't right, what they done to them young-uns," she said. "Just ain't right." She waited again. "I know what goes on. The Reverend and the Mrs. give me thirty-five thousand dollars to keep my mouth shut, what all about how them kids had been used. But I jus' can't. The Lord jus' won't stand for it. I got to tell somebody," she said, her eyes now filling with tears.

"They gave you money to keep you from telling what they were doing with the children?" ("Thirty-five thousand!" I thought.)

"That plus what they pays me ever' week. That Mrs. Brandyworth said she could get me into the Junior League, but I had to keep my mouth shut. Hell, didn't matter no count—they didn't never have no meeting 'til you come."

"Then why did they have a Junior League?" I asked. "If they weren't going to have any meetings, why ..."

"Mr. McCrae," she said, turning cynical, "you's from that New York City. Thought all y'all up there was supposed to be so smart."

"Trust me," I said, "you come visit sometime and you'll see, there's not that much difference. A few tall buildings and ..."

"I jus' got sick to my stomach that first time I saw it—what they'd put the youngest ones though," she went on, oblivious to my take on the Big Apple.

"Jus' sick," she said. "One of the fourteen-year-olds come up and ask me how she kin stop bleedin' ... between her legs, you know. I's thinkin' she meant her ... you know ... girly-time and all, but twernt so. Mr. McCrae, she and all them others had been ruined. And I don't mean jus' once."

"But the paper said ..."

"Shit, that durn paper. What do they know? I know 'cause I was *there*, and why else they give me that money if-in there twernt nuthin' wrong?"

"You do have a point."

"Them Brandyworth's as bad as the rest of 'em."

"Weems, I'm guessing, you don't like."

"That's another'n."

"Yes, I've heard some talk."

"You want talk, or you want to see?" she asked

"What do you mean?"

"I got a key. I go in to clean. I know what goes on there. Seen it myself."

I thought about it for a moment. It did sound intriguing, catching Jecko and Weems in a compromising position. Then I thought better of it. "Let's just let that one go for a while," I said.

"Well, anytime you wants to see it, you jus' lets me know. I kin sneak you in. Unnatural—that's what it is. Totally unnatural. A freak show if-in you ask me."

My good breeding (what there was left of it) wanted to preclude me from asking about the rest of the hen house, but my writer roots were showing and I wanted to know more. Plus, Mrs. Childers was opening up, probably for the first time in her life.

"What did Weems give you?" I asked.

Mrs. Childers thought a moment, adding it up. "Seems like it was somethin' like seventeen thousand five hunert and ..."

I just about fell off the bed. "Seventeen thousand, five hundred forty eight dollars and thirty-five cents?"

"How'd you knows?'

"Don't worry. Let's just keep going, if you don't mind," and with that Mrs. Childers shrugged. "Don't make me no never mind."

"Just out of curiosity, did any of the other women give you any money ... to, you know ... not say anything?" I asked.

"All of 'em did, 'cept I guess now that I've shot my durn mouth off, I'll have to give it back. That was the deal. 'You jus' keep your mouth shut, Mrs. Childers, 'bout everythin' you sees, and we'll take good care of you' they all said."

"No. Now wait a minute. No one else knows what you've told me, so you don't worry—you just keep that money."

"You think?"

"Look, don't worry about it. They're not going to ask for it back, and if they did, how would they get it?" I saw a light bulb go off in Mrs. Childers's head.

"Then I should keep it where no one would ever look," she said.

"That would be a good idea. It was cash?"

"Pure 'n simple."

I thought of the money I had in my laptop computer case, hoping it was safe there. I never went more than a few feet from my room without taking the portable computer, so I didn't worry. I had even carried it with me to the Weemses' dinner. And where were these women getting this cash from anyway, this money they were throwing at me and Mrs. Childers? The Weemses I could see—they were rich. Then the Brandyworths—well, they had been prostituting their children in Florida, so that was where their healthy (or unhealthy) income flowed from. But Mary-Ellen and Shelby? If Shelby was giving anything it probably wasn't much, though five dead husbands and their life insurance policies could fetch a pretty big sum when added together. Then there was Henrid—how she figured into this entire equation I hadn't deduced yet, but she had a cash flow of her own.

"Just how much money did Shelby give you?" I asked as innocently as I could.

"Purt near eight thousand dollars."

Hmmm. Not as big a sum as some of the others, but then, perhaps she was keeping the insurance money mainly for herself. Plus, everyone in town knew, or thought they knew what had happened to her husbands. There wasn't that much for Mrs. Childers to keep quiet about.

"And Mary-Ellen?" Mrs. Childers sat in thought. She looked up at the ceiling.

"Hard to tell," she said.

"Why?"

"Well, she ain't like the rest."

"How do you mean," I asked.

"She didn't give me no lump sum. She sort of doles it out, in addition to paying me each week."

"Doles it out how?"

"Well, she give me the usual ten dollars a week fur the cleanin' [I wanted to choke at the low price], then she give me two hunert more on-a top of that. Said the extra would total up to sixteen thousand by the time she finished."

"Holy be-Jesus!" I thought to myself. "I need to move down here and clean people's houses." I calmed myself and deliberated: Mary-Ellen was not able to come up with the President Grants and Benjamin Franklins the way the other ladies were. But then she didn't have a bevy of dead husbands or a brood of underage prostitutes to supply her with greenbacks. One could do only so much teaching at the local high school.

"Where did she get that number?" I asked. "Sixteen thousand."

"Ain't got no ideee."

I let this information roll around inside my head. Each of the women was paying Mrs. Childers to keep her mouth shut about something, and so far she had—up until now. I had another question I wanted answered and so I asked: "Mrs. Childers, if these women have given you so much money … and I don't want to be rude or judgmental here … but why do you live in a … the way you … why do …"

She cut me off. "Why do I live in a dirty trailer like white trash?"

"Well, if you want to put it that way."

"Now, how's it gonna look if all of a sudden I come up with a brand new house, new clothes, and what-not? You don't think peoples is gonna suspect sumpthin'? 'Sides, I got alls I needs. When them women is poor or they's dead, then I might move on up. And to tell the truth, Mr. McCrae, that money is tainted. I lives simply and I've got what I got from the insurance from my houses burning down."

"Accidentally."

"So I'm jus' a-holdin' on to that money. And who's to say they ain't gonna accuse me of something and want it back? Plus, I got my eye on a thing that might jus' make 'em all squirm."

"Such as?"

"There's this great big old plantation house over way out of town—on the other end from where I lives."

"I've seen it."

"Might buy it up someday. Fact is, I looked into it, but it's in some sort of po-tate . . prob-mate …"

"Probate?"

"That's it. You know 'bout that stuff?"

"Not that much, but I know about the house. I've seen it."

"That my ideee," she said. "Might buy that place up and show the whole town—tell 'em all to kiss my ass."

"I can't say I blame you," I said, thinking that I really wanted to ask one more question but wasn't sure if I wanted to press my luck. But then, the woman was sitting right before me.

"Mrs. Childers," I began, that fertilizer of yours …"

"Salinger's."

"Salinger's, quite right. I've seen what it can do and I was wondering if …"

199

"You want me to bring you some?" she asked. I thought perhaps she read minds as well as grew gigantic vegetables. It was exactly what I had planned to ask and she had saved me the trouble.

"Well ... yes, if you don't mind I'd ..."

"I seen that puny little old African violet over there you got and figgered you'd be wantin' some."

I could have corrected her and told her that the plant wasn't mine—that it had come with the room via Tuck's decorating, but I held back. Besides, she was doing most of the work for me.

"Why ... yes, that's exactly what I want it for," I said, completely wallowing in deception. "It looks so pitiful and all ... and, well, I just thought ... well, I didn't want to ask Salinger himself because he might think I'm ... you know ... that way," I said, making a limp wrist. "I mean, what would people say if they knew I raised African violets?" and I tried to blush.

"Don't make no never mind to me," she said. " 'Sides, Salinger's got some of the purtiest ones around."

"Salinger raises African violets?"

"Sho nuf. Won some prizes, too."

"And you'd think that winning the chili cook-off five years in a row would be enough," I said, and left it at that.

200

32

Shapley Bent Cigars

"You sure you don't need me to clean yur room today?" Mrs. Childers asked after I had gotten up and walked to the window.

"Quite."

" 'Cause if-in you do, I'll be glad to clean it."

I stared at the remains of the Weems Town Hall. If I leaned slightly out the window, I could see the smoldering ashes of the church. All this information Mrs. Childers was giving up further piqued my interest in Chalybeate Springs. What if, instead of just a cookbook about the town, I wrote about the people, everything; the scandals, the twisted relationships? What if I put it all down while I was here, in my laptop where it would be safe? I had already stored a lot of it in my computer, not including it in the binder that traveled around. These women, and Salinger, had no idea what I was doing. For all they knew I was simply helping with a cookbook. And the money from Weems and Henrid was a blessing, though I was smarting from the fact that Mrs. Childers had managed, by my estimate, $76,548.35 from the women, simply by existing. And that wasn't counting what Childers had gotten for the five times she'd burned down her house, plus her husband's insurance money. She lived like a church mouse but probably had more on-hand cash than anyone else in the town.

I turned from the window and looked at her, still sitting in the spindly wooden chair. "Mrs. Childers, did a ... Miss Henrid ever give you any money."

"Miss Henrid," she said, putting her finger to her temple. "No, can't say as she ever did. That's that new woman ain't it?"

"That would be the one."

"No, none that I kin recollects. Only seen her in town from time to time. Don't think anyone really likes her if-in you ask me. She goes around with that Salinger—the one that come out with you that day to see if it was me burned the Church of Christ down."

"I remember."

"Tick, ain't that her name?"

"Tuck," I said, "Tuck Henrid."

"What the hell kinda name is 'Tuck' anyways?"

"Evidently she was named for Tuckahoe, New York," I said, "though her family lived in the southern part of the state for a long time."

Mrs. Childers sat in thought. "Ain't never heard tell of that. I got relatives all over the southern part of the state and ain't no Henrids down that a-way."

"Do tell?"

"Swear on the Bible. Don't know what J.D. would want to go and get mixed up with her for anyways, not after what he been through."

My ears perked up. Anything on Salinger was like honey to a bear. "What did he go through?" I asked. "You mean losing two deputies—that Adams that married Shelby and then that Dick Hunter that got shot?"

"Naw, not that. Everybody knows that. That ain't no news."

"What then?"

"That business with his daddy and all—when J.D. was sixteen. Don't care what nobody says, it was his daddy that done it to him and all. Made him git married."

"Salinger was married before?"

"Only oncet. They, them Salingers twernt what you'd call the best of the crop. Daddy up and made J.D. marry that Slattery girl over in Bugger Hollar. Lucky-wise she died in childbirth, but J.D. twernt never the same."

"Because of his wife's death?" (I marveled that a Chalybeaten had actually died of natural causes.)

"No, 'cause of the baby."

"There was a baby?" No wonder Salinger was so filled with pregnant pauses. I mused over his long stretches of silence until Mrs. Childers went on with her story. Then my musings stopped. Cold.

"What you could *call* a baby," she persisted. Now, she was up, walking toward the window as if to get some air. She took a deep breath. "Lord knows the town treated him badly all his life, but after that happened ..."

"The baby?"

"He just got mean-like."

"But what happened to the baby? I mean, did it die too?"

Mrs. Childers turned toward me. Her eyes narrowed and her head seemed to shake for a moment. She seemed undone by the remembering.

"Thank Jesus it died. If-in it had lived, there's no telling what this town would-a been like; and what poor Salinger's life woulda been like. He never wanted to git married no ways, and his daddy a pressurin' him an all."

"Let me guess, he didn't give you any money to keep the story from circulating."

"No, he ain't give me no money. Didn't have to. Whole town knowd it. Knows it still. Though some have tried to forget." She looked down at the floor, then up at me. "Mr. McCrae, Salinger's daddy was the biggest ruttin' animal this side of hell. Didn't seem like there was a woman he didn't have his way with behind a barn, in the hen house, or in the backseat of a car when he was in high school."

"I'm not following."

"He shoulda knowd better than to push J.D. on that Slattery girl. He shoulda remembered that he'd gotten her mamma pregnant seventeen or so years ago when his own wife was all big with J.D. The man couldn't keep it zipped—J.D.'s daddy—not even for the time his wife was pregnant."

"So you're telling me that Salinger's father was the father of the Slattery girl? The same girl he forced J.D. to marry?"

"Sure enough. Though nobody knew it at the time, least-wise 'cept Salinger's daddy and the Slattery mother."

"And they didn't say anything?" I asked.

"Say anythin'? Hell, they pushed them into it, like it was some sick game. Well, that, plus seemed like it wouldn't have mattered who Salinger got married to. Anyone he'd a-picked woulda been related to him, just because his daddy got around so much. And most of the men folk not knowin' nothin' 'bout it back when it was happenin', well, they didn't suspect nothin' until it was too late." (My spell-check is having a field day with her language as I type this, trying to remember it all word-for-word as she's now left the room—back to the narrative.)

"So Salinger and Slattery were brother and sister," I said.

"Half-so." Mrs. Childers sat back down, seemingly exhausted from the story and her morning with me.

"Mrs. Childers, up until now you've not said much—I mean, before today. Why are you telling me this, at this point in time? Is it because the ladies of the Junior League have left you out, or rather, *want* to leave you out?"

"Partly." She seemed to be returning to her old terse self. I feared I had said something insulting, asked the wrong question; committed some Chalybeaten *faux pas*.

"You didn't say why you were glad the baby died," I blurted out, trying to get back to Salinger in the hope that her well of information wasn't yet dry.

"Oh, that. Sad, so durn sad." She bowed her head. "As I said, thank Jesus it died."

Part of me wanted to ask, and part didn't. I jumped in. "Why? What was so wrong with it?" I was aiming for something between nonchalant and slightly interested. What came out was gauche and wrong.

She took a full minute before answering. When she did, her eyes had narrowed and her color had changed. "Four legs, Mr. McCrae. The thing had four legs, two heads, no arms." She paused again. "Ain't that enough?"

"Oh, my God."

"God, I suspect had darn little to do with that," she said, and gave a curt nod.

"How awful for everyone, especially the child. Thank God it *did* die," I said, stunned by the realization that Salinger had gone through such a horrible experience.

"That's not the really bad part," she said, and I waited for the other shoe to drop.

"The thing lived for six months that way. With the mother dead, Salinger had to care for it; feed it, change it …"

" …before it died," I finished.

We both waited, her for the remembering of the thing, and myself for the additional facet it now gave the sheriff, his jocular square-jawing nothing more than a cover for his past pain.

"Not sayin' nothin' 'bout whether or not he killed it, mind," she said, looking me square in the eye, "though wouldn't have blamed him if he had of. Woulda been doin' that child and everyone a favor. Forced into that marriage, then made to take care of that baby. Seems to me that if he'd wanted it dead, he coulda done it when it came out— right when his wife died. Wouldn't nobody a-knowd. But somethin' in him couldn't do it—kill that child. Don't know if he thought it might change or get an operation or what …" She trailed off, far into the land of memory. My morbid streak was raising its head. I wanted to let the subject drop but had one more question.

"Mrs. Childers," I began, as gently as I could. "I've seen Salinger go to the cemetery, well, every day. To visit Dick Hunter's grave." I didn't add that Salinger had cursed the man. "He goes there and then leaves. I've never seen him once visit any other grave—his dead wife's or the baby's."

It was then that her mood changed, as if she were coming back from a land she had not initially intended to visit. She got up and started to the door. I feared that I had lost her; that my question would go unanswered. Finally, at the door, she turned.

"Mr. McCrae, the wife ain't buried there, in that there cemetery. She's buried over at that big old plantation house. The one I told you I'd like to buy someday. The one you done seen."

"So the baby's buried there too," I said, thinking *that* was the end of the story.

"Nope." She waited. "The baby ain't buried there. Not in the cemetery either."

"I don't understand. Was it cremated?"

"Mr. McCrae, I've said too much already. You've done got me runnin' on at the mouth for too long. That Mr. Hastings is gonna take it outa my hide if-in I don't get some work done 'round here."

She left, making her way back downstairs, not cleaning my room, but I didn't mind. I thought of her, of the ladies that made up the Junior League. I thought of their jobs, their perceived senses of self-worth. And I thought of Mrs. Childers and what she did for a living. Mrs. Wash Childers, it seems, was not only appropriately named, but she really did have the "dirt" on just about everyone in the town.

33

Playing Bare Chests

A fter the fiasco at the Weems house I was reluctant to accept any dinner invitations. I had washed and eaten most of the vegetables that Mrs. Childers brought, and while they were fresh and delicious, raw foods don't sit as well with my stomach as they used to. A blue-cheese dip wouldn't have hurt any either. At any rate, I was torn once again between sampling some of the town's *possibly* good cuisine and fearing another disaster of Weems-like proportions. Then again, it did make for a good story.

The first invitation I accepted was from Shelby. I wanted to go prepared with several antidotes for the various poisons that might be ingested, but when she told me that all we were having was frozen TV dinners, hoping I wouldn't be insulted, I went without hesitation. I was able to watch her pop them in the oven (no microwaves here) and serve them, so I could see if she added any additional "spices."

I feigned interest in the preparation, constantly on the lookout for small vials or bottles with no labels. Nothing much came of the meal, but afterwards she asked if I'd like a glass of wine. I said yes as the bottle hadn't been opened, and by the time we had consumed two glasses each she was quickly snuggling up to me on the sofa, for what reason I couldn't imagine, unless it was to get some information on the other ladies or to have her recipes featured in some special way. I assumed she wasn't husband-hunting as she had now completely spelled "D.E.A.T.H.," and unless she was starting another word, I didn't feel the need for any special protective armor.

Then again, if she was starting on the word "Murder," I might want to rethink the rest of the evening. I made a mental note to get in touch with Paul Udell (the town barber), Robert Randford (the owner of the Chalybeate Springs Café), Sam Delahaunty (retired), Bob Ewell (no idea what occupation, and no relation to the other Ewell that Shelby had married), and Alton Reynolds (former owner of the pig farm and now airstrip), just to let them know they might want to be on their guard.

I have to admit to being more than a little worried. I didn't think Shelby was planning to spell "Magnanimous" as she, a) wasn't, and b) couldn't, and c) would wipe out what was left of the town if she decided to make that particular alphabetic journey.

As we sat, she tried (optimal word here) discussing books.

"I find Hemingway to be the world's most fascinating writer," she oozed in my ear, obviously having no idea that I detested the man's work.

"Are you *kidding*? He's a complete boob! Talk about the emperor's new clothes! You can't tell who's saying *what* in any of his stories and he's boring as hell." I do have to admit to actually drinking more than my share of wine, so there may have been good reason for my unabashed honesty. I did and do intensely dislike Hemingway. He's just such a *bore*.

Shelby retreated and attempted to reload, thinking that another weapon might work. She chose the elephant gun. "Faulkner is nice," she tried, sipping from her oversized brandy snifter—obviously not made for the particular beverage she was drinking.

"Oh, what have you read by him?" I asked, thinking we could delve into *Light in August* or possibly *Absalom, Absalom!* Where my mind could have been, I have no idea.

"Well, I, uh, haven't actually *read* any of his books," she said, uncomfortably getting closer. By the time her tongue was in my ear, she had completely unbuttoned my shirt, was playing with the hair on my chest, and her hand was scrubbing my crotch. I had pretty much gotten the idea: No books, just sex.

"What books *do* you have in the library?" I asked, inching away from her. "You know, I want to keep this relationship, and all my relationships in this town, on a strictly professional basis," I said.

Her tongue went deeper. I couldn't help but think she was trying to glean some knowledge (literally) from my brain as she obviously had none herself. The evening came to an end when I declared that it was waaaaaay past my bedtime and could sleep only with the peace and quiet that the Inn provided (it was only seven o'clock at night). She didn't buy it, but I didn't care.

The next evening was spent with Mary-Ellen Killchrist, whose invitation had been strictly for drinks on the porch. It seemed a safe enough bet.

It wasn't.

Skipping any talk of books (for obvious reasons) she went directly to "Maybe we'd be more comfortable in the bed." Her subtlety was not lost on me. "I'm not sleepy," I said, playing an opposite hand of cards from the night before.

"You probably need some more gin," she said, and retreated to the kitchen to refill my glass. I followed, worrying that she might have taken a tip from Shelby's personal cookbook. I watched as she refilled a normal gin bottle from a large ceramic jug.

"Are you sure that's gin?" I asked. "It tasted a little more like vodka."

"Not really either one," Mary-Ellen said. "It's sort of a special family recipe."

My third-grade math was coming in handy once again. One: Mrs. Childers was asked to keep her mouth shut and was paid for it on a regular basis. Two: A house out in the country with several large metal tanks in the backyard and what appeared to be a giant chemistry set. Three: Homemade liquor. Four: Large jug in kitchen with no recognizable label and a liquid inside that would burn a hole through the average gasoline tank. I stopped there.

"Boy, I bet if you struck a match to this stuff, it would go up in a second," I said as Mary-Ellen finished pouring.

She smiled demurely (is there any other way for a moonshiner?) and answered slyly, "You have no idea."

I hated to tell her, but I did. I wasn't sure who had burned *what* down yet in regard to the Town Hall and the Brandyworth Church of Christ, but it was clear that all the women had access to flammables.

I was uneasy.

"You look uneasy," Mary-Ellen said when we were once again on the porch. I had tugged away as she attempted to drag me into her bedroom (fake fur bedspread, shag carpeting, and silver "orb" lamps— it was a 1970s decorator's wet dream and enough to make any man with taste lose his erection regardless of his sexual preference or need).

"I've got to get up early in the morning," I said, and noticed a pout coming over her face. She stepped up to me and did Shelby's play-in-the-chest-hair-routine.

"What is it? Am I not attractive?"

"What? No. Why would you …"

"Are you afraid that Salinger might find out? Is that it? Because I can tell you that there is nothing between us. He's stuck on that Tuck Henrid and frankly, I'm jealous. I think she has big feet anyway," she added. She turned the small umbrella in her drink with one finger. It chased a floppy mint sprig around and made the ice cubes swirl in their aqua-colored textured prison. I did have to agree with her on the foot point—the woman had abnormally large feet, but I suspected this

208

appearance was because of her odd choice of footwear and not her natural most southerly-directed attributes.

"She is rather pretty," I ventured. I at once realized my mistake.

"So that's it! You like her better than me!" It was a bad play in which I was cast as the object of some over-sexed schoolteacher's desire. I kept waiting for someone to call "curtain" but nothing happened.

Why I had not realized this before I do not know: Once a Homecoming Queen, always a Homecoming Queen. Mary-Ellen could not fathom being rebuffed by any man … for any reason—biological, chemical, mineral, spiritual, or vegetable. She had wanted Salinger at one time, but he had agreed only to date her. And this was before his horrible mistake of marrying his half-sister. Evidently he had seen something or some inner bell had gone off with Mary-Ellen (perhaps they had the same jaw?). Or maybe he just knew she was a brainless and blackmailing fruitcake.

With Mary-Ellen and Shelby hot-to-trot it was becoming clear why I was the target of the affections and affectations. That, plus the lack of children in town and Salinger's curt comments about "rugrats" the day he had showed me the homes of Weems, Brandyworth, and Shelby fit perfectly with why I was now being sought after: Inbreeding. The main part of the younger population in the town belonged to the Brandyworths (when they weren't farming them out for quick cash to Florida's pedophile population), and *those* had been adopted—safe bets for sure, gene pool-wise.

Evidently everyone in the town was related somehow, and with Old Man Salinger sowing his seeds like a fully-matured dandelion at puff-ball stage during a tornado, it was anyone's guess as to who was related to whom or, since this was farming territory, what. (Even the sheep had an odd look to them.) In short, I was being imported as a sperm bank; a penis with a brain (though the two are sometimes confused by their owners) to provide fresh outside irrigation to the gene pool. Wading pool was more like it. Or hot tub. At any rate, the town was desperate to go on; to reproduce. *Why*, I could not fathom. So far, the only one not to make a move was Miss Henrid. But then, she was from someplace else already and could be counted on not to be related to anyone, male, female, or livestock-wise. I ended up calling it an evening with Mary-Ellen—it was, after all, night.

Bisect Gay Shrapnel

I suppose I hadn't been paying attention to the degree that was required, for I hadn't noticed a certain theme developing each time the binder made its way from Junior Leaguer to Junior Leaguer. The first go-round had been a few pork recipes, some overblown bread-and-fish mixture, and a dash of local color and spite thrown in for good measure. The second time had been bitchiness with a good helping of hatred. The third time the booklet had made its way through the land of recipes, I had suggested a vegetable theme as the town seemed to be a cornucopia of legumary (Faulknerian influence again). So it didn't come as much of a surprise when the dessert section came about. And wouldn't you know that I would be heavily mentioned?

Just Desserts

Mrs. Helen Weems here.

♦CHANGE OF PACE SUNDAE♦

1 ungrateful writer
1 sense of remorse
1 moment of gladness that I'm not this week's target

Take one uppity, know-it-all-author who showed up UNINVITED to your town. Let everyone know that he is totally ungrateful and be thankful he never accepted an invitation to stay in your home. Distance yourself as much as possible from this outcast and vow to regain your title as President of the Junior League. By-the-by, I DO NOT feel Mrs. Brandyworth has the proper, how shall I say, "credentials" for the job, even though I have been informed that she now holds the position. I will NOT bow to her in any way, shape, or form.

Mrs. Wash Childers added her take on nature and the recipe that goes with that discourse.

♦EVEN EDUCATED BEES DOES IT PUDDING♦

1 can of that there common sense
4 bitches
1 writer whose room at that Inn is a mess (not my fault)
1 can cream of mushroom soup

Take the four bitches I works for and let them clean their own damn houses. Also, let that durn writer pick up after himself (in more ways than one). As far as what he does with his private parts, I live on a farm and I can tell you, them animals will do one another at the drop of a hat, so it just seems natural to me. Frankly, I don't see what all the fuss is about. I gots bulls in the pasture that do each other all the time. And you kin put cream of mushroom soup in just about anythin' if-in you wants.

This "light" number comes by way of Mary-Ellen Killchrist. As the saying goes, "A woman scorned ..."

♦TOOTIE-FRUITIE SALAD♦

1 can of pineapple
1 apple, chopped finely
1 can of maraschino cherries
2 large oranges
1 teaspoon lemon juice
4 cups of sugar
2 pears, cored and chopped
1 bag of those dinky little marshmallows

Peel and pull apart oranges. Cut pear up. Combine all other elements in large bowl and chill overnight. Or, better yet, just use Mr. McCrae as he seems to be fruity enough.

Shelby is our next Junior Leaguer to enter a recipe. It seems that the male population of Chalybeate Springs is dwindling to such an extent that she is prepared to offer her "services" to just about anyone for just about anything. While I personally wouldn't touch this particular dessert, perhaps it could be fed to a few of the other ladies.

♦FLAMING AUTHOR PIE♦

Apple pie
Gasoline
Author

Take one apple pie. Douse it and a particular author with gasoline. Set on fire. Enjoy.

Mrs. Brandyworth felt it necessary to add her two cents' worth, even though she and her husband had been arrested (they're out on bail) for running one of the largest child prostitution rings in the country. It seems that hypocrisy is not at all in danger of being killed off in this area—in fact, it is rampant, and Mrs. Brandyworth, while a drunk and a liar, is still an extremely religious woman.

♦SMITE-THE-SINNER DESSERT SOUFFLE♦

Information from Shelby and Mary-Ellen
1 author (from New York)
1 BIBLE
1 very good attorney (from out of state, though able to practice here and in FLORIDA)
1 clear conscience
1 decision NOT to resign from the Junior League and NOT to give up the presidency
3 bottles of the best vodka you can find

Drink all three bottles of vodka first, then write this damn recipe for that McCrae "person." Take the Bible and open it to Exodus 21:7. See the passage where it says that you may sell your daughter into slavery. I interpret this to really mean ALL children, and that SLAVERY is just another word for prostitution. After all, didn't Jesus minister to the prostitutes? (Hold on now, I've got to

212

have a refill.) And besides, the MONEY these kids brought in went directly to the church and for foundation repairs on our greenhouse. And I had NO IDEA that marijuana was growing in that enclosed structure. As for Mr. McCrae, the BIBLE says to "Go forth, be FRUITFUL and multiply." Mr. McCrae seems to have misunderstood this passage and I am more than happy to enlighten him. First of all, he is in his forties and NOT MARRIED. Now, it doesn't take a rocket scientist to figure THAT one out, does it? So he is NOT married and NOT multiplying. Secondly, it says, "Be fruitful." Obviously Mr. McCrae has *grossly* misunderstood this passage. And let's not even get into Leviticus as that thing is littered with references to butt-fucking and having sex with SHEEP! It was rumored that the other day, while visiting the town café, that Mr. McCrae held his little finger out while drinking his iced tea. WHAT MORE DO YOU PEOPLE NEED???!!!!!! And as everyone knows, all men who are not married are pedophiles. You stay away from my kids, you pervert! And as for all you mother-fucking-assed bitches, I don't give a shit what you think of me. And for whoever burned the church down, I WILL get your sorry ass. Maybe it was ALL of you damn bitches. I hate all y'all's fucking asshole guts and I hope you all DIE!!!!!

Well, that went well. Secretly I worried about the African violet incident and hoped Childers hadn't said anything. Word got around quickly in this town and anything was possible. Good news travels fast; bad news even faster. And pernicious gossip at the speed of light, coming with steamer trunks, banners waving, and a big cruise ship honking into the harbor. For all Chalybeate Springs's lack of cell phones and modern auditory devices, they had the communications situation very much in hand when it came to spreading a rumor. It was almost telepathic, or tele-*pathic*, if you will.

In order to test the pipeline at one point, I stated to Mrs. Weems, quite emphatically, that I had discovered the cure for cancer and was keeping it under wraps until I could release the news to the world when I got back to New York—that the whole thing was very hush-hush.

Nothing.

Not a word.

Then I pretended to let slip a small item that I had just maybe, just *possibly*, probably not, couldn't remember, *might* have, wasn't sure, but *could* have, *maybe* had sex at one point and gotten paid for it, though I had been drinking and possibly performed the act on a dare. The headline in the *Chalybeate Springs Times* the next day read: MCCRAE WORLD'S BIGGEST WHORE AND DRUNKARD—SYPHILIS SORES VISIBLE TO GENERAL PUBLIC! AUTHOR FOUND NAKED IN GUTTER—PASSED OUT!

I would have to be more careful. And more guarded.

35

Blanc Pegs Hysteria

Mrs. Childers was back to clean my room. She knocked and entered as usual. Her demeanor was such that one never would have guessed we had previously conversed about the townspeople. She swung from open-book to shut-in hermit like a rusty-looking but well-oiled gate. I couldn't read her and so let her alone. Besides, I was smarting from the last recipe entries and trying to stay under the radar. It was one thing to watch five women take shots at one another; something else entirely to be the object of their scorn. I stayed in the room as Mrs. Childers straightened up, thinking that today would not be her day to converse. I worked on the recipes and my impressions of the town, trying to put them in some order.

Just as she was wiping down the bathroom, Mrs. Childers stuck her head out and called to me. "Mr. McCrae," she said, in a matter-of-fact tone. "I don't like what they done to you."

"Huh?"

"The book. Them recipes. I seen it. What they done to you. What they said."

"Oh, that." I attempted silence, thinking she would drop the subject. I certainly wanted to.

She didn't.

"Been thinking," she said. While I now liked Mrs. Childers, the thought of her ruminating over any subject other than cleaning or growing planet-sized vegetables scared me. But she did have valuable tidbits on the townsfolk. I had experienced a taste of her exotic gossip and my brain wanted more.

"It doesn't really bother me, Mrs. Childers. Besides, they just wanted to get in good with me and some of them think I've failed them. They probably just wanted only *their* recipes in the book. You have no idea what some of these women are capable of."

That was a red flag for her. "Oh yes I does," she said, meanness coming from every pore. "They only let me into that League so's I wouldn't tell on 'em."

"I thought they paid you," I said, taking off my reading glasses and setting them down.

"That too. But the way they been a-treaten' me is down-right disrespectful."

"Do go on," I said, my arm now draped over the back of the simple wooden chair she had done so much confessing from that first day when she opened up to me.

"Now, I don't mind bein' the housekeeper for 'em, but they promised me I'd be a part of that Junior League and I'm *not*."

"But they've given you quite lot of money."

"Money ain't everythin'."

I was caught between a guffaw and agreeing with her. Money was *most* things to *most* people, *most* of the time. Without it you were as good as dead, either figuratively or literally. I coveted the stuff as if it were a canteen and I was marooned in the Mojave. But I knew what she meant and let her continue after I mentally confirmed what I thought her real reason was for being so despondent and acerbic—a wanting to belong to something, anything.

Before I could speak, she jumped in: "Oh, and I forgot," she added, reaching into her apron pocket. Got this here fertilizer fur you like you's asked." She produced a dog-eared envelope that contained what looked like dirt mixed with powder.

"This is it?" I asked.

"Don't need much. Plant ain't that big. You need more, you let me knows."

"Oh, okay. Fine," I said, and put the envelope on the table, thinking that I would later send it to one of my friends in New York and get it analyzed.

"What were we talking about?" I asked. "Oh, yes. So being a part of their group is more important to you than just getting paid?"

"Exactly right, Mr. McCrae." She was leaning on the handle of her mop, eager to get me on her side. She didn't have to try that hard— I wasn't that enamored of the ladies at this point.

"Well, what would you like me to do?" I asked.

"You could put in a good word fur me, and maybe ..." but she stopped.

"No, go on."

"Well, maybe if I told you some things you could use, showed you things ..." again she stopped.

"To get even with them?" I asked.

She leaned the mop handle against the doorframe and came closer. "I don't want to be mean-spirited like they is, but I was promised somethin' and I aim to *git* it."

216

"Fair enough. I certainly know how you feel; been there. But, to tell the truth, why would you want to be a part of this group anyway? They're not what they appear to be."

"You don't have to tell me that," she said, picking her mop back up. "I knows all about it." I wondered how much more she could tell than what she already had. Certainly I knew about the Brandyworths and their child prostitution ring. Then there was Mary-Ellen's moonshining business. Shelby's foibles were known state-wide, though no one did anything about them. And Mrs. Childers herself had confessed to burning down her own house five times for the insurance money. Plus, she'd taken bribes to keep her mouth shut—something she wasn't doing very well at the moment. Then there was ..."

"That Weems woman," she said, breaking into my reverie. "Like I told you afore, what she's doin' ain't right."

"Mrs. Childers, I know all about that and evidently so does everyone else in town."

She smiled impishly. "I don't think you do. Like I said, I got a key. I take care of the house. I's seen it for myself. If you want, I kin *sneak you in*." She stuck her neck out on the last three words for extra emphasis. It worked.

Unhealthy thoughts made their way into my brain. Weems was the equivalent of a bad painting costing several million dollars—a rip-off at a New York auction house where the buyer didn't know what he was getting. That was one layer I knew of. Then there was her not-so-well-hidden relationship with Jecko. And now, after what she had pulled at her dinner party, the whole town was talking.

"When would this ... um, show, take place?" I asked.

"They goes at it about ten-thirty ever mornin'." She was riveted by my interest, thinking that she had her hooks into me and that I was on her side. And she was right.

"Where exactly do they ...well ... do it?" I asked. I was expecting her to be shocked by my straightforward manner, but she wasn't.

"Right there in the kitchen. On the *durn kitchen table*."

So that was it. That was why the ladies had been upset about Jecko's cooking the food. Perhaps they knew what went on atop the table as well. While not the most squeamish person, I did have to admit that it was a bit unappetizing. I had heard of married couples doing it in different places to try and spice things up, but Mrs. Weems being taken on top of her very own kitchen table while her butler-playing husband was at his now non-existent Town Hall job (his offices had been moved to the library), was a bit much.

"What time is it?" I asked, not having my watch on.

"It's ten. If we go now, in a few minutes, sneak up on 'em 'round the back, we kin *catch 'em*. Better walk. I kin show you a back way so's nobody'll know what we're a-doin'."

A few minutes later, after I had told Mrs. Childers to wait downstairs while I put myself together, we set out for Weems-land. Around the back of the Inn, behind the café, the barber shop, and several other stores, we made our way to the lush green part of town where the Weems mansion was.

"We got to go right around here, behind these big ole bushes," she said, obviously enjoying each and every minute of the Hardy Boys-like escapade. Finally, we were at the back garden of the house, amid a large clump of hydrangeas. Pink blossoms the size of our heads hid our faces while Mrs. Childers sketched out the plan: "I'll go up first, git my key out, and let myself in through the laundry room," she said.

"Can't we just look in the window and see them?" I asked.

"Can't. Won't be able to see 'em from there. You got to go through the laundry room, past the pantry, and into the sunroom. There's a winder that you kin see 'em through plain as day. She's got a lot of plants in there, so you kin hide behind 'em."

"How do you know they'll be doing it right at ten-thirty?" I asked, wondering about the bizarre punctuality of the deed.

"Always the same. Been the same for six months now. Was that way when Jecko was a-workin' at the Inn, and is the same now he's got more time on his hands. Plus, Old Mayor Weems is always away at that time. He come home for lunch sometimes, so this is the best time fur 'em."

"All right. Whatever you say." I followed close behind her as she stealthily soft-shoed her way up the walk and eased the key into the door. It was amazing how quiet she could be and I thought about her ability to come and go without being noticed, wondering if she had indeed set the fires that had burned the Church and the Weems Town Hall. It *was* possible. After all, she was sneaking me into her employer's home for the purpose of spying. Then again, I was a part of that equation and couldn't really point fingers.

I also wondered if I was being set up. Could she be tricking me into planting my fingerprints all over the house—in places I wouldn't normally go? Maybe I was just being paranoid. Besides, I wanted to see Weems and Jecko together. I couldn't picture them *ensemble* at this juncture, but we had come this far, and the ladies of the Junior League had been sharpening their claws on me, so I rethought the escapade. I wanted to get even with them, and Weems seemed the most likely place to start.

We traversed the laundry room and then the butler's pantry just as Mrs. Childers had said we would. Then we eased into the sunroom. Tropical palms and gardenias crowded each other and a humidifier hissed uncomfortably in one corner. A window between the sunroom and kitchen was open and with the right amount of camouflage and positioning I was able to see the kitchen table.

Just as Mrs. Childers had promised, Jecko and Weems were there. "See," she whispered, "I told you. You didn't believe me, but there they is."

They were indeed together, but not in the way I had been led to believe, for Mrs. Weems had taken Jecko's large black hand and placed it on her throat. She was making sounds, doing her best to impersonate Anne Bancroft in *The Miracle Worker*.

"Ith a 'Guuuuhhhhh' tound," she said. "Oow oooh tie," she warbled on, and with that prodding, even though he couldn't hear it, Jecko, his hand still in place, made the effort.

"Gaaaaaaahhh," he uttered, attempting to repeat the vibrations. The sound was heart-wrenching. Like a baby calf trying to *moo* its first time. I wanted to cry but held back.

"Now tie did one," Mrs. Weems continued. "Ahhhhhhh."

Jecko tried again, this time doing better.

Mrs. Weems went on. "Peeeeennnnnn. Tie dat un." Jecko tried again, almost getting it.

Mrs. Weems pressed on. "Ahhhhhhhh-peeeennnnnissss," she said, and Jecko attempted it: "Ahhhhhh-peeeeeenis."

It was then that Mrs Childers added her commentary while hiding behind a rather large and overflowing tropical fern. Her whisper was tinged with perniciousness: "See, it's like I done told you; unnatural, them two. She's got him trying to say 'Ahhh, *penis!*"

I turned to her, brushing away a large palm frond that was poking me in the eye. Irritated that I'd been dragged into witnessing a scene that was more touching than corrupt, and having an entirely new appreciation for Mrs. Weems, even though her attempt at teaching a deaf-mute to speak was somewhat like a man with no legs trying to teach ballroom dancing, I spoke with as much severity as I could, but in the lowest volume possible.

"Mrs. Childers," I said, my teeth gritted, "she's trying to get him to say 'Happiness,' not " 'Ahhh, *penis.*' "

36

Blather Cagey Spins

Getting back to the Inn, I dashed off a note to my friend in New York and enclosed the envelope containing the fertilizer, putting both in a larger-sized manila one. I took it down to Mr. Hastings and asked if he would mail it. Surprisingly, he agreed and the thing was on its way.

That evening, after the field trip to the Weems sunroom and the mailing of the package to New York, the Killchrist High School burned to the ground. The fire consumed the building within a few minutes (it wasn't that big anyway). There was no siren this time, and I was totally unaware of the incendiary activity until a copy of the *Times* arrived at my room the next morning, care of Mr. Hastings. The article stated that the structure had gone up in ten minutes, evidently as a result of a large amount of some "alcoholic" substance stored in the basement.

Salinger, miraculously, didn't show up, and no one sent me a note. I passed the rest of the day and that evening rummaging through a box that I had thrown together and borrowed from the library, care of the assistant who didn't like Shelby. It was one of those fold-up moving boxes that you can find everywhere—those put-together things usually seen being carried by some employee who has just been fired and has barely managed to clean out his or her desk before being escorted by security out of the building. You know, those faux-wood boxes that usually contain a picture frame, a pair of shoes, a stuffed animal, some books, and all the paper clips, staplers, and toilet paper that the fired employee can carry?

But in this case the box held copies of the *Chalybeate Springs Times* and a few clippings from other area newspapers with items that were pertinent to the Springs. As nothing in the library was in any kind of order, I had figured that I would just scoop up whatever I had not already read, and go through it leisurely in my hotel room.

EGGPLANT SAID TO HAVE PICTURE OF VIRGIN MARY ON IT, one headline beamed. I *had* to read the article—it was just too good to pass up.

A migrant worker at the Reynolds's farm dropped dead Friday after seeing what he believed to be the likeness of the Virgin Mary on the surface of an eggplant. The vegetable, weighing thirty pounds, was located on the right side of the southern-most field, next to the property of "Imma" and "Withhim" Bellenmoth--the Siamese twin brothers who are joined at the buttocks. Workers reported that Jose Vasquez-Ramirez-Alejandro-Garcia-Xavier-Pallardo, the migrant worker who saw the image, collapsed of a heart attack about three-thirty p.m. after crossing himself and kneeling in the dirt. When Vasquez-Ramirez-Alejandro-Garcia-Xavier-Pallardo's friends went to investigate his collapse, they found the man facedown in the mud, next to the large vegetable. Then, seeing the image themselves, they stood amazed for two hours with no one getting help for the vegetable's victim. Dr. Crapinthrop of Westerville arrived on the scene too late to provide needed medical attention. Vasquez-Ramirez-Alejandro-Garcia-Xavier-Pallardo was pronounced dead at the scene of the vegetable, and services will be held at the Brandyworth Church of Christ, outside as migrant workers are not allowed in, this Sunday from one o'clock until two o'clock p.m. His body will be shipped back to Mexico in a refrigerated truck--the same way he came to this country. The vegetable was relocated to the Weems Town Hall where it was displayed in a glass case for two weeks until it began to show signs of decomposition. The eggplant was then cooked and eaten at the church's Holy Communion this past Sunday, substituting for the usual crackers. Grape juice was served to compliment the large vegetable in not only taste, but color as well.

Another article gave insight into the lack of youth in the town—a condition I had noticed and one that had been commented on by several others:

CHALYBEATENS NEED TO ALLOW MORE OUTSIDE INFLUENCES, the headline ran. That particular writing assignment went on to admonish the residents for being xenophobic, though it didn't use that particular word.

It has become clear that too many
Chalybeatens are related to one another
and are therefore unable to marry and bear
children without the horrible consequences
that we all have witnessed over the years.
For reasons which should be obvious, this
reporter begs the people of this good town
to form a chamber of commerce for the
purpose of drawing larger crowds to the
area. Attractions that could prove useful
to lure in tourists are: The John L.
McClanahan Memorial Barbeque Pit, right
off I-84, and the Civil War shoe that was
found in Mallard Pond last year. In
addition, we have a lovely Town Hall ["Not
anymore," I thought to myself] and many of
the older homes are in fine condition.
Chalybeate Springs could easily become *the*
tourist attraction of the South with its
fine gardens and lovely public park. The
Yoke-Wacko-Hunter State Park [so that was
the name] is probably the best-kept secret
in this area and could easily serve as a
stop-off point for travelers between
Titusville and Clearwater if money could
be found for the sign that the mayor has
agreed to ask the county to put up. "SEE
YOKE-WACKO-HUNTER STATE PARK," the billboard
would read, and the appropriate exit
number could be displayed underneath.

I kept reading, pulling out papers and articles.

SAYERFIELD MAN KILLED WHEN WIFE'S LITTLE FINGER
ENTERS BRAIN. Well, that headline got my attention.

A Sayerfield man, living just west
of the Springs area, died almost instantly
when his wife's little finger became
lodged in his left nostril and entered his
brain. Mrs. Francis Burdock injured her
hand last Tuesday night and was hurrying
up the stairs and rounding a corner of her
home, when her husband, John Burdock,
emerged from the couple's bedroom.
Evidently the force with which Mrs.
Burdock ascended the stairs, accompanied
by the upward positioning of her hand,

223

caused the smallest appendage to lodge in
her husband's nostril with such vigor that
it ripped his nose apart. I must also be
noted that Mr. Burdock sneezed at the
exact moment he rounded the corner, adding
to the intensity of the accident. The
downward thrust of his head, accompanied
by the positioning of Mrs. Burdock's wrist
and hurrying nature of her journey, caused
her little finger to thrust itself into
Mr. Burdock's frontal lobe and areas
beyond, killing him instantly. Law
enforcement officers on the scene some
time later determined the cause of death
to be a "freak accident" and no charges
have been filed against the Sayerfield
woman. Services are to be held tomorrow at
the Sayerfield Baptist Church. The funeral
is to be closed-casket. On a side note,
Mrs. Burdock's hand is healing nicely.

As usual, the rest of the reading was below third-grade level
and good material for those having trouble falling asleep. I was about to
do just that when I came across something that set off a "ping" in my
brain. It was from a very old copy of the *Times*—one from at least
twenty years ago.

CHALYBEATE SPRINGS YOUTH HELD IN OUTHOUSE ARSONS,
the headline read. The article went on to say that a young man from
one of Chalybeate Springs's oldest and most respected families had
been caught in the act of burning down an outhouse that belonged to
one of the town's farmers. It added that the youth had confessed to the
act, along with nineteen other outhouse burnings, and that he had
pleaded guilty. The judge in the county sentenced said youth to
probation and community service as he was underage, and also because
he was from such a well-established Chalybeate Springs family. The
article also added that, while this was a serious offense, part of the
reason it was being treated so lightly was that the youth's family had
agreed to a cash settlement for the residents of the town, and had also
agreed to have the outhouses rebuilt free of charge. One of those
residents whose outhouse was destroyed was a Mrs. Wash Childers.
And the youth who set the fires? His name was Dick Hunter. Address?
The Yoke-Wacko-Hunter Plantation.

The next morning the library burned (that was quick, wasn't it?—nothing like a good old transition) and, if you'll pardon the expression, things really started to heat up. While I had thought gossip was the town's most notable activity, it seems that arson was also high on the list. And while I would have thought Dick Hunter (I still can't type it with a straight face) was the culprit, he'd been dead now for a year or two and incapable of the act.

For nothing more than the reiteration factor of hate, cookbooks, and fire, let's look at what had happened so far: Brandyworth Church of Christ burned; The Weems Town Hall burned; The Killchrist High School burned; and now, after changing the lettering on that immense book depository for everyone's literature (but mine) to read, "THE SHELBY D.E.A.T.H. MEMORIAL LIBRARY," *that* structure was in ruins.

Five women were in the Junior League and I suspected each and every one had had something to do with one or more of the conflagrations, and well, Mrs. Childers *had* burned her own house down five times. (That "five" number keeps coming up. Me, I like "sevens." What can you do.)

My guess was that the fire-starter was Childers. The other possibility was that each of the women had pointed their flaming arrow of hate at one another's eponymous structures in an attempt to get even, vie for attention, or just psychologically wipe one another out.

So now, the four main buildings, the anchors of the community, were gone. Caput. And while Salinger hadn't shown up after the Killchrist High School burned, he did make an appearance after the library went up in smoke, or rather, while it was going up.

I became aware that he was standing next to me as I, along with everyone else in Chalybeate Springs, watched the library walls cave in. Salinger's arms were crossed, and while he wasn't looking at me, he spoke to me nevertheless.

"Is this going to be the final one you burn down?" he asked, still gazing at the orange flames as they leapt higher and higher.

"Uh, I don't know if noticed or not, but right over there," I said, pointing to Helen Weems, "Is the mayor's wife."

"Yur purnt?"

"She's holding a copy of Ray Bradbury's *Fahrenheit 451*," I said. "Doesn't it strike you as a bit ironic?" Then I remembered he hadn't even read *The Catcher in the Rye*—by the man with his (somewhat) own name. I suppose Ray Bradbury would have been totally out of the question for Deputy Dud. I felt it necessary to clarify. *"Fahrenheit 451* is the temperature at which paper catches fire and burns," I said. "Paper, you know, as in a library with a lot of that stuff between book covers?"

"Naw, I don't know nuthin' about that," he said, still looking straight ahead.

"And you're just going to stand here? Not even any garden hoses to try and fight the thing this time?" I asked.

"The only hose is the ones by the Café and that other building. Too close to the flames. Ain't no use no-how as the thing's too far gone. Sure is a shame," he said, and took his hat off to scratch his head."

"You're telling *me?*" I said. "That was about the only place I could get any work done. And all the historical documents and old newspapers were in there—everything I was using for research."

Salinger paused. He looked at me for the first time that day. "That's not what I meant," he said. "Didn't mean it was a shame about losing all that."

"What then?"

"Shame I'm going to have to arrest you for arson," he added, and began to bring the handcuffs out from behind his back. "Mr. Jackson Tippet McCrae, you're under arrest for burning down the Town Hall, the Church of Christ, the Killchrist High School, and this here Ly-berry," he said with as much dramatic volume as possible—evidently for the benefit of everyone within hearing range. "You have the right to remain silent ..." he went on, completing the so-often-spoken Miranda Rights, and ... believe it or not, for once in my life I did.

37

Reshaping Cab Style

Since the jail had been in the Weems Town Hall, and since that particular building was no more, the place to keep such a dangerous individual as myself had not been properly thought out. Not that I minded. Salinger had slapped the cuffs on me in front of the entire town and they had cheered. Evidently I was not the most well-liked person for several reasons, the least of which wasn't the fact that the Junior League ladies had been spreading vicious rumors about not only my uncooperativeness, but my alleged sexual proclivities, along with my supposed penchant for burning down the most important edifices in town. Misguided though it was, the mob and its mentality (or lack thereof) turned into the ugly behemoth it can so often become. Salinger—thinking of my safety, I'm sure—and having no place to keep me, stuffed me into his patrol car and took off, sirens blaring and lights flashing. He sped away from the angry crowd, which had now been brainwashed into thinking that I was the reason for the town's bad luck.

"Got to keep you safe," he said as he turned from Main Street onto the highway. Then he took some smaller roads and circled back to town. He came in through a lesser street and then pulled into an alley, carefully traversing the gravel and dented garbage cans.

"Ain't no use you stayin' at the Inn. They know you was there. Besides, the way the town feels right now, you ain't welcome and some of them has guns."

"You don't honestly think I did this," I said. "Burned down all those buildings."

"Son, I don't know what to believe. I've got to take somebody in before those people's head's blow off, and you've got to admit that you're the most likely suspect."

"So you *do* think I did it?"

"Naw, I ain't sayin' that. But it does look that way."

"But you saw those recipes in my book," I pleaded. "Those women are crazy. Each and every one has some reason to have burned at least one of the buildings."

"And where is that collection now; that book with them recipes?" Salinger asked.

"It's being passed around again," I said, slumping back into the seat. I worried that the ladies would remove any evidence of their frustrations with each other. Then I remembered that I had already transcribed the recipes into a computer file. At least some record of their hate-fest would still exist. It was peculiar, this being arrested: the first weeks I had been escorted around in the back of Salinger's car as a guest, and now I was a wanted criminal, handcuffed and pleading, in the same location.

"If I can find any evidence to the contrary, I'll let you go. But you do have to admit that it looks suspicious," Salinger said.

"So, if the Weems Town Hall is gone, where are you taking me?" I asked, as we turned down a smaller residential street. It looked familiar and then I realized that the last time I'd seen it, it had been by way of the other end.

"Tuck Henrid's house?" I asked, as we pulled into the drive.

"Listen, nobody in this town likes Tuck, and since you two have been avoidin' each other like the plague on account of her wantin' to get into the League, this is the only place I can think of." He waited, then turned around. "You got a better idea?"

"No," I said, dejectedly. I couldn't complain too much. Tuck was, after all, one of the nicer people in town and she did have a restful home and know how to cook.

"Look," Salinger went on, turning more in his seat, adjusting his bulk, "I'll see you get to be as comfortable as you can, get your stuff from the Inn. What is it you need?"

"Just my clothes, a box of papers and stuff, and my laptop," I said.

"You just leave it to me. I'll take care of everything." After helping me out of the car and taking the handcuffs off, he escorted me toward the house.

"You aren't afraid I'll make a run for it?" I asked, massaging my wrists. "And did you have to put those things on so tight?"

"Mostly for show," he responded. "The townsfolk needed to think you were no longer a threat. They won't look for you here, and if they ask, I'll tell them it's none of their business as to where I'm a-keepin' you."

We were now making our way to the front door. Salinger rang the bell and we waited. After a few moments—a little longer than I thought it would take—Miss Henrid appeared. The look on her face was priceless. Salinger jumped in:

"Look, Tuck, you've got to help me out. The whole town thinks McCrae here has burned down the Church of Christ, Town Hall, and the ly-berry and high ..."

"The library too?" she said, looking crestfallen.

"Point is, I had to handcuff him in front of the crowd who was watching Shelby's place of books go up in flames."

"Oh, my goodness," she said, adjusting her hair and then holding the door open for us. "Y'all come on in." We swept past her. She was perfectly coiffed with large white clip-on earrings and a strand of white pearls to rival Wilma Flintstone's. Her outfit was a clingy but not overly-so sun dress, showing just the right amount of neck and upper chest—freckles and a bit of age (she must have been in her late thirties or early forties.) The usual pumps were on her feet and she was wearing an apron.

Salinger continued: "Figured that he could hide out here until we find out what exactly went on. Plus," he added, looking at me askance, "I ain't exactly sure he didn't do it."

"Mr. McCrae here?" Henrid asked, looking at me as if I was incapable of such an act.

"Well, hell, Tuck, you never know. And somebody's been doin' it."

"But Mr. McCrae was asked here by me; to help out with that cookbook so that ..."

"Know that, Tuck," he said, holding up his hand. "I don't want to hear no more about it neither. Like I said, I got to figure this thing out and I ain't sure he ain't done it. If you could just keep him here for a while until things blows over."

"Well, that's not a problem," she said to Salinger while looking at me. Then: "Jackson," she said, and then an aside, "I may call you Jackson?"

"Sure."

"... and I get along quite well and we can catch up on gossip anyway. Besides, he can sample some of my cooking and see if my recipes are fit for his book."

Salinger looked from Henrid to me, then did a reverse of the move. "Y'all ain't plannin' on gettin' too friendly, is you?" he asked, his eyes narrowing.

I turned to him, face-to-face. "Look, I just want to get this book done and get out of here. You don't think I'm going to screw up my chances any more by making a pass at your lady friend, do you?"

Miss Henrid put a shocked hand to her breast and stood open-mouthed.

Salinger took a minute to think about it. "Guess you got a purnt. And I'll leave them handcuffs off. Way I figures it, where you gonna go, and how you gonna get there?" Then he turned to Miss Henrid. "You keep an eye on him a make sure he don't go anywheres."

"Will do, J.D."

"I got to get back to town and see if there's any evidence on the burnin'. Y'all take care and stay out of trouble. And Tuck, you keep him out of sight for now. If anyone comes by …"

"You know the whole town hates me, J.D. Who would come by?"

"You got a purnt," he said. "Anyways, keep him out of sight. I got to go by the Inn and get his stuff."

I turned to the sheriff. "You *really* don't think you need to handcuff me again?" I asked, jokingly. Then I realized he might.

He paused and looked at me with a strange smile. "Nope. Think Tuck can take care of that. She's got her own set of handcuffs," and he smiled even more.

"Kink in Chalybeate Springs," I said. "Who'd-a thunk it."

"Well, we might not be quite as provincial as you think," Salinger said. I marveled at his ability to know the word *provincial*, when it wasn't attached to some ugly reproduction furniture that had been popular in the 1960s.

"We'll have a grand old time," Tuck called out as Salinger made his way back to his patrol car. "With or without the handcuffs." She turned to me and smiled the same smile I had seen on Salinger's face.

"God, I hope so," I said under my breath, and with that, Salinger pulled away.

As Tuck led me through the house, I followed, dejectedly. But then she added one more note to the already burgeoning bizarrity (Faulkner from the grave) of the situation, changing her tone: "And Mr. McCrae, while I like you, don't think of trying anything. I have a Colt .45 and I know how to use it." She stopped and turned directly to me. "And I'm not talking about a can of beer or my cookies," she added, and sashayed back into the kitchen, leaving me in the living room.

Part IV

The heart is deceitful above all things, and desperately wicked: who can know it?

Jeremiah 17:9

And some other organs aren't much better either.

Jackson Tippett McCrae

38

Psych-Belting Areas

Salinger was nice enough to bring me the binder that had made its most recent pass through the hands of the Junior League. Thankfully the group had calmed down and were not attacking me quite as much. And thankfully Salinger had not looked inside my laptop case and found the large stash of money. He might have taken it or questioned why I had it. Then again, I could have lied. At any rate, I got the two most important things: the money and the computer. Here you'll find the latest addition to the priceless tome that Chalybeate Springs high society was working on.

Canning and Preserves—or as I like to call it . . . Things in Jars

A history and short essay on canning and putting up preserves by Mrs. Wash Childers.

As many of y'all knows, canning and preserving them there vegetables and other food items has been around with us folks for years. Our grandmothers and mothers "put up" vegetables and other foods, just as we-uns do today. Pressure canning is the only known safe method for a-doin' this and the only way to be sure that them there foods is good to eat. You gots to be careful of that there food poisoning. I can't remember the fancy name it goes by and all. But you want to avoid this at all costs as it will not only make you sick as a dog with worms, but it shore-nuf kill you.

What y'all is gonna need:

Standard canning lids, ring bands, and jars (lids should be two-piece)
A pressure cooker

Take some of yur best vegetables and try to can them as soon as possible for freshness.

I won't go into the entire thing here, as you really needs to have someone help you the first time you do this. Just make sure you cook them vegetables first. Place them there vegetables in jars and remove air bubbles. Put that durn ring band and lid on the jar, along with top. Lids can all be diff-ernt, so check with each person who made the thing. Put about four inches of water in your pressure cooker. Use a rack and put the jars on this, inside. You will need to look for a dent on the lids after they's done as this is a sign that they has a vacuum inside. If that lid has a bulge, or if there is an odor or the food appears to foam, git rid of it and DO NOT EAT! The result could be real bad!!!

The recipes below is for the preparation BEFORE they goes into the canner. You may vary these as you like.

I read on, thinking that the ladies of the Junior League had gotten over their many falling-outs and tête-à-têtes. No so. It appeared that, while their anger was no longer *mostly* directed at me, it was still there—at pressure cooker levels. Mrs. Childers added her introduction to the recipe, taking away my responsibilities for the moment.

Mrs. Weems give us this first recipe in this section. It speaks for itself ... even though I ain't read it yet.

◆CAN-HER-ASS-BEANS (FOR MRS. OTIS BRANDYWORTH)◆

Take some string beans, oh, I don't know, say about forty bushels (enough to feed everyone in the state prison where you're going), and separate and snap their nasty little ends off. Cook to death. Place in jars and follow the procedure that Childers dictated. It doesn't matter whether or not you kill anyone as you're already going to be put away for *very* long time.

233

Shelby is next, providing us with a special recipe for, as she calls it ...

♦PICKLED AUTHOR♦

1 author whose books I haven't read
4 backstabbing women
1 town that doesn't deserve me
Some Botox
Plastic surgery
Hair transplantation
Arson
1 claim to the Presidency of the Junior League

Take one author (preferably from New York) and give him a face lift, some Botox, and a hair transplant so that he can look younger than he is. Check his bio and do some simple math. Figure that he's too old to father a child in the town, even if he could or wanted to. Suspect he burned down the library because they didn't have any of his books. Try dating outside your own county. Let him know that you feel used and underappreciated. Hope he rots in jail. Claim Presidency for self after Mary Ellen is caught with underage boy from high school in a compromising position. Oh, wait ... is there an epidemic of this stuff going around?

Mary-Ellen interjects her comments here:

♦CHICKEN SOUP AND ONE CRACKER (FOR MRS. WASH CHILDERS)♦

1 jar of chicken soup that you put up last year
1 dirty housekeeper
1 sponge
No brains
1 bitchy librarian

Use the same sponge to clean my kitchen that you used on everyone else's bathroom. Make sure I get some horrible bacterial infection. Don't come to clean on the

234

day you're supposed to while I'm sick, forcing me to eat nothing but chicken soup for *three days*. Don't worry about having crackers with it as you've got the biggest one already in the county coming to your house almost every week. Note to self: Pull each and every hair out of Shelby's head. *I'm* sorry—*I* forgot she wears a wig. Guess I'll have to come up with another way to get even. Perhaps I could teach her to spell correctly—that would ruin her as she'd have no claim to anything! Oh, wait, I forgot again—she's killed five husbands, so she's known for that. Better watch out, fellows!

Mrs. Brandyworth again, though this one has nothing to do with canning. The phrase "Needs no introduction" comes to mind ...

◆DOO-DOO BARLEY CAKES◆

17 lbs human excrement (this is really the key)
13 eggs
4 cups flour
7 very strong Martinis
5 cups barley

Mix flour, barley, and eggs in large bowl. Take approximately 17 lbs of the excrement and mix in well. (Note: Since Delilah will not make this particular recipe, I do it myself.) After mixing ingredients, mash into small hamburger-sized patties. Bake at 400 degrees until golden brown.

It says in Ezekiel 4:12 "And thou shalt eat it as barley cakes, and thou shall bake it with dung that cometh out of man, in their sight." (Another note: Cow's dung *may* be substituted for this, though I'm not sure—Ezekiel 4:15 is not clear on this point. It's not apparent if God is speaking here or not.)

While Childers had offered her tips on canning and "putting up" vegetables and preserves, she hadn't given a specific recipe. It didn't matter. I was so distracted with my recent arrest and incarceration at Tuck's that I wouldn't have been able to do much work

235

anyway. I settled in after typing this latest section into my "thing you got in the bag" as Salinger had called it, and then sought out Miss Henrid, who was now in her kitchen.

39

Her Playact Bigness

"Why don't you have a seat in the living room?" Miss Henrid insisted as I stood in the kitchen doorway. Her back was to me and I couldn't see what she was preparing. "I'm just putting the finishing touches on something and you can be the first to try it. If you like, you can include it in the book."

"Yeah, about that," I said, making my way toward the living room. "I've been meaning to talk to you. You know, it's not exactly turning out to be a plethora of good old-fashioned Southern cooking."

"Oh?" Again, from the kitchen. I was attempting to direct my voice through the dining room and around the corner, into the area where she was cooking.

"No. As a matter of fact, it's turning out to be quite bizarre. Seems these ladies are quite a peculiar bunch."

"What?"

"The ladies," I said a little louder. "They're a peculiar bunch."

"What did I tell you?"

"Well, you were right. What I don't get is this: You want to be in the Junior League, and so does Mrs. Childers."

"She's already in it," she continued from the next room. "My, you've got to taste this."

"Well, she's in it, but she not—really. See, they only let her in because she knows something about them."

"Interesting. Ooooh, yummy!"

"What, the fact that Mrs. Childers has something on them?"

"No, the frosting. It's really yummy."

"Oh. Right." I sat down in the dark-green velvet chair and fingered a small ashtray on the side table. Curiosity rather than rudeness overcame me and I picked it up to see who had made it. "Limoges," I said to myself. "Not bad." At least Miss Henrid had taste. Her clothes, hair, house, cooking, and even knick-knacks were high-class. Nothing too showy. She didn't live in a mansion like the Weemses, but she was well put together and always appeared polished.

Henrid entered the living room still wearing the apron and carrying a beautiful three-layer chocolate cake on a tray with two glasses of water, forks, a knife, and napkins.

"Happy birthday to you," she sang, and my mouth fell completely open. Where had I been? It was evidently my birthday, but with all that had been going on, and with the book and the fires, and, well, everything, I had completely forgotten—or not.

"How did you know? Even I forgot," I said, completely lying. Okay, so it wasn't my birthday—she had gotten the date wrong—but I never correct people when they do this. It is, after all, a free cake. I prayed that presents were also involved. Unfortunately, they were—just not the kind I had hoped for.

"I know a lot about you, Mr. McCrae," she said, and set the cake down on the coffee table. Then she pulled open a drawer and retrieved a copy of my first book: hardcover with a tattered dust jacket. It had obviously been read more than once.

"You've actually read my book," I said, as she handed it to me with a pen.

"Yes, and I want you to sign it," she said. Someday it will be worth a fortune."

"Lady," I said, as I made my signature, "from your lips to God's ears." Then I handed the book and pen back to her and eased into the comfortableness of the chair.

"So, you actually read it?" I asked, amazed to find the one person in town who had dared to acquire a copy.

"Yes I read it."

"Well, I hope you know you're the only one in town who has."

"How do you mean?" she asked.

"Even Shelby at the library hasn't, and the library doesn't have a …" but I stopped, "*didn't* have a copy," I said, remembering that the building was no more.

"Oh, poo, what do you care?" she said, taking a seat on the sofa and sticking a knife into the cake. "They're such a bunch of know-it-alls who really don't know *anything*. That Mrs. Weems, who travels everywhere, yet somehow manages to be cultureless. I know she's not read it. And Shelby and Mary-Ellen are too wrapped up in themselves to read anything, even with Shelby being the librarian and all. And that Mrs. Brandyworth—should have been in prison years ago. Holy-roller and a fake."

"Yeah," I said. "And the way she treats Delilah is awful. Do you know that Mrs. B makes her wear rubber gloves to do everything, just because she doesn't want the woman touching anything with her hands?" While I said this, it wasn't lost on me that Delilah had probably been asked to make Doo-Doo Barley cakes at one time and had run screaming from the house. The gloves were probably a compromise. Sure enough, Miss Henrid confirmed this—sort of.

"Mr. McCrae, you've got it all wrong. For your information, Delilah doesn't want to touch anything that a *white* person owns. Mrs. Brandyworth just makes it known that it's *her* idea and not Delilah's. She wears gloves here too."

"Oh? Delilah is your cook also?"

"Well, no. You see, for Brandyworth, she's a cook, but *here* she works as my housekeeper. And she's not perfect by any means. She'll clean any and everything but refuses to touch the kitchen and bathroom."

"But aren't those the two things you'd really want cleaned?"

"You think?"

"I see your point."

Miss Henrid continued. "And that's fine, I guess. I'd rather do them myself as I can have both done the way I want. That way I know what sponge has been where, if you know what I mean."

"Right. No Mrs. Childers trying to pull anything."

"Yes, but back to the ladies of the Junior League, and Mrs. Childers in particular," she said, using a red-nailed finger and the edge of the knife to lay one thick and moist piece of the cake on a plate. "She's got her own problems. I almost feel sorry for her. Has a good heart, but a bit of an arsonist, if you know what I mean," she finished, handing me the plate and birthday cake.

"You know, you seem to have these people nailed down pretty well," I said. "I feel about the same as you do. Childers isn't a bad person; just a bit backward. She brought me the most delicious vegetables from her garden."

"No doubt helped by Salinger's remarkable fertilizer," she said, as she cut herself a piece of the cake.

"No doubt. I've been wondering how he does it." I didn't let on that I had sent a soil sample to New York for testing. I wasn't going to steal his formula—I was just curious as to the contents; you know, so I could use it if I ever had a garden of my own.

"Oh, that's a secret you'll never get out of him. That Salinger is a sly one. But he's got a good thing going and he makes a fair living from it."

"Seems like everyone in town makes money on something, other than what they're *supposed* to do," I said.

I sampled the confectionary concoction she had prepared and wasn't ready for the shocking effect it had on my taste buds. "This is incredible," I said, mouth full and still chewing. "I can't believe you made this." I dug into the cake, eager for another bite. "This has got to go into the book—I don't care what they say."

"Well, I'm glad you like it."

About that time, Salinger pulled up in front of the house. He was unloading my belongings that had been in my room at the Inn.

"Who is it?" Henrid asked, not getting up. I turned and looked out the window—I had an easy view of the man.

"The three wise men," I said, "bearing gold, frankincense, and myrrh."

"No, really. You writers have such a colorful way of speaking. It's what I liked about your first book."

"It's Salinger," I said. "He's brought my stuff and that African violet that was in my room. So I can have a muse while I'm incarcerated here."

Miss Henrid batted her eyelashes and looked up at me as she licked a few crumbs from her perfectly manicured hands. Then she turned her fingernails inward, toward her palm, and scrutinized them. "Mr. McCrae, my place is hardly a cot with a slop bucket in the corner," she countered, and just as she said it, I took note of a particular action she had just performed and a thought popped into my head—and it was not a good one. Instinct summoned something from my psyche once more—as it had done the first day I had met her.

"I was just kidding. I'm actually looking forward to it." I tried to sound as normal as possible, but it was a strain. I had just seen something—some sign that things weren't exactly right—and it bothered me. Maybe I was making too much out of it, or perhaps she had just been a bit "off" at that particular moment, letting her guard down. Whatever it was, a bell went off, or rather *on*, in my head. I worried a light bulb was showing, suspended only inches from my hair.

"You look strange," she said, catching my mood and its sudden change.

"Strange? No, why? I don't feel strange," I said, trying to smooth my reaction over. I didn't want to say anything until I was sure.

"No, just now, you looked at me as if you saw right through me," she continued. "I'm a little skittish, I guess. Worried that writers have a bit more perspicacity than most people. Worried they're going to find out things about a person that a person might not want them to."

I wanted to change the subject. I wanted Salinger to come into the house with my belongings. I wanted to know who Tuck Henrid was and where she came from. I wanted to dismiss my suspicions, but first

I had to play it as if I hadn't noticed anything out of the ordinary. I changed the subject back to her cooking. I took a drink of my water, finished swallowing, and wiped my mouth. "You know, I'm eager to get a taste of something else you've made. I've had those cookies, the ones shaped like guns, and then this cake, but I'd like to try some more substantial fare if you wouldn't mind."

"Well, since you're to be my, um, *guest*, then I suppose you'll get your chance."

"What, no bread and water for thirty days?" I said, attempting to add levity into the present situation.

"Mr. McCrae," she said, and smiled. "I certainly don't think you'll be here for thirty days," and with that, Salinger opened the door and made his way to the back bedroom where I was to stay, carrying the box of newspapers, my clothes, my computer, and the African violet—a cherry on top of a sundae, as if it were life itself.

40

Help Snags Acerbity

The next day, the sound of Salinger's car pulling up in the drive woke me from a nap. I knew the sound as I had spent far too much time inside that particular mode of transportation. The wheels made a "clickety" noise that told anyone within hearing distance that the sheriff was on his way. Not exactly the thing to have if your plan was to sneak up on someone. I crawled off the bed and ran a brush through my hair.

As I came out of the bedroom, Salinger was already standing in the small foyer between the living room and dining room. "Got some good news for you," he said, thumbs hooked into his belt.

"I can't wait."

"Oh, you're gonna like this one. I researched it out and all. Seems that I've got no hard evidence that you set them fires, but both you and me knows you did."

"I did not set …" but Salinger held up his hand.

"Now, just hear me out on this one. Fine, you say you didn't. I say you did. Who do you think has more pull around here? And I ain't lookin' for no answer from you. So here is what I'm figurin'." He stood there, with arms now crossed, and then raised up slightly on his toes. "Pretty fine thing too, if you ask me."

"What? What? Would you get on with it?"

"You're to do some community service."

"Great," I said.

"Now, hold on. This here is serious. You gots to pay for what you done, least-wise it's got to *look* like you're doin' that—to the town anyways. Everybody's in an uproar and they're out for blood—and it'll be mine if it ain't yourn. And it ain't gonna be mine. I got a plan, but you gonna have to play along."

"I'm listening."

"You're gonna do two things. First off, you're gonna fix a complete dinner for the entire Junior League, and serve it yourself—cooking, clean up, everytin'." He had my attention and I wasn't happy.

"There's no way," I said. "Haven't you got something like breaking rocks or a chain gang? I'll even be Bubba's boyfriend for a week. Anything but an evening with those hens, especially after what they've done to each other and to me."

"No, and that's that. You're to do what's been agreed on and I've spoken to each and every one of the ladies and they think it's perfect. In fact, they's the ones who mentioned it—brought it up first. Thing is, *they* want to put together the menu."

I couldn't believe this. I was going to have to share one more evening with the witches of Chalybeate. I imagined that Salinger had put the idea into their heads, regardless of what he'd said about it being the ladies' brainstorm.

"That's great," I said, sarcasm reeking from every pore. "What's on for the evening, bird-dog stew?"

"No, now don't get your panties in a wad. They's gonna pick the menu, but said you could pick one thing—a side dish or some what-not. See, trouble is, you got to do it all, and by yourself—no help. And, you got to serve them and clean up."

"Okay. Fine. You already said clean up. But you said there was another thing. And I'm not worried as it couldn't possibly be any worse than the evening you've just described."

"Oh, yeah, that. Well, you remember how I told you about the chili cook-off?"

"Right."

"It's the Fourth of July at three o'clock in the afternoon, in the park, and you're gonna judge."

"And you're still going to win," I said. Then I remembered: The day after tomorrow was the Fourth of July. "That's in two days—a day and a half!"

"You got that much right."

With the epoch of good times that had been happening, I had completely forgotten what day—or month—it was. Not that I actually celebrated the Fourth of July with anything other than reading a book or trying to sleep while fireworks went off over the Statue of Liberty or New York's East River.

Salinger turned to Miss Henrid. "He's right smart for a city boy who's been up north all these years." Henrid nodded and smiled. I couldn't tell if she felt sorry for me or was smirking at my situation.

"Don't worry," she interjected. "I can help with the dinner if you want."

"No. No help from you on this." Salinger cut his hand sideways in the air. "He's got to do it all himself," the man retorted, almost angrily. "And I better not catch you over at the Inn, in any way, shape, form, or fashion," (pointed finger, scowl on face, leaning in slightly).

"Inn? Why would she be over at the Inn?" I asked.

"That's where you're gonna cook for the ladies. Hastings scrubbed the place down so all of Jecko's germs is outa there and it's the only neutral territory we ... uh ... *they* could think of."

"So you did have something to do with this," I said, finding my way over to the sofa and sitting down. Salinger and Henrid continued to stand.

"Now don't get on my case. I'm tryin' to get you out of trouble, not *into* more. I still think you're responsible for them fires, but I can't prove it, and without that proof, judge over in Titusville says I got to let you go. The next problem comes in the way you's stirred up trouble with the Junior League. Way I figure it, whether or not you done the deed—them fires—you're paying for things one way or another. Plus, I get to win the chili cook-off this year ... again, and that'll be worth them buildings burning."

"You're charming. That's what you are," I said, sarcasm spilling forth.

"No need for the compliment," Salinger answered.

I put my head in my hands and addressed the green carpeting between the sofa and coffee table. "So when is this dinner supposed to happen—the one I'm going to cook for the ladies of the Junior League?"

His answer was quick and short. And most unwelcome.

"Tonight."

I sat bolt upright. "Tonight! Are you frickin' nuts? There's no way I can fix a dinner for five women tonight, and I don't even know what I'm fixing!" I couldn't believe this. Not only was the town full of crazies, but they expected miracles that normally would have taken days to perform. They couldn't even get a cookbook together without outside help.

Salinger piped up. "Just so happens I have what they'll be wanting to eat right here," and with that he pulled a sheet of paper from his hip pocket and handed it to me.

As I read, it hit me that the ladies were not without a sense or humor, for the dishes all required something with which the town was most familiar: Fire.

```
┌─────────────────────────────────────────────────┐
│  ♦MR. MCCRAE'S COMEUPPANCE♦                       │
│                                                   │
│  Appetizer: Flaming kabobs of bell peppers,       │
│  onions, and chicken livers wrapped in bacon.     │
│                                                   │
│  Main course: Flame-broiled Red Snapper           │
│  (prepared tableside)                             │
│                                                   │
│  Side dishes: Your call, Mr. McCrae               │
│                                                   │
│  Dessert: Bananas Foster                          │
└─────────────────────────────────────────────────┘
```

Everything they had asked for required fire in its preparation. I would make certain that the things I chose for the side dishes *didn't*. All that I needed was one more reason for Salinger to suspect me as the arsonist. I knew the women had decimated each other's eponymous buildings, but I couldn't get the sheriff to believe it, and perhaps if I performed this menial chore of making dinner and judging the contest, all the bad things would just go away and I could coerce Salinger into taking me back to the pig-farm-slash-landing strip to catch an ancient propeller plane to Atlanta, then on to New York. I longed for the irritable people and smog-filled canyons of the city where you knew that everyone hated everyone else and that they were all out to get you; that it was all out in the open, right up front. Not this small town *pastoral* with quirky recipes and even more quirky residents.

Fine. I would cook their meal, and I would wait on them, but after that and the judging of the chili cook-off, I was out of here.

As I had to get started right away I needed the help of Salinger (once again) and he knew it. But, for all his finger-pointing and readiness to have me drawn and quartered as the guilty party of the arson-fest, he was surprisingly helpful when it came to the dinner. He and Tuck promised to find the needed ingredients and bring them to the Inn after they had dropped me off there, under the watchful eye of Mr. Hastings. The townspeople had long ago surmised that I had left or been sent to the county jail, and after a few had insisted on checking the one room at the Inn, they were satisfied that I was nowhere to be found. I would be safe as long as the Junior Leaguers kept their mouths shut—something I wasn't sure they could do.

But two hours and myriad ingredients later, in the small but well-established and totally "Negro-free" kitchen, I was ready to prepare the meal. I have to say, I still would have preferred the chain gang or splitting rocks, but the choice wasn't mine.

The chicken livers were grilling while I coated the Red Snapper with olive oil, salt and pepper, and a fine dusting of dill. I also had an excellent cooking sherry on hand which I planned to use when I seared the fish, tableside. All ingredients for the dessert were prepared beforehand and ready to be set aflame.

As the dinner time had been specified at exactly six o'clock (this, from the paper Salinger had brought out) there was little time for angst of any kind. I was so busy concentrating on the meal that every other worry fell to the wayside.

The women were seated in the dining room and already tongues were wagging—mostly about me. I could hear snippets through the metal swinging door while the bacon crisped and the onions became somewhat translucent on the kabobs that held the livers. I partially cooked the fish in a large oven so that the tableside flame show would be nothing more than that—a show. All that remained was to serve the side dishes and ...Oh, my God, I had completely forgotten the side dishes. I was panicking when the backdoor to the kitchen opened and I saw Tuck's head poke through.

"Hi, I know Salinger told me not to help, but I thought you might want some of these," she said, holding up two jars. One contained string beans and the other harbored pickled eggs (something I never touch but evidently were a favorite in this area of the country).

"You're a Godsend," I said. "I had completely forgotten about the side dishes."

"I figured you might. Noticed that you didn't ask us to get anything like that when we went shopping, and since I canned these last year, thought they might come in handy, and, well, here you are!"

"You put these up yourself?" I asked. "Canned them?"

"Sure enough. Ate some last week, and if you don't like the pickled eggs, then you haven't tasted *these*. Incredible, if I do say so myself."

"I can't thank you enough."

Tuck blushed and rolled her eyes. "As Mrs. Childers says, 'Twernt nothin'," and we both laughed.

"Listen," I said, I've got to get out and serve the *Flying Monkeys* bread and water, and do my spiel about what we have on the menu tonight. I'll put these string beans in a pot and let them simmer."

246

Tuck jumped in. "Oh, don't worry about tasting them right now—they're already salted and you've got a lot to do."

"Thanks. I'd better get going," I said, and with that she tiptoed back out the door. Just before she left she added a warning. "Whatever you do, don't tell Salinger I was here. He would *kill* me," and she wrinkled her nose in that "I'm cute as a bunny" way.

"Gotcha," I said.

I threw the beans into a pot, took out some of the pickled eggs and placed them on the nicest tray I could find, and made my way through the swinging kitchen door to the dining room where the ladies were gathered around one table. I carried a large serving tray just the way I'd seen waiters do in New York and amazed myself at how quickly I picked up the balancing feat.

"Coming through," I said, even though no one else was in sight. Frankly, I was already exhausted. I couldn't figure out how cooks did this *with* help, much less alone. I hadn't even had time to taste anything and see if the seasonings were correct—not that I really cared. As I made an appearance, they started in.

"Just when *will* we be getting the chicken liver kabobs, Mr. McCrae?" Mrs. Brandyworth bellowed, obviously having already had more than a few drinks.

"In just a moment," I said, with as much civility as I could muster. I had determined not to let them get the better of me. "We have a lovely tray of pickled eggs for you this evening as one of your side dishes, and here's the water ... and the bread ... and ... is there anything else you need right now?"

"I need the damn appetizer," Mary-Ellen snapped. "And I need a refill on this Harvey Wallbanger," she added. I noticed Mrs. Childers as she sat quietly; the only one not abusing me. She looked down at her plate, an obvious outsider to the group. "And make it snappy," Mary-Ellen added, bringing my attention away from Mrs. Childers.

I paused. Never being one for mixed drinks, I had choked when Mary-Ellen had ordered her first libation. I hadn't planned on negotiating the kitchen *and* the bar, so I had been caught even more off guard. Fortunately, the other ladies were having wine, with the exception of Mrs. Brandyworth, who was drinking straight vodka—directly from the bottle.

"When *will* we be getting the chicken liver kabobs, Mr. McCrae?" Mrs. Brandyworth repeated, even more loudly than the first time, and Mary-Ellen leaned over and put her hand on the old woman's arm.

"You already asked that, Mrs. B," she said, more gently that I would have.

"Just let me check on those appetizers and I'll freshen up your glass," I said to Mary-Ellen as I whisked it away and navigated the bar.

"Bitches," I said under my breath. "Not a damn person here to help and they're going to try and run me to death."

Then I heard Mrs. Weems's voice over the others, calling to me. "Oh, Mitah Mah-Taahy? You-hooooo!, Mitah Maaahhh-Taaaahhhy, I've pilled my mat-uh and me need tome more na-kins an a noooo tabe-uh cot."

"Spilled water, napkins, and a new table cloth. Jesus Christ," I said to myself as I wrestled with the liquor and wine bottles—a veritable Manhattan skyline of glass and colored liquids. They clanked against each other like glass slaves on a ship making a rocky voyage across the sea.

"And some more butter too," Shelby rang out.

"WHERE ARE THE DAMN APPETIZERS?" Mrs. Brandyworth bellowed.

I managed Mary-Ellen's drink and then went to the kitchen to get the butter, napkins, and new tablecloth. I checked on the kabobs and looked in on the fish. Thank God for Tuck and her homemade canned vegetables and eggs. She had really saved the day.

Finally, the tablecloth was changed, the napkins given out, the butter set on the table, and the wine glasses refilled. As I had to run back and forth so much to get the food, the women had little time to harass me but for a few barbs thrown in now and then. I managed to serve the appetizers, finally.

"They say he drinks, that Mr. McCrae," I distinctly heard Shelby say, just loud enough for my benefit, as I was reentering the kitchen. Mrs. Childers said nothing, but she shook out a "no" with her head in response to Shelby's outburst. I'm assuming it was for the last statement and not for something she was being offered, as she was not being offered anything. The ladies acted as if she didn't exist. I couldn't help but feel envious.

"He made a pass at me and I had to practically call Salinger, that's how much he frightened me," Mrs. Brandyworth was heard to say as I brought in the red snapper and set it ablaze. I found her comment ironic as she had accused me in print for having a proclivity for "unnatural" choices where lovemaking was concerned.

Once the fish was on fire and served, the ladies made mince meat of the poor thing, and finished every bit of the string beans and pickled eggs. I frankly didn't think they'd have room for dessert. Unfortunately, they did.

Back in the kitchen, I was putting together the bananas and other ingredients, adding just the right amount of liquor that would be used to set the confection on fire. As I appeared with the Bananas Foster (a dish I had enjoyed many times in New Orleans and was quite familiar with), Shelby commented how lovely the presentation looked. Then I set the dessert aflame and Mary-Ellen remarked, "My, you look as if you've done this sort of thing before!" At that point all the women roared and I felt my grip loosening on what little sanity I had left. I was trying to control my temper and had just gotten over the comment when Pedophilia & Co. slurred a criticism my way that pushed me over the edge. Mrs. Brandyworth shot her remark in my direction, all the while spewing vodka foam like a tsunami hitting a seawall: "Faggot New York writer anyway. I thought this food tasted like shit. And I never did get any appetizers."

Everything went black. I lost it. The room seemed to spin. It all piled up—my anger over the last weeks, these women with their inflated senses of self-worth, all of it. I screamed at the top of my lungs, "I HATE ALL YOU MOTHER-FUCKING BITCHES AND I WISH TO HELL YOU'D ALL DIE! I'D KILL YOU MYSELF IF I COULD!"

Suddenly there was silence. The women looked aghast. All turned in my direction and stopped cold. Mrs. Weems had her hand to her chest, and Mrs. Brandyworth's mouth was completely open. Mary-Ellen's jaw was somewhere under the table, and Shelby's lips were pressed together so tightly and her eyes bulged to such a degree that I thought she would explode. Only the reverent Mrs. Childers was silent, as she had been through the entire meal.

It was then that I felt it rather than saw it. Actually the "it" was a "him"—Salinger. Everyone in the room felt the intense energy and turned toward the door leading from the dining room to the kitchen. There stood the sheriff, arms crossed, with a scowl on his face. He had evidently come in through the back right after I had started my Bananas Foster performance and had heard the last exchange of words. The blackness was breaking up around me and my anger was quickly dissipating with his appearance. I was trying to remember exactly what I had said, and with how much sincerity it had registered, when he motioned for me to come into the kitchen, and … I did.

41

Change Player's Bits

After a scolding from Salinger over my remarks, I cleaned up the kitchen, put everything back as it originally had been, and went out to tidy up the dining room. Nothing; no one. The ladies had left with not so much as a "Thank you." And they had left a mess. I cleaned that up also and left the place the way I'd found it. Looking at Tuck's jars I thought, "To hell with it, she can get more," and threw them in the trash, then put the garbage out back. I turned off the lights and made my way outside where Salinger was waiting. He escorted me back to Henrid's and then left. It seemed to be the end of the sheriff for a while, but the next morning he was once again at Tuck's house. I could hear whispering but wasn't able to make out what he and Henrid were saying. I tried listening at the door but nothing came through. Finally, I made my way into the hallway.

"Can I get some of this?" I heard Salinger say. The comment sounded forced—the way one does when someone changes the subject and they don't want you to know they've been discussing *you*. Then I saw it: Tuck was going back and forth between the kitchen and living room and my birthday cake was in plain sight.

"That's Mr. McCrae's birthday cake," Miss Henrid scolded, all the while cutting him a piece. As Salinger took the plate and tasted the cake they both looked at me with wide eyes, as if they'd seen a ghost.

"Damn, woman, you're good!" Salinger said, addressing the cake and not its maker after he'd regained his composure.

Miss Henrid flashed a droopy wrist in my direction, wrinkled her nose, and pressed her legs together as she sat. "He says that to all the girls."

"No I don't!" he hooted. "This here is one fine woman. Best in the country. Had to go way out of town to get her, but she's worth every penny." Again, something seemed forced, as if they were putting on a show for me.

"Oh, stop. You make it sound like you paid for me." Miss Henrid was blushing and both her hands were now on her knees—one leg over the other.

"Well, I sort of did," Salinger said, mouth full, no humor in his voice.

Miss Henrid's demeanor changed, then she caught herself and pulled in the reins. "All I meant was, that you don't have to make me sound like a whore or something." She fingered the back of her hair, twirling one strand around her index finger—a common Chalybeate attribute among its female population. "Mr. McCrae here might suspect all kinds of things if you keep saying off-color remarks like that," she continued, addressing Salinger but looking right at me.

"He behave while I was away?" Salinger asked, jerking his fork at me. He was still standing and holding his plate.

"He's just been the perfect house guest."

"Then there ain't no reason to cuff him to the bed," Salinger said, scraping the icing from the plate and licking the end of the fork.

Miss Henrid tried to look demure. "Well, not unless he's into that sort of thing," and with that both she and the sheriff guffawed heavily.

I didn't.

"Oh, dear, we didn't offend you, did we?" she asked. Her arm was outstretched toward me and the hand attached to it waved up and down.

"Oh, no, no, sorry," I said, and with that her wrist went limp and she made another bunny nose—all wiggly and snuggly. "I'm so glad." Then to J.D. "I just think we're going to have the *best time* here, with him hiding out and all." Then to me. "Don't you?"

"Hmmm."

Salinger then looked at me sideways. "You feel all right?"

"Fine, why?"

"No reason," he shrugged. "Just that you looked a little peaked to me."

"No, just got up late."

He started toward the door. "Well, that making dinner last night was punishment enough. Suppose you're feeling the results of it today." Then he turned to Tuck and commented, "And you should have heard what he said to those ladies, Tuckie!"

Then he left and things calmed down in the Henrid household. I charged the battery in my laptop and sorted out my clothes. I placed the box—the one containing the only known remains of the history of Chalybeate Springs—under the bed for later viewing and readied myself in the bathroom. The day was quiet enough, the exception being that every few minutes or so Miss Henrid asked me if I was feeling all right and this sent me, more than once, straight to the bathroom mirror. Salinger called twice that day and he and Henrid whispered something which I assumed was about me. As far as I knew, everything was okay. I couldn't make out what they were saying, but a few words filtered through: new plans, cook-off—that sort of thing. I assumed they were trying to arrange my appearance at the chili cook-off tomorrow and somehow get the town to change its mind about killing me in the process.

As the day wore on, I recorded my thoughts on my laptop, and transcribed some of the latest recipes and events from the binder onto my computer. Then I recharged the batteries once more. By that time, it was nearing dinner and I would finally have the chance to be waited on, making up for the horrible evening I had endured yesterday. Below is what was on the menu—what Miss Henrid served, along with a neat little card that carried her title for it:

♦FOOD FIT FOR AN AUTHOR♦

Roast beef (main course, and nothing like Jecko's)
Potato salad (side dish)
Pickled beets (optional)
String beans (the evening's vegetable)
Chocolate cake (made especially for Mr. McCrae's birthday, though partially eaten already)

I'm actually leaving out the recipe for this as, a) you're not going to want to make it, and, b) it won't matter after you're finished reading this book and find out what happens.

The evening was perfect. The food was the best I had tasted in my entire Chalybeate Springs experience (even better than that at the Weemses' house, with the husband playing butler), and the presentation was perfect. Miss Henrid was an excellent hostess, conversationalist, and just plain good company. In fact, she was the one bright spot in my stay in a town that now hated my very insides. We finished the chocolate cake (second go-round) with fresh coffee, real cream, and an after-dinner mint. If anyone in the town deserved to be in the Junior League, it was Miss Henrid. She was a model-perfect woman for each and every feminine thing she attempted.

Being a good Southerner at heart, and wanting to show my gratitude, I offered to clean up. She, of course, refused. As the game is played in the South, I again insisted. She refused. I insisted. She refused. I insisted. And finally, pulling rank with "I've got a taste of bad

Yankee manners comin' on and I'm cleaning your damn kitchen, woman, now sit down!" I managed to win out. And I really wanted to, so impressed was I by her homemaking abilities and professionalism. But this is where the trouble started.

I scraped the plates into the garbage and stacked them in the sink, preparing for the by-hand wash/dry cycle. Miss Henrid was over me, insisting that she at least help. She seemed almost paranoid about my presence in her kitchen. I had to laugh to myself, thinking how protective she was being of her domestic duties. Maybe that was why she wasn't worried about Delilah cleaning that area or the bathroom.

Finally, I managed to get her out of my way by promising that I would call if I needed any help and not just rummage through her cupboards looking for whatever I wanted—that I would allow her to show me where things were. She agreed, half-heartedly, and I continued to clean up.

"I'm not hearing another word about this," I said, rinsing the plates on one side of the double sink and filling the other side with dishwashing liquid in preparation for the good scrubbing I was about to give them (she didn't have a dishwasher—at least not one other than me).

"You just promise that if you need anything, that you'll call me. On second thought, why don't I stay here and ..."

"No," I said firmly, pushing her out of the door with my yellow rubber gloves on, doing my best Delilah impersonation. "I'm not having the prettiest woman in Chalybeate make me the best dinner I've had in ten years, and then not let me clean up." I fully understood her over protectiveness with her house. It wasn't a large house, but it was immaculate and her cooking was superb.

"Really, this is the least I can do. Please, I insist on it. I want to show my appreciation for what you've done. And staying here with you will be a joy. You won't have to worry about me running away," I tried to joke, "not after a meal like that!"

"Well," she said, glancing nervously at the cabinets and then the floor, "if you're absolutely certain. Just remember, call me if you need anything so I can help you find it."

"I promise," I said, once again pressing her into the dining room and then the living room. "Now you just sit down and read a magazine or something and I'll be done in a minute."

"Well, okay, if you're really sure," she nervously answered, and seated herself on the sofa. I went back into the kitchen and began the cleanup. I could hear her in the living room, spasmodically flipping through a magazine, page after page, not really reading anything. Why was she such a mess about someone else being in her kitchen? And especially if she wanted to be in the Junior League so badly and I was her key, shouldn't she have been doing a bit more in the cooperation department? I wrote it off as her fear I'd escape out the kitchen door and over-zealousness at wanting to play hostess, and continued my scrubbing of the china. Perhaps that was it: she thought I might break something. I walked to the door, gloves upturned as if I were about to perform surgery, slightly dripping, and called to her.

Seeing me, she jumped to her feet. "Oh, you need ..."

"No, no, I don't need anything. Will you calm down? I just wanted to assure you that I wasn't going to break anything. I figured out that was what you were worried about."

She sat back down. "Oh, that. No, that's okay. I trust you." She opened a small silver box on the coffee table and took out a cigarette, lighting it and inhaling deeply. Still standing in the doorway, dripping, I commented: "I didn't know you smoked."

"Don't very much. You want one?"

"No thanks."

"Just sometimes," she said, still nervous. She tried to laugh. " 'Fraid J.D. might come in and think we're being too domestic," she said and blew a long column of smoke toward the fireplace. She was now sitting, one leg was crossed over the other, and the foot attached to said leg was flailing up and down to beat the band. I tried to assure her again from where I was standing.

"Really, everything is going to be fine. You just sit there and smoke and I'll clean up in two seconds."

She didn't respond but nodded at the coffee table and then played at fixing the back of her hair with her free hand. I resumed my duties in the kitchen, making my way through the silverware, dishes, and crystal she had used for that evening's feast. I positioned the cleaned items on the draining board and was looking around for some fresh towels to dry the silverware with, but none were in sight.

"No," I said to myself, "I will not ask. I'm here to clean up. I'm a man. I'm self-sufficient. I know my way around a kitchen. She's cooked this lovely dinner for me, and I'm perfectly capable."

I reached for one of the eighty-year-old cabinets and it silently came open—the closing mechanisms completely worn out from years of use. I imagined the previous owners and all the meals that had been prepared in this kitchen, then the delicious ones that Miss Henrid had made for Salinger. No wonder the man was putting on weight.

Opening one of the upper cabinets I found no towels, but there was an array of prescription bottles. Now, I'm not one to snoop, but there were quite a few, and Miss Henrid looked healthy. I thought they might be Salinger's or maybe Henrid was ill and that was why she was in such a hurry to get into the Junior League. And I was, after all, brought here under less than honest pretenses, so I really didn't feel it was much of an intrusion to look at one of the labels. Besides, the bottle was turned just so, so that I could read part of the name. "Prema ...something" the label read. Strange, Miss Henrid looked about thirty-five or a little older—and healthy enough. But then, this really wasn't any of my business. I closed the cabinet ... and she heard it.

"What do you need? What are you looking for?" she asked, and came running to the kitchen.

"Look, I don't need anything. If you have some clean towels, that would be great."

"Okay," she said, opening a drawer (where I would never have thought to look), and procured for me several lovely hand towels (fruit, bee, and butterfly motifs; also assorted yellow-and-white checks, and even one with bananas on it—the kitchen was a sunny yellow). "You just promise you'll call if you need any help."

"I promise," I said, lying through my teeth, and ushered her back into the living room. My curiosity had been piqued. What was it she didn't want me to find? Ordinarily I would have let the thing drop, but with discovering the many personality delights that the ladies of the Junior League owned, I wasn't about to let *this* go. Plus, everyone in the town had enough skeletons in their closets to supply every medical center in the Western hemisphere, and still have a few left over for Halloween.

When I was sure Miss Henrid was out of hearing range, I started the water in the sink, full force. It gushed noisily downward and I put a glass underneath, just for extra sound distraction. Then I opened the cabinet with the prescriptions and took one out. "Premarin 1.25 mg twice a day," it read. I had no idea what it meant and was about to give up, when it came to mind to look at the cabinets underneath the counter directly to my left. I don't know why—perhaps it was some intuitive element, or maybe it was because she had glanced in that direction nervously while trying so hard to get me out of domestic ground zero. For whatever reason, I bent down and eased open the door.

Nothing too interesting there. Pots, pans. An electric skillet with the Teflon almost all gone. Two pieces of a canister set. Totally boring and just what you'd expect. I eased the door closed and opened another one. At first I wasn't sure why the difference in items was so great. "This must be, what is lovingly known in many homes— especially the kitchen—as the *junk* place," I said to myself. You know—everyone has a space such as this: a drawer or a cabinet where useless things go to die.

Waffle irons, old phone books, rubber bands, and even a spoon rest in the shape of a rocket ship filled this particular cabinet. A plaster-of-Paris spoon and fork (big enough for the Jolly Green Giant—avocado green with "antique" finishing) huddled to one side. The contents consisted mostly of things that were waiting for the garbage dump or next yard sale. That is, with the exception of two medium-sized jars in the very back.

"Strange," I thought, as I eased my hand through the land of dead objects, careful not to make any noise. "Why would there be two jars of food items this far back, and in this type of environment?" I looked up to make sure the sink wasn't running over and listened for Miss Henrid's footsteps. Nothing. I was safe.

I grabbed one jar and gently brought it out. "What the ...?" I thought, as I set it on the counter. Perhaps the other jar would yield a better clue—you know, fill in the blank of the first one. I eased my hand back in and brought *that* one into view, setting it next to its companion. Interesting, but why would something like this be in a kitchen cabinet, underneath, back with all this throw-away junk? And what *were* they? They looked almost identical, though one was slightly bigger than the other. I looked at the first jar. It appeared to house an over-grown Vienna sausage or some type or an organ from an animal. A pig, perhaps? The second was so similar that it only further confused me. Its only real difference was that it had some sort of discoloration— a dark stain of sorts, shaped like the country of Thailand, only upside down. (Oh, get the Atlas out—it'll be fun.) So why not put them in the same jar?

While the containers were sealed, opening one wasn't much of a feat. The second after I did this, I regretted it—Formaldehyde, and boy, did it smell. This looked like something I'd seen swimming around in an aquarium in Chinatown in New York. I replaced the lid and peered harder into the jar. It looked almost like a ... oh, God ... no ... it couldn't be. I was recoiling from the jars when I heard a rustling in the other room. Miss Henrid was coming, and if these were what I now suspected them to be, I surely didn't want to get caught.

But it was too late. I had my hand on the first jar, trying to remain calm, realizing what it was, when she suddenly entered the kitchen and let out the loudest scream known to mankind. I immediately dropped the jar I was holding and the formaldehyde splattered everything. The object that had been inside lay forlorn on the floor.

Both Miss Henrid and I were now in a panic, breathing heavily. Then she screamed again ... at me: "I TOLD YOU NOT TO GO THROUGH MY CABINETS! TO CALL ME IF YOU NEEDED ANYTHING!"

I felt, at that moment, like a butterfly pinned to the wall (perhaps it had something to do with the smell of formaldehyde).

"I'm sooorr ... rryyy ..." I stammered. "I jus ..."

Miss Henrid was hysterical, her eyes bulging, and I was hyperventilating. I knew now what the objects were. Then she saw the other jar and she let out a sigh that sounded like a tractor tire being punctured. She put her face in her hands and began to make inhumane sounds.

"I'm really sorry. I'm sorry. I'm soooo sorry," I said, and made an attempt to move toward the pickled object on the floor.

"No! Don't touch it! Let me get it ... in a moment ..." she said, breathing hard. "I was afraid of this. Damnit! That Salinger bringing you here." Her mood was going from hysterical to angry. It was a *most* uncomfortable situation.

Finally, we both tried to calm down and take deep breaths. She was still standing in the doorway, and there I was, with my back to the kitchen sink. The water was still running so I reached around and turned it off. The silence was deafening.

"Miss Henrid, I found those," I said, gesturing toward both the jar that was extant and the one that was smashed on the floor along with the pickled object inside.

"Obviously," she seethed. I felt like a five-year-old who'd been caught with his hand in the cookie jar.

"Is that what ..." I started to say.

"Yes. Yes, Mr. McCrae. That is ..."

" ...what I think it is?" I said, trepidation coming over every fiber of my being.

She waited and caught her breath. "Yes, Mr. McCrae, that," and she pointed to the five-inch-long object on the floor, amid the smashed glass and formaldehyde, "that is a penis."

I stood there in shock. It was all becoming clear now—the prescriptions in the cabinet, the size of her feet and hands, the "something I couldn't put my finger on." Then I remembered the way she had looked at her hands.

I waited for what seemed like a full two minutes. It actually felt like a lifetime. I looked at the penis on the floor, then at the one in the jar. I had to ask. After all, I'd come this far.

"But whose is it?" I questioned, my windows to the soul wide with horror.

She rolled her eyes, put one hand on a hip, and shook her head. "Whose do you think?" She asked, looking me straight in the face.

"I ... I don't ..."

"It's mine, Mr. McCrae," she said bending down to pick up the poor limp organ. "It's *my* penis ... okay?"

42

Grab Penis Chastely

"Miss Henrid ... Miss Henrid?" I began. "I don't want to be any more nosy than necessary." I waited, unsure. "Do you mean "*My* penis" as in "I got it at a garage sale kind of thing," or "*My* penis" as in "I had it cut off and saved it in a jar?""

"The latter," she said.

I had to let this sink in. I had suspected something was "off" with regard to the lady of the house, but this was *way off.* The town's most feminine woman, the only one with any taste, and the only really fine cook was a ... man, not a woman.

"Does Salinger know?" I asked.

Miss Henrid (we'll keep the name to ward off that pesky condition known as "confusion," not that you weren't being afflicted by it already) responded: "Of course he knows. He went up there with me to New York to have it done. The operation. On me, not him." She was now cradling her/his penis gently in one hand, searching through the cabinets for another jar. "I'll have to get some more formaldehyde for it." Then she put a finger of her free hand to her lips. "Or maybe I could just put it in this other jar, with the other one." She waited, giving the idea some thought. "No, that would just be sick."

"Nothing like priorities at a time like this," I said, still in shock. Then it hit me—the other shoe that was to drop, or penis, if you will, or not—drop. I don't know.

"But, if that's *your* penis," and I nodded to the object she was still holding in her red finger-nailed hand, "then who does *this* belong to?" and I pointed to the smaller version that was floating quite peacefully in the jar on the counter. "Why the *Two Gentlemen of Bologna?*"

"That's a long story."

I looked at the penis—the second one—actually bent down to stare at it through the glass. "I don't think it's that long."

"The story, not the penis," she said. "It's too long a story to tell. It gets complicated."

"I'll bet."

Finally she found another jar and relegated her guillotined member to it, sans formaldehyde. "This will have to do for now."

"I don't want to pry, but ..."

"Really, Mr. McCrae, why stop now?"

"I'm sorry," I said.

"I told you not to go through anything. And now this. You've ruined it all."

"All I'm asking is, if that is your penis," and I once again gestured to the new jar that was keeping her former male organ, "then please tell me you didn't have two of them removed."

"Okay. Fine. The second one belongs to Harry Killchrist."

"Who?"

"Mary-Ellen's brother. That twit who tricked Salinger into taking her to the prom when they were in high school—her brother."

"Mary-Ellen, the one who screwed Shelby out of the date with Salinger? That penis belongs to her brother? Don't you think he might miss it?"

"Pieces beginning to fit now?" she asked, turning her jar from side-to-side as if it were a flower arrangement and she was looking for the best angle. Miss Henrid was, if nothing else, the consummate homemaker. "Poor thing," she continued, "looks so sad just slumped like that."

I tried to steer the conversation—if you could actually call what we were having intellectual intercourse, seeing that she was now incapable of ... oh, I'm not even going to finish the thought—back to the additional penis. Finding one in a jar is bad enough (just my opinion here, don't quote me on that), but two—really, that's a bit much.

I peered at the second organ again—Harry Killchrist's penis with a birthmark shaped like Thailand. That was the discoloration on Harry's member, and where he would have urinated was longitude and latitude Singapore. I ruminated on the mark and its positioning. If you were the owner then it was Thailand going the *wrong* way. It all depended on whether you .were the proprietor of the penis (an unfortunate thing now), or simply viewing it as I was, museum style.

"So Salinger cut off Harry Killchrist's penis because Mary-Ellen tricked him back in high school?"

"No, silly. That would just be stupid."

I wanted to say, "Like having a pair of penises in your kitchen is not?" but held back. Besides, what, exactly is the plural of penis, and how many times would you ever need to use it outside of an all-male orgy?

Miss Henrid continued. I was most grateful. "Salinger caught Harry making moonshine more than a year ago, two years ago; I don't know. I can't remember now."

"I know that story," I said. "Or at least I thought I did. Wasn't it one of the Childers clan who shot at Salinger?"

"No," she said. "None of the Childers were involved. We just wanted everyone to think that. Harry shot at Salinger but missed."

"Okay. Wait. So, does Mary-Ellen know that Salinger cut her brother's penis off?"

"I'm guessing, 'No' on that one. She also doesn't know that Salinger … well …" but she stopped.

"Salinger what?" I asked.

Henrid paused. "Perhaps we'd better sit down and discuss this. It's not a simple story. Would you like some coffee?" I thought about her handling her … his own penis that had been pickled for God-only-knows-how-long, and declined. I shook my head "No."

"Fair enough," she said, and sighed. "Let's go into the living room and I'll tell you what happened. Might as well now as you know this much," and with that I followed her out of the kitchen.

"You see," she began, before we had even sat down, "Killchrist …"

"Harry."

"Shot at Salinger but hit his deputy, Dick Hunter."

My mind was spinning. If only the man were here now, with his ironic name, he would fit in perfectly. The only thing more bizarre would have been finding out that I had amnesia and that *I* was indeed Dick Hunter—then the whole kitchen scene, myself included, could be smacked with a rubber "Therapy" stamp.

She went on: "Harry shot Hunter twice. Once in the face and once below."

It was my turn. "Okay, that much makes sense and coincides with what … I don't know … read … go on."

"Read? Where?"

"In an old *Chalybeate Springs Times*," I said. "But it didn't say who the shooter was."

"Oh, right."

"Go on. The story," I said.

"So Harry misses and shoots Dick Hunter. Salinger shoots Harry. Salinger is left unharmed, but Harry is not. Salinger killed him—Killchrist. It was strictly self-defense and no jury would have ever convicted him.

261

"But wait a minute. I heard that Harry was never found. That was why Mary-Ellen was so mad at Salinger," I said, trying to make sense of the whole drama.

"Oh, he was found all right," Henrid continued. "He was quite *found.*"

It was all beginning to make sense now, or so I thought.

"So it's Harry Killchrist that's in the grave of Dick Hunter," I said, deducing that the reason Salinger went to that spot each day and cursed that pink marker was because he had been forced to dispose of the body.

"Well," Henrid responded, "not exactly."

"What do you mean?"

"Charles Adams is in the grave of Dick Hunter. He was Salinger's first deputy."

I squirmed in my seat for myriad reasons, most of which you can probably figure out.

"Wait a minute. Let me see if I can follow this. First, Salinger shoots and kills Harry Killchrist."

"Right."

"Then Charles Adams is put in Dick Hunter's grave."

"Right."

"But this doesn't make sense. I thought all of Shelby's husbands, including Charles Adams, were cremated."

"They were supposed to be," Henrid said, "but Salinger needed a body to go in Dick Hunter's grave."

"Then why didn't he use Harry Killchrist?"

"That, I can't tell you, just now," she said.

"Can't, or won't?" I sat in stunned silence. Then it began to make a bit more sense. I had to ask. "Why wasn't Dick Hunter in Dick Hunter's grave?"

She looked at me with a completely blank face. If we had been playing poker, I would have lost.

"Because, Mr. Jackson McCrae, I *am* Dick Hunter," she said. My jaw hit the floor, went through the foundation of the house, entered into the land of molten lava, came back up through the earth, and may presently be found somewhere in the outermost recesses of China. (I imagined impoverished field workers coming home from a hard day of planting rice, san-pan hats wobbling, yokes across their shoulders, shouting in amazement as an American jaw jutted up from the rice paddies.)

262

Miss Henrid, it seemed, was not only the perfect June Cleaver with pearl strands, cake-baking skills, and a demeanor that was equal to America's most famous housewife—though no Ward, Wally, or even Eddie Haskell was in sight—but she actually had the beaver now to prove it.

43

Psyche Baring Tales

Just when you think things are beginning to make sense in life, something comes along and slaps you upside the head. And it was doing that to me right at this minute.

"But Dick Hunter died and he's buried ..." I started to say. Then I hit the rewind button. "Ooooohhhhhhhh, I get it."

"Right."

"I think."

"Right." Miss Henrid brought out another cigarette from the silver box and lit it. I couldn't blame her; I wouldn't have minded having one myself except that I didn't smoke. I tried taking deep breaths in the hope of getting some good old-fashioned second-hand cancer fumes. It wasn't working that well.

"Would you like one?" she asked, holding the box in my direction.

"No. No, thanks. I'm trying to quit. Or start. I don't know." I looked around. "I'm confused."

She exhaled a long column of smoke, this one pointed straight toward an oil portrait over the mantel. I looked up at it and she followed my gaze.

"Colonel Bismirch Hunter," she said, flicking her ashes into a tasteful receptacle designed for that purpose.

"His parents actually named him 'Bismirch?' "I asked.

"Sad, isn't it?"

"Truly. But I'm still trying to figure out this game of grave swapping." It was like one of those little puzzles where you have to move a bunch of squares around and get them into a particular order—get them to make sense—only I was never good at them, and I certainly didn't feel good at this one.

"Let's recap, shall we?" she said. "Harry shot at Salinger, and hit me, Dick Hunter. I got shot in the face and crotch. Salinger shot Harry and killed him. Salinger used Charles Adams's body in the place of mine at the closed casket funeral. With me so far?"

"Hmm. Go on."

"Charles Adams is buried in the grave marked 'Dick Hunter,' and I went to New York to have plastic surgery and a sex-change operation." She paused for another lengthy and dramatic draw on the cigarette. "You see, Mr. McCrae, I knew you would have an appreciation for my story after I read your first book."

"Well, it's certainly right up my line."

"Indeed."

"But why the elaborate ruse—the sex-change, the plastic surgery, the New York trip? Why didn't you just admit to being injured and to the fact that Salinger's shooting of Harry was in self-defense?"

"This is where things get a bit tricky," she said, and stubbed out the cigarette. She sat back and crossed her arms, looking up at the ceiling. "You may or may not have heard stories about me and Salinger; stories about us in high school. That buddy-buddy routine."

"I did hear something about a sort of *Cat on a Hot Tin Roof* kind of Brick-and-Skipper ..."

"Exactly." She took another cigarette from the case and lit it. "Sure you don't want one?"

"No, please go on."

"So, where was I? Oh, yes. Salinger and I were, how shall I say, close in high school. I was the quarterback for the high school team. Quarterbacks are smaller than the other players and I always had a slight build for a man. But Salinger and I hit it off and went drinking and carousing together, just as any red-blooded American male football players do."

"So, what went wrong?"

"Well, I wouldn't actually say anything went *wrong*, but we did get extremely drunk one night and pulled one of those '*Boy I don't remember a thing about what happened and I hope you don't either*' excuses that are so prevalent among experimentation in male youth."

"You guys had sex."

"If you insist on being so blunt, yes."

"Boy," I thought, "I just found two penises in your kitchen and you're worried about me putting a name on the dirty deed you and the star linebacker did back in high school?" As is rarely the case, I didn't say what I was thinking.

Miss Henrid continued to verbalize the rest of her story. "So there we were, acting as if nothing had happened. For a long time. Then Salinger's father—you may know about him—forced J.D. to marry that Slattery girl. He'd heard the rumors and was furious."

"I heard something about that."

"A disaster," she said, flicking her ashes dramatically into the small tray. "A lot of people don't know this, but some do ..." she trailed off somewhat, looking out the window.

"The baby," I said.

Her head turned to me and her eyes focused. "You know about that?"

"Well, I've heard all kinds of things. You've got to admit, this town is pretty small."

"What, exactly, did you hear?" she asked sucking on the end of the white cylinder that she so deftly held between two of her perfectly manicured fingers.

"That it was born with four legs and two heads."

"And no arms," she added, quite matter-of-factly. She waited, then continued. "Poor J.D. was so upset over that, he tried to commit suicide. You have no idea how horrible it was for him."

"I can imagine."

"No. No, Mr. McCrae, you can't." She leaned forward, putting her knees together and holding the cigarette over the small ashtray. She looked me straight in the eye. "The baby lived for six months and he took care of it. That's the kind of person he is ... or was."

"What do you mean *was?*"

"Things like that change a man, Mr. McCrae."

"Jackson, call me Jackson," I said, thinking that, with all the information that was being volleyed back and forth between us, we certainly could be on more intimate terms. After all, I had seen her penis.

"Very well ... Jackson. As I was saying, things like that will change a man, even a man with as strong a constitution as Salinger's. His wife was dead, thank God, but he was left to care for that child. You don't go through something like that and not come out the other end a different person."

"Okay, that brings me up to his bad marriage and the baby. He changed. This is not something I haven't already heard," I said, "or figured out."

"I'm just filling you in on everything. I don't want you to judge the man too harshly before this is all over."

Something in me wanted to ask "Before *what's* all over?" but I put myself in denial and hoped she meant the cookbook and her entry into the Junior League. Then I thought about it—how badly most of the women in the League had treated me. What a wonderful trick to play on them; getting a transsexual into their club with them not even knowing that the person used to be the star quarterback for the town's high school football team. I was more in sympathy now with Henrid than she imagined and wanted to be a part of this intricate and clever

266

plot of hers to get back at the town. She continued with Salinger's saga as it was also a part of her own.

"So, you would have thought that the town would have rallied around a man who had the guts to take care of a child that horrible, and especially one that had lived. You know as well as I do that he could just as easily have killed the infant at birth, but he wasn't that way. He believed that it was God's will and that he needed to do the right thing—that was what he was like at that time, deeply religious. That's why it crushed him that the church denied him membership. They said it was over some away-game drinking that happened, but I was here then and I *know* the Brandyworths—they're mean people. Look what they did to those kids. Then there was the guilt factor that played on his mind—about what we'd done together and the way we felt about each other."

"So the town didn't stand behind his decision to try and keep the child?"

"Stand by him? My God, no. They persecuted him. They believed God was punishing him because of what his father had done."

"Yes," I said, "I've heard the stories, the ones about his father's promiscuity."

"Well, they're true, all of them. His daddy *did* have sex with just about everyone in the county and now no one knows who their real father is, or whether or not they're related to the Salingers."

"What about DNA testing?" I asked.

"Mr. McCrae, how long have you been here?"

She did have a point. The place didn't even have a cell phone—where were they going to get DNA testing, or even hear of it?

It made sense. Salinger could never marry and have children with anyone in the town for fear of what might happen; fear that the horrible incident that had taken place so many years ago with the Slattery girl might repeat itself. And he had experienced how the town had treated him because of his father's actions and his own decision to try and keep the child alive. His hate had festered all these years and he was going to get even with the town no matter what. It was only a matter of time, and the elaborate ruse to marry his old high school buddy and have her enter the Junior League with the town's most prominent and influential women would be the ultimate slap in the face. I had to wonder if and/or when Mr. and Mrs. Salinger would make the truth known.

"So what happened to bring about this sex-change … and the extra penis in the kitchen?" I asked, eager for information but not sure

267

I really wanted to know—that whole "bad accident on the highway" kind of thing.

"When I got shot, when we were making the raid on the Killchrist still, Salinger killed Harry right then and there. I was in pretty bad shape and we didn't have a doctor in the town—still don't. I wasn't going to die, but I did need immediate attention. Salinger rushed me over to the next county, to a doctor nobody knew. Since he …"

"Salinger?"

"…yes, was a sheriff, the doctor didn't question anything except the fact that we were from another county—right over the line. Salinger gave him some story about chasing a fugitive and getting shot at and not realizing we had crossed the line; something like that. The doctor bought it and fixed me up so that I wasn't going to bleed to death."

So that explained the new backseat in Salinger's patrol car—the one that didn't match the rest of the vehicle. That must have been the reason for it being replaced—all the blood from the accident. "But you must have been a mess," I said.

"Mr. McCrae … Jackson … mess doesn't begin to describe it. Salinger had to hide me, and the logical place seemed to be that old plantation my parents had."

"I've seen it," I said.

"Since they'd been dead for six months and I'd moved out long ago, the house was just sitting there empty. I stayed there until Salinger could sneak me out and drive me over to Atlanta where I got on a plane with most of the money my parents' had left me, and headed to New York."

"But why would Salinger cut off Harry Killchrist's penis? That still doesn't make sense."

"Mine was shot off and Salinger didn't know if it could be sewn back on."

"Nothing like thinking fast on your feet," I said. But I waited. "No. You're telling me that Salinger thought that if yours wasn't in good enough shape, that a doctor could use Harry Killchrist's penis in its place?"

"You and I know that you can't do that kind of transplant, but J.D. didn't, at that moment, and he panicked."

"But why keep it? In a jar, I mean? In the kitchen?"

She waited a moment and then spoke. "Well, I kept mine because, it was … mine. His was kept on a whim. We meant to get rid of it—bury it—something. It just never happened."

"Wouldn't that be a top priority—you know, getting rid of an extra penis that doesn't belong to you? Especially one that was just hanging, if you'll pardon the expression, 'out' in your kitchen?"

"No, the top priority was getting a sex-change, getting my face fixed, and getting into the Junior League. A girl does have her most immediate needs. I hadn't given it that much thought until you came to stay. Delilah never goes into the kitchen and no one in town visits. It just wasn't an immediate concern. And it hasn't been that long since the events happened."

"I see," I said, even though I didn't. "And the reason Salinger curses Charles Adams, who is really in your grave, is because ..." and I left a space for her to fill in.

"Because Salinger hated him for running off with Shelby and getting himself killed, thereby putting me next in line. If Adams hadn't messed with Shelby, it would have been *his* privates that got shot off by Harry Killchrist."

At least some of this was making sense: Salinger had put Charles Adams's body in the grave because if Harry's had been found, penis-less, it might have raised some questions. But Henrid said Killchrist's body *had* been found. Where was it then?

I had to wonder at the story; why she was telling me all this. I asked: "Miss Henrid, I really appreciate you filling me in on your history and all (I lied again—it was becoming a habit), but aren't you *afraid* of telling me? Afraid that I'd tell someone else? The town? The authorities in the next county?"

She smiled impishly and tilted her head. Then her tone changed from matter-of-fact to coy Southern belle. "Why, Jackson Tippett, you old sly dog. Now you don't actually think anyone is going to believe you if you tell them, now do you?" Then she changed again, to a more straightforward mode. "Besides, you're a prisoner in my home, Salinger is the only law enforcement within fifty miles, and you have no way out of this town."

She made a very good point. An uncomfortable one, but a very good one nevertheless.

44

Blatancy Pegs Heirs

One generation away from White Trash will get you perfectly coiffed hair, a suburban home (comfortable and a bit beyond your means), a steady income, one copy of a book on manners (spelling out which fork goes where), and an almost insane and palpable urge to erase and/or provide a disclaimer for each and every relative that came before.

The next generation will burgeon, fecund with college drop-outs, teenagers who want to grow up to actually have a low-paying job, and a desire to dress with such a disregard for the latest styles and hygiene that it is possible to mistake them for, well, White Trash.

The generation directly following this one—the grandchildren of the original I'm-Not-From-The-Land-Of-Want, will dig into their family history, become horrified at their parent's lack of family tree knowledge (or denial), and do everything they can to repair the damage, once again covering their tracks so that no one will know they came from people who took a bath once a year (whether they needed it or not) and thought marrying your sister was a safe bet so as not to introduce foreign blood into the family line.

And this brings us to Miss Henrid, whose tale, though somewhat similar, is far more twisted and curvaceous than any country road—the design constructed so as to confuse the traveler and lead him in the direction directly away from his desired goal. In short, Miss Henrid was a product of her environment and a family history that stretched back for over a hundred years.

It was all making sense now (in a Chalybeate Springs kind of way), and the signs had been there all along: the Colt .45-shaped cookies, the fact that she actually owned a real gun, the history with Salinger, her desire to manipulate each and every citizen in town because of what they had done to the man she loved (first as a good friend, then as more), the fact that her relationship with Salinger had to be hidden and the only way they could live together in such a small and judgmental place was as a real (all terms are relative here) husband and wife—albeit ones without any children of their own. But then, given Salinger's father's history, the town probably would have cheered the couple's option not to reproduce, fitting in perfectly with the "I have a vagina but not the rest" factor as it related to Miss H.

And the fact that Lady Mac-Peter-Gone had tried to reclaim the old plantation on the outskirts of town now made perfect sense. It was where she … *he* had grown up—it was the Hunter family home. Like thunder inside my head, what I've just related to you rumbled on as Henrid excused herself and went to the kitchen. I could hear her whispering on the phone, and while curious, couldn't imagine that she was imparting any information that I didn't already know. Then she glided back into the room and sat down across from me. She could see the wheels turning in my head, and she seemed changed since the phone call. I tried to rationalize that being afraid of her was not an unnatural reaction and continued the dialogue in an attempt to keep a line of communication going—just in case things got even more bizarre.

"So, you went to New York, had the plastic surgery, the sex-change, and now you're taking hormones. You've tricked the town …"

"But not been accepted yet," she butted in.

"But not been accepted yet. Right. Okay. And I'm assuming (God, I hate that word—especially now) that you named yourself Tuck because you really were born in Tuckahoe, New York, while your parents were away."

"Now, what do you think?" She started to turn cynical with a dash of mean underlying the whole façade.

"I don't know."

"As I said before, I read your first book. I know how you work." She was becoming downright hostile now. I knew women could have more mood swings than men, so I figured that her regime of meds was causing the reaction. Plus, I hadn't been around her before as much as I was now. And I *didn't* understand. What was she talking about, "I know how you work?"

"Anagrams?" she said.

"Huh?"

"Mr. McCrae, Tuck Henrid is an anagram for Dick Hunter."

I sank several feet down emotionally. How embarrassing. I, who was so into this sort of thing, had never put the two names together. But then, how could I have known? I quickly did the alphabet rumba in my head and confirmed she was indeed correct. "Dick Hunter … Tuck Henrid. And all along I just thought you were related to the actor."

"Well, he spelled it differently. *Henreid*, I think, with an extra "e." As I told you when you first came here, I tried to get a movie night going but nothing happened. I do actually like the actor Paul Henreid and I'm a bit of a movie buff, as I know you are, so it all fit, somewhat. Nothing's perfect, I guess. And the epitaph on Dick Hunter's—*my*—gravestone, the one Charles G. Adams is actually buried under, is an anagram."

I pulled a blank look.

"Caged Marshals."

"Right. I remember," I said.

"An anagram for Charles G. Adams. You see, his name really *is* on the stone, just, well, sort of rearranged. Nice touch, don't you agree?"

"Amazing."

"Not really," she said, "when you think about it. And 'Caged Marshals' seems to be about the gist of Salinger and myself—at least for the moment. But you've probably figured that out because of what you've done plot-wise in some of your books."

"I don't quite get your inference."

"Well, come on, your books are pretty 'outside' if you know what I mean."

"No," I said, emphatically. "I don't know." She was just plain snotty now and it was becoming irritating.

"The first one, then those short stories in the second? And the third," she said. "You've got to admit, there's some edgy material in there. You always have your characters do some pretty weird things."

"Listen, there's some edgy material right here in this town," I responded.

"You've got that right. Which is why I wanted you here," she snapped.

"Yeah," I said, "I've been meaning to talk to you about that. You want to get into *The League*," and at this point I held out my hand making that stop-sign-gesture, "and you're secret's safe with me, especially after that little discovery ..."

"It's not that little," she interrupted.

". . . in the kitchen, but what I don't understand is how I'm suppose to accomplish this. I mean, these women hate me right now. Nothing I could say would get them to accept you. And from what I've heard, they don't like Salinger much, either. So how do you plan ..."

"Jackson. Dear, sweet Jackson. If you would only think about it. First, Mrs. Weems is forced to give up her role as President because she's thought to be hiding the banana with that African-American man."

"And you know that all she's doing is trying to teach him how to speak," I said.

"And you know that I know how much you like irony."

"Go on," I said.

"And then Brandyworth became President, and her reputation was shot to hell over that child prostitution ring."

I looked at Miss Henrid for a moment. "You wouldn't by any chance have helped that story along?"

"I most certainly did," she said, and seemed quite pleased. "And it was one hundred percent true. So there." The cigarette she was now smoking was held aloft by one hand which rested upon one slender arm whose elbow rested in the cup of the other hand. She continued: "Then Mary-Ellen got the post and screwed it up, but what do you expect, sleeping with a fifteen-year-old boy? That left Shelby, who had it for a week, which is longer than most of her marriages."

"She doesn't still have it?"

"Heavens no! They voted her out last night," Henrid said. "Mrs. Childers, God bless her soul, is next in line and wouldn't be given the job if she were the last White Trash Cleaning Lady on earth."

"You planned this whole thing out," I said.

"Every bit."

"So them tearing each other to pieces ... you knew that would happen? To this extent?"

She snorted. "Well, look at them! You've met them. They're all crazy!"

She did have a point, or a "purnt" as Salinger would have said.

"So, let me get this straight; your plan is that they'll be so starved for some new blood that you'll get in?"

Henrid hesitated. I didn't like it—the hesitation. Something about that particular delay made me very uncomfortable. "You're not answering my question," I said. "You think they're just going to accept you now? Won't you have to do something first—get them to notice you? Like you? Invite you in?"

She looked up at the ceiling and clicked one red nail against the other. "Not really," she responded, rather dreamily.

"What exactly do you mean, 'Not really?' " I asked, getting more concerned by the minute. But at that moment the silence was broken by the noise of car wheels on the pavement outside. As I said before, I had come to know the sound: Salinger's car. But something was unusual. The car sped up to the house with unusual velocity and force. Then, no Salinger. He was inside the vehicle, doing something—

I had no idea what. Miss Henrid sat calmly on the sofa, not interested in getting up to greet him. Something was going on. Something I didn't like.

After a few moments, the sheriff got out of the police car and walked slowly to the front door. He didn't bother to ring, and, since the door was open, walked right in. He looked at Miss Henrid, then at me, then back at her. She continued to coolly sit back and smoke. Too coolly for my satisfaction.

" 'Fraid I have some bad news, he said. Some *really* bad news."

We both waited: me on pins and needles and Miss Henrid with no emotion at all. Salinger continued even though neither of us said anything.

"Got a call a few minutes ago from Old Doc Patterson over in Swillville—only doctor within fifty miles."

Henrid looked at me between puffs on her cigarette, then spoke: "A hundred and one if he's a day. Can't hear. Stone deaf. Shakes like a leaf. I give him two weeks, tops, to live."

Salinger looked at her. "Well, you're right about that, but he was here all last night and this morning."

"Why," I asked. "What's the matter? Who's sick."

"Mr. McCrae, it's not who's sick … it's who's dead."

"Dead? Who? What now?" I asked, sitting straight up. I looked at Miss Henrid and she was quite composed, still smoking.

"Would anyone like some tea?" she asked, as if she had just received news that her pet poodle would need to be clipped tomorrow (she didn't have a pet poodle—I checked).

"Who's dead?" I asked.

"Here's the bad part," Salinger continued. "It's more than one."

Henrid spoke up. "Why, my dear J.D., do *not* keep us in suspense any longer, you must tell us who it is … who *they* are." She was cheerful, almost ecstatic. Salinger looked worried and *quite* upset.

"Seems that Weems, Brandyworth, Childers, Killchrist, and Shelby D.E.A. …"

"We got it J.D., do go on …" Henrid interrupted.

" … are all dead. Patterson says food poisoning."

"That's silly," I said. "This is some kind of joke. Food poisoning can't kill people. They might get really sick, but they wouldn't die. Nobody dies from food poisoning." Satisfied with myself, I leaned back. "Good joke," I said to him sarcastically.

Then I saw the sheriff's face. "It's no joke," he said. I looked at Miss Henrid. She was still clicking one fingernail against another. "I simply must get these done next time I'm over in Memphis," she said, totally unconcerned. I swallowed hard. Salinger looked solemn and I knew where this was going.

"What kind of food poisoning? Did the doctor say?" I asked, the breath almost knocked out of me.

"A Botticelli something," Salinger said.

I was caught between the hysteria of him actually pronouncing an artist's name correctly, and the realization of what he was talking about. "Botulism?" I asked.

"That would be the one," he said. I realized that it was indeed the one food poisoning that could kill a person, and sank lower in the chair.

Miss Henrid continued the fascination with her nails. "The actual name, I believe, is *Clostridium botulinum* and it is most often found in home-canned vegetables that are not prepared properly."

I balked, turned white, and found it hard to breath. Miss Henrid, while not all what she appeared to be on the surface (anymore, at least) was, above all, well-educated.

45

Thy Escapable Rings

I now found myself handcuffed to the bed. "Isn't this a bit drastic?" I pleaded to Salinger.

"The charges have been upped to murder," he said. He was neither angry nor abusive. He simply … *was*.

I tried to whisper—keep my voice low—as Miss Henrid was in the kitchen, preparing lunch (can you believe?). "It came from those jars she gave me, the ones with the string beans and pickled eggs," I whined, desperate for him to understand that Tuck had intentionally murdered the women, albeit indirectly via me.

"Now, I told her not to go near you or help, and if it's one thing she does, it's obey me. She might be a lot of things …" (he paused and thought), "though she's a lot less these days," and he let out a laugh, "but she wouldn't lie to me."

"She told you I know about the …" I started to say.

"Operation? Sure. Called me on the phone. Ain't nobody gonna believe you if you tell." He paused again, ominously. "And believe me, brother, you ain't gonna tell. I didn't know them organs was here or I'd a brought you some place else, though where, I have no idee."

"But those women," I said. "They're all dead. What's going to happen? Is there going to be a coroner's investigation?"

"Now, I done told you, we's short on help in this here town. I'm the coroner since Shelby did away with …"

"So you *do* think she killed the first coroner."

"I'm just sayin', and who am I to question? Besides, it's a done deal. He's dead and I'm the body-looker-atter, and Doc Patterson says that it was that bottle thing …"

"Botulism."

"Right. You seem to know all about it. Anyway, it was *that*, that killed 'em."

"Can he come here, Doc Patterson? Can you bring him here?" I pleaded. "I don't feel so good. I think I need help."

"Now, you're gonna be just fine. Tuck will take care of you and everything will be okay," he said.

I was cuffed by one hand to the bed frame. Salinger stood back and looked me over. "I left your right hand free so's you could do your writin' or anythin' else you need," he said. Then he laughed. "If you know what I mean," and with that he turned and left the room. I hated to tell him, but giving myself personal sexual release wasn't foremost in my mind right now. With two penises in the house already—separated from their owners—the last thing I wanted to do was have mine flailing around in plain sight.

"Now, you just keep quiet and I'll see what Tuck is doin'," Salinger said, already on his way to the kitchen. And, as I really had no choice, I did just that.

The unfortunate thing about being handcuffed to a bed is that it gives one quite a bit of time to think. I was trapped. Salinger didn't believe me and Tuck had purposely provided me with botulism-imbued vegetables to feed to the Junior League. But how did she know that I wouldn't eat any of it—taste any of the tainted food she had given me to serve? Had she planned for me to die as well—to eat the canned goods? It had only been my extreme agitation, accompanied by a lack of caring what the ladies ate and the fact that I had been too busy to ingest anything myself, that had saved me from the same fate as those in the League. Was that what she and Salinger had been whispering about this morning? Also, they had persisted in asking me how I felt. Was that a coincidence because I looked so worn-out after the horrible evening I'd spent, or was it because they thought I should be dead?

Salinger didn't seem to believe that Tuck was capable of such a thing and had once again pinned the deed on me, like some faded and out-of-date blue ribbon for the world's largest and most memorable dope. Or was that an act too? And God only knew what I'd been given in the food that I'd eaten last night—before I found out what Tuck was really up to.

Then I remembered—what I'd said to the women: "I HATE ALL YOU MOTHER-FUCKING BITCHES AND I WISH TO HELL YOU'D ALL DIE! I'D KILL YOU MYSELF IF I COULD!"

Oh, God, why had I done that? And in front of Salinger. He now thought I was responsible not only for the fires, but for the murder of the Junior League women as well.

Then, with my head once again spinning like some out-of-control Vegas Roulette wheel, I remembered the item I had seen in the *Chalybeate Springs Times* about Dick Hunter burning down the twenty outhouses. It was, unfortunately, all making even *more* sense now. Dick Hunter, who was really Tuck Henrid, had burned the Town Hall, library, high school, and church out of spite. Only I was made to look like the culprit, just in case the deed wasn't pinned on one of the Junior

Leaguers. Tuck had played me like a termite-ridden cello until I was almost sawed in half. And here I was now, handcuffed to a bed in her house while she made lunch. I could only imagine what poison she would be serving me. The sound of Salinger getting in his car and driving away jolted me back to reality.

I tried to wiggle out of the cuffs. They were on solidly. And the bed frame was one of those early 1900s wrought-iron jobs with no hope of breakage. I was secured with zero possibility of escape—an innocent mouse on a glue trap. Just as I was reaching a state of heightened panic, Miss Henrid came into the room. "I've got a lovely cream of tomato soup and some cold roast beef," she said, "for lunch."

"I'm really not very hungry," I managed. Then she walked over to the cuffs and surveyed them. "Why, J.D. has these on so tight. It's going to cut off the circulation and you could die of gangrene."

"How good of you to notice. You wouldn't have the key by any chance?"

"Now, Jackson, you know I don't. And besides, I would never go against J.D.'s wishes." My mind went to an image of myself—a writer without a hand—one that had been amputated because of gangrene. I sighed heavily.

"You've got to eat something," Miss Henrid pressed.

"You've *got* to be kidding," I said. "You think I haven't figured it out?"

"I'm quite sure you have, but there's really nothing you can do about it." She smiled and put on hand on her hip. "What could you do anyway? If you got free, I mean. Call the police? Besides, he doesn't believe I did anything wrong."

"He'll figure it out."

"I wouldn't be too sure," she said, moving to the window and looking out over the small side lawn. "I do love Salinger, but there are limits to what I'll put up with. Besides, you're cuffed to a bed in a town that doesn't like you. There are no cell phones, no faxes, no way to communicate with the rest of the world ..." (She adjusted her hair.) "Thank God," she went on. "And the ladies of the Junior League are dead, so there's *that* little bit of nuisance out of the way." She turned to a mirror that hung over an antique bureau, again adjusting her hair. "Guess we'll just have to start a new Junior League," she said.

"Who is this 'we'?" I asked.

"Well, myself and a few of the other girls I'll rope into joining me. You know, those lonely individuals who were shunned in high school or made fun of, or perhaps never given a chance to compete?"

She paused dramatically, on purpose, full of show. "Oh, wait, that would describe *Moi!* The rest of the town made fun of me and Salinger—those ugly rumors. And now they have to pay."

"Who is 'they'?" I asked. There were a lot of "they's" and "we's" being thrown around lately.

"*They* are all the ones who did me wrong, did Salinger wrong, did everyone like *us* wrong." Now we had added an "us" to the equation.

"But everyone's been wronged at some time in their life," I said, trying to find a soft spot to appeal to her decency, if any such place did indeed exist. He/she had gone to the trouble to change into a woman for his/her best friend, so there had to be one there somewhere. Or maybe it had been removed along with "Dick" (read that any way you want).

She put a red-nailed finger to her lips—a Henrid trademark. "Hmmm. I don't know. I don't really think anyone has been as wronged as Salinger and me." I wanted to point to myself, but, being the generous person that I am, decided not to turn this particular conversation around.

"Look, you planned this elaborate scheme to get even with the Junior League and some of the town. Why not just move away? You were in New York. You had a chance to stay there. Salinger was up there for a while with you. You said so. Why didn't you move there for good? If not there, then to another small town where no one knew you? I don't understand this elaborate dog-and-pony show."

"Now, you really are being a bore," she said, and sat down on the edge of the bed. I moved my legs over, accommodating her, for what reason I have no idea. But then, I wasn't exactly in a position to argue. Her persona began to change once again. With all the mixed-up estrogen and testosterone flowing through her body, it was a wonder she was able to function at all. She was becoming mean.

"How? How am I being a bore?" I asked.

"Moving away would be, well, sort of like running away, don't you think? And besides, I grew up here. This is home. You know, at one time that big old plantation that you saw—that house that belonged to my family—was the only thing in these parts." She had a far-away look in her eyes now—another mood switch—she appeared sad. Then she brushed off her dress. "Should have stayed that way. But then the others came."

"But if the others hadn't come, then Salinger wouldn't be here either," I said, trying (God only knows why at this point) reason.

279

"That not totally correct," she said, tilting her head. "And we—my family—were here first. That house is mine. And if I have my way, it will be mine again and I'll be the, and I know you'll pardon the expression here, 'Queen' of this town."

I looked at her, really *looked* at her, possibly for the first time. I mean *really, really* looked at her—not the physical being, but the person. Dick Hunter, picked-on quarterback who Salinger had probably taken up for in high school. An outcast in the town along with his best buddy. Two friends in a town that had snubbed them, and now they were paying the three hundred or so individuals back with a joke.

But the fun had turned deadly and I couldn't tell if Salinger was in on the prank or if Henrid had her own plans in mind. Then again, these two weren't exactly open books when it came to the truth. A part of me felt sorry for Miss Henrid—we can all know how she felt if we think about it; we've all been made fun of or shunned in one situation or another, been made to feel inadequate in some way. And who hasn't wanted to get even and had fantasies about killing certain individuals who have made our lives miserable? But Tuck hadn't just fantasized; she had actually concocted an elaborate scheme to take down some of the town mentally and physically.

Coming out of thought, I spoke: "Why me? Why did you pick me?"

Henrid looked at her nails, the way a man does, the way that had tipped me off in the first place—with her fingers curved toward her. A woman looks at her nails by holding out her hand in front, with the back showing up. A man would never do this, and while Dick Hunter had taken the trouble to have certain organs removed, he/she still had male attributes—a last vestige of what *quarterback Hunter* had been; a part that he couldn't let go of.

"Why did I pick you?" she asked, leaning in slightly. "Like I told you, I read your books and your sense of fair play appealed to me. That and your warped sense of humor." Her face looked friendly enough, but there was something underneath the expression that unnerved me. It was a twitch at the corner of one eye, a tilt of the head, an unseen energy that emanated from her body.

There was something else she wasn't telling me. It wasn't just that she'd read my books. She had factored additional numbers into her equation of the Henrid Universe, and searching her visage now, I felt an uncomfortable remembering wash over me. I hearkened back to the first day of our meeting and that instinctive thought that had said, "I've met this person before." We've all had it happen at one time or another, and have either written it off as a past-life experience or some common attribute the person has that is similar to that of someone else we know. At the time, I suspected that her Joan Crawfordishness had been the reason. I wasn't so sure now. I looked at her again, seeing her in a different light. Yes, something about her struck me as familiar, but then that happens a lot when you've seen as many people as I have.

She continued. "Let's just say that you made me really angry one time and I thought your involvement in this plan might be the way to get even for what you did."

"I made you … angry … how?"

"Oh, you probably don't remember." She forced a smile that was full of sarcasm.

"Obviously I don't," I said.

She looked into space and the smile faded from her lips. "Think back. To New York. Where you worked while you were waiting for your third book to be published."

My mind hit rewind and I tried to piece together where I'd been at that time. Magazines, newspapers, free-lance stints. "I give up," I said. "I can't remember."

"Where were you working July 3rd, two years ago?"

"July 3rd? How the hell would I remember that? And what would that date have to do with anything, especially anything I would want to remember?"

"Think," she said. "Right before you went away to Aruba that year for the Fourth."

"Aruba? How would you know about that?" I blew out some air and tried to remember. "Okay. New York. Two years ago. Writing assignment on the mayor, article in the *New Yorker* … ghost writing for that idiot who paid me in cash. . . magazine stint with … a New York newspaper … trip to Aruba …" and then something clicked for me. It was as if my life had suddenly been jerked back to the past—a rabid dog on a leash needing to be trained.

"Oh. My. God. No. It couldn't be."

"It could," she said crossing her legs at the knee and joining her hands over them. "Receptionist at the paper? Tall guy who was working to make extra money while the rest of his inheritance came through for his sex-change?"

A pause. An uncomfortable silence ensued while she let her last statement register. Then she did her innocent, finger-to-the lips routine once again and played at *cute*. "Oh, but you didn't know that

281

then, did you?" Then quickly back to anger: "That I was *working* and *living* in New York so I could get a sex-change."

"It wasn't ..." I said, trying to remember bits and pieces; seeing someone, seeing the office in my mind—the gray carpet of the area where the receptionist sat, the dead corn plant by the window, the phone, the walk from the elevator bank to the double glass doors that led to the newspaper's offices.

She was standing now—angry. "Wasn't your fault? You got me fired! You told personnel that I wasn't 'front desk material.' And every day I had to listen to you squawk on about that damned novel of yours to whoever you were walking through the area with. Oh, you thought you were so much better than everyone at that paper, and especially me.

"Perhaps you don't remember what you said one day, as you got into the elevator, waiting to go down to lunch with your buddies. July 3rd. I remember that day. July 3rd. Perhaps you thought I didn't hear. Or maybe you *wanted* me to hear. Maybe you *wanted* to be that cruel. Should I refresh your memory?" She was on the verge of hysteria. Her fists were balled tight and her eyes threatened to pop out of her head. I tried to think back, but whatever I'd said didn't register and I couldn't remember, especially now, being handcuffed to a bed by the town's botulism murderer.

"Ringing phone, carpet, corn plant, elevator's 'ping' ... strange person at desk ..." I mused to myself. I had to speak: "I don't remember. I have no idea. The receptionist, just sitting out front? But that ugly person's name was a Tech something. We never could tell if they ... Aruba? I was going to Aruba? We didn't know what *they* were. We were only joking around. I just remember being amused that anyone would have the name Tech," I said, and then put *Tech* and *Tuck* together.

"Uh-oh," I said. "No, it couldn't be. I remember thinking that someone had probably come up with that name because they were good with computers or something such as that. But the last name was ... I can't remember. That person couldn't even *use* a computer. I remember how inadequate they ..." I was staring at Henrid, trying to put together yet another piece of the Chalybeate Springs puzzle.

"I was a person," she seethed. "I was using the name Tech Durkin while in New York."

"Not the most attractive of names either," I said, then wanted to kick myself for taunting a woman capable of murder; one who had just poisoned five women and burned down four large buildings.

"Damn," I said to myself. "Wait, that was you? You were the ugly ... I mean, you were the ..."

"Shall I refresh your memory? Shall I?" she interrupted, picking up steam. "As you walked into the elevator, on July 3rd ..."

"You *would* have to remember the date," I said.

"It was the day before the Fourth of July. May I continue?"

I nodded.

"As you walked into the elevator, and yes, it is imprinted on my mind for all eternity, you joked to your friends, jerking your thumb toward me and glancing back. You said, 'If *it* doesn't watch it, *it's* going to end up in somebody's book someday.' Then you added, 'With a name like that and a face and body to match, everyone would want to read about *it*,' and you all laughed. You all laughed at me! Do you know how much that hurt? Do you know how bad I felt, after being treated the way I had been by this town and then trying to find someplace else to live and being given a hard time in New York?"

"Tech Durkin?" I said, thinking that ... "Oh, my God."

"Clicked, huh? Finally clicked for you," she said, both hands on her hips now.

And it had.

Dick Hunter, Tech Durkin, and Tuck Henrid were all the same person—and all the same name. She had told me that Tuck Henrid was an anagram for Dick Hunter, but so was Tech Durkin (in my mind, equally unfortunate as Dick Hunter had been), and the joke had been on me. Me, Jackson Tippett McCrae, who used anagrams in his books, had had one final joke played on ... him (partial out-of-body experience happening here for author). It was as if present and past were happening at the same time, for I was immediately back to *that* day in *that* particular New York office, walking once again toward the elevator, joking about the homely and badly-named receptionist. And now here she was—the quarterback turned ugly duckling turned swan—right before me.

"Miss Henrid," I said, "you had no intention of ever actually getting into the Junior League, did you?"

"None whatsoever," she replied and looked me squarely in the face. She was calming down, but her breathing was still heavy.

"You only wanted me to start something with these women so they could tear each other apart."

She waited. She was cooling off. "Exactly," she said. "Did it work?" she asked, even though she knew the answer to the question.

"Like a charm," I said, feeling ashamed, embarrassed, afraid, worried, paranoid, helpless, and upset. (Did I leave anything out?)

Henrid had regained most of her composure by this time and was standing in one spot. I was perfectly still, waiting for her other pump to drop.

It did.

"Well, Mr. Jackson Tippett McCrae of novel fame, be careful what you say, for it may come true, especially the part about 'If *it* doesn't watch it, *it's* going to end up in somebody's book someday'. . ." and she paused again, catching her breath. Then she finished: "Because *it* just *has*."

46

Yes, Graphical Bents

Have you ever been unlucky enough to look out a window, just in time to see a bird fly directly into the glass; the poor thing not realizing that there was something transparent in the way? The little bundle of feathers usually makes the most God-awful thud and then drops like a stone. If you have any human attributes at all, you at once feel a sick twist in your gut—a sort of "this is not right" kind of response to the incident.

I give you this image not to disturb you (that will come later), but rather to paint a picture of how I felt at a particular moment. In case you've been wondering, in my mind (a scary place to be—but you knew that), I was not only the chirping little Tweety-Pie flying directly into the window of Miss Henrid's little shop of horrors, but the bystander as well.

I avoided all foods made for me by the impressive "Lady" of the house (wouldn't you?) and tried to make polite conversation, throwing in the occasional "I'm so sorry" (and really meaning it), and the often repeated "Can I do anything to change your mind?" but nothing seemed to work.

As the chili cook-off was that very afternoon, I allowed myself time to ruminate over my present state. It amazed me that a receptionist (a temp no less) had been so offended at my comments that she had followed my career (what there was of it) and set me up to be the perfect pawn for her plan to get even with one small town that had done her and Salinger wrong. But then, as she said, she'd read my other works and knew what I was all about.

So now, a day later, with not much to occupy my time, and being left alone after our rehashing of my insensitivity in New York, I sifted through the box of newspapers and typed (with one hand) on my laptop. Trying to keep my mind off all the possible situations involving Henrid, handcuffs, anger, and what they could blossom into, I caught up on the cookbook, made notes (including these chapters you are now reading), and went over some newspapers that I had not yet seen. Miss Henrid didn't seem to mind as it kept me quiet and I wasn't trying to escape. And, like she said, what would I have done anyway if I could have gotten free? Picture me, the fox at a hunt with less-than-well-dressed townsfolk, sans thoroughbreds and riding gear.

It's surprising how interesting the contents of a small town paper can become when you don't have anything else to do and have no access to the outside world. Think back: Try and remember a time with no Internet, fax machines, cell phones, or e-mail. See? You can't. Those things have so become a part of our world that we simply couldn't get along without them. But in Chalybeate Springs, this was not the case. The world had passed the area by. By Chalybeate standards, dinosaurs had been extinct only a few months and Jesus was still coming (for the first time). With no church, town hall, library, or high school, the good people of the Springs area focused on my foibles and a small part of me gave thanks for being hidden so well in a house where the town's oddest couple chose to spend their spare time. While Salinger had his own place—one which I had never seen—he was at Tuck's more and more as she was helping him with his chili recipe for the big cook-off that was to come—only a few hours away. Call me crazy, but this was not how I had planned to spend this year's Fourth of July.

So it came as a surprise when Tuck announced that she had to go off to work.

"Work? What work? You never said you worked. Go off where?"

"Now, Jackson ... I'm assuming we're still on a first-name basis?"

"I've seen your penis, you hate my guts, I know you burned down half the town, and you killed five women. I'd say we're friendly enough."

"Good! Now, I'll be gone only a little while, and when I get back, I'll keep you company until time for the judging. Then Salinger and I will take you over to the park. You're not going to be any trouble now, are you? And then after you judge his chili to be the best, we'll bring you back here."

"Here for what?" I asked.

Henrid came over to me and put her hand on my chest. I lay down the newspaper that I'd been reading. "Let's not get ahead of ourselves," she said, and I looked at her hand. It now sported Mrs. Weems's enormous ring that I had seen on the night of the infamous dinner where Mrs. Brandyworth had made a nosedive into the pink arctic fruit salad.

"You don't waste any time, do you?" I said, looking at the ring.

She jerked her hand back and frowned. "Wasn't going to do her any good now anyway," she pouted. Then her demeanor changed again. "Besides, looks better on me, don't you think?"

I remembered the evening where Mrs. Weems had told me that the one on her hand was a copy—that the original was kept in her Bible. I kept my mouth shut, not knowing if Henrid had taken it from Weems's hand, if Salinger had procured it for her, or if they had somehow gotten into the enormous house and ransacked the place. Whatever the case, Henrid had the reproduction and not the original. I still wasn't sure if Salinger knew or believed that Henrid had killed the Junior League women via me, and I certainly wasn't going to get the truth out of Tuck right now. But it seemed certain that Salinger had been a part of procuring the enormous boulder that now resided on Tuck's hand, fake though it may be.

"No, really, it's lovely," I said, glancing at the gargantuan stone once more. "But you still haven't said where you work. And you never mentioned it before."

"Well, I don't actually have to go 'off' to work. Rather, I go over to Salinger's and use his old Remington typewriter."

"Oh, no. This doesn't sound good. You write?"

"Why, a bit."

"Tell me it's not books."

She smiled. "Heavens, no! You see, I freelance, for the *Times.*"

I looked at her askance. (Was there any other way?) "But everyone in the town hates you. Why would the *Times* let you work for them?"

"They wouldn't. And they don't *know* I work for them."

I was confused—once again. "I don't get this. In a town this small ..." but Miss Henrid cut me off, picking up the newspaper that I had just put down.

"Hmmm. May issue of this year. Let's ... just ... see," she said, thumbing the pages. "Here, on page three," and with that, she pointed to an article on the merits of steer castration. How I had missed it, I will never know. I gave the article a once-over and then set it down.

"I don't get it."

She pointed to the end of the page. "The writer. The initials. T.D.," she said.

I thought I was a quicker study than most, but given the inordinate amount of stress, being handcuffed to a bed, and not knowing my fate in the town, I had obviously slowed down and events had taken their toll. And it was showing.

"Just fill me ..." but once I'd said it, it came to me.

"Do I see a light bulb over your head, or are you just happy to see me?" Miss Henrid asked.

"Damn!" I said. "T.D.—Tech Durkin. You work for the paper. You wrote those articles and bits on the town."

"Well, some. Only the ones for the last year. The *Times* is so starved for news that they take any and everything. I just mail them in and they print them. They have no idea that Tech Durkin is really Tuck Henrid slash Dick Hunter. You see, my fame as a receptionist in New York has yet to make its way down to the Springs area."

"God." I sat back, stunned once again.

"You obviously didn't write those bits about the good things the ladies of the Junior League did."

"They did something good?" she asked.

"Aren't I keeping you from your day job?" I said.

"No, seriously, what, if anything, did these women ever do that was good?"

I reached into the box—the one containing some other copies of the *Chalybeate Springs Times,* and brought out a copy printed ten years ago.

"MRS. HELEN WEEMS TO GIVE $300,000.00 FOR CANCER RESEARCH IN CHARLESTON," I read. The headline said it all.

"She was just showing off," Henrid replied.

"Oh, and what did you, with all your inherited money, give? Oh, wait. I forgot. You spent it on a sex-change operation because you wanted to get even with a town of three hundred people and live with your linebacker boyfriend."

"You're really in no position to ..."

"And how about this one," I continued, "MRS. OTIS BRANDYWORTH DONATES TIME AND MONEY TO CARE FOR NEEDY IN NEIGHBORING TOWNS."

"When she wasn't drunk," Henrid replied.

I went on. "And here's a bit on Shelby, when she wasn't killing her husbands I might add: 'A Mrs. Shelby Dipsey-Ewell-Adams ...' " I stopped. "I guess she hadn't gotten to Tellerman and Hatton yet," and then continued, ". . . was part of a committee dealing with the improvement of the town. In an interview with Mrs. Dipsey-Ewell-Adams, she admitted that she would put to good use the insurance money that Mr. Ewell had left, contributing funds in excess of 8,000 to beautify Hunter Park, located just to the north of the town's cemetery." I paused and looked up. "A park named for one of your relatives."

"Stop it," Tuck snapped. "I don't want to hear it."

"You don't want to hear that these women, while so *off* that they make a Picasso painting look normal, had other facets to their lives? Were human? Were capable of things other than just sharpening their claws on each other, on me, on you, on anyone?"

"What about Brandyworth? What about that entire child prostitution thing?" Henrid seethed.

"Well, other than explaining her alcoholism over the guilt factor, brought on even more by your needling her via the *Times*, you might want to consider this," and I read from the back page of an edition that I had used for research: "The Reverend and Mrs. Brandyworth will visit the sick and disabled at Veteran's Hospitals in Memphis, Nashville, and Jackson, Mississippi. The couple has also donated rehabilitation equipment to several care facilities. In addition, they have spent countless hours personally reading to the veterans in an attempt to keep them company and lighten their spirits." I held up the paper. "And here's a lovely picture of the couple doing just that," I said.

"A photo opportunity if ever there was one," Henrid snarled. "And where do you think that money came from anyway? From those kids being sold for sex. You want to torture me? You think you can make me feel something for these women, for this town? Let me tell you Mr. McCrae, you're in no position to play a hand such as this."

While she did have a point, I wasn't sure what I had to lose. Things weren't exactly looking up. Playing nice with the other children hadn't gotten me any additional toys and so I was trying the antagonistic method. It *does* work from time to time. It didn't now.

I had a sinking feeling, remembering the two penises in the jar in the kitchen. While Henrid had elected to have hers cut off, obviously Harry Killchrist hadn't. And I was handcuffed to the bed and Miss Henrid knew how to use a knife. I saw her eyes narrow. I became worried. Perhaps I had pushed things a bit too far. And I remembered how warped her mind was. It might not be just a knife, but a very dull one—she might be planning to make the operation as painful as possible. Then my thoughts ran to something even more horrible. No, she wouldn't—she couldn't. No one could be that cruel. No one could torture someone, hate someone that much. And she *would* know just where to get me. Everyone in the town talked and eventually *everything* about *everyone* got around. The Junior League women had endured horrible deaths that included vomiting, diarrhea, and pain. There was no telling what Henrid was capable of when it came to *my* torture or demise.

"Don't you have to get over to that Remington and do some typing?" I offered up, hoping to change the tone of the day.

"I don't think so, just yet. I think ..." and I could see the wheels spinning, "that you need a bit of torture yourself. Yes. I think torture of the most horrible kind might be just what you need," and with that, she quickly walked out of the room. I could hear her going through drawers, cabinets, shelves. I began to panic. Then she reentered my bedroom and when I saw what was in her hand, I started to fall apart.

"No, not that! Anything but that! Come on, please. Tuck, please, I'm sorry. Miss Henrid, I didn't mean to ..."

"Shut up, you!" she growled over me, holding the one dull item I'd hoped she wouldn't find. I had no idea she was capable of anything this bad. Even my wild imagination wouldn't have dreamed up torture of this magnitude.

"You're going to pay for what you've done to me," and with that she sat on the edge of the bed and leaned over my legs.

"No, please! Not that! Anything but that! I'll do anything you want! I'll keep my mouth shut! I'll say anything, just please don't ..." but the room started to spin and I could see in her eyes that she was going to go through with the act.

Tuck Henrid—poised over me with her weapon of torture— began as slowly as possible, making the process as painful as she could.

"Robert Cohn was once a middleweight boxing champion of Princeton," she began, reading from Hemingway's *The Sun Also Rises*.

"Please, not that! Not his *most* boring book!" I screamed, a regular Ronald Reagan in *King's Row* when he discovers his legs are missing.

"Do not think that I am very much impressed by that as a boxing title, but it meant a lot to Cohn," she continued, savoring the words as she brought them to light off the page, enjoying the incredible pain she was inflicting. I writhed in agony, but she kept it up, kept going at this agonizing book until it was like water torture. By the time she finished, I was a zombie—willing to do anything she wanted. She had me in her complete control.

47

Let's Hang A Spicy Reb

That afternoon I was all hers. The Hemingway had taken its toll (*For Whom the Bell ...*) and I was completely broken. Well, that plus the fact that both Henrid and Salinger had guns. I begged to take my laptop with me to the cook-off and miraculously, they agreed. Being electronically challenged and self-absorbed, neither had looked in the case, and in the event that they had actually been able to start up my computer, it contained enough passwords to thwart even the most experienced crook.

The three of us made our way to the park where the festivities were under way. Long tables were placed perpendicular to the walkways, and a tent had been set up at one end of the green oasis. In the very middle was a makeshift stage. It was small, supporting a podium with a red-white-and-blue skirt-material around the bottom. The backdrop was a thirty-by-forty-foot canvas, painted with the words "CHALYBEATE SPRINGS ANNUAL CHILI COOK-OFF!," along with a bad representation of a bowl of steaming chili. Cheesy canned music poured from two large black speakers on each side of the stage. A clown was juggling bowling pins, and off to the side, a man dressed in black-face and minstrel attire waited to go on. In addition, there was an enormous fireworks display set up not far from the cooking stations— not the best placement in my opinion, this gunpowder and propane combo.

"Day's entertainment, before the big announcement," Salinger quipped, seeing my gaze follow Al Jolson and the clown on stage as the police car pulled up next to the entrance to the park in a spot marked subtly, RESERVED FOR THE SHERIFF—DO NOT PARK YOUR ASS HERE.

"Exactly how many entrants are competing this year?" I asked, looking for each and every angle to escape. I scanned the park, seeking unfamiliar faces from neighboring towns, people who didn't know me and with whom I might stand a chance at telling my story.

Salinger must have been equipped with mind-reading capabilities also, for he appeared to know what I was thinking. "Don't get no fancy ideas about running away or tryin' to tell anyone what's gone on, other than what they already know," he said. "Tuck and I'll be watching your every move."

Tuck, who was sitting in the front seat with J.D., turned toward the scratched Plexiglas and wire mesh partition. "And *do* try and make it sound real—when you announce J.D. as the winner," she said. I could see her reach over and squeeze Salinger's free right hand. We all sat in the car a few moments and then the sheriff and Tuck got out. They opened my door, and with one of them on each side—showing me their guns (Salinger's on full display, Tuck's hidden in her purse)— they ushered me into the park.

"So, who's the competition today now that you've gotten rid of the Junior League ladies?" I asked.

Salinger responded, cigar in mouth: "None of that crap. You keep your trap shut until it's time to announce me as the winner. Then this town's gonna see who's the boss."

I looked around the park. By this time, most of the people in the hamlet of Chalybeate Springs had seen us, and they made a point of staring at me and gesturing. I could hear bits and pieces of the remarks. "Arson," "He's the one," and the classic and grammatically incorrect, "Outsiders is always the cause of trouble," floated by us. One part of me was glad for the escort. If not, I might have been torn to bits. Salinger had certainly done a good job of convincing the town that I was not only an arsonist, but a murderer as well. Just as we neared the first row of tables, one brave Chalybeaten called out, "Yankee killer!" and Salinger held up his hand. I wanted to jump in and interject that his comment was unclear. Did the unnamed man verbally assaulting me mean I killed Yankees, or that I was a Yankee who killed people? Not even one of my beloved commas could have fixed *that* problem.

"Now we don't want to go causin' no trouble till there's been a trial," Salinger said to the man, but just at that moment the Reverend Brandyworth appeared next to us, puffing and angry.

"How dare you bring this piece of *filth* to this cook-off!" he said, and Salinger made a move to hold the good Reverend back. The Reverend's fists were balled and he was beet red.

While not in the best of positions, I couldn't resist. "Don't you have some kids you should be prostituting?" I asked, and Salinger had to work harder to restrain Reverend Platitude.

Tuck actually snickered and attempted to cover it up by using a tissue to blow her nose. "Watch it," she said through the thin, soft white covering, and it was unclear if she meant it in a friendly way or not. Now Mr. Weems was on us, himself chastising Salinger for his blatant display of the town's most despised perp.

292

"I'll see you hanged, boy," he said to me, pointing a plump finger directly at my face. It was odd to see him outside of his subservient butler role, and I let another comment go in his direction. "I'd wath-uh be ee-wek-tuh-kooted (I'd rather be electrocuted)" I said to him, and Tuck quickly herded me off in another direction.

"Jackson, you have to behave," she admonished, when she had pulled me away.

"Oh, let me get this straight: You get to kill people and I have to behave."

"You just watch it. Besides, nothing you could do would convince these people that you're innocent."

I looked right at her. "You really believe that. You really believe that everyone hates me at this moment more than you." I pulled my laptop case closer and adjusted the strap over my shoulder.

She smirked and relaxed. "Okay, you want to play? Fine. Just try it. I'll even stand by and keep my mouth shut. I don't think you realize how deep you're in this thing."

Not being sure if she was kidding or not, I moved toward one of the townspeople to try my knowledge out on them. Tuck stood, just a few feet away, arms crossed. I sallied up to a man I had never seen and spoke: "You've got to help me," I started out. "Tuck killed the Junior League women and she was the one who burned down all the buildings. She's not really a ..." but the man cut me off by shoving me to the ground.

"You piece of filth," he spat out. "Why they let you in here today is a mystery to me. I hope you get life for what you've done to this town." Then he stormed off. I looked up to see Tuck standing over me.

"See, we're not worried. And that was someone you've never met. Imagine what the ones you know think of you." She took a pack of cigarettes out of her purse and tapped them. Then she took one out and lit it. "Want one?"

"No. Thank you though. You are most generous." I got up and dusted myself off.

Tuck spoke: "You're through here. Just judge the competition and we'll see about getting you off with a light sentence."

"You still haven't informed me who the other contestants are, not that it matters," I said.

"You're right. It doesn't matter, but for the sake of making this thing look like it's on the up-and-up, I'll tell you." She took me by the arm and walked me around the tables. They all sported those red-and-white gingham checked tablecloths. "Paul Udell, the town barber," she said as we stopped by the first pot of chili.

"I know him. Saw him once, anyway."

"Robert Randford—the owner of the Chalybeate Springs Café," she continued, stopping by the next station. This time, the cook was behind his kettle and he scowled in my direction. I waited for his hateful comments, but then realized that he actually thought he might have a chance of winning. Funny, what people will put up with for that blue ribbon. We walked on.

Once again, the cook was next to his enormous kettle of chili. "Sam Delahaunty," Henrid explained and nodded to the man. He said nothing and I counted myself lucky. That was it for the first row. We walked around a set of generators and coolers toward the next aisle.

"I have to ask a stupid question," I said to Tuck.

"Shoot."

"Why does everyone have such a large kettle? These things are enormous. Each one must hold five hundred gallons."

Tuck smiled. "They're actually sugarcane kettles from down near the Gulf coast. We had them brought up years ago when this whole thing started. Some people have their own; some rent them. The idea is that whoever wins gets to feed the entire town. She looked around the park. See all these people? The whole town? Everybody's here today. This is the biggest thing we do and no one has ever missed it."

"So, what happens to the losers? What happens to all that chili they made?"

"Freeze it, most of them. Everyone has a big old side-by-side freezer in these parts and they won't let it go to waste."

"Well, at least that's a good idea."

"You might want to start the tasting, so that Salinger's can be last. Take your time," and with that she smiled again. "After all, you haven't eaten anything all day."

That much was true. So afraid was I of Henrid's cooking now that I wouldn't have *dared* to eat anything she'd touched. Besides, I knew too much and I wasn't sure what she and Salinger were going to do with me. I walked up to one of the tables and looked at the card on the front: "Bob Ewell—no relation to Shelby's dead husband," it read. I looked up to see the man himself standing behind his kettle with a chef's hat on.

"Guess I'd better get started," I said to Tuck.

"Mr. Ewell," she said, leaning over, "won't you keep an eye on Mr. McCrae for me? See to it that he makes it to Mr. Birdwell's station, right there next to you, and then on back to table two where the others are? I don't want him cheating or anything."

"Will do, Miss Henrid," Ewell said, and gave me a most unpleasant look. He ladled out his concoction into a bowl and I dipped my spoon in. Then I blew on the stuff, to cool it off. It was actually pretty good. "That may be the first I've tasted, I said, but it's really good. Mind telling me what's in it?"

Ewell snorted and then sneered. "The recipe's a damn secret, moron. Ain't no author gonna get this for that cookbook you a-doin'. Probably come down here to steal all these recipes anyways."

"Friendly," I thought, and moved on to Mr. Birdwell's kettle. By now, Tuck was secure in the fact that I was busy with the judging and that the town was not about to let me get out of the park alive. She evidently felt it safe to leave me off leash, though well within her sight.

Mr. Birdwell did his best Mr. Ewell impersonation, so much so that I couldn't tell their comments *or* their chili apart. I was about to move to table number two when a man grabbed my arm.

"Mr. Reynolds!" I said, shocked to see him, remembering the man from my first meeting at the airstrip. He still smelled faintly of pigs and dirt. I drew back; afraid he might hit me with either his fist or his comments. Okay, partially from the smell. He wasn't the most pleasant man to be around, at last olfactory-wise.

"You're not afraid to be here?" he asked. His comment seemed just what it was—a question; without malice or scorn. Genuine curiosity was my guess. I looked over at Tuck while she conversed with another of the townsfolk. She seemed satisfied that I wasn't going to bolt.

"I'm not thrilled, but they asked me to do it, and, how should I say … 'made me an offer I couldn't refuse.' "

"That so?"

" 'Tis."

"That a purse you got there?" he asked, seeing my case with its shoulder strap.

"Computer. Carry it everywhere," I said, thinking that it would be best to leave out the fact that a large amount of cash was hidden inside. Why, with all that had gone on, Henrid hadn't bothered to take her money back, along with that given to me by the other women, was beyond me—it was all there; in the case. She's certainly had the chance and there'd have been nothing that I could have done.

The thought that she hadn't even brought it up bothered me—stuck in the back of my mind.

Reynolds and I stood looking at one another. An uncomfortable silence settled in. Finally, he asked: "Did you really kill those women?"

"Nothing like being blunt," I said. "Do you think I did?"

"Don't know. But I've heard some mighty bad things about you. And Salinger said you convinced him not to buy from me this year—again."

"Buy from you? Buy what?"

"Pork. Pig. For his durn chili."

"I didn't have anything to do what that. I've got problems of my own. He told you I convinced him?"

Reynolds laid one arm over the other and slumped, evidently ready for a more lengthy conversation than I had in mind. "That's what he said. Said you told him to go over to Titusville and get his pork there. He only uses pork in his chili."

I looked over at Tuck. She was still involved with one of the people from the town, evidently doing better socially than either she or I thought capable.

"I had nothing to do with Salinger or his pork," I said.

Reynolds waited. "Well, I wasn't sure. Salinger is an odd one. Makes good chili, though." He paused. "Funny thing is, I checked with the pig farm over in Titusville and they said Salinger hadn't been to see them. Way I figure it, he musta changed his mind."

"Must have," I said, "or maybe he's using beef this year."

Reynolds looked around, squinted at the sun, looked back at me. "Don't think so. It's a tradition in these parts. No one's ever used beef—only pork. It's a thing we do. People can taste the difference."

"I'll keep that in mind," I said, and watched Tuck as she made her way back over to me.

"Having a nice chat?" she asked, but before Reynolds could answer, she tugged me toward the end of row number one—the very place where Salinger was setting up.

48

Ah, Abler Spicy Gents

"How come Salinger is last to set up? These other people have been cooking all morning," I said.

"He's not going to cook his recipe right here in front of everyone—let them see what he puts in his." Tuck looked at me as if I'd grown an extra head.

"But that doesn't violate some rule or something?" I asked. I looked over at the police car we'd arrived in. Salinger was now struggling with two enormous tubs of chili that had been in the trunk of the vehicle. I watched from a distance as he tried to manage one of them.

"You'd better go help," Tuck said.

I squinted. "That wouldn't be another violation of some sort?"

"Like this is an honesty contest anyway," she quipped.

"Point made," I said, and walked over to where Salinger was wrestling with the large containers.

"I'm supposed to help you," I said. He looked up at me. Then he looked around. The sun was getting hotter by the minute and it was well past noon. It seemed as if our nearest star was bearing right down on top of us. Salinger was sweating profusely and large stains were appearing under his arms and spreading to his back. He wiped his brow and removed his cap, wiped it again, and then replaced his headgear.

Finally, he looked down. "You grab that side and I'll get this one," he said, and we lifted the large container out of the trunk.

"How did you get these in?" I asked.

"Tuck," he said, then looked around. "It was okay when she came over to the house, but we can't let people see she's that strong here."

"Right. Gotcha." It did make sense. Tuck, despite the operation, was still a man in many ways and could easily handle heavy objects. I looked back at her, a safe thirty feet away. She waved daintily.

We lifted both tubs out of the trunk and set them down on the grass. Then we took the first one to the cooking station and I helped Salinger dump it into the large kettle. We went back for the second and placed it behind a partition that was in back of the tables. "Leave this one for later—when we run out of the first one. Besides, it won't all fit in the kettle right now."

"Works for me," I said, and started to walk back to the car to close the trunk.

Salinger called after me as he was tying on his apron: "Oh, son?" I turned. "Don't think about doing anything funny," he said, and held up the car keys. While the thought had not occurred to me, I wanted to kick myself now that it hadn't. I did need to find some way out of this situation or at least someone who believed I was innocent and would help me. My prospects looked bleak, and as I made my way to the car to close the trunk I heard yet one more comment from a loving Chalybeaten: "Hope you rot in hell."

I tried as best I could to shrug it off and had my hand on the trunk lid when something caught my eye. Could it be? No, surely not. Cocaine? It certainly looked like it. There was some white powder spilled in Salinger's trunk. I looked back at Salinger. He was busy setting up his station. Tuck was with him, only occasionally glancing over at me to make sure I was within eyesight. I bent down and looked closer. Heroin? Couldn't be. But then, consider what Tuck and Salinger had done so far. Then I saw them: two large plastic jars shoved up under the spare tire. There was still some of the white powder residue in them—some of the same powder that was spilled on the carpeting of the trunk floor. Salinger's fertilizer? No, that wasn't it. I had seen a whitish substance in the envelope that Mrs. Childers had brought, but this wasn't the same thing.

"Oh, my God," I said to myself, "these guys are trafficking in heroin as well as everything else." While I had managed to stay out of trouble in New York with regard to drugs and drinking (okay, just the drug part), most of my friends hadn't. I had been to numerous parties where cocaine and heroin were served the way pigs-in-a-blanket might have been at some Midwestern shindig. I didn't partake on a regular basis, but I knew what they tasted and looked like (the heroin and cocaine, not the pigs-in-a-blankets).

As nonchalantly as I could, I wet my index finger and stuck it to the white powder, some of which had spilled close by. I tasted it. No, this wasn't cocaine. And it wasn't heroin. PCP? Some type of speed or barbiturate? I didn't know, but Salinger and Tuck were trafficking in something and I could possibly use this to get the upper hand if I could only figure out what it was. I sniffed the substance and then tasted it again. Bitter-sweet. And no odor. What *was* this? And what would I do once I figured it out? Who was I going to tell? Still, knowledge is power and I needed anything I could lay my hands on.

A voice jolted me back to reality. "Hey, McCrae, over here!" It was Salinger calling me to his station. I shut the trunk and obeyed. By the time I was back at his table, the sheriff had set up and was heating his chili.

"You still have some others to taste before mine," he said, indicating those in his line who waited with cynical looks on their faces. I wanted to tell them how lucky they were simply to still be alive, much less losing, but they wouldn't have believed me, and the town's two main miscreants (now that the Junior League ladies were dead) were standing right next to me.

As people milled about and I made it to two other stations, I started noticing a strange feeling. At first it was just dizziness, then a slight nausea, but in a few moments it went away. I wrote it off to the latest circumstances, having not eaten for a day, and putting spicy fare into my system at this late date. I did have to admit that I was hungry, and most of the recipes were exceptional though similar.

I walked about a bit, letting my taste buds rest. Salinger's chili was the only one I had yet to ingest and so, to make it look less forced—make it look as though I was enjoying each and everyone's station and not just doing this for show, though God only knows why—I waited. As the people milled about, talk was heard of the recent deaths in the town. Heads turned in my direction and people looked over one another's shoulders to get a glimpse of me. More comments floated about.

"Heard anything about the Brandyworth funeral?" one person asked.

"Nope. Reverend's too tore up to perform the service and then do it for them other four women." This was accompanied by a scowl in my direction. I moved through some parked cars and leaned against one. I was sweating profusely but wrote it off to the sun and the intense humidity of the day.

"Sheriff said that when he'd heard Weems and Brandyworth were dead, that he went straight to Killchrist and them other two women, just to see what was up with them," I heard over the hood of one of the cars. The sun beat down on the chrome trimmings and the reflection momentarily blinded me. I had the most tremendous headache.

"Did they say he found them all dead?" another person asked, and I felt my stomach doing somersaults.

"All but Childers. Said she died while he was there," a companion of the first voice answered.

"Wouldn't want that job for all the peanuts in the world," a farmer-type said, joining the conversation. "Having to do that sheriff work and then pick up them bodies and take them over to the funeral home in the next town."

I felt as though I was going to pass out and staggered over behind a rusty pickup truck, retching out my stomach contents on the grass.

"Lord, God, somebody's puking," I heard a voice say, but I didn't care—my head was killing me and I was feeling weak. I tried to think back: Had I eaten anything at Tuck Henrid's? Nothing I could think of, other than the dinner sometime before. Then a rather upsetting suggestion placed itself in my mind. These townspeople hated me; in fact, thought of me as an arsonist and murderer. Wasn't it possible that one of these cooks had poisoned me? After all, I was to taste the chili, then decide who was the winner. No one else was eating or *could* eat until I'd made my "decision." It was only after I had declared the winner that everyone would eat that particular kettle of chili.

I clumsily made my way back to the first table.

"Man, you look like shit," Salinger said, as he stirred what was before him.

"Hail to thee, Thane of Glams," I said.

"What?"

"Nothing. It's from Shakespeare," I said. "Can I get a glass of water?"

Tuck and the sheriff looked at each other. "Course you kin," he said. "And you still got to taste mine," he added. Then he bent over the table. "Just remember that it's the best damn chili you ever ate and say so when you announce it."

"I'll try," I said, regaining my legs. The purge behind the pickup had helped and I felt that I was recovering. Salinger dipped his ladle into the kettle and dished me out a large bowl of his special recipe. It was twice as meaty as the others and, in fact, did look better than anyone else's.

I took the bowl and spoon, and turned away from Tuck and Salinger, looking into the crowd. Perhaps eating something that I knew wasn't contaminated would make me feel better. After all, Salinger had made this and he certainly wasn't going to poison me or the town. Who else would give him first prize and who else could he blame everything on?

300

I put my spoon into the bowl and was bringing the implement up to my lips when a shot was heard several feet away. Everyone turned, momentary chaos took over, and Salinger, being the only law enforcement official, stood up straight and sniffed the air, then instructed Henrid to watch his station while he went and investigated. I put the spoon down, more curious about the shot, and forgot to actually taste Salinger's concoction.

Salinger returned with the news that "It was only one of them Roman candles going off, behind a pick-up," and we all turned our attention back to the judging.

"Time to get up and announce the winner," Salinger said, and shoved me up a set of steps and toward the microphone at the podium. On the way, I once again began to feel dizzy but wrote it off to the heat. Finally, I made the announcement to tepid applause and the people in the crowd began to file over to Salinger's station.

"Fill 'er up!" I heard Mr. Ewell say. "I want to see if you beat me fair and square." I scanned the crowd, looking for anyone who might be sympathetic to my plight or at least listen to the story and believe it. I wasn't optimistic. Just as I was about to leave the stage, I caught sight of Jecko, standing in the back, behind the last row of parked cars, near the very pick-up truck where Salinger had investigated the "shot."

"I'm gonna git me some of this durn chili and I swear if it's not as good as mine, I'm gonna kick that McCrae man's ass," Mr. Birdwell was heard to say, a little too loudly and a little too much in my direction.

As I left the stage, someone handed me another bowl of Salinger's chili. By now, between the sickness and the amount of the stuff I had consumed by tasting alone, it was the last thing I wanted to see. But I absent-mindedly took the bowl and picked up a spoon, watching the crowd at the same time.

People swirled around Salinger and Tuck, taking them in as never before. It must have been the combination of the excellent food and the fact that they had caught the world's most wanted criminal— me—that gave them the extra caché they needed. Whatever it was, I was grateful, for there were now so many people between Salinger's station and where I was that there was no way he and Tuck could catch me if I tried to run.

I feigned nonchalance and dug my spoon deep into the bowl's culinary landscape. But just as the eating implement went into Salinger's award-winning chili, it hit something hard. "Must be an uncooked

301

bean," I thought, glad that I hadn't tasted the stuff and bitten down on it. I fished around for it while Tuck and Salinger exchanged pleasantries with the rest of the crowd. The sheriff and his future bride were a good distance away and seemingly unconcerned with my whereabouts.

Bringing the spoon up, I noticed something shiny. "What the...?" I said out loud, and then hoped I hadn't attracted attention. I put the spoon to one side of the bowl and picked out the object. It was covered with chili and so I shook it off, slinging the food away from it. But when I saw what the item was, my head started to spin.

"No," I said to myself. Just then, someone walked by and said "Asshole" to me. I let it go. "This can't be," I said, taking a closer look at the shiny thing I had extracted from the bowl. If what I thought had happened *had* indeed happened, I and everyone else had bigger problems than name calling.

Caught up in my analysis of the object, I was unaware that a man was standing next to me. I looked up just in time to hear him speak, and, thankfully, he didn't see what was in my hand. I closed my fist around the prize.

"I'll see to it you rot in the county jail for what you did to my wife." It was Mayor Weems, a bowl of chili in his fat and age-spotted hands. Evidently the sight of me had not ruined his appetite.

"I'm sorry, Mr. Weems, I really had nothing ..."

"I don't want to hear your excuses," he said. "I'm so angry." Then he shifted from foot to foot. His rage seemed to be looking for a place to settle in his body. "I hope to God, for your sake, that they find you *didn't* do this," he continued.

"Mr. Weems, please believe me, I didn't. But I have something really important to ask you."

"You? Ask me something? What could you possibly want?"

"Was Salinger in your house yesterday or today, or was Miss Henrid?"

"Why should I answer you? Why should I have anything at all to do with you? You're ..."

"Please, it's important. *Really* important."

He sighed heavily and looked about, then answered. "Salinger was there to take Mrs. Weems's body, that was all." He looked at me hatefully. "I thought you and she were friends."

"I thought we were also," I said, but my legs were starting to give way again and I felt dizzy. "Could you answer one more thing for me?" I asked.

Weems, while frustrated and angry, replied: "What? Get on with it."

"Was anything missing from Mrs. Weems's Bible?"

"What the hell are you talking about? And you look sick."

"The Bible," I said. "Mrs. Weems's Bible. Was anything missing from the inside of it? I know about the hiding place."

"Mrs. Weems didn't even *own* a Bible. We're not religious like the Brandyworths. I thought you knew, Mr. McCrae, knew all the secrets. Mrs. Weems was an atheist. She just insisted we go to church every Sunday to be accepted in the town. Now I guess it doesn't matter much if everyone knows or not. Me, I believe in religion, but we don't even *have* a Bible."

That was it: the one thing that put me over the edge, for I slumped to one side and around the corner of one of the cars, vomiting heavily into the grass once again.

49

A Chap's Grisley Bent

Just as I finished my regurgitation session, I heard my name being called. "What now?" I thought, and looked up to see Mr. Hastings from the Inn.

"Glad I caught you," he said. "Didn't know where you was and all. This here letter came for you, along with this other envelope, and now I can get rid of 'em." He held out the envelopes and I took both. I wanted to ask if he hated me also, but if what I had discovered about Salinger and Henrid was true was, it didn't matter. I muttered a "Thanks" and he nodded and moved away.

Left alone now, I tore into the first envelope. It was a letter from my friend in New York—the one I had sent Salinger's fertilizer sample to.

> Jackson,
>
> I don't know what kind of joke you think you're playing on me, but these tests are expensive and I don't have time for your usual pranks. You obviously thought you'd get one over on me, but I hate to tell you, guy, you failed.
> Did you actually think I'd be shocked to find that ninety-eight percent of that stuff you sent was human matter—mostly bones? Where did you get someone to grind up a human being? Man, I knew you liked to play pranks, but this one's a little far out. See you when you get back to the city.

The letter was signed. I looked at the postmark just to make sure it had actually gone through the mail and come from New York. It had. As if everything up until that point had not been disturbing enough, I now had my proof as to what had happened to the former chill cook-off contestants. The list of those missing—the one I had gleaned from the *Times*—matched the ones who had also entered former contests: Kinderson, Gallonheimer, Murphy, and Shelkins among others. They had all disappeared. And those years they had come up missing had been the very ones Salinger had won the competition—using his own recipe. That also explained the vegetables of enormous size and Salinger's special ingredient for making them grow. He had used some of Chalybeate Springs's very inhabitants to nurture the mammoth specimens along. Then I tore into the other letter—the one with no address or postmark. Several scraps of paper were inside, each with a cryptic message—or not. "A Chap's Grisley Bent," one read, complete with the word "grisly" misspelled. Then, "He brings Catalepsy," and "Cab Gal, She Try Penis." Ah, an oriental motif? I crumpled the collection and put them and the letter into my case.

The evening was descending over the cook-off. A circus-like atmosphere invaded the crepuscular lightening-bug air and someone started up a stereo in one of the cars. Country music twanged from the speakers and filtered in with the murmur of those partaking of Salinger's winning recipe. I looked at them—all unsuspecting people, not knowing what was about to happen.

I staggered toward the back of the stage where the generators were. Neither Salinger nor Tuck had noticed I was gone, or, if they had, they hadn't found time to get through the crowd. Then again, if what I thought was true, it wasn't going to matter … for any of us.

I opened my hand and looked at the piece of jewelry I had extracted from Salinger's chili. It was unmistakable: Mrs. Weems's gigantic ring. But I had just seen Miss Henrid wearing it earlier today. Then it all made sense. Salinger had taken the ring from Weems's finger when he was removing the body. A distraught Mr. Weems wouldn't have noticed. That meant that Henrid was indeed wearing the copy, and that I had just dug the original out of my bowl of chili.

I thought back to the dinner party where a drunken Mrs. Weems had let me in on her secret—where she had hidden the *original* ring—while she showed me the copy on her finger. The conversation surfaced like a dead body that had been weighted down in a river, jettisoning to the top with ugly force, shooting out of the water, geyser-like … then falling back.

"I'd never expect? A place I'd never expect?" I'd said at the party.

"Hmm," Mrs. Weems had answered.

"Are you going to tell me?" I'd asked.

She had waited demurely. She had smiled and then rolled her eyes.

"If you-ah wewwy good boy," she had said, and had started to lead me back into the room where Mrs. Brandyworth had just arrived. But just before we re-entered through the French doors, she'd pulled me closer and whispered into my ear the answer.

"I ide ith in my bu-bi-nuh."

"My bu-bi-nuh." That was it. I had thought she was saying "In my Bible," when what she was really telling me was that she hid the original ring in her "vagina." (Hey, it was her idea, not mine.)

"Bu-bi-nuh; Vagina" I said, over and over. And there was only one way Mrs. Weems's vagina could have gotten into Salinger's chili. (Hey, it was Salinger's idea, not mine.)

It all came together in a second. Everything. The object, the powder in Salinger's trunk, the chili, Mr. Reynolds from the pig farm. It piled up and I was more than just physically sick. Salinger hadn't bought pork because he'd used another meat source—the Junior League ladies, and the powder in the trunk wasn't heroin or cocaine—it was some so-far unknown substance, but it was clear that it was poisonous and had been added to the chili he was cooking.

As if I wasn't sick already, the thought that I had just almost tasted one, if not all of the Junior League ladies, made my stomach perform another gymnastics routine. So far I was gold medalist in this year's Olympics. I would have been more than happy to let that honor go to some third world country. I hurled everything I could (literally) come up with between two electrical generators which bellowed their exhaust and noise around me. Normally, when I do this physical feat, it sounds like a large farm animal exploding, reverberating within a white porcelain commode. Now it was more reminiscent of someone being choked to death.

Catching my breath for a moment, I thought to myself, "Junior Leaguers—the other white meat." Then I let loose another dry heave and felt the soreness in my abdominal muscles. When I was done, I knew I had to stand up fast—and think. Now it was clear that Salinger knew about Henrid's escapades with the botulism and had probably helped. But did that mean that Henrid was aware that Salinger had used the women as meat in his chili?

At that moment, the phrase "I'll take care of you" no longer held for me the warm, fuzzy connotation that it once had. Salinger had uttered it that first day on my ride into the town, and I had believed him. And he wasn't kidding.

Now the expression took on an entirely new meaning. I was reminded of the long-told story of an American couple visiting China. It's a story that has been repeated many times, elevating itself to myth status. I'd give credit here for its creation, but by now it is so a part of our handed-down storytelling that finding the originator would be impossible. Suffice it to say that I'm not taking credit for it myself—though I would like to.

Back to the couple visiting China; the story goes like this:

They had brought with them to the land of rice and exotic dishes, their pet poodle, and, not wanting to leave it in the hotel room (God only knows why), took it to a restaurant with them that evening.

After being served water and a menu, they discovered that the dog was becoming a bit rowdy and asked the waiter if he could "take care of it" for them. Said waiter did, and some time later, Fido was served with an apple in its mouth. It seems that the lack of rudimentary Chinese language, coupled with a dearth of cultural facts (they *do* eat dogs in China), had caused a most unpleasant situation for not only the couple, but the restaurant, and especially Fi-Fi, who no longer had a say in the matter. Oh, and as a special touch, the dog's rhinestone collar had been placed on top of the well-done pooch, just in case the couple might think that the restaurant owners were trying to pass off another lesser-quality barking machine as that evening's dinner. How thoughtful.

This all has something to do with food, Salinger, and this book—just keep going.

So now, with the discovery that Salinger had not only gotten rid of those individuals who had so threatened his winning the chili cook-off, but had actually included them as part of the recipe along with poor castrated Harry Killchrist (an explanation finally for the reason that Charles Adams's body was used in Dick Hunter's grave instead of Harry's—don't worry, I'm having trouble too), I feared for my life. While I sported no rhinestone collar (I had a ring—does that count?), I did have vast amounts of information on him, Miss Henrid, and the rest of the town. Not to mention the reason he'd won the contest for the last five years. To be blunt, I didn't want to be on the menu, so I played it close to home. Thinking about the possibilities and permutations the situation could follow, I was reminded of the initial reason I'd come to Chalybeate. It was to write a cookbook (okay, it was for the money); I just hadn't planned that some of the ingredients would be so exotic (or not). Right about now, Mrs. Childers's *Road-kill Sou-flay* was sounding pretty good compared to Salinger's winning chili recipe.

Reeling from the revelations, I climbed up a set of back steps to try and get a look at where Salinger and Henrid were, to see if they were still surrounded by crowds of adoring fans. Sure enough, there was Miss Henrid with Mrs. Weems's fake ring flashing in the setting sun's rays, and she *wasn't* eating. But Salinger was nowhere to be found. Partially hidden behind the tacky canvas screen, I searched the crowd.

Just as I was about to give up, something cold and hard pressed itself against my head.

"If you move, I'll blow your brains out," a voice said, and I unfortunately recognized it as belonging to Salinger.

"Turn around slowly and don't make any fast moves," he added, not that it was really necessary.

Part of me wanted to laugh at his dialogue, and part wanted to throw up again. I settled for doing as he asked. He moved the gun and pointed it at my stomach as he stood on the back of the platform, just behind the canvas. I was outside the material backing for the stage. If anyone came walking along they might see me but not him. The sound of the generators was almost deafening.

"When did you figure it out?" he asked, the gun sill pointed at my middle section.

"Just a while ago," I said. I was light-headed again and felt my tenacity going. Being poisoned and realizing you've almost eaten a Junior Leaguer will do that. "Did you put botulism in the chili too?" I asked. I was wheezing, barely able to breathe.

"Huh?" he asked, and I remembered Salinger was deaf in one ear and that with the generators creating their din, it made it even harder for him to hear anything.

"Did you put botulism in the chili too?" I repeated at a louder volume.

"No need to, them Junior Leaguers was full of it. And cyanide works much better—chili's got both in it. What don't kill 'em now would surely kill 'em later," Salinger retorted loudly over the generator noise. From where I was standing I could still see Tuck, holding court over at Salinger's chili station.

"How very Jim Jones. So you ground up the ladies of the Junior League for your meat," I said, almost doubling over with pain (and a little disgust).

"Well, not all," he replied.

I looked up at him. I was now bent over: a geometry problem for fifth graders who had to determine how straight-up-and-down had turned into a perfect ninety degrees.

"I left out Mrs. Childers. Even we sociopaths have our limits," he said. "Besides, you are what you eat, son." He waited, obviously in no hurry, then continued: "Seriously, would you want to eat somethin' that dirty anyways?" and with that he cocked the hammer of his pistol.

"Wait!" I said, out of breath.

"What, you need more info? So I used the wood chipper from the next town to grind up the bones and parts I didn't cook with. Let's see … am I leavin' anythin' out? Oh, yeah, how else you think them tomatoes gets to be big as basketballs? Bone meal. Makes a damn good fertilizer," he shouted over the noise, obviously not worried that anyone would hear him.

"I see you lookin' in the direction of the crowd," he went on. "Don't worry. They'll all be dead soon. And even if old Doc Patterson could come …" and here Salinger paused and smiled, "he'd never be able to treat 'em all. Plus, there ain't no real antidote for botulism that I knows of. And there ain't no Doc Patterson no more neither."

"Double negative," I said, dry-heaving.

"What?"

"You used a double negative. A couple, I think." I was stalling for time. Anything.

"Lord, God, son. You is more fucked-up than I thought. Who gives a shit about the way somebody talks when you're getting ready to die? And just in case you're wonderin' about that cookbook and your binder and all? Burned. Did it this afternoon. Ain't nothin' left of your stuff 'cept that computer you got in that fairy case you carries around with you, and I'm gonna take that off your body as soon as I put a bullet right between your eyes. That is, unless you drop dead right in front of me and save me the trouble. And I don't guess it matters much since you'll be dead anyways in a few minutes since you ate some of my chili. (I didn't correct him on that point.) Oh, and I'll be takin' that money that Tuck done give you, along with any other you might have. Figger it's in that case as we couldn't find it."

Normally he would have raised his gun, but since I was now bent over, the gun was already pointed between my eyes. He made a clicking sound with his mouth (which I found totally unnecessary and a tad torturous). He was about to splatter me onto the back of a bad artistic rendition of a bowl of chili. Funny, the things that go through your mind when you're about to die.

I saw his finger start to squeeze the trigger. "No! Just a minute," I managed to shout.

"Son, I've give up just about all my secrets, and I ain't about to let you slide on outa here with 'em, even if you could. 'Sides, these townsfolk love my ass right now, and they hate yourn."

"Hey, what did one cannibal say to the other when they were eating a clown?" I asked, still trying to buy a moment. There was some movement behind Salinger and I was trying to see if it was a person or

309

just the wind from the generators as they blew their exhaust into the air. If someone was coming, they'd see the sheriff with his gun drawn, see that I was helpless and perhaps do something—anything.

"Oh, you poor bastard. Tellin' jokes when you're gettin' ready to die. And I'm doin' you a favor, takin' you out a-for that cyanide does. Okay, I'll play. It's the least I kin do for a stupid city boy like you. So, tell me about the two cannibals eating the clown. What did one say to the othern?"

"Does this taste funny to you?"

"Does what taste funny?"

"No, that's ... the punch ... line," I barely managed to get out. I was staring death in the face and my life rushed before me. It (my life, not death) had become one big parenthetical insertion. I imagined standing before The Maker, summing up my existence and a list of things I'd done (or not)—a first-day-of-school-type scenario with me about to wet my pants. We'd all have to stand before this Greater Being, this God-Teacher, and explain who we were, what we'd done, and say something interesting about ourselves.

There I was (in my mind), summing up my life in one moment: "I found two penises in a jar, was tricked by a transsexual into killing five horrible women, escaped botulism poisoning, almost ate some of the women who were made into a bowl of chili sprinkled generously with cyanide, came close to choking on a $40,000 ring, and got shot between the eyes by a mass murderer." Then, turning to Rodney Dangerfield, in front of God, I would say, "Your turn." The poor bastard wouldn't stand a chance in this one-upmanship competition to see who'd been metaphorically fucked in the ass the most. Respect can't be earned—it needs to be bought.

"I think we're done here," Salinger said, completely void of humor. (I thought it was a pretty good joke—the one about the two cannibals.) He stretched his arm out toward me and prepared to shoot, but out of the corner of my eye I saw the main rope that was holding the canvas up. It swayed and the backdrop came loose. Someone must have done it on purpose, for the large sheet of heavy material came sailing down, right on top of Salinger's head. Because of the generator noise and the general mayhem of the crowd, Salinger was unaware until it hit him. I jumped (okay, I fell off the platform—I was very sick) and as he fired the gun, the bullet missed, sailed into one of the cooking stations, hit one of the enormous cast-iron kettles, ricocheted off it, and flew directly into the gas tank of a 1965 Chevy. The car exploded. (What, I ask you, *is* a 1965 Chevy really good for besides blowing up?)

The crowd screamed, I rolled into the brush in back of the stage, and General Mayhem reported for duty at the nearest recruiting station.

Within minutes I had gotten control of myself (and my stomach) and determined that Salinger was still alive and not going to give up, especially since he'd told me what he'd done with the Junior League (honestly, I wasn't all that upset). I lurched off into the undergrowth and followed a footpath into the nearby woods. Taking a moment to get my bearings, I headed, as best I could, as far away from town as possible.

I had made it to the other side of a small forest and come into a field when I thought the end was upon me. While managing to regurgitate most of the cyanide, I had nevertheless retained a good deal in my system and was quite ill. My legs would barely hold me up. As if things weren't bad enough, it began to rain—nothing too heavy; a sprinkling, really. In the distance, through the trees, I could still hear the sounds of turmoil at the cook-off. The flaming car had now evidently set a decorative overhang on fire and the conflagration was getting bigger. It was nearing sundown and the glow competed with the orange and red display just opposite me. I squinted at something large and white up in front, not sure what it was. Pressing on through the field, I came to a line of trees, then another clearing.

The old Yoke-Wacko-Hunter Plantation confronted me. There seemed to be no getting away from the family who had been some of Chalybeate Springs's first settlers, and my heart sank once more. The domicile stared back at me—shuttered eyes not willing to see the truth, rotting roof, peeling paint, and cracked stucco: an aged dowager with no feeding tube, will, or power of attorney—but one who refused to die. The only thing completely untouched and looking as it probably had when originally built were the gargantuan columns that held the house up. Stoic Greek "We're better than you are" monoliths, witnesses to a time ... (dare I say it?) *Gone With the Wind.*

I stretched out my hand toward the house and started to run, remembering that no one lived there any longer, thinking that it would be a safe refuge. But as soon as I had taken four or five steps, I collapsed. I lifted my head momentarily, looking at the darkening sky, and at that moment the greatest roar was heard.

The Civil War had come to life again and shots were being fired all over. Two fields and a small forest away the din competed with the roaring in my head. Troops rushed over the landscape. Grays against Blues, muskets firing. Rebel yells. Windows breaking. Women being raped. In my mind I heard *Dixie* and tried to sing along. Just as

311

the sky darkened with rain clouds, a fireworks display shot onto the overhead blackening canvas, with reds, yellows, whites, and blues. The 1965 Chevy and its flaming friends had evidently reached the gun powder in the Fourth of July rockets, sending them hurtling into space. I watched for one brief second as they exploded above me, and before they had time to fall to earth, I was face-down in the dirt.

I remember feeling something pelting the back of my neck and thanking God for the coolness, thinking it must be rain. I remember smelling the goodness of the earth, thinking how nice it was to be next to something that was not a gun or a cooking pot. I remember feeling the weight of my body press against the earth, the rain becoming momentarily heavier, and the scent of wisteria and boxwood. Then a large bolt of lightening illuminated the atmosphere, and I journeyed into the land of "I forgot."

50

He Brings Catalepsy

The sound of rain awakened me. The dripping did also, only this time it wasn't on my neck—it was on my face. Something was wrong. Either I had turned over in the field, or heaven (I'm making an assumption here at this point, regardless of some of the things I've done—and that person I hit with my car wouldn't have lived anyway as he had cancer) … or heaven, as I was saying, had some serious roof problems.

A face as black as night appeared over me, saying nothing. "I should have known God would be a Negro," I moaned, putting my hand to my head. My mouth tasted like a garbage can and I felt as if I'd been run over by Salinger's police car, then dragged all the way to Mobile. Oh, no. I remembered him—Salinger. Survival mode kicked in and I tried to sit up, but God's big black hand pushed me down. (Nothing all that new in my life.) Then his large index finger made that "Wait just a minute" gesture in front of my face: the Sistine Chapel with a color change, only pointing up and not sideways. Personally, I didn't feel like playing Adam at this moment.

"Great," I thought, "you have to wait even in heaven." I shifted my eyes from side-to-side, aided by what slight movement I could get out of my neck. I was in a room of gigantic proportions. The ceiling was a good fifteen feet high and the entire chamber looked as if it had been at the bottom of the sea for decades. Furnished opulently at one time, it was now a broken, dusty, and decaying mess. It was, in short, a bad Faulkner novel come to (for lack of a better term)…life.

The thunder rolled overhead. God had just gotten a strike. He was doing quite well from the sound of things. But wait, he was in the room with me, so who was bowling upstairs? The phrase, "It was a dark and stormy night," comes to mind, moth-eaten and clichéd though it may be. Lying still and being subjected to water torture from the leaking ceiling, I had time to gather my thoughts, if not my wits. Some of it was coming up to the surface—some of it wasn't. I tried to backtrack: Face-down in dirt. Fireworks. Civil War generals. A battle (theirs and mine). Before that, taking a few steps. A field. A line of trees? A field. A park? Canvas falling. God's big arm cutting a rope. Salinger with a gun. Bad joke about cannibals. Discovery that I had almost eaten some portion of the ladies of the Junior League. (Memory is a curse.)

I stopped.

That was far enough.

My head was splitting and I once again brought my hand to it. But this time God beat me to the punch with a cool white washcloth. His large hand smelled like that of one of our housekeepers when I was a child. I remembered her touch as she nursed me back to health from a bout with the flu—the texture of her dark flesh, the smell, the sensation, and the cool water and white washcloth. I felt comforted. I felt alive. I felt safe. Time was past, present, and future all rolled into one. And then ... I slept.

Morning arrived in the form of seventeen slants through a window-length plantation shutter. Most of the sunlight landed on the floor and was absorbed immediately by the bare wood planks. The rest of it ran onto a faded and worn oriental rug, up the sides of the colossal mahogany bed I was in, across the sheets that bathed my feet with their softness, and onto the wall. Massive pieces of wallpaper hung loosely from the sides of the room. The water-stained plaster played tricks with my eyes, forming monsters, waterfalls, cast-iron kettles, dancing cherubs, and maps of Thailand. I was ill—I knew that much. I was Jem in *To Kill a Mockingbird*. I was the Truman Capote character in *Other Voices, Other Rooms* after he is bitten by the cottonmouth (I could actually taste the turnip and feel the water, see my legs beneath the mullioned glass-like surface before the snake sank its fangs into me). I was Huck Finn, Tom Sawyer, even Beth from *Little Women*. I was any and everyone, but I wasn't me. Something was different. Life had changed. My mind had changed. I had reached a fork in the road. A "go this way, and not that way" type of experience had occurred. And I was now lying in some bed, in some enormous room, coming back to life, slowly, but coming. A second time, if you will.

The door to the room opened and the most enormous African-American man I had ever seen walked in. It was God—the very one who had taken care of me the night before.

"Jecko?" I said meekly, trying to rise up. A good Lazarus I was not. My head agreed and I lay back down. The great man nodded. I was thankful he didn't try to speak à la Mrs. Weems's vocal lessons. The sound had been heartbreaking that day as Mrs. Childers and I listened, and that was the last thing I needed at this moment. But I felt some need to let him know I was his friend. Some need to say something, however weak I might be.

I tried to make my lips move so that he could read them. He smiled, setting down a large tray he had brought in. My head hurt too much to see what was on it, but I could tell by the *ping* of glassware and the *ka-ching* of silver that I was being served with the real thing. I smelled chicken soup and was drawn to it. A spoon the size of a shoe fed me and water was given to me in a crystal goblet. After managing a bit of nourishment, I turned to the man. Knowing he couldn't speak or hear, I tried to enunciate as much as possible so that he could read my quivering lips.

"Am I ... in the Hunter ... plantation?" I asked. Even talking hurt.

He nodded.

"Does anyone ... know ... I'm here?"

Nothing.

I tried again. "Does anyone know ... I'm ... here ... now?"

He shook his head "No."

"Am I ... safe?"

He nodded a "Yes."

That was enough lesson for one day. I sank back, mentally and physically, and Jecko carried the tray from the room. It was only as he was closing the door with one hand while holding the tray with the other that I observed the flat silver object to be covered with the whitest and most starched cloth I had ever seen. Jecko had obviously been busy.

Most of that day and the next night I slept. If I went to the bathroom, it was news to me. I remember water from time to time, but not more food. Finally, my second morning came. I know it wasn't the first because rain lightly peppered the aged glass and there were no more sunlight slants. Dirty streaks ran down the glass and changed the shadows on the patina-laden walls. Everything smelled slightly of smoke, old wood, and wet rugs.

Able to sit up for the first time, I took five minutes to stand, then another ten to cross the room. Now at the window, I threw open the sash and pressed on the cypress shutters. Rain pelted everything, hitting the ground with great force. I looked toward the town. Everything seemed black and ruined—just like my psyche. Looking down at an antique table which was covered with a tattered sepia-colored doily, I saw my laptop case. I managed the energy to open it

315

and find my computer inside, along with the money that had been given to me by Mrs. Weems, Mrs. Brandyworth, and Miss Henrid. I shut the case and turned.

I managed the room and the door, then made my way to the top of the stairs. Below me curved an immense staircase. From the ceiling hung a chandelier the size of Saturn, its splayed and shattered remnants askew with age and neglect. Jecko rounded the corner and came to the foot of the steps. He motioned for me to go back.

"What? I'm not going to try and come down," I said loudly, and with as much lip motion as possible. I remembered how Mrs. Weems had tried to teach him to speak by holding his hand on her throat. He certainly couldn't have read her lips as she had none. Either my message squeaked through or he gave up, for he left the entrance hall and I returned to my room. As I mentally waded through the remnants of my life I physically came to the white rumpled bed sheets. I had evidently hit my head at some point between being poisoned and being carried into the house as there were faint blood smears and stains on my pillow case—a regular shroud of Turin without the deity-imbued benefits or guarantees of absolution. I fell back into the land of warm-white and drifted off again.

Later that day, Jecko brought more broth and water. Both tasted of iron. I construed that he wasn't poisoning me and that the water had come from a well. I went back in my mind to my childhood days with my mother's relatives and their lack of running water. They had lived in the country and something about it, while backward, seemed simple and appealing. Now I had no choice.

I tried the question-and-answer session with Jecko again.

"Did everyone die in the town?" I asked, thinking it the most morbid of questions but remembering the cyanide, the chili, the body parts used to make the award-winning recipe.

Jecko nodded a "Yes."

I breathed a sigh of relief, pernicious though it may have been.

"Are Salinger and Tuck Henrid dead?" I asked, just to be sure "everyone" included those two.

"Yes" again—with a nod.

I looked down at the floor, thinking: Good, that meant I was safe for a while. But these people had relatives and the town was not totally unknown.

"Are we the only two left?"

A pause. A confused look. Then a "Yes."

316

"One more question," I said. Exhaustion was coming over me like heat waves rising out of a sugarcane field on a mid-August day in southern Louisiana.

Jecko nodded.

"Did you ever have sex with Mrs. Weems?"

Jecko paused for a moment. I made a motion—sticking one finger into my other hand's fist. He jumped back.

"No," he shook his head dramatically, and with that I passed out on the bed.

51

Cab Gal, She Try Penis

hen I came to again, I do not know. I do not know if it was the next morning or a week later. I had lost all conception of time. All I *did* know what that I was feeling much better. It was as if a doctor had come upon me during my sleep and administered something that had transformed me. I felt Rumplestiltskinish (will Faulkner *never* die?) and I had a good growth of beard to prove it.

Once again I made my way out of the room and to the top of the stairs. I was wearing the same clothes, covered with mud. Evidently I had worn these since my rendezvous-gone-wrong with death, not noticing when I had first been nursed back to health by Jecko. For some reason, I worried that the wet mud on the bottom of my shoes might cause me to fall. Then I saw how dry the dirt was and descended the steep staircase, trying to calculate how long it would have taken my shoes to reach their present state. The stairs creaked under my weight, and as I landed in the entrance hall I surprised Jecko. I looked right at him so that I could be sure he understood.

"I want to go out and look around."

He shook his head a "No." This upset me. It wasn't raining and I had already been a prisoner more than once in the past week.

"I'm going *out*," I said more emphatically.

This time Jecko said nothing, but hung his head. He watched as I started for the door, then came after me. I assumed it was to stop me, but instead, he pressed ahead and pulled the door open.

Stepping out onto a wide verandah, I surveyed what was before me. A dirt road (now mud) led from the front of the plantation down to the highway. I had seen the route from the other direction, but never from this end. I had viewed it the night Salinger brought me home from Mary-Ellen's—when I had seen Mrs. Childers turn into the drive. Now I saw it through another's eyes, for I was no longer Jackson Tippett McCrae sent to help with a cookbook, but an author who had barely escaped death. Shelby would have been irritated, no doubt.

Jecko stood behind me looking worried. I shouldered the steps by leaning on a railing and made it to the earth. Finally. The ground was muddy and steamed even though it was mid-morning. As I began to turn to the left and make my way around the house, Jecko jumped to my side. He attempted to tell me something, making a sign with his arms; a sort of criss-cross as if to say, "No, don't."

"You don't want me to go around this side of the house?" I said to his face.

He nodded "Yes."

"Well, if that isn't a red flag to do something, I don't know what is," I said, not caring whether he understood or not, and stomped in that direction. At once my head ached from the pounding and I slowed down, but no sooner had I done so than my foot hit something soft and fat lying in the weeds.

My eyes focused in the morning light and I tried to decide whether to be relieved or worried. There, lying supine before me, were the bodies of Salinger and Henrid. Both were quite dead and bloated (I must have been asleep for longer than I thought), and both had a surprised look on their faces (who wouldn't, being killed and all?) with their mouths wide open.

Looking closer, I noticed that their speaking orifices weren't so much opened as stuffed with something. By this time, Jecko had procured a stick and had walked to where their heads lay. He motioned for me to come. What could I do? I went, side-stepping their outstretched arms and the wild burs that grew in the yard. The scent of Queen Anne's lace filtered through the air with a trace of cow dung, completing the country-scent tableau. Then the wind shifted. The bodies had begun to decompose.

Poking at Salinger's lips, Jecko pried open the mouth even further, moving the object that was stuck down the man's throat to one side so I could see. Then he did the same for Tuck Henrid.

"Okay. I get it," I said, looking right at him. Then I thought about his voice lesson with Weems where Childers and I had witnessed her trying to teach him how to speak. "Haaaaaaaa-penis," I said, and it didn't matter this time whether he got the double entendre or not.

With his stick, Jecko had shown me that, not only were Tuck and Salinger quite dead, but that they had been choked with two penises. I surmised that they were the exact two which I had seen in Henrid's home, and turned away, quickly walking back to the house. I could hear Jecko following. He caught up to me and I turned to him.

"Did you do that? Kill them? Stick those … things in their mouth?"

He said nothing but simply looked at me, completely blank.

"You *do* know that someone is going to come eventually and want to know what happened," I said.

He nodded a "Yes."

"We have to do something."

Again a "Yes." Then he motioned for me to follow and I did once again, this time to the other side of the house. Parked there, in a muddy gullied-out drive, was a 1953 turquoise Buick (did anyone in this town even *know* what an SUV looked like?). While I've never liked Buicks (see first book), I was grateful for the transportation.

"You drive?" I asked, turning toward The Jolly Black Giant.

I got a non-verbal "Yes."

"So do I. Which one of us is going to drive?" Jecko pointed at me. Thank God. This time I would be behind the wheel. At this point, all I needed was a black chauffeur driving Miss Daisy. We got in the car and I started it up. It had that ... old car smell: real leather, real fabric, real plastic, real 1950s. It was like driving a boat. Turning to Jecko, I asked, "Is this the Weemses' car?"

No.

"Is this the Brandyworth's car?

No.

"Is this the Killchrist car?"

No.

Finally I gave up. "You know, I don't give a shit whose car it is," I said, and we drove toward town.

52

Rebel Ashcan Pigsty

Before we had traveled less than a half a mile, I notice something shiny in the road. Something silver. Whatever it was, another one appeared. I recognized a china plate, smashed, and another in pieces. I stopped the car and got out. There was silver cutlery and china all along the road. Whoever had thrown these items out had done so with great abandon and even possible anger, but, like a tornado, the force had been unpredictable and one solitary fork had landed straight down with such gusto that it had stuck directly into the soft, sun-heated asphalt surface, evidently at midday when things were at their hottest.

I reached down and pulled the culinary implement from the highway—a regular "sword-in-the-stone" scenario without all the glory and nifty knights-of-the-roundtable costume, and got back in the car. Jecko and I made our way once again toward the town, following the broken brick-a-brac like a squirrel follows peanuts. "Nothing like a good metaphor," I said out loud to myself.

While Chalybeate Springs had been small to begin with, it was much more so now. I'll be blunt: Not a building was standing. Every house, every store—everything except the plantation house that I now occupied—was gone. Blackened, like a piece of Cajun catfish, each house told only part of its story. A piece of a toy, a headboard of a bed, a sink, a bathtub, even a washer and dryer; they all stood sentry over the remains of the homes, while nothing remained of others. "Uneven" would be a word to use here.

"When did this happen?" I asked. Then I deduced that I was looking ahead and not at Jecko who was riding shotgun. I realized I'd asked my question as if I'd been expecting him to volley up paragraphs on the last few days. Stopping the car, I reached out to him and touched his arm. "Did this happen the night of the chili cook-off?"

A "Yes," was given up.

"But it rained that night, didn't it?"

Jecko made a "so-so" motion with one of his hands.

"Not that much?"

He nodded in agreement.

"But later it rained heavily, and put the fires out?"

Affirmative.

"Did Salinger and Henrid do all this?"

"Yes" again.

Silly me, I thought of my computer at a time like this. "Is everything burned in the park? The generators too?" I asked, hoping I might find power for the laptop and finish my writings. (Come on—what else was I going to do?)

I got a "Yes," unfortunately.

We looked around. Nothing was left. There was no one to arrest, but sooner or later someone would come from outside to investigate, and with Jecko and me the only survivors, we'd have some explaining to do.

"You know people will come?"

A blank look was all I got.

"Has anyone else been seen?"

"No," was indicated by a shake of the head.

I started the car and we moved through the streets of Chalybeate Springs, taking in the destruction. It was as if an enormous black-smoke tornado had descended upon the town and wreaked havoc with lives and property.

"The plot sickens," I said, to no one in particular as we turned down the street where the Weemses had lived. Jecko looked out the window and raised a hand, putting one index finger to the glass.

I stopped in front of the house and touched him again to get his attention. "I'm sorry," I said, realizing that I'd said it loudly, as if Jecko was only partially deaf. He nodded and looked sad. Putting the car into drive once again, we headed back toward the plantation. There was nothing I could do now for the people of the town, but then, hadn't I done enough?

It's funny how a place that has been a part of you, even for a few moments or a few days, can become so important in your life. Walking back from the driveway to the front door of the plantation felt like coming home after a long vacation that had included amebic dysentery and no air-conditioning. Jecko and I made our way into the cavernous living room and sat down—he in an over-stuffed smoking-chair, and me on a tattered velvet sofa. "Beltzer," I said to myself, noting the woodwork and construction. "Must be worth a fortune."

Swags and drapes still clung to the window frames, attempting to keep the hot Southern sun at bay, and the sheer material underneath moved unsteadily, like some medicine-laced, sherry-drunk dowager waiting for death as if he were a late-coming guest. The fabric occasionally bowed into the room with the help of the wind—a swirling petticoat at a ball given too many years ago by then-already ghosts.

I turned to Jecko and waved to get his attention as he appeared to be nodding off. Who could blame him after all that had happened?

"We need to get out of here. To the next town," I mouthed.

A definite shaking of his head told me "No."

"Why not?" I asked. Stupid me. What did I want—an answer? I tried again. "Is it because you *want* the police from another town to come here and find out?"

He didn't seem to understand—perhaps the sentence was too long. I went at it again, slower. "Is it ...because you *want* ... the police ... from another ..."

But he stopped me with a violent shaking of the head, indicating that he wanted *no* police of *any* form.

"We can't live here," I said to him, emphasizing my words with hand gestures.

He understood but nodded a "Yes." He pointed to the floor.

"No," I said. "People are going to come. We need ... money ... we need food ...we would need to fix the ... house up. Do you understand?"

An affirmative response was given. While I remembered the currency that Weems, Henrid, and Brandyworth had (ahem) donated (cash, thank God, from Henrid and Brandyworth—can you imagine how useful the Weems check was now?), I knew that if the police came, we'd need more than that amount for attorneys, and if for some insane reason I decided to stay, the house would take much more money to make it inhabitable. I needed to get back to New York, anyway. Or did I?

With no one to interrupt my thoughts, I gave in to the fantasy. I had always wanted a house like this, just, well ... not acquired in quite this way. It would be a Southerner's dream, that is, when it had been fixed up. There was no running water and no electricity, the water situation evident by the iron taste in the food that Jecko had brought me. I had discovered the lack of electricity when I had searched for a plug to recharge the battery in my laptop.

In mid fantasy-slash-rumination, Jecko stood up and motioned for me to follow him. As there was precious little else to do, I tagged along behind. It was all very Mark Twain. He led me through the ballroom-sized foyer and down the long hallway to the back of the house. We traversed several steps and he walked me over to a garden that was hidden behind a fence made of willow branches and some brush. Turning the corner was like walking into the land of *Oz*.

Gigantic vegetables of every size and shape lounged around in the sun while a swarm of bees buzzed in and out of squash blossoms.

"Did you do this?" I asked, looking him straight in the face.

I got a "No." Then he made an up-and-down gesture.

"Up and down? I don't get it." He looked around and then ran toward the house.

"Hey, wait," I said, gingerly picking my way out of the land of plenty. But before I could get out of Brer Rabbit territory, Jecko was back with an old-fashioned washboard. Okay, so this was going to be charades. I had nothing else to do but wait for the state patrol to haul my ass off to jail.

Jecko then made his up-and-down motion on the board again.

"Clothes?"

Up-and-down.

"Wash? Oh, *Wash!*"

Next he cradled his two arms together.

"Childers" I said. "I ... get ... it. Wash Childers. Mrs. Wash Childers planted this." I wondered why, but *that* explanation was long gone. She didn't live in the house—that much I knew, but Salinger and I had spotted her one night driving her mule and wagon up the road that led to the plantation, so there was some reason she came here. Evidently this was it. Salinger had just figured she was crazy. Maybe she was, tending to vegetables in the middle of the night. Perhaps she was paranoid, I don't know. Maybe Chalybeate Springs was going to start a "Largest Vegetable Competition." A sort of spin-off of the chili cook-off.

"Too late for that now," I said to myself.

Then Jecko tugged at my arm. I followed again and he led me to a well.

"Water, I get that too." Starting back to the house, he led me into the kitchen. He threw open the cabinets next to the stove and revealed jars of preserves and homemade vegetables. The doors to the storage space were glass—that non-see-through type—you know, like a million little snow flakes? The kind you might see in doors of old-fashioned offices from the 1930s.

"Oh, no," I said, making a cutting motion with my arms. "No. No homemade canned goods for me. I know all about them." But Jecko was not to be placated. He pulled me toward the cabinets and ran his hand over the foods.

324

"I'm ... not ... going ... near that ..." but I stopped mid sentence. While there were about twenty jars of every shape and size, containing every preserved fruit and vegetable known to mankind, there was one particularly large one in the back. Jecko was pointing to it.

"What? You're hungry now?"

He looked totally confused.

"Are ... you ... hungry *now*?" I tried again, even attempting fake sign language. (I probably said something like, "Me handcart France see anteater panties," not that he would have known.)

"Okay, fine, let's get it out if you're so interested in it," I added. I said this more to myself really, as I was getting frustrated with whatever game we had been playing. Where he was going with this I had *no* idea.

"You take these green beans," I said, handing him a jar, "and then this small one of ... looks like peach preserves ... and then this one of ... tomatoes." I paused. "You know, these don't look half bad."

We continued emptying out the cupboard with me handing the jars off to Jecko and him setting them on a large and badly-worn-out kitchen table.

"This one of beets and this one ..." but I couldn't finish. Most of the jars were out of the way now, and the one Jecko had been pointing to was partially revealed. The kitchen was not the best-lit area of the house, but just at the moment I was moving a large home-canned jar of pickled okra, the sun shot through the tattered curtains and put nature's spotlight directly on the jar in question.

"What the hell?" I said, as my eyes tried to focus. There was some kind of small jar floating in the larger jar, supported by whatever food the owner of the ... house ... had ... "Oh, my God, no."

I stepped back.

It couldn't be.

The jar was extremely large—five gallons by my estimate. I had moved it slightly as I was taking the pickled okra from in front of it, and now, with the sunlight hitting the container, the liquid swirled around inside, loosening particles of debris so that the effect was like that of a giant snow globe. A smaller jar bobbed at the top, inside the larger one—a life-saving buoy that would make much more sense once its own contents were revealed.

"Please God, tell ... me..."

I couldn't finish. My eyes had adjusted as the object inside the jar turned slowly in the liquid. It floated effortlessly in its surrounding

325

atmosphere, not touching the bottom or sides, but perfectly suspended. And this seemed most odd, especially when I stopped and considered that a baby with four legs, two heads, and no arms—one that had been so crammed down into this jar, this final resting place—could look so at peace now that death had been sent mercifully so long ago, and that the horror of its life had been preserved for all time.

53

Hyper Glass Cabinet

As I was incapable of moving at that point, Jecko started for the jar. I couldn't have lifted it at any rate, nor would I have tried. "What are you …" I began to say, but realized he was facing away from me. I backed up in disgust, one hand resting on the farm sink and the other on a rusted pump. Jecko gently transported the jar (Thank you, Jesus), bearing it against his stomach and holding it with both arms, cradling it like what it was—a baby. He set in on the kitchen table and looked at me.

"What? What next?" I asked. I couldn't decide if I was upset, mad, disgusted, sad—or just felt sorry for everyone in the world. Maybe all of the above. Jecko pointed to the jar, his large index finger shooting down at the top.

"You don't actually think I'm going to let you open that, do you?"

He ignored me and began to screw the lid off.

"No! Don't … oh, my God, what …"

Too late. The lid was off. The room filled with the familiar smell of formaldehyde; an uncomfortable reminiscence of the two penises found at Miss Tuck Henrid's, God rest her soul (what there was of it).

"You can't be serious," I said as Jecko reached into the jar and pulled the smaller one from it. "What now? Is this an Egyptian thing? They bury the heart separately?" I said, and started for the door, but Jecko jumped at me and blocked my path. I held up both hands—an indication in any culture not to touch a person—and backed away.

Again he did his "Hold up one finger; wait a minute" routine. I watched, fascinated and disgusted. Jecko sat the smaller jar down on the table and then looked around for a towel or piece of cloth to wipe off the top (he was at least neat.) I spotted one next to the sink and threw it to him. "Might as well use this," I said, "I'm not staying here now, and I certainly won't be using the kitchen before I go."

He gently unscrewed the lid off the smaller container and reached in with his index and middle finger, pulling out the largest wad of cash I had ever seen in my life.

"Money," I said. He nodded. This was good.

"But where? Where … did it come … from?"

Jecko once again made the up-and-down motion, and then did his babes-in-arms number.

"Irony," I said. "It's everywhere." He looked confused. "Never mind. I'll ... tell ... you ... later."

So Mrs. Childers had not only been paranoid about her vegetables, but her cash as well. Then I figured it out: If you were going to burn your house down five times, you certainly wouldn't want to keep your money at *home*. And what a perfect place to hide it—in the very jar that housed the baby that had ruined Salinger's life. I thought for a moment: J.D. Salinger—an anagram for "Singled Jar." Iro ... no, I won't bring it up again. Even if anyone had thought to look there, in the glass jar with infant, they wouldn't have had the nerve to open the thing and take it out. Well, no one but Jecko. But how did he know? I could always ask ...

"How ... do you, did you ... know? About the money?" I said, so that he could see my lips clearly.

He once again made the scrub board and baby gesture.

"No. How did you find *out* ... for the ... *first* ... time?"

I received a confused look and not much more. I repeated the question again, hoping for better results. Then Jecko beckoned to me and began to move to the door.

"Hadn't you better ...close...that up first?" I said, indicating Baby Gooey and his glass house. (I wasn't worried about him throwing stones—he had no arms.) Jecko closed the jar—I felt better. I'm sure the human pickle appreciated it also, especially since that pesky smaller jar had been removed.

I followed Jecko up the staircase, and then up another flight to the floor that had lower ceilings and dormer windows—an attic, really. He moved boxes and barrels out of the way, sending the dust flying about the area. Shafts of sunlight streamed in through the filthy windows and the dust swirled inside them. It was very "baby-in-a-jar" all over again, only drier. The God-beams of sun illuminated sections of old clothes, books, sewing machines, dolls, and boxes. A crate closest to me contained books and I reached in and picked up the first one I saw. Not able to read the cover because of the thick dust that coated it, I wiped it off with the palm of my hand while Jecko did some digging of his own.

"Wouldn't you know it," I said, resignation filling each word. "Hemingway. *A Moveable Feast.* Boy, our old friend Mr. Irony is working overtime today."

By now Jecko had found what he wanted and he waved me over. He sat on a large barrel in the sunlight and motioned for me to sit down near him on one of the large flat crates. He was holding a worn velvet-covered photo album—like those from the 1800s. He gently opened it and began to delicately turn the thick pages. Sepia snapshots, black and white photos, and daguerreotypes looked back at us—flat and dead. Women in hoopskirts. Women with bustles. Men with slicked-back hair and mustaches, and then … a group of black men and women. Jecko showed me the photos, the ones that were more toward the back of the album. He pointed to one in particular and then to himself.

"That's you?" I asked.

"No." He shook his head.

"Who?"

He made a gesture with his hand held above his head.

"Taller?"

He made a face.

"Older?"

He nodded in the affirmative.

"Oh, these are your relatives?"

He was ecstatic. I took the album from him and looked at the picture. Then I discovered that I could bend the thick cardboard casing apart and remove some of the photos. I did. On the back of the aged and brittle photograph Jecko had picked was a date and inscription: "1878. Yoke-Wacko-Hunter Plantation. Children of slaves who chose to stay. Myra and William Washington, Edna Pickard, Samuel Larson and wife, Anne and Henry Childers." All those represented in the photograph were black, and none looked too happy.

"Childers," I said so that he could read my lips. "So her family was rich too … at one …time. They owned slaves too." I said.

I got a "No."

"Then why is her family name here, with the others?" Jecko got most of it. He made bizarre motions and, probably because I had been around him now for a bit, I understood.

"They worked here? As what?"

Again, the odd pantomime.

"Oh, the cooks," I said, and Jecko nodded.

"But Mrs. Childers is … was white," I said. This face-to-face thing was getting tiring. Still, inquiring minds …

Jecko shook his head.

"No?"

Then he pointed to himself, and then to me.

"Half black, half white," I said. (I'd seen this kind of thing before.) And on top of that, she'd kept her maiden name. Or married a relative.

I got a "Yes," and studied the photo in the swirling dust-light. The sun began to sink and I adjusted the book so that it was still well lit. Then I looked at Jecko's face again, the light bulb over my head finally going on.

"She worked here at one time," I said.

I thought Jecko would jump out of his skin. I had hit the nail on the head. I was on a roll. "And you did too?"

Again, the ecstasy. You couldn't blame him. It was probably the most communication he'd had in years. "So that's why she knew this place so well," I said to myself, not really caring whether Jecko could read my lips or not. "You always come back to the place you know," I mused. And that was what had brought Dick Hunter back as Tuck Henrid—the desire to return to the place where he was from, even if it was as a *she*. Obviously Mrs. Childers, as well as Jecko, had felt the same tug from the house. I looked at him. "You worked here too," I reiterated.

A nod.

"When you were small. Mrs. Childers was much older," I said.

A nod, again.

"She didn't like you."

A nod.

"But you liked her."

Same response.

We were getting good at this. It all made sense. Jecko and Mrs. Childers had returned from time to time for various purposes and sometimes just because they had missed the place. Dick Hunter was trying to do the same, although with a much more elaborate (and painful) plan. Then I thought of Hunter and Salinger, out in the yard, their bodies bloating in the sun, flies laying maggots in their eyes—it all seemed sad. Two people who had wanted to be together and weren't able to achieve it because of small-mindedness. And Hunter, who had loved his best friend so much that he was willing to have a sex-change, accompanied by the idea that he might be able to return to the house he'd once lived in and start all over, had set the wheels in motion.

Or maybe I had, that day in New York when I had made fun of a temporary receptionist whose sex none of us had been certain of. Then there was Salinger—tormented by the town—loving the one

330

person he couldn't have had openly in the one place he wanted to be—Home. The only way to accomplish it was for Hunter to change his sex, and that's what had been done. Some say marriage can only be between a man and a woman. What could they have said about Henrid and Salinger now that Hunter/Henrid was indeed a female?

Then there was Weems and Jecko, attempting to unite in their own way, a marriage of sorts, both without proper speech and one of them without hearing, still connecting innocently, though still forbidden in the eyes of many. But in some way the entire town had been deaf and dumb to each other's problems, pain, love, hate, and possibilities: Shelby with her many marriage attempts; Killchrist wanting to relive high school forever; the Brandyworths doing what they did out of guilt and shame, becoming overly religious to hide their faults and sins—their attraction to one thing leading them in the opposite direction, hoping for salvation, delivering up hypocrisy. And now Mrs. Childers, wanting to hide her miscegenetic past, ashamed of it, knowing that if it were found out, that she would be ruined—more so than she already was.

I wondered why Miss Henrid had not tried to deal with Childers in some other way—blackmail or some such manner, but then it became clear that if she had, she would have exposed herself as someone else: Dick Hunter. As small as the town was, it was still segregated by race, class, and every other possibility.

"Did Mrs. Childers live here when she was young too?" I asked Jecko.

"Yes," he nodded.

I made a note in my mental margin. But I had one more question.

"Why was the baby kept—in the jar? Downstairs, in this house?" I asked and mimed cradling my arms, a cylinder shape, and two fingers on my palm as I pretended to descend a set of steps.

He got it. Within moments he was digging through another box—this one full of old papers, magazines, and newspapers. Ah, the *Chalybeate Springs Times*, I said as he brought out a yellowed and dog-eared version. I recognized the Gothic typeface; the heavy black letters at the top of the page. He brought it to me and I began to read. Nothing. Then the next few pages. Nothing. There was nothing at all about the baby, about my question. I struck my forehead with the palm of my hand. Jecko couldn't read. I kept forgetting.

"The answer is in the paper? *A* paper?"

331

I got a nod. Jecko began digging again, and brought out another album of photos. He opened it up, then closed it. Then he held it up.

"It's a paper in one of these albums?" Evidently it was. Jecko did the happy dance.

"Okay," I said to myself, now we just have to find it. I got up and searched the box. Album, album, newspaper, magazine, album. I was looking for that magical combination of album with papers stuck in it, but nothing surfaced. While rummaging, I ran across old photos of Dick Hunter. There were ones of him on his first tricycle, later ones as a youth, ones fishing, and even one of him and Salinger, arms draped around each other, still in their football uniforms. Then college, a new car, one girlfriend (a foil, no doubt), and a few at Christmastime and other holidays.

Sad. All gone now, regardless of sex, love, desperation, and fear. I set the photos down and looked up at Jecko.

"Is there another box?" I asked, full-faced. He pointed to one in a corner and the process started all over again. After a good thirty minutes and one sinking sun, I came across a more modern version of the collection in the worn velvet album. This one was some cheap plastic job from the sixties or seventies and sported a marlin being caught with a fishing line on the front—no fisherman in sight. "Guess taste doesn't run through the generations," I said to myself, thinking how beautiful the house must have been at one time, and how tacky and unfortunately up-to-date some things had become as the years progressed.

Finally I hit pay dirt. A *Chalybeate Times* news item:

```
        The   infant   of   John   Dillinger
Salinger  [they  printed  this  with  a
straight face--I'm not kidding] and Tinky-
Ernestine Salinger--maiden name Slattery--
[As if this was an improvement] was stolen
yesterday  from  the  Titusville  Funeral
Home, about nine-thirty.
```

Nine thirty? How did they *know*? I read on.

```
        The  infant,  grossly deformed with
four  legs,  no arms, and two heads, should
be   easily   recognizable   ["no  shit,"  I
thought]   and   anyone   knowing   the
whereabouts  of  the  child  should contact
```

the funeral home, the Salinger family, or
any law enforcement official.

I looked at Jecko. "The Hunters stole the baby?"
I got a "Yes." This was good information-wise, but bad,
well ... information-wise. I was going to ask why, but realized I had to
come up with the answer and see if I would win a prize.
"They wanted to ... how do I say this ... blackmail Salinger?"
A puzzled look followed. I wasn't sure if he understood and
didn't know the answer, or if "blackmail" had thrown him. I repeated.
Before I was even finished he was shaking a "No" out of his head.
While the nonverbal exchange was exhausting, I remembered the lack
of television and electricity, and placated myself with the realization
that this was now the only form of entertainment that Chalybeate
Springs offered—what was left of it.
"They didn't like Salinger."
Affirmative.
"They took the baby to cause him more pain?"
Affirmative.
A moment more of digging through the history of the Hunter
plantation revealed numerous copies of a letter, evidently anonymously
sent out when needed, to Salinger & Co., alerting them that "someone"
had the baby and would see it displayed in a circus if the former
football player did not stay in line.
It made sense in a perverted sick sort of way (the information);
like I *needed* any more. The Hunter family had evidently learned of the
rumors about Salinger and Dick (Hey, his parents came up with the
name, not me), and didn't like what they were hearing. It wasn't too
much of a stretch to figure out that they had probably paid a large sum
to have Salinger's father force the young son to marry the Slattery girl,
knowing somehow that there would be a debacle. Ten more minutes of
rummaging through what was left of the Hunter legacy let me know
that that was exactly what had happened. A letter, addressed to (I'm not
kidding) Monsieur Slattery, and post-marked about the same time
Salinger and his sister-bride would have been doing the horizontal
mambo, surfaced amongst a pile of tied-together love letters or some
such perfumed whatnot.

Dear Monsieur Slattery,

I am under the assumption that you are a logical man
who is, judging by your circumstances, in need of money. It is

333

therefore with great pleasure that I enclose a check in the amount of $17,548.35.

I put the letter down. $17,548.35. What the? Where had I ...Ohhhhhh, the Weems money. I had wondered why the bizarre amount. And here it was again. But why? I read on:

> My only condition is that the marriage of your daughter Tinky-Ernestine and J.D. Salinger take place at once, that the marriage be consummated [always sounds like a weak soup to me] before the end of the month, and that I have your word that nothing will interfere with this agreement.

> I am, faithfully yours,

> Brandis Hunter, sole proprietor and owner of Yoke-Wacko-Hunter Plantation

But if the letter was sent to Mr. Slattery and his unfortunately-named daughter—sent from Brandis Hunter in order to put an end to the relationship between J.D. and Dick Hunter—then why was it here? There was additional correspondence attached. I turned the page.

> My Dear Mr. Hunter,

> I am in receipt of your letter and check and feel it necessary to return both to you immediately. I have no intention of Tinky-Ernestine marrying J.D., and you may keep your money, your fancy stationery, and your insults to yourself. I return your letter as I will not have such a thing in my home.

> Good day, Sir,

> Yours,

> Monsieur Bonko Wallace Slattery, Jr.

I don't know which was worse: the letters, or the fact that there was evidently a Monsieur Bonko Wallace Slattery, *Sr.* at some point in time. And Wacko Plantation and Bonko Slattery? Talk about a screwed up bunch of people ... and names. Bonko, Wacko, Jecko? A pattern or just a coincidence? Plus, this still didn't explain the strange amount that not only Weems had come up with, but that Brandis Hunter had used as well.

I looked at Jecko and asked the last question of the evening as the sun sank lower and lower.

"They were complete assholes, the Hunters?"

Jecko opened his eyes wide, threw his head back, and brought it down, then up, then down, the up, with such ferocity that I thought it would come off.

54

Ancestral Big Hypes

With fading light and a box of letters, I did what any writer would do: I snooped. Hunter's letter had been returned, along with the check, but that didn't explain why Salinger and Slattery had indeed tied the knot in addition to doing some tension release. Or why they had *kept* the results of their original sinning. (Hey, I can't read minds—only other people's mail.)

The love letters, the ones tied with a pretty bow and scented with perfume, I only glanced through. Nothing of interest there. Finally, just as I was about to give up, more sludge came to the surface from my insistent dredging: The original deed to the Yoke-Wacko-Hunter Plantation. It had been sold, all six thousand acres of it at the time, for $17,548.35. There was that amount again. Further digging provided the reason for the connection between the deed and the amount offered to Slattery. (Hunter had obviously made much more by that time.) A document from granddaddy—Horace Bismirch Hunter— specified the "luck" factor in using the amount. (Note: obviously no longer applicable.) Horace went on to say in a letter to his son that *his* father had won the plantation in a poker game for this exact amount (who plays for thirty-five cents?), and that any monetary dealings that he should have in the future, regarding large sums, should include the same number.

Okay. Fine. That explained the poker-game-slash-plantation-slash-bribery amount. But where had Weems gotten it? Ordinarily I wouldn't have cared, but given the odd circumstances of the past month, I now had a vested interest.

There's a saying, and I'm not sure where it comes from, so forgive me if I do not give credit here to the originator. It goes something like this: "You should know when to stop." The bad news for me was, I didn't. But who could resist boxes of letters, old newspapers, and family history that had come down to a transsexual, a baby in a jar, and a deaf-mute, all connected to the only still-standing house in a small town?

Deep breath. Here we go.

Exhausting the letters and newspapers, I was left with nothing more than dust and a few old leather pouches, loose photos, and one ancient shoe. They say it's darkest before the dawn, and perhaps this could be a metaphor for my plight through the land of murk and dank, for I was just about ready to give up when I pulled the *last* item from the *last* box. (Isn't it always that way? Is that some type of God-joke on us all?)

A weathered cardboard-and-leather binder-type-folder with a thin string cord wrapped around it was all that remained. I moved to where the light was best, expecting to find disappointment inside. It would prove to be prophetic, this binder, and I suppose, with all that had happened, I should have seen it coming. I unlaced the thing's strap and opened it up.

A letter—a note—popped out, with a date and small introduction; written by Mrs. Horace Bismirch Hunter. This is what followed:

Yoke-Wacko-Hunter Plantation, 1887

It is my intention to put together a cookbook gleaned from the small farming community that is to be incorporated this month (why we have waited this long, I do not know). We have decided (mostly myself and one other person) on the name of "Chalybeate Springs," as the town's water supply is very "irony." ["Lady," I thought, "if you only knew …"] And, as this has been said by the local and remaining Indian population (the smallpox blankets only did *part* of the job) to be a cure for melancholia and fainting spells, I think this most appropriate. Though the water's taste is not pleasant (we are slowly getting used to it), we have found, in the area, that by cooking with certain spices and in certain ways, the taste may be masked. I am asking only a select few in the town (the prettiest woman, the Reverend's wife, and one or two others, including a woman who cooks here on the plantation) to participate in this project, and my hope is that a large publisher in New York (seeking to know more of our history and culture after the Civil War and the period of reconstruction), will publish the book (it's not very extensive) and make it available (why would they not?) to the world at large.

Sincerely, Mrs. Horace (née Tippett) Bismirch Hunter

Odd. The woman liked to use parentheses as much as I did. And her maiden name was Tippett. I knew I had been given the middle name because it was a great grandmother's or some such relative—a Bodice Marjorie, Marion, Maraschino Tippett, or some variation thereof—but I hadn't really looked into it. It wasn't an uncommon name—Tippett—but neither was it Smith or Jones. The recipes that were included in the binder read like a book themselves, though most were sedate compared to the modern version I had been working on. And none contained Bird-Dog Stew or Flaming Author Pie.

The only thing left now to look at was a large, many-times-folded, and almost turned-to-dust paper—yellowed beyond anything I'd seen in the attic, and inscribed with a quill pen. It could have been the original Declaration of Independence for that matter. I opened it as carefully as I could, and laid it out on the floor, in the fading rays of the sun.

It was a tree of the Hunter family. The branches stretched back to Europe—1549 to be exact, but ended with the birth of Brandis Hunter, over eighty years go. Scanning the map of genes-and-progeny-laced materials, a name caught my eye. It snagged like a hook in a fish's mouth—my mouth—and I had no choice but to read it.

"Miss Bodice Marionette Tippett marries Mr. Horace Bismirch Hunter." There was a date, and a line that descended to Brandis Hunter. But it couldn't be. My family had never mentioned the Springs area, and whenever that branch of the family had been talked about, if ever, it had been …(Oh, my God) hushed up, as if something …

Dear me, Marionette Tippett was a relative, and not even a high quality one. Evidently puppetry and parenthetical insertions ran in our family—not to mention alliteration (and ill-iteration for some), for I had been used—a wooden thing with joints and string—to perform the pernicious deeds of one J.D. Salinger and Tuck Henrid (second or third cousin? Tenth if I was lucky). The parenthetical part should speak for itself at this point. If not, you need some serious social psychological substitutive strategy, which would bring in the alliteration and … oh, never mind.

It couldn't be (being related to Dick Hunter, not the parenthetical insertion or alliteration part). Dick Hunter would *have* to have known this. Had he/she come to New York for just the operation, or because he/she knew we were related? But she hadn't mentioned any of this, especially when we were sharing secrets, penises, and birthday cake. Could it be that he/she had lived in this house and never bothered to look at the family history, or at least play dolls (I'm guessing things started early) in the attic?

But just as I was about to practice more dry heaves, things got even worse. There, just to the right of the Tippett-Hunter connection, was another fork: "Colonel Wilfred Wormwood Weems marries Chassy-Mae Tippett (sister of Bodice Marionette Tippett)—1906."

My stomach lurched upward, into my throat. Oh—My—God. I was related to the Weems family. And I had thought the *Fourth* was bad. Evidently the $17,548.35 had been handed down through several branches of Tippetts, Hunters, and Weemses. It was one thing to be connected to a single loon in the town, quite another to find out that I was genetically bonded to a flock of them. But had Weems known? Surely she had known there were Tippetts in her family, somewhere. Then again, she hadn't read my book and wouldn't have seen the entire name on the cover. I had, after all, in *her* mind, written to her, requesting a visit.

I let the paper fall from my hands, not wanting to know if Jecko was my uncle and Mrs. Childers my sister. At this point, anything was possible. I just wanted out.

Suddenly the room began to spin and I found myself reeling backwards. I felt my head hit the floor. A cloud of dust appeared around me. It was as if cyanide had been introduced into my system all over again. It was all too Oedipal; too incestuous. It was too sick, too twisted. But it was all there, in ancient script, on a piece of paper that had been found by, as is said in the movie *Apocalypse Now,* " ... an errand boy, sent by grocery clerks, to collect the bill." It was truly my *Heart of Darkness*—my journey into the night, a traveling into my own soul. I was caught *Comin' through the Rye*—a body meeting a body, several in fact ... and it was terrifying.

55

Let Shy Sir Beg NAACP

The money in the smaller jar—the one that had been babysitting Salinger's very own personalized home-grown vegetable—added up to over $90,000. Mrs. Childers had been keeping not only the hush money from the Junior League ladies, but she had been adding some of her own, the insurance money, and maybe even a blackmailer's take or two. As it was now early morning, and the sun—which had so helped in the discovery of Chalybeate's social infrastructure the afternoon before, began to creep into the kitchen—the thought of neighboring law enforcement officials arriving on the scene and demanding an explanation from one large African-American and one New York City writer with not-so-very-good alibis, raised its ugly, misshapen, and pointy head.

Something had to be done.

I was certain Jecko had killed Salinger and Henrid, and maybe even a few more people of the town who might have gotten in his way. And I was sure that he had rescued me and brought me to this house. This much I knew: He had fed me, nursed me back to health, and shown me more about the town and their skeleton collection that I had ever dreamed. So now I feared for him. While I wasn't squeaky clean by police standards, this was still the South, he was black and couldn't hear or speak, and everyone was dead but us. Did I mention something had to be done?

I sat the large man down at the kitchen table, after requesting that he very carefully replace the bobbing infant in its original location, and had the "Come to Jesus" talk with him. For those not familiar with the term, a "Come to Jesus" discussion isn't what it sounds like. Rather it is a "Let's get things straight here" term, and if you tell someone you're going to have one … they listen. Or in this case, watch. I gave my mouth a few stretches and prepared for the speech I was about to give.

"Jecko. We have ninety thousand dollars here," and I pointed to the wad of money that lay on the table. (I wasn't counting my stash as it was, well … mine). "I want you to take this ninety-thousand and get very far away from here. Do you *understand*?"

"Yes," he nodded. But then he shook his head "No."

"No what? No you don't understand?"

A "No."

"No, you're not going?"

I got a "Yes." Part of me wanted to strangle him and part wanted to ... well, that was about it—I just wanted to strangle him. This was like playing "Who's on first?" with Helen Keller. I was tired, barely recovered, worried, and unable to eat meat or go near canned vegetables ever again—how would you feel? And Salinger's and Henrid's "Jim Jones impersonation" was weighing heavily on my mind.

"Jecko, listen ... I mean, read my lips." (It was hard not to say "No new taxes," but I managed.) "You have got to get *out* of here now. If they come ... and they *will*, you will be tried for murder." I expected a shocked look but none came. Then he pointed to me.

"Yes, I know that I will be tried for murder, but I can defend myself," I lied. I continued. "I want you to do this one thing for me, okay? Take the car, and this money, and get very far away from here. I'm begging you to do this."

He made no movement with his head, but instead narrowed his eyes. I thought I had made him mad, but in an instant I knew I was wrong. A solitary tear ran down one cheek, but other than that he showed no sign of emotion.

I swallowed hard.

"Why not?" I asked in reference to my statement.

Jecko again made no motion either way with his head, but he stretched out his arms and then hugged himself.

"Jecko, listen, I want to help you," I said, and got up to take his arm. He jerked away from me. I looked him straight in the face and started again, but he cut me off with his upheld hand. Then he shook his head "No" violently.

I grabbed the money, pulled him up by one arm, furious that he was being so stubborn, and tried to drag him toward the door. There was precious little time left and I didn't want to have to answer for myself *and* him. While he couldn't see my lips at this point, I spoke, more for myself than his benefit, "You stupid bastard, you've got to get your sorry ass out of here." He jerked away again and stood in the middle of the kitchen.

What to do. I felt a rush, and panic overtook me. If Jecko didn't leave it would be all over for him. He let out a hostile puff of air, like a bull in a pasture, and stomped off onto the back porch.

I sat back down to think, sticking my hands into my pants pockets. In my right one I felt something and dug it out.

"What could this be?" My question was answered soon enough. It was Mrs. Weems's enormous ring from the bowl of Salinger's chili. The *real* ring, not the fake one that Salinger had procured for Henrid after he'd taken the body away from the Weemses' house. Jecko was pacing on the porch and I was becoming sick to my stomach as I knew what I would have to do.

Slowly, I got up and walked over to his jacket that he took everywhere with him—rain or shine. I gave the ring a quick brush with my shirttail and then slipped it into the right breast pocket. He would find it at some point, perhaps when he needed it most. Maybe after what I was about to do he would forgive me someday.

As I was still standing when he reentered the kitchen, I chose that moment for the confrontation. I was so eaten up inside with anger, sadness, and contempt for what had happened that it was a cakewalk to bring up the forced hostility I was about to display. I thought back to my few acting lessons in New York, channeled the energy to where it was most needed, and took an aggressive stance.

Jecko's look was one large question mark—underlined.

Drawing a deep breath and narrowing my eyes, I began. "Jecko, I lied. I didn't want to hurt your feelings and was trying to get you out of here, but you've left me no choice." He watched, not moving. "As much as I'm grateful for you doing what you did—saving me and all—I can't associate with you."

He made an upturned gesture with both palms—a "Why?" if ever there was one.

I narrowed my eyes and breathed hard. "Because you're a God-damned nigger!" I said (well, all but the "N" word—which I just mouthed). "I'd rather you had left me out in the field to die. I couldn't do anything about it while I was sick, but I can now. And it makes me sick again, all over, to think that I actually ate some food you touched. I was just playing nice until I was well, but I want you gone. I won't have a 'nigger' (lips moving, no sound) in this house, and when they come, I won't be associated with one. And you can forget about taking the money too. Just get out of here and ..." but before I could finish he lunged at me. He had his hands around my throat and was moving me around the room, lifting me slightly off the floor.

"Jecko, no, wait," I squeezed out. My lips were moving but sound barely came through. Quick realization came that luck was not on my side in this fight. I had just called him the "N" word, thinking he would bolt. He hadn't, and the situation was going from bad to worse.

342

Then, just as quickly as he had grabbed me, his strangle turned to softness. He had me pinned to the kitchen wall—a butterfly with no options. It was then that the painful thing occurred. I had heard it only once before, when Mrs. Childers and I had spied on him and Weems as she attempted to teach him how to speak. And here it was again, face-to-face. Now he moved one of his hands to his own throat in an attempt to get the thing right. I stayed pinned by his other hand; terrified, fascinated, and morbidly curious.

"Aaahhhhh," he moaned, trying to coerce his vocal chords into a sound. "Doooonnn whaaaaa," and the pitch and wavering tone of it tore into me. Finally, he managed the last word: "Gaaoohhhh." We stayed locked in our embrace for several moments, then he let go of my throat with his one hand.

My heart was breaking. I felt a tearing inside, realizing that I had used that awful word, nigger, for the first time since I was a child, when I had hurled it at a housekeeper, not even sure what it meant at the time. But I knew that I couldn't let up now if I was going to get him to leave.

"Did you understand me?" I said, forcing the hostility into my face.

Jecko didn't move.

"I said I don't want any of your kind around here, so get out!" I coerced all the blood I could manage, to flow, attempting to get it to pump itself through my system. I tensed my fists. "If you want, then take the damn money and go—that'll be your payment for what you did for me, but get the hell out!"

Jecko looked at me. It was all I could do to keep up the act. I was actually getting angry now—angry that he was forcing me to continue playing a role I so loathed.

The large man moved slowly to the farmer's sink and pump in front of the windows. He looked out across the fields in back of the house, past the vegetable patch, past the old slave quarters. This was his home, the same way it had been Mrs. Childers's and that of the Hunter family. I understood what he was going through, but I wanted him out of this mess.

He turned to me. There were no tears in his eyes and no real expression of regret, thanks, or anger. Jecko was now a blank. He took the money from the table, slowly, and put in into his pockets. He paused. Then he carefully picked up a large butcher knife—the only one the house had—and looked right at me. I couldn't read him and froze solid. But he only turned, with the knife held by his side, and made a long, painful walk to the front of the house, and out the door.

I fell into a chair, exhausted after my performance, sitting perfectly still at the kitchen table. Then, when I was sure he was at least sixty feet away, I let out a heavy sigh.

The car started—it seemed to idle for hours though I'm sure it was only a moment or two. The sound of the wheels let me know it was moving over the ruts in the yard, and their reverberation progressed to the bumpiness of the drive. My ear followed the car's progress as it left the yard and turned onto the highway, now nothing more than a soft wisp of sound that blended in with the chirping of the birds outside.

I listened for minutes, then hours. I listened until darkness fell. I listened all through the night. And then, sure that Jecko was not coming back, and with the sun rising on the next day, I got up from the kitchen table and made a slow and sad journey up the winding staircase, to the second story of the house.

56

Planatary Big Chess

With Jecko gone, I wondered how I would survive. And what would be my fate when "they" came to find out what had happened to the town? Then there was the pesky problem of Salinger's and Henrid's bodies on the side lawn. One good breeze and they were in the room with me.

My main focus had been getting Jecko out of harm's way, and now that that particular job had been accomplished (with more trouble and acting than I had ever expected) I turned my attention to survival and piecing my life back together.

Food wasn't a problem. Well, okay, it was. If it's true that "You are what you eat," then what can any of us do? If one decides to be a vegetarian, will that person slow down to the point of complete incapacitation, becoming in essence, a vegetable? Or maybe I'd become bovine in my middle years because of the incredible amount of hamburgers and steaks I had eaten. Were my nipples going to lactate? Would I eventually moo? I once stopped eating fish after graduating from college, noticing that I had gained a proclivity for crowds and the direction they were always turning, and enrolling myself in one refresher course after another, unable to break the "school" habit.

Chicken was one of my favorite foods, but now I was afraid of, well, everything—I was scared of my own shadow (think about it). Folks, there's a reason most of the world doesn't eat snakes, worms, or rats (knowingly). And anyone who would feed you one of those pesky critters could be called any of those same names.

So now the conundrum: What would I subsist on, here in Tara-land? This, accompanied by the agony of knowing that I was related to the very people whose plantation I now occupied (the cyanide poisoning didn't help, beating a dead horse though it may be) gave me a feeling of helplessness with a side dish of depression. But fear is easy to let go of once you're dead. Perhaps I should have let Salinger and Henrid finish me off. Maybe I'd have been better off not knowing the things now haunting me. The truth will indeed set you free. Trouble is, it doesn't taste very good.

But back to eating—why you're here. While the pantry and kitchen cabinets held myriad vegetables and preserves in jars, I had no desire to die a slow and painful death, and any appetite that surfaced was quickly quelled by the sight of Baby Two-Heads. I was seriously considering ending it all, but put the thought out of my mind for the moment and returned it to the theme of food. There were vegetables enough in the back, and I didn't need any meat products now as I was strictly a vegetarian since the chili cook-off. But I wasn't really hungry. Having not eaten for days will do that to a person. My stomach was probably the size of a peanut.

What was I to do as the day wore on? Not having my charades partner, I succumbed to what is normally called "the blues" (feelings, not music), and trudged upstairs, then back down, then up. There was sun enough left to avoid the kerosene lamps, and so I turned my attention to the laptop, determined to fill in the last part of my book if there was indeed any power left in the batteries. I had charged it days before, before the cook-off, and as far as I knew, Jecko hadn't used it to locate porn on the non-existent Internet. I flipped up the lid and booted it up. It worked, and I set about finishing the story—the parts you're reading now.

Thankfully, I had transcribed all the recipes (wouldn't want to lose those) and even the newspaper clippings into this most-modern form of notebook. Saligner had burned the actual hard copy, and now, with this being the only record left, having limited battery supply and a desire to put down the truth in the hope that it might help Jecko and/or me, I began to type. I finished up and then shut down, saving what battery power might be left.

Sleep came easily for me, but its landscape was fraught with nightmares, remembering, colors, death, bottled babies, and recipes. I awoke in a sweat, the sheet wrapped tightly around my legs. Lying on my back, I took in the ceiling, the peeling walls, the moldy air that circulated (or didn't) in the room. Solitude and silence worked their evils, and by three o'clock the next morning I was a wreck. What would I do? Wait for someone to come? And what if no one did? What then? What if I lived here for the rest of my life? The thought was both frightening and comforting: simple life, well-water, farm-fresh vegetables fertilized with previous chili cook-off entrants who had been unlucky enough to actually have a good recipe. And wasn't that why I had been called here? For the recipes? But no, it hadn't been. That was just the foil for Henrid's elaborate plot to get even with me, Chalybeate Springs, and the world. It had been to avenge a town that had destroyed two individuals' lives and I had played a most intricate part. I would have to look at myself in the mirror each day for the remainder of my life (they say that this is a common thing) and the thought weighed on my now-deranged gray-matter.

Maybe it was the morbidity of the house; the loneliness, the lack of Jecko. Maybe it was the iron content of the well water, supposed to cure mental illness but having the opposite effect. Whatever the cause, I had time to think. And this was dangerous.

The ladies of the Junior League were taking up permanent residence in my head, and why shouldn't they?—they were now a part of me. Mrs. Weems, who had been a snob but had found the time to try to teach Jecko how to speak, floated up first. She was much more than her recipes let on. So was Mrs. Brandyworth and her holier-than-thou tributes to Jesus and pedophilia. (A bad cliché—think of all the priests in Boston.) She had vacillated between sin and righteousness like a possessed see-saw.

Then Shelby: illiterate librarian who liked her town enough to help beautify the park by donating money to that endeavor. She had also been easy on the eye, perfectly put together—on the outside at any rate.

Childers—another member—had so sweetly brought me bounty from her garden when she wasn't preparing road-kill or burning down her houses for the insurance money, and there was some part of me that felt sorry for her; sorry because of the simplicity of mind that God had bestowed on her, though in reality she was a much more complex person than her exterior demeanor illustrated: honest to a fault, certainly down-to-earth (perhaps a bit too much), and a giving person in her own way.

And Mary-Ellen. I'd like to tell you that I discovered some great secret about her; that she could speak seven languages or that she had a Ph.D from Harvard or had once done a great service for some noble cause. Alas, she was simply flat—without dimension. She was what she had always been—a Homecoming and PromQueen, and the most beautiful girl in her class; vacuous, vain, and, well, just plain stupid.

As for Salinger, Henrid had pointed out earlier that death and suffering can do odd things to people, and such was the case with the sheriff. For some, a death transforms them, changes them for the better, into someone new; gives them a whole new appreciation for life and the simple pleasures that daily living can bring. For others suffering can be another kind of death: a death of the soul, of the spirit, of hope—an emotional sarcophagus from which there is no escape. These individuals fester, vampire-like, wanting to destroy. Couple this with a good helping of grief and throw in some remorse, disgust, and a horribly deformed infant and you have a recipe for disaster with two feet, a gun, a position of power, and a proclivity toward a sexual orientation that is none too popular in areas such as Chalybeate Springs. Such was the definition of Salinger. And while he and Henrid never *ate* anyone themselves, they were warped enough to turn the town's cannibalistic emotional tendencies into real ones, feeding the town to itself in the most literal way, letting them "become what they ate." Almost all of us seek love at one time or another. Not finding that, we settle for sex or friendship. If that fails, we gravitate toward abuse, power, insanity, anger, or any combination thereof. What happens when even those possibilities start to unravel is the very definition of evil.

But last and surely not least, let us not forget Miss Henrid, née Dick Hunter, for he/she is our star witness in this debacle that Chalybeate Springs once called life. As she had so deftly pointed out, the sex-change was not the first option in the burgeoning relationship with Salinger, but Harry Killchrist's aim—whether intended or not—had taken care of an integral part of Hunter's lower anatomy, and somewhere, sometime, in someone's mind, the decision had been made to transform Dick Hunter into Tuck Henrid.

Yes, Henrid and Salinger had loved one another, and they had tried to figure out a way to make it work in the one place they wanted to live—Home. Small town America-Anywhere would never have stood for a couple such as that, especially one that counted among its participants the sheriff of the town, and not only would their sexual preferences have been offensive, but hitting a nerve more so would have been the fact that both Salinger and *Hunter-now-Henrid* had been football players—the ultimate taboo in the South, this combination of same-sex love and pig-skin parades—for if anything is still sacred even above religion in the Southland, it is football. So they had attempted to conform, at least in the eyes of Chalybeate Springs. They had played at being a normal couple for the sake of staying together. Played at being accepted; tried to love and live in the place where they had grown up.

But Chalybeate Springs had been no *Mayberry* with a bungling Barney Fife, along with the other cast members. No, it had been small-town America at its worst and it wasn't pretty—small-town America ruined by corrupt politicians and a police state of one. People think that one person can't make that much difference in the world. Think again. Look at Hitler, Gandhi, Mussolini, Jesus, or any other good and bad people who have shaped the planet. Look at yourself.

So how to compete in this world? How do we make it work? Salinger and Henrid had asked themselves this when they weren't seething about all the other religious, emotional, spiritual, intellectual, and physical limitations that a small town places on its occupants. They had found the only way they could, given the circumstances and wants of all parties involved. No, it hadn't worked—for anyone—but they had tried, realizing at some point that the plan was doomed. Probably accepting defeat fully for the first time when it became clear that nothing they did would garner them respect in the Springs area.

Someone once said, "Those who cease to love, seek power." I believe that. But let's carry it one step further in thought, shall we? What do those who have ceased to love and then lost power do? Each of us has our own version of that last-ditch scenario and Salinger and Henrid certainly had theirs. Now, the knowing, the realizations, the participation, and the help that I had given, all piled up on me.

Had I been the catalyst for the whole adventure? Had my one nasty comment, that one day in New York, July 3rd, set off Dick Hunter to serve up revenge and use me as the table's centerpiece? Or had he read one of my books, realized we were related, and sought to open a line of communication? Tuck Henrid's words, quoting me, now seemed prophetic. I thought back to them; to our conversation in her home:

"As you walked into the elevator, and yes, it is imprinted on my mind for all eternity, you joked to your friends, jerking your thumb toward me and glancing back, you said, 'If *it* doesn't watch it, *it's* going to end up in somebody's book someday.' Then you added, 'With a name like that and a face and body to match, everyone would want to read about *it*,' and you all laughed. You all laughed at me! Do you know how much that hurt? Do you know how bad I felt, after being treated the way I was by this town and then trying to find someplace else to live and being given a hard time in New York?"

And so Dick Hunter's, Tech Durkin's, and Tuck Henrid's words came back—a gasoline explosion in which I had not properly calculated the amount of fuel involved. I remembered her final shot that day: "Well, Mr. Jackson Tippett McCrae of novel fame, be careful what you say for it may come true, especially the part about 'If *it* doesn't watch it, *it's* going to end up in somebody's book someday'. . ." and she had paused, catching her breath. Then she had finished: "Because *it* just *has*."

And what of the cryptic pieces of paper? The ones I've included at the beginning of each chapter? "Beneath Classy Grip," "Perishable NYC Stag," "Psyche Baring Tales," and all the others? See anything unusual? Each and every one contains the same letters. And each and every one is an anagram for Chalybeate Springs—the same way Percy Abel Hastings is an anagram for the town's name (which is how I figured out he'd sent them). Good old Percy. "Why," you ask? I can hear you. The reason should be obvious: he's a relative; a foil, a signpost in the night, a guiding and not-so-guiding light, and the very one who sent or left lying around those scraps of paper. He knew he didn't have long to live and, having figured out at least part of the Henrid-Salinger plan, wasn't concerned with any of the possible outcomes the chili cook-off might have for most of the town.

And the same attic-discovered fading and aged family roadmap that told of the Hunters, Tippetts, Weemses, and others? It also told of the Hastingses, and yes, the Salingers, for even Betsy Chap Salinger (another anagram for Chalybeate Springs) had married into the one line that was the town.

So, was Mrs. Horace Bismirch Hunter's claim correct that the town had been named for an iron spring? (I'm talking water, not bed here.) Or had she used Betsy Chap Salinger's name as an anagram, knowing some darker connection would be made in the future? And could she have foretold that, at some point Yoke-Wacko-Hunter Plantation would be an anagram for Tuckahoe, New York? Could any of us?

It does seem odd when you consider that Yoke-Wacko-Hunter and Tuckahoe, New York, are also anagrams for the phrase, "Co-author knew key," especially since Tuck Henrid is, in a way, the co author of this work—for without her note I would never have made it down to Chalybeate Springs.

Whatever you choose to call it, the remembering and the piecing-together of the last month had become painful. The muse was relentless now, but the batteries on my computer were low. I needed to leave something; a legacy, a history, a record. Something, anything to let someone know—if anyone found this—what had happened. The true story as told to me, found out by me, and lived by me. I also remembered the words I had used to my editor: "Barring some unforeseen accident, I should have you the manuscript in about a month." Oh, there had been an accident all right. And boy, was it ever unforeseen. I opened my laptop and started typing once again, thinking how visionary the name of Mr. Reynolds's place of pig worship had been—*That's All Folks!*" (With or without a comma after the word "all.") It seemed appropriate not only for Chalybeate Springs, but for this book as well.

"You have limited time left," my laptop screen read, letting me know that fast typing was of the essence. I began a note to the publishing house in New York.

Note to my editor: By the time you receive this manuscript, I will have committed suicide.

Publisher's note: McCrae's manuscript ended shortly after his entry about the many ways he could kill himself. If you like, go back to the beginning of the book and read it once more.

McCrae did not actually die but his batteries *did* succumb to that particular fate. Once it was determined that he was missing and no communication could be made with the town, efforts were put in place to find him. True to his word, Mr. McCrae had picked a most horrible way to commit suicide (his opinion, not ours): by reading Hemingway's *A Moveable Feast.* Evidently Mr. McCrae, thinking that the title would somehow connect with the epicurean efforts as they related to *The Chalybeate Springs Junior League Cookbook,* attempted to bore himself to death while tying in his *modus operandi* with the food theme.

The individuals who found McCrae managed to revive him with adjectives, sentences that were interesting, and some resemblance of plot, using some handy first-edition Dickens, Proust, and Faulkner, and he was resuscitated within minutes. His laptop computer was found *Anne Frank*-style on the floor—an innocuous-looking small case containing the password-protected file that would tell the world what had really happened.

Because of the unusual happenings surrounding the town, the killings, and the author himself, the judge at McCrae's trial was lenient, citing the unusual circumstances of his experiences in Chalybeate Springs and giving him two years probation with the caveat that his next book have nothing to do with food.

Jecko returned when he found Mrs. Weems's ring in his pocket, realizing that Mr. McCrae didn't mean what he'd said, and was able to "tell," via a series of question-and-answer games, such as the ones he and the author had played, exactly who had done what to whom.

Through the queries put to Jecko (using occasional hand puppets and drawings), it was established that Delilah, surmising that Salinger and Henrid were on their way to the plantation to do away with Jecko (her brother, by the way—hey it was a *very* small town), killed the sheriff and Miss H with an assortment of heavy cooking utensils as they approached the Hunter home. Delilah's size-thirteen tennis shoes were imprinted at the crime scene and excessive traces of *Bon Ami, Pine Sol,* and *Clorox* bleach were found. Not a single fingerprint was located; the authorities determining that whoever had done the deed had worn heavy rubber gloves. As far as the two penises stuffed into the mouths of the victims, Salinger's contained Harry Killchrist's, obviously recognizable by the birthmark resembling Thailand, and Henrid's contained her own. Delilah, it seems, had been doing a bit more snooping in Miss Henrid's kitchen in the last few days than suspected, and was not at all squeamish about transporting the aforementioned organs to the crime scene after she'd done Henrid and Salinger in. Unbeknownst to anyone else, Delilah had also been receiving those cryptic slips of paper from the duplicitous and not-so-what-he-seemed Mr. Hastings—the ones with the anagrams on them that McCrae had been collecting—and had deduced what was about to happen to everyone. She is serving time at a state correctional facility (she gets to wear rubber gloves every day) and Jecko is a free man.

When McCrae had asked Jecko if they were the only ones alive, and Jecko had responded with a nod "Yes," he was evidently factoring in that Delilah was now far away—in Texas to be more specific. Jecko, having been to that state at one time, felt that living there was pretty much equal to death, and wrote Delilah off. So his statement was, while misleading, not entirely false.

Mr. McCrae now lives comfortably in Chalybeate Springs, in an enormous old plantation house that he is currently remodeling. His editor, not wishing to leave New York, and learning of the bizarre way in which the author gained possession of the house, chose to decline the most generous offer of ownership.

Jecko returned to the plantation as a paid full-time cook, and he and Mr. McCrae now live quite happily and without fear of encroachment by neighbors. While Jecko's culinary repertoire includes some of the most sumptuous ribs, chicken, beef, and pork dishes, Mr. McCrae is now a strict vegetarian and extremely happy about it. He wanted us to add that the Hemingway he attempted to commit suicide with made him more ill than any combination of botulism and cyanide could have.

But perhaps the most disturbing event occurred after the first printing of this novel, for, over seven hundred small towns in the South came forward in an attempt to sue, claiming that Chalybeate Springs was based on their fine hamlet, even though the entire population of

Chalybeate Springs was dead, the exceptions being Mr. McCrae, Jecko, and Delilah.

One addendum: McCrae's laptop ran out of battery power before he could finish the last "P.S." We asked him what he was going to say, and this was it:

"Please do not drink the water."

Jackson Tippett McCrae has worked for various magazines and publishing companies in New York. Educated at the University of Texas and the Juilliard School in New York, he originally made his living as a composer. His books include *The Bark of the Dogwood: A Tour of Southern Homes and Gardens, The Children's Corner*—a collection of short stories—and the novel *Katzenjammer: Soon to be a major motion picture.* He currently writes fiction full-time, dividing his time between New York and Connecticut.

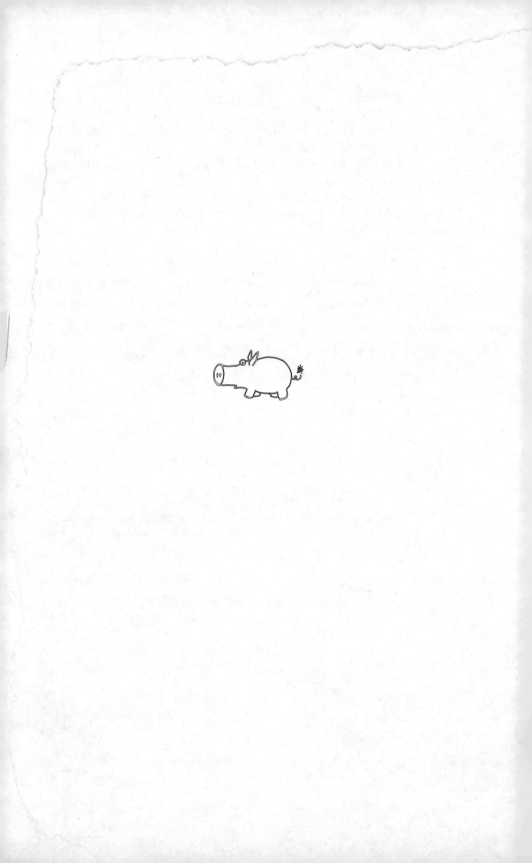